Where the Larkspur Grow

To Marie,
with Best Wishes
Niall x

A Novel

Niall Illingworth

Grosvenor House
Publishing Limited

This book is published by
Grosvenor House Publishing Ltd
Link House
140 The Broadway, Tolworth, Surrey, KT6 7HT.
www.grosvenorhousepublishing.co.uk

A CIP record for this book
is available from the British Library

ISBN 978-1-78623-332-5

For Helen, Erin and Sarah

Prologue

For weeks the weather had been unseasonably hot and now the air hung heavy and still. Rain, intense rain, was not far away.

It was late April 1967 and Cathleen Heggerty sat on the porch of her farmstead clutching a postcard in her hands. It was from her friend and former work colleague Vernon Schilling. On the front of the card was a picture of a pelican sitting on a bollard behind which some small boats were moored to a jetty. The water was cerulean blue. The slogan read 'Greetings from Longboat Key, Florida'. Cathleen turned the postcard over and as she read the words tears welled up in her eyes.

"Dear Cathleen,

Lorri and I are settling into retirement, can't believe it's been three months already! We're very much enjoying spending time with Norma and the grandkids. Longboat Key is a lovely spot and our new house looks onto a jetty just like the one in the picture. It couldn't be more different than W. Virginia. Expect it won't be long now till you stop work and the big day must only be a month or so away. You must let me know when baby arrives, I'm betting it's going to be a boy. Wishing you & Frank all the best for the future.

Regards, Vernon."

As the early evening light began to fade, Cathleen could see the lights of Fairlea twinkling in the distance. Blinking back tears her thoughts turned to the county hospital, just beyond the town in the foothills of the Allegheny Mountains, where she had worked as a midwife for the last fourteen years. Except for the last three months, all that time had been spent working with Vernon Schilling, the resident Obstetrician. Just about every baby born in Greenbrier County during those 14 years had been under the care of Vernon and Cathleen.

For a brief moment Cathleen wondered if things might have been different if he had been with her. On countless occasions at work she had been sure that they had lost a baby, but Vernon would never give up on the child. Every ounce of effort and nearly forty years of professional experience were focused on one outcome; delivering healthy babies. For every one he lost dozens more were brought back from the brink and many a family in Fairlea had cause to thank the skill of Vernon Schilling.

Midwifes are pragmatic people, they have to be. Deep in her heart Cathleen knew that Vernon would not have been able to save her child. Two days had passed since she had been crippled with pain while kneading dough in the kitchen. Severe cramps and abdominal pain had swept over her and within minutes she was losing a significant amount of blood. She knew immediately what was happening as she had seen it many times before. She knew there was nothing anyone could do for her. In less than an hour it was over. Her baby was dead. Aching with despair and sobbing uncontrollably she had desperately checked for the heartbeat she knew wasn't there. She noted that the baby's lips were very red and small water blisters covered the baby's wrists and ankles. Cathleen's midwifery training had taught her what a stillborn baby looked like. But in that moment her baby looked serene and perfect. She carefully wrapped her precious son in a sheet and held him to her heart. She wanted him to know that she loved him and even though she was overwhelmed with grief, all through that first night she cradled him in her arms and spoke to him gently about her hopes and dreams.

It had most likely been the trauma of the miscarriage and the certainty that nothing could ease her pain or her crushing feeling of loss. Whatever the reason, Cathleen had been unable to lift the phone and call for help. She had desperately wanted her husband Frank to be with her but, like the last time, Frank wasn't there.

Nearly three years had passed since Cathleen had lost her first son, she had been thirty-three at the time. Then, like now, she had gone into spontaneous labour during her eighth month of pregnancy. On that occasion Cathleen had been rushed into hospital but there had been nothing that Vernon or his staff could do to prevent the loss of her child. Thinking back to that time Cathleen could remember being told that her son had been stillborn. Shortly afterwards a nurse took the baby, whom Cathleen had named Peter, wrapped him in a blanket and gave him to her to hold. But within a few minutes a midwife had taken the child from her and she never saw her baby again. Although she had been heavily sedated Cathleen recalls that moment with absolute clarity. The pain of that parting was seared into her heart and often, when she was alone or awake in the small hours of the morning, she would think about Peter and sob quietly.

It was the silence that she found most shocking. In the weeks and months that followed her miscarriage nobody spoke a word to her about her baby, not even Frank. Sure, her husband, Vernon and other friends went out of their way to enquire as to how she was feeling, so she always tried to but on a brave face and sound positive. But no one ever spoke about her baby, her son, her Peter. It greatly unsettled her and in some strange sense made her feel guilty. It was as if it was dirty and this dreadful event about which no one would speak had to be expunged. To everyone other than Cathleen, it was as if her baby had never existed. It broke Cathleen's heart.

At the time of her first miscarriage Frank had been contacted at their farm and asked to attend at the hospital immediately. But he arrived too late and never got to see or hold his son. Cathleen often thought that lack of physical contact had deeply affected him and, painful as it still was to remember, she cherished those precious moments spent cradling her son. She vowed that this time Frank would see his son.

*

Frank Heggerty was due to return home in a couple of days. For the last week he had been helping with the lambing at his brother George's hill farm just outside Hinton in Summer County. George raised sheep and grew apples on a 200-acre farm on the gentle slopes of the Allegheny Mountains which ran like a spine down the eastern border of West Virginia. In truth, George did little more than scratch an existence from the farm and with no other help, except from his sheepdog Bess, he was dependent on Frank to help out during lambing and again when he harvested his apple crop.

George Heggerty was somewhat stuck in his ways and over a period of time had gradually slipped out of normal social conventions. Now fifty-two, he was twelve years older than Frank. He had never married and was shy and awkward in the company of people he didn't know. When you saw George and Frank together you could tell they were brothers as they both had the Heggerty trait of smallish ears but quite large, slightly bulbous, noses. George was much the taller and slimmer of the two being over 6' and stick thin. Frank was only 5'8" but quite stocky and muscular in build. He walked with a pronounced limp; the result of a mining cart running over his right foot a number of years ago when he worked as a hewer at the Middleton mine. The accident had not only affected Frank physically, it had also had a significant impact on his mental health. Having to work on Cathleen's grandparents farm was never a job that Frank would have chosen for himself, but it was a means to an end and put food on the table.

Unlike George, who still had a good head of dark hair, Frank was balding, and his reddish-brown wispy hair had been the bane of his life since school days. His classmates continually teased him about it and his Irish roots. Like many Irish Americans, Frank's great grandparents had emigrated from Ireland during the potato famine. The Heggerty's hailed from Dunglow in Donegal and had arrived in America in 1850 at the height of the famine. The family had not had it easy since arriving in the States and for three generations, most of them had scraped a living working as poor labourers picking tobacco and working on fruit farms in the Virginia's. Unlike his wife, Frank found it difficult to take pride in his Irish heritage and would seldom, if ever, talk about it.

George led a slightly unusual and isolated existence as there was no telephone at the farm and he'd never owned a television. His only regular contact with the outside world was from an old battery-operated transistor radio in the living room that was permanently tuned to ABC News. Despite their age gap and different lifestyles, the brothers had always rubbed along just fine and Frank often remembered with affection how George had looked out for him when he was a small boy after the premature death of their father when Frank was just six.

*

Fifty miles away in Fairlea, Cathleen stood in the kitchen of her farmhouse. She was thirty-six, four years younger than Frank, and at 5'2" with a light wiry build she cut a diminutive figure. She had light brown hair that she kept swept back from her face in a tight pun at the back of her head. She was dressed in a pale green summer dress over which she wore a cream coloured cotton pinny with two large purple and gold butterflies embroidered on it. The pinny had been a present from her beloved grandmother, and Cathleen treasured it. On her feet she wore a pair of flat brown leather shoes. Cathleen bent down and opened the trap door next to the kitchen table that led down a narrow flight of steps into a large basement which ran the length and breadth of the house. It was by far the coolest place in the house and it was here that she would store the apples and vegetables that they grew on the farm. With its well-ventilated air supply and lack of natural light the produce would keep for months if stored properly. She felt the cool air on her face as she descended the steps and tip toed the fifteen feet or so across the room to a small gate leg table that was standing in the corner of the room. On top of the table was a wooden apple crate. Cathleen gently pulled back the grey coloured blanket that covered it and peered into the crate. All was well, baby was quiet and asleep.

Back in her kitchen Cathleen noticed two small spots of blood on the floor close to the stove. Yesterday she had spent over an hour scrubbing the floor which had erased all physical traces of what had happened only forty-eight hours before. These were fresh blood spots. She felt physically drained. She hadn't eaten for two days and she was barely in control as her hormones surged wildly. She badly needed to get fresh pads and some provisions as there was no milk or bread in the house. The local convenience store was only a couple of miles away but if she left now she would get to it before it closed and before the rain started. She shut her eyes and took several deep breaths exhaling slowly each time. She thought of her grandmother and pictured her standing washing dishes at the sink. Cathleen yearned for her warm embrace and her words of wisdom. She could almost hear her grandmother saying, "You can do this, Cathleen, you can do this." Moments later Cathleen felt a sense of calm and peace come over her. She picked up her handbag, put on her jacket and took the keys for the old Ford pick-up from the hook by the side of the front door and headed outside. It had started to rain.

Chapter 1

At their lakeside home on the shores of Lake Tuckahoe, approximately eleven miles east of Fairlea, David Saltman was loading his wife Jennifer's carefully packed suitcase into the back of their Edsel station wagon. The suitcase had been ready for more than a fortnight, but this evening Jennifer's waters had broken, and her contractions were coming thick and fast. One every two to three minutes, regular as clockwork. It was time to head to Fairlea and the county hospital.

David and Jennifer had first met seven years ago at a convention centre in Charlotte, North Carolina. David had been attending a conference for mining engineers while Jennifer had been at the annual conference of the American Association of School Librarians. They had bumped into each other in an elevator at their hotel and that was that really. It was love at first sight and the two of them had married barely a year later.

David and Jennifer had been married for six years, for the last four they had been trying to have the baby that would make their lives complete. Jennifer was the middle of three sisters, her older sister Elaine still lived with her husband Howard in Atlanta, Georgia where Jennifer had grown up. Her younger sister Ruth lived about forty miles away in Marlinton with her husband John. Neither of her sisters had children.

David Saltman worked as the Operations Manager at the nearby Middleton coal mine while Jennifer had only recently stopped working as a librarian in Lewisburg Public Library. By West Virginian standards they were very comfortably off, their four-bedroom chalet style home, with its sweeping glass balcony that ran the entire front of the house, provided them with spectacular views of the lake. Their property was the envy of many in the town. But for all their material wealth there was a void in their lives which would only be filled by the arrival of their baby.

David carefully folded two delicate white shawls and placed them on top of the suitcase. They had been knitted out of the finest Merino wool by Elizabeth, David's mother, and they had been used for David's, and his younger Sister Elspeth's baptisms nearly forty years ago. When Jennifer found out that she was pregnant Elizabeth insisted that they should have the shawls and said that they should choose the best one to use at their baby's baptism.

The last couple of years had not been easy for the Saltman family. Fourteen months ago, David's father Bert had passed away only months after being diagnosed with lung cancer and now his mother, who was only in her early seventies, had been diagnosed with Alzheimer's. No longer able to look after herself properly, Elizabeth had recently moved to Tallahassee in Florida, so she could be cared for by Elspeth and her husband Paul. Having to leave the family home so soon after the death of Bert had been a real wrench for Elizabeth, for like most family homes it was a treasure trove of memories. When he was growing up, David remembered how the house was always filled with music and friends. In the early 1940's his parents had been part of a very successful Bluegrass group called Three Top Mountain. Bert had played banjo and mandolin while Elizabeth sang vocals and played the fiddle. They were in demand throughout the state and David and his sister spent a great many of their childhood weekends in smoky concert halls and clubs listening to their band. David remembers fondly one weekend when he was about ten. His father was almost beside himself with excitement as Three Top Mountain found themselves in Beckley as the supporting act to Bill Monroe & His Bluegrass Boys. Monroe was Bert's musical hero and the night was made complete by the fact that Earl Scruggs was playing banjo with the Bluegrass Boys. For Bert Saltman it didn't get any better than that.

David smiled at the thought of those childhood days with his parents. It was somewhat ironic that David, while loving listening to music, couldn't play a note. Growing up it nearly drove his mother to distraction. Try as he might he just didn't have the wherewithal to play an instrument. David was 6' tall with a shock of thick blond hair, broad shoulders and an athletic build. He had always felt more at home on the football field or baseball park than in the music room. His hands were large, and his fingers were thick and quite stubby: too big for piano keys or delicate stringed instruments. Jennifer wasn't musical either, but she liked to think that the musical gene would skip a generation and that their baby would inherit the gift.

Although her memory was slowly deteriorating, Elizabeth Saltman knew that David and Jennifer were expecting a baby and she was over the moon at the thought of being a grandmother for the first time. What she and the rest of the family didn't know was that she was expecting twins. Jennifer had been unusually tired during the early stages of her pregnancy; her weight gain was higher than expected and her blood pressure had significantly increased. Twins were suspected but only confirmed when Vernon Shilling detected two heartbeats in the fourth month of the pregnancy. David and Jennifer were of course thrilled, but they had decided to keep the news a secret. Only they knew that both shawls would soon be needed.

By the time David closed the trunk of the station wagon the rain had started to fall quite heavily. He called to Jennifer who was putting on her jacket in the hallway. "Better grab yourself an umbrella, this rain is only going to get worse."

As Jennifer got into the car, David leaned across and kissed her gently on the cheek. Placing his hand on her bump he thought he could feel the kick of one of their babies. He whispered into Jennifer's ear, "I've never loved you so much as just now, I'm so excited."

Jennifer reached across and squeezed her husband's hand. This was finally it. David set the gear lever to drive and slowly drove down the gravel driveway to the road. It would take them about twenty-five minutes to reach the hospital.

*

It was dark now and raining so hard that Cathleen had her windscreen wipers on double speed. The last hundred yards to the junction of the Fairlea to Lewisburg road was sharply downhill. She braked gently as she approached the junction, but as she did, she immediately felt her front tyres skid underneath her. Peering through the misted-up windscreen she could see torrents of water streaming onto the highway. Several large stones had been washed from the track and were now strewn across the road. She thought about turning back but she knew that if she left it till morning there was no guarantee of making it to Fairlea at all. The road by the river was prone to flooding and this rain showed no sign of letting up. Anyway, she desperately needed the pads and provisions, so knew it was best to press on.

*

On the other side of town in class 2B of Ridgemount Elementary School, Susan McDowell was finishing preparing for her parents' afternoon the following day. Susan had newly turned twenty-two and this was her first teaching job after graduating from college. With only three months teaching experience, Susan knew how important it was to make a good impression with her children's parents. For the last three hours she had been busy making sure every child had at least one piece of work displayed on the wall. Above her desk she had hung a mural that the class had made out of plastic bottles, egg cartons, and just about anything else that was capable of being stuck onto a large sheet of cardboard. The mural depicted an enormous yellow dinosaur standing on two legs and wading through a swamp. Making it had involved the whole class and taken several hours as well as quite a few tears to complete. Susan felt the dinosaur had a Mona Lisa like quality, as no matter where she stood in the classroom, the dinosaurs eyes seemed to follow her. Anyway, she thought it looked great and hoped that the parents would too.

In one corner of the classroom Susan had laid out a tambourine, cymbals and other instruments that she used each day with the children during music time. Susan was a gifted musician playing both the guitar and piano and she liked to encourage the children's musical talents as much as possible. So far it had proved to be very popular with the children and tomorrow she planned to show some of the parents how the children had been learning to play basic rhythms and beats.

There were still one or two things to do but they would have to wait until the morning since the rain that had started half an hour ago was now thundering off the roof of her classroom. Susan wanted to get back to the flat she was renting above the baker's shop in Fairlea. She hadn't eaten since mid-morning and was hungry and weary after a long day. Susan didn't know Fairlea well as she had not long moved to the town from Harpers Ferry in Jefferson County. Harpers Ferry is one of West Virginia's most popular tourist areas and fisherman, kayakers and rock climbers throng to the area to enjoy its spectacular mountains and fast flowing rivers. She had developed her love of the outdoors while living there and though Fairlea was a beautiful town, it didn't have the bars and restaurants that gave Harpers Ferry such a buzz. Susan was finding being away from home difficult. It was fine when she was at work: she loved her job and the children. The evenings and weekends could tend to drag a little as she hadn't met many people yet. She knew she would have to give it time, but at the moment, when the weekends came around she loved to head back home and spend time with her family and friends. Her Aunt Claire's lodge was her favourite destination as it sat on a hillside looking over the beautiful Shenandoah river.

In the few weeks she had been in Fairlea, Susan soon found that living over the baker's shop had its compensations. Steffen Moller owned both the shop and the flat Susan rented. He was the second generation of German immigrants and his family hailed from Mainz on the banks of the river Rhine. Steffen would speak for hours to anyone prepared to listen on all things German; their world-famous engineering, beer and cars being his favourite topics. Susan was too polite to walk away, however, her patience was usually rewarded with a large bag of rolls, croissants or occasionally a slice of apple strudel. Steffen never took any money for them but always said, "That's alright Susan, just make sure you keep paying the rent."

On one of the rare occasions that he hadn't been talking about Germany, it had been Steffen who had told her that the river outside the town was prone to flooding in heavy rain. When it did, it usually closed the road which meant an eighteen-mile detour to get back to Fairlea. Remembering Steffen's words, and keen to avoid that possibility, Susan switched off her classroom lights and headed to her car that was parked near to the front gates of the school. By the time she reached it she was soaked through. She would be glad to get home for a hot shower and a glass of wine. The food would have to wait.

*

In the distance Cathleen could now see the lights of Fairlea quite clearly and the store was less than a mile away. Two sharp bends lay ahead as the road weaved its way along the banks of the Greenbrier River to the metal bridge. Many years of experience had taught Cathleen that if the river had burst its banks it would be here. As she slowly approached the first bend the headlights of her pick- up truck flashed across the river. The river was high, very high, but it had not yet burst its banks. She sighed in relief. The rain continued to lash down and large ripples of water pulsed in waves across the surface of the tarmac. As she carefully rounded the second bend she noticed the red taillights of a car. Slowing to almost a halt, she could see that a vehicle had left the road and careered down the riverbank striking a willow tree by the edge of the river. It had come to a stop inches from the water. Cathleen stopped her truck, leaving her headlights and hazard warning lights on, and ran down the slippery bank to the car.

The front end on the driver's side appeared to have taken the full impact of the crash and was badly smashed. She noticed that the car's engine was still running which made her think that the accident must have only just happened. She peered apprehensively through the steamed-up window on the driver's side. Inside she could make out the figures of two people, a male driver and a female passenger. She could see that the driver was slumped forward with his chest crushed tight against the steering wheel. Alarmingly, she could see that he had suffered a significant injury to the left side of his head. Blood continued to ooze from an open wound. Frantically, Cathleen pulled at the door, but it wouldn't open, it had been badly dented during the impact. She could feel her heart racing as she desperately tugged at the door. Finally, the door opened a few inches. Bracing herself against the bank, Cathleen began kicking the door hard with her right foot. Eventually, she was able to prise the door back far enough to allow her to wriggle into the front of the vehicle. She switched off the ignition and pushed the driver off the steering wheel and back into his seat. She knew the man was already dead. Blood covered the left side of his face and his beige open necked shirt was a violent pink colour. By the interior light Cathleen could see how the fatal injury had occurred. Blood and blond matted hair was smeared onto the 'A' pillar of the car. Instinctively she lifted the man's left wrist to check for a pulse. His arm was still warm, but his heartbeat was already a distant memory.

It could only have been seconds, a minute at most, but it felt like an eternity. She knew she had another casualty to help but time seemed to stand still. Every action she had taken from opening the car door to checking for a pulse had seemed to have been done in slow motion. She felt sick, her head was throbbing, and she could feel her energy levels slowly draining away. A voice inside her head was telling her to save the living and leave the dead. She longed for someone, anybody, to be there to help her, but she was alone, and things were not going to get any easier.

As she scrambled her way round the rear of the car, Cathleen noticed the suitcase and shawls through the misted window of the tailgate. The passenger door opened without any difficulty and she stared in disbelief at the woman in the passenger seat. She turned around and vomited violently. She recognised Jennifer Saltman immediately. Jennifer had been attending her antenatal classes at the hospital for the last 12 weeks. Just last week they had joked how Jennifer's bump appeared to be twice the size of hers even though their due dates were not much more than a month apart. She remembered Jennifer saying, "Of course, I'm getting two for the price of one but please keep that to yourself we're going to surprise the family."

Jennifer was unconscious, but she was breathing. She had a large abrasion and swelling on her forehead. The windscreen in front of her was cracked where her head had hit it. A trickle of blood was coming out of her right ear, Cathleen knew that wasn't a good sign.

She put her hand on Jennifer's belly. She could feel her stomach hardening under her touch as a contraction intensified, moments later it would soften slightly. The babies were coming. She bent down to see how far advanced Jennifer was, but the interior light was too dim for her to see anything. Instead she placed her hand between Jennifer's legs. She could clearly feel the crown of a baby's head. The first baby was delivered only minutes later.

Cathleen worked quickly to clear the mucus and blood from the baby's mouth. It immediately took a breath and started to cry. She reached into her jacket pocket for her pen knife, Cathleen seldom went anywhere without her knife. Living on a farm you never knew when you might need a knife and while she mainly used it for cutting vegetables, it wouldn't be the first time she'd had to use it to cut an umbilical cord. This time it would be for a baby and not a lamb. Cathleen opened the knife and cleaned the blade with some wet ferns that were growing next to the car. Carefully she cut the cord about 4cm from the baby's stomach. With some more ferns Cathleen tried to wipe the baby clean. She gazed at the baby, it was a beautiful baby boy. She opened the trunk of the station wagon and grabbed one of the shawls. She wrapped the baby tightly in the soft wool and carefully made her way up the river bank to her pick-up truck. She opened the passenger door and placed the precious bundle carefully on the front seat. Then she raced back to the stricken vehicle slipping on the soaking bank and sliding the last few feet. No more than five minutes had passed when Cathleen felt the head of the second baby appear. With one leg kneeling in the footwell and using her other leg to brace herself she was able to free both her arms so that they could support the baby. She could feel painful spasms in the small of her back; she wouldn't be able to maintain this position much longer.

Suddenly, from the road above her, Cathleen heard a woman's voice shouting, "Is everything alright? What can I do to help?"

Susan McDowell had pulled over when she saw Cathleen's truck at the side of the road and the taillights of the station wagon at the water's edge.

"Yes, yes! Down here!" cried Cathleen. "I can't see properly, I need some light! Do you have a torch in your car?"

"I've got a flashlight!" replied Susan.

"Can you grab it? Please get down here! This poor lady is having a baby!" shouted Cathleen. "And be careful the bank is very slippy!"

Susan grabbed the flashlight from her car, switched it on, and headed down the treacherous slope. As she arrived at the passenger door the beam from her flashlight lit up the front of the station wagon and the full horror of the accident was revealed. She gasped and instinctively recoiled. She wanted to run away, but she knew she must stay and help. She had seen a dead body

11

before but not like this. Some years ago, she had seen the body of a canoeist who had drowned after he hit rocks on the Shenandoah River near her aunt's lodge. This was altogether different. Blood and bits of body tissue were everywhere, she was just inches from a bloodied corpse. It was horrific.

"Can you hold the light steady? This baby is nearly with us," shouted Cathleen.

Susan placed the flashlight against the top of the passenger door and held it steady with her arm. For a brief second, the beam of light shone directly onto Jennifer's ashen face. The bright white light gave her a ghostly, almost ethereal, appearance. It was as much as Susan could bear. She tilted the light down and shut her eyes.

Cathleen could now see the baby's head and shoulders. She desperately wanted to stand up as the spasms in her back gripped her like a vice. Seconds later she felt the weight of the baby in her hands. With great care she backed herself out of the doorway and stood up. It was another baby boy. She cleaned the baby's airway with her finger and the baby took its first breath and started to cry. Cathleen took her knife and just as before cut the baby's umbilical cord. Susan wanted to cry too but no tears came. She was stunned by the intensity of the moment, she had seen the start of one life and the end of another. Her heart was racing, and her hands were shaking uncontrollably.

Cathleen could see Susan was in shock, but she needed her help urgently. Holding the baby across her right arm she grabbed Susan by the shoulder and looked directly into her eyes,

"I know this is difficult, but I need you to focus, I need your help. Can you do that for me?"

Susan didn't reply but nodded in acknowledgement. Cathleen added, "I saw a shawl in the back of the car. I need you to get it for me."

Susan nodded again. As she made her way to the back of the car Cathleen scooped up the bloody placenta that was lying in a pool of blood in the passenger footwell and with one heave tossed it into the dark waters of the river. Best not be keeping that, she thought, just to be on the safe side.

Susan opened the tailgate and picked up the shawl. As she closed the trunk, a series of piercing cries split the still evening air. The cries were coming from the direction of the road. They sounded like the cries of a baby.

"Did you hear that?" asked Susan, "It sounded like a baby crying."

Before she could say anything else, Cathleen cut her off, "It's a Fox crying. I heard it twice before you got here."

Susan looked confused. "Are you sure? It sounded like a baby to me."

"Quickly bring me the shawl," said Cathleen, "I need you to take the baby, so I can try to help his mother. I'm sorry I don't even know your name. I'm Cathleen, I'm sure glad you showed up!"

"My name's Susan, Susan McDowell."

Cathleen wrapped the baby in the shawl and handed the infant back to Susan. Then she picked up the flashlight and shone the beam of light at Jennifer. There was still work to do. She looked at Jennifer's chest, it was no longer moving, and her head had tilted further to the side. There was no sign of life. Cathleen put two fingers to the side of Jennifer's neck in the hope of finding a pulse but there was none. It was too late, Jennifer was dead. She had clung to life just long enough for her babies to be born; now it was time to let go.

Susan held the new-born in her arms. She pulled him tight to her heart and tears filled her eyes. It was just so desperately sad. She was holding a baby who would never feel the loving touch of his mother or the comforting hug of his father. She had never experienced such raw emotions and she felt completely overwhelmed. Still holding the baby Susan leant into Cathleen's shoulder and both women wept.

It was Cathleen who broke their embrace first.

"Susan, I need you to get the baby to the hospital and get help."

The drive to the hospital was a complete blur. Susan remembered running into the entrance and shouting for help. She recalled that a nurse quickly came and took the baby from her. She knew she must have given someone details about where the accident was and that the baby's parents were both dead, but she couldn't remember much else. For several hours she sat in the hospital canteen nursing a cup of coffee. She was completely numb.

*

Over in Ike's Diner on the outskirts of Lewisburg, Ewart Wilder and his partner Phil Coutts were finishing their coffee break and returning to their patrol car just as the radio crackled into life. They were being directed to attend the scene of a suspected fatal road accident near to Greenbrier Bridge on the Fairlea Road. The radio controller informed them that an ambulance was already en route and that a member of the public, Cathleen Heggerty, had come across the accident and was waiting at the scene.

"Surprised it took this long for a car to go off the road in this weather," said Ewart Wilder in a cold and rather matter of fact way. "We'd better get over there Shads, before some other idiot does the same thing."

Shads was short for Shadow, or The Shadow, as Wilder habitually referred to his partner. Phil didn't exactly know why. It was something to do with the fact that he was rather quiet, and he preferred staying in the background. Taking the initiative didn't come naturally to him. He hated the nickname, but if he showed any sign of weakness, it would be leapt upon on by Wilder and the name calling and ribbing, would only get worse.

At twenty-seven Phil Coutts was two years older than Wilder and had been with the Lewisburg Police Department eighteen months longer, but it was Ewart Wilder who called the shots in this partnership. Wilder had joined the police service four years ago. He had followed his father, who had recently retired after thirty-one years' service with the Lewisburg department, into the job. It was partly that that had given Wilder his confidence, but it was also the fact that he was a naturally outgoing type and his stocky muscular build gave him a physical presence that he frequently used to his advantage. He had quickly gained the reputation of being a capable officer, but in the quiet backwaters of rural West Virginia, he was a little too quick with his fists when things turned ugly especially for Phil's liking. There was only one way of dealing with resistance in Wilder's book and it didn't involve debate or diplomacy.

Experience had taught Phil how to get along with Wilder. Once in their early days he had made the mistake of answering back after Wilder once again called him the shadow. Phil countered by calling him, Bull, or Little Bull, to be precise. Both Ewart and his father had gone by the nickname of Bull on account of their bullish characters and their powerful build. Phil thought it would be funny to christen Wilder, Little Bull. That turned out to be a serious mistake. Wilder had immediately flown into a rage, grabbed him by the throat and smashed him against a metal locker at the station. Phil swears his feet never touched the ground as he hurtled backwards into the locker. That was the first and last time that he called Wilder anything but his name. He was a bully and while they would never be friends away from work, Phil didn't mind working with him. Wilder was hard working and knowledgeable. His natural confidence gave him the ability to deal efficiently with incidents in a way that didn't come so easily to Phil. He also knew that as long as Wilder didn't fall foul of his temper, it was very likely that he would rise quickly through the ranks.

*

By now the rain had stopped and Cathleen was starting to feel cold as her jacket and dress were soaked through. She had no idea how long it would take for help to reach her. It must have only been ten minutes since Susan had left for the hospital, but it seemed much longer. Grabbing onto tufts of wet grass and ferns she carefully made her way up the sodden riverbank to the road where her car was parked. She opened the passenger door to check on the baby. His eyes were tightly closed, and he appeared to be sleeping contentedly. Cathleen fetched some newspapers and a couple of old towels that were lying under a tarpaulin in the back of the pick-up and folded them in several layers in the floor in the footwell of the passenger seat. Being careful not to disturb him she lifted the child and placed the shawl and baby on top of the towels and papers. It was not a cold evening, even so the newspapers would provide some insulation and stop the baby from getting damp or chilled. More importantly he needed to be out of sight for the time being.

In the back of the pick-up Cathleen also found an old, grey gabardine coat belonging to her husband. It was far too big for her, ripped and covered in oil and goodness knows what else. Frank used it around the farm when he was mucking out the hogs. It smelt terrible but for now it was welcome. It would help keep her dry and warm. The zip was broken so she wrapped it around her and held it closed with her arms. The sleeves were so long they completely covered her hands.

Cathleen could now hear sirens in the distance. Moments later she could see the blue flashing lights of the ambulance as it rounded the bend. She watched nervously as two ambulance men exited the vehicle. Her head started to spin.

What if they recognised me and notice I'm not pregnant thought Cathleen. She stared at the men as they approached the top of the bank. Dozens of ambulance drivers worked out of Fairlea and Lewisburg depots and through her years working at the hospital she had got to know many of them. Fortunately, she didn't recognise either of these men.

Calmly Cathleen explained the circumstances to the men. They were already aware that a baby had been rushed to the hospital and that the parents were thought to have died in the accident. They quickly made their way to the station wagon where they confirmed the inevitable. Both occupants were dead. There would be no call for their medical skills this evening. This would be a recovery and conveyance to the mortuary, a service they had provided many times before.

The police arrived as Cathleen was talking with the ambulance crew. Having surveyed the wretched scene for themselves, officers Wilder and Coutts spent some time speaking to the paramedics. When they came over to speak to her, Cathleen she was struck by how calm and emotionless they both seemed to be. By now she was feeling exhausted and desperately wanted to be back home at the farm. She felt irritated and annoyed at how routine this appalling event seemed to the officers and ambulance crew. She understood that these men had a job to do, but she still felt shocked at how detached they appeared to be. Cathleen had felt a deep sense of attachment to every baby she had lost as a midwife. She cared, she had always cared.

While officer Coutts took photographs of the station wagon, Ewart Wilder recorded brief details of the incident and noted Cathleen's name and address in his notebook. She told him about Susan McDowell and apologised for not knowing her address.

"Not a problem," said Wilder, "I'll be able to get her details from the hospital."

Wilder told Cathleen that he would need to get a full statement of the circumstances later, but that could wait for now. Several hours of work lay ahead recovering the bodies and tracing next of kin and more photographs would need to be taken in the morning.

Cathleen said she would be happy to attend at the police station tomorrow if that would be helpful. Officer Wider said that would be fine and they arranged for her to attend at Lewisburg Police Department at 7 o'clock the following evening.

Nobody had asked if Cathleen was in a fit state to drive, but as she drove away her mind was already turning to other urgent matters. She needed to get to the store and now she had one more item to add to her list of provisions, a tin of infant formula. The baby must be very hungry.

Chapter 2

It was shortly after 9pm when Cathleen drew up outside Jed Gosling's convenience store. She had expected to find it shut and she was already resigned to the twelve-mile journey to White Sulphur Springs where Desi Singh's store stayed open till midnight. She noticed that a light was still on in the shop and as she approached the front door she could see that Jed was sitting at the counter writing. She had known Jed since their school days. The Goslings had run the store in Fairlea for over forty years and Jeff and Roselyn Gosling, Jed's grandparents, had been good friends with Cathleen's grandparents on her mother's side. She tapped on the window of the door with her car key. Jed Looked up from the counter and waved at Cathleen standing in the doorway. He unlocked the door and let her in.

"Lucky you caught me," said Jed, "I was just catching up on some bookkeeping." Jed stood for a moment and looked Cathleen up and down.

"I've seen you better dressed Cathleen! What on earth are you wearing?"

Cathleen started to explain that she had been on her way to the store when she had come across a serious road accident at Greenbrier Bridge. As she described what had happened her voice started to tremble, and it became clear to Jed that Cathleen was getting upset.

"Oh, that sounds terrible, no need to explain any further," said Jed before asking, "What is it you're needing?"

"I need bread, milk and some, I need some pads and infant formula too, I've had my baby Jed."

"You've had the baby!" Jed's voice sounded surprised. "I thought it wasn't due till next month? Wow, that's great news Cathleen. What did you have?"

"A beautiful baby boy. His name's Josh."

"Congratulations! I take it Frank is thrilled?"

"Over the moon," said Cathleen, "Just over the moon."

"I nearly forgot," said Cathleen, "do you have any baby bottles? One of mine has a crack in it."

"I think I may have a couple left. I've sold quite a few recently," replied Jed as he pulled over a stool and stood on it. Stretching on his tip-toes he reached into a large cardboard box on the top shelf. "Yep, just as I thought, still a couple left. You'll have to bring the baby in to see us next time you come into town," said Jed as he gathered up and bagged the rest of Cathleen's shopping.

"Of course I will," said Cathleen. Jed handed her the brown bag of provisions.

"No charge," he said. "Have these as a baby gift. A baby boy! That's just great, Frank will be made up."

"He sure is. You didn't have to do that Jed, it's real kind of you," said Cathleen.

"My pleasure," replied Jed as Cathleen turned to leave the store.

Cathleen climbed back into the pick-up and started the engine. Baby was still wrapped up tight and fast asleep. As she reached the crossroads at the edge of town she didn't turn left to head for home, instead she took the right turn and headed towards the hospital. There was something that she needed to do, and it wouldn't wait.

The main drive rose steeply towards the front entrance of the hospital. Cathleen drove past the staff and visitors' car park and took a sharp left turn at the top of the hill. It was a route that she had taken hundreds of times before, but she now found herself feeling apprehensive and nervous.

The hospital seemed very quiet, visiting was over and all the dayshift staff had headed home long ago, so there were few people about. As she made her way to the maternity wing at the rear of the hospital she didn't pass another vehicle. As the unit's lights came into sight she switched off her headlights and reduced her speed. She needed to be quiet. She parked the pick-up in dark shadow under some trees at the far end of the car park near the boiler house. She got out of the vehicle carrying her bag of provisions and walked round to the passenger door. She opened the door very carefully, picked up the sleeping baby from the footwell and wrapped her coat over her precious bundle.

Cathleen made her way to a recessed doorway about fifty yards from the rear entrance of the unit. The door led to the clerical office where Cynthia Lehman worked. Cynthia was Vernon Schilling's secretary. She was hardworking and extremely efficient, Vernon thought the world of her. Except for one thing; she chain smoked. Cigarette ends littered the ground outside her door. Cathleen wondered if any of them had been hers as she had been known to have the odd one at the back door with Cynthia when she could catch a quiet five minutes. She didn't like to let Vernon see her smoking as she knew that he didn't approve. Cathleen had stopped smoking completely after she had discovered she was pregnant. Vernon was always preaching about the perils of smoking during pregnancy. Not everyone listened, certainly not Cynthia, but Cathleen did. Vernon was the smartest man she knew.

Being careful not to drop the baby Cathleen shuffled her bunch of keys with her left hand until she found the one she was looking for. As far as she knew she was the only person who Cynthia had given a spare key to. Over the years they had become firm friends. Cathleen would often take her lunch break with Cynthia and they would put the world to rights about a whole range of issues. Cynthia would take a long draw of her filter-tipped Kent Cigarette purse her lips and blow three large smoke rings before giving her thoughts on the latest crisis or political scandal. Blowing smoke rings was Cynthia's party trick, that and being able to drink large quantities of Old Mister Kentucky Bourbon. Cynthia always said that having two older brothers taught her many things, smoking and drinking bourbon being just two of the more acceptable ones.

Cynthia was an intelligent woman who had originally wanted to be a lawyer. Having to care for her elderly parents had curtailed that ambition but Cynthia remained interested in world affairs and politics was a particular passion. Cynthia was a confirmed Democrat, which set her at odds with Cathleen, who, while not being particularly interested in politics, had always voted Republican. That was until she switched sides and voted for John Kennedy. Cathleen used to tease Cynthia by saying she only did it because he had lovely hair. That infuriated Cynthia who always thought deeply about important issues and disapproved about anyone treating serious matters frivolously. Deep down Cynthia knew that Cathleen was only kidding about the hair, but she was never entirely sure whether she had really voted for Kennedy.

Cathleen walked past Cynthia's office and the Consultant's room to the end of the corridor where there was a small kitchen comprising of a sink, kettle, cooker and a small refrigerator. Next to the window were a formica table and four chairs each of which had a yellow coloured plastic seat.

Cathleen carefully closed the window blind. She didn't put a light on but by leaving the door open there was just enough light from the corridor for her to see. She took off her coat, folded it several times and placed it on top of the table. She carefully placed the baby on top of the coat. He was starting to stir and was now making repeated soft cries.

"Hush now, baby Josh," whispered Cathleen. "I'll have this milk ready for you in just a minute." She boiled the kettle and rinsed out the baby bottle a couple of times. Using a table spoon she scooped out three spoonsful of the formula and tipped them into the bottle. She half-filled the bottle with hot water before topping it up with cold. After shaking it vigorously she replaced the rubber teat on the top of the bottle and squirted a little of the warm milk onto her forearm. It seemed fine, it certainly wasn't too hot. She picked up the baby and sat on one of the chairs, resting the baby against her right arm. Cathleen looked lovingly at the child. Gently she presented the bottle to the baby's mouth and said, "You've had to wait a long time for this Josh, I hope you enjoy it little man."

The baby sucked enthusiastically at the teat. He was clearly hungry and after only a few minutes the bottle was empty. Cathleen felt a warm and contented glow inside her as she stared at Josh. She stroked his flawless soft skin and with her fingers traced the outline of his tiny hands. She wanted to sit a while in the quiet stillness of that room and hold her baby. However, she still had one more thing to do and it needed to be done now.

The door to Cynthia's office wasn't locked. Cathleen went across to the window and closed the blind. The light from the corridor was insufficient for what she needed to do so she switched on the lamp on Cynthia's desk. To the side of the desk stood two large metal filing cabinets each of which had three large drawers. Taped onto the top left-hand corner of the first cabinet were the words Patients A-L. On the second cabinet were the words Patients M- Z. Cathleen opened the middle drawer of the second cabinet and started to leaf through the manila suspension files that hung neatly in rows. The tab on the last file in the drawer said Perryman. She carefully closed the drawer and then opened the bottom one. Seconds later she had found what she was looking for. She removed the file and placed it on the desk. Handwritten on the tab on the top of the file was the name, SALTMAN: JENNIFER, DOB. 19.3.36.

Cathleen opened the file and started to read. The file contained some typed pages meticulously prepared by Cynthia as well as several handwritten notes. She broke into a smile at the familiar spidery writing of Vernon Schilling. Many years of practice had taught her how to decipher Vernon's writing. Not many could, and Cynthia was always threatening him that he would have to learn to type if he couldn't make his handwriting more legible. As she read on she noted that Jennifer's projected due date was the 24th of April which would be next Tuesday, her babies had arrived five days early. As she turned to page three she found what she had been looking for. The page contained three short handwritten paragraphs describing Jennifer's sixteen-week assessment. Vernon had recorded that Jennifer had presented with unusual weight gain, extreme fatigue and hypertension. Her blood pressure was recorded as 159/109 mm Hg which was much higher than would be considered normal. Towards the end of the third paragraph Vernon had written that during a doppler examination he had detected two foetal heartbeats and as a result he had determined that twins were expected. Vernon had signed the entry which was dated October 27th, 1966.

Cathleen had hoped that she could have retyped the page and then forged Vernon's signature. That was something she had done a number of times before as he frequently forgot to sign off notes or prescriptions. She knew it was wrong but sometimes needs must. Vernon was aware it went on but turned a blind eye as after all, it was his forgetfulness that necessitated it. But these notes were handwritten so retyping clearly wasn't an option.

Having read the remainder of the file Cathleen could find no further mention of twins anywhere. Furthermore, the last entry by Vernon had been in December just a couple of weeks before he retired. The last entries that had been signed off by doctors were Doctor Hannah, in January, and Doctor Simmons, in March. Both doctors had been providing locum cover at the maternity unit after Vernon retired and she was confident that neither would particularly remember Jennifer Saltman. So, the solution seemed obvious, she would just remove page three from the file. It would disappear. It would be as if it had never existed and nobody would notice.

Cathleen took out the page folded it in half and put it in her jacket pocket. She closed the file and returned it to the cabinet taking great care not to make any noise. Having switched off the desk lamp she opened the window blind and headed for the door. Baby Josh was awake but appeared content. It was a little before midnight when she got into the pick-up. She switched on the engine and drove slowly out of the car park. She didn't switch on her headlights until she was sure she was out of sight of the unit. As she turned right onto the main road to head for home she felt content and at ease, after all, she was just like every other new mother who left the hospital with their new-born. Full of hopes and dreams for the future.

The journey home was uneventful. As she approached Greenbrier Bridge she noticed a yellow police sign at the side of the road that said, 'Caution: Road Accident'. Even before tonight's events Cathleen knew how dangerous the bends at the bridge could be and she couldn't have been doing more than thirty kilometres per hour when she passed the accident scene. A police patrol car was still parked on the verge of the road and an officer was standing near to the crashed vehicle. Yellow and black barrier tape had been erected to stop any unauthorised person from getting too close. She could only just see the rear of the vehicle, so she couldn't tell if the Saltmans had been removed from the car. She expected that they had but as she passed the station wagon she glanced at the sleeping baby and whispered, "Don't you be worrying Josh, you've got a new mom now and I'm going take good care of you."

Although the rain had now stopped, small torrents of water streamed down the farm track and large puddles had formed in the numerous potholes that littered the track. Cathleen knew where most of the deepest ones were so took great care to avoid them as she had lost a wheel once before driving into a pothole. She was anxious that there would be no repeat tonight. She parked the pick-up next to the hen coop and made her way to the house carrying baby Josh and her bag of provisions. The rain had freshened up the air and mercifully the temperature was a few degrees cooler than it had been for several weeks.

Once she was back in the house Cathleen hung up her coat and went into the back bedroom. She placed the baby gently into a wooden cot that sat against the far wall of the room. The bedroom itself was sparsely furnished but it was clear that it had been decorated to be a nursery. The walls were painted powder blue and all the wood, including the door, window frame and skirting boards were bright white. Apart from the dresser the only furniture in the room was the cot and a mahogany rocking chair that stood next to the window. On the chair sat an embroidered cotton cushion that depicted a variety of colourful spring flowers. Two bunny rabbits, one blue and one pink had been painted onto the panel on the end of the cot. The pink bunny's ears looked a bit peculiar as some of the paint had flaked off the top making it look more like a teddy bear than a rabbit. A plain set of dark blue curtains hung from the window that had been double lined to keep the light out.

Hanging from the ceiling above the cot was a mobile of brightly coloured fish. There were seven fish of all different sizes each with its own design. They had been roughly cut from hardboard and hung together using fishing twine.

Frank had made the mobile more than three years ago in preparation for the arrival of baby Peter. The mobile, cot and other items in the nursery had stood unused but in a state of readiness for those last years.

From the top drawer of the dresser Cathleen took out a dark green knitted baby grow. From the bottom drawer she removed a linen diaper and a safety pin. She carefully unwrapped the delicate woollen shawl that had keep Josh warm for the first traumatic hours of his life. Looking down at Josh, Cathleen felt overwhelmed by love. On the top of the baby's head she could clearly see the two fontanels under tiny tufts of straw blond hair. His eyes were a blue grey colour. His skin was still a little wrinkly but beautifully soft with a reddish tone. Looking at his chubby arms and legs she thought the baby weighed about six and a half pounds. Cupping her hands underneath the child she lifted him and nodded to herself, definitely over six pounds, not bad for a twin she thought.

The shawl was now smeared with blood, it was wet and on one side there was a large yellowish-brown stain. Good healthy colour thought Cathleen just what you'd expect from a new baby. She smiled to herself as she always thought that the colour and texture of a new-born baby's poo looked rather similar to peanut butter. She lifted up the shawl with her fingertips and discarded it onto the floor, in much the same careless manner a young child discards paper from a lovingly wrapped gift.

"We'll need to get you a nice new shawl; this smelly old thing won't be any use no more."

Cathleen cleaned the baby, put on his diaper and slipped him into the baby grow that was clearly a couple of sizes too big. It covered his hands and feet, but it would do for now. Cathleen carried Josh back into the kitchen and switched on the kettle.

"I think you could do with another feed before bedtime Josh, what do you think?"

Cathleen fed him the bottle which again he accepted with relish. In no time it was finished, and she tucked her baby son into his cot. She sat on the rocking chair next to the cot and quietly started to sing the words of an old Irish lullaby that her grandmother had often sung to her when she was a small child.

"Over in Killarney, many years ago

My Mother sang a song to me in tones so sweet and low

Just a simple little ditty in her good Irish way

And I'd give the world if she could sing that song to me this day

Too-ra-loo-ra-loo-ral, Too-ra-loo-li..."

By the time Cathleen got to the chorus the baby was asleep. She leant into the cot and kissed her sleeping child. Her heart swelled with love and her body tingled with excitement. Things are going to be just fine, she thought to herself. Back in the kitchen she washed out the dirty milk bottle and left it drying on the draining board next to the sink along with the tin of formula and a fresh linen cloth. She expected to be up at least once through the night as her son appeared to have a healthy appetite.

Cathleen looked at herself in the bedroom mirror. Her hair was bedraggled and no longer in its usual neat bun. Her dress was still damp and as she turned to the side she could see that the back was covered in mud where she had slipped down the river bank. She longed to lie down and sleep but before she could she had one more task to do.

Cathleen opened the front door and went out into the cool night air. She left the door slightly ajar, so she would still be able to hear Josh if he started to cry. At the smaller of the two outbuildings which sat at a right angle and a few yards from the house Cathleen reached up and removed a large key that was hanging on a nail underneath the overhang of the roof. She unlocked the rusty padlock and pulled back the hasp. The outbuilding contained a number of pieces of farm machinery and a large selection of tools. Cathleen had forgotten to take a torch and it was so dark she could hardly see. As she stumbled about in the dark she got increasingly frustrated as she couldn't find what she was looking for. She picked up a garden fork, then a hoe and a rake before finally putting her hands on the wooden shafted shovel she'd been looking for. It had a rounded end and Frank often used it for cutting trenches. It would be just the tool for the job in hand.

A couple of hundred yards from the front of the farmhouse, at the top of the field that marked the boundary and high point of the farm stood a very large chestnut tree. It must have been at least eighty feet tall and as far as Cathleen knew it was a couple of hundred years old. Its massive branches spread out in all directions and in the fall, it produced hundreds of sweet chestnuts that she loved to roast to make stuffing for the Thanksgiving turkey.

It was a special tree in many ways, not least because it was the only one left on the farm that hadn't been contaminated by a deadly blight that had seen nearly all the chestnut trees in Greenbrier County succumb and die.

The biggest of the branches hung only about twelve feet from the ground and it was from this branch that Grandpops had hung a rope swing for Cathleen to play on when she was a child. Grandpops was her grandfather Sean McClung whom Cathleen had loved dearly. Her own father had been killed in the battle of Okinawa during the Second World War when she was only fifteen. He had been in the Navy for ten years before that, so she hadn't spent much time with her father growing up. Her mother died an alcoholic when she was seventeen. Her relationship with her mother had suffered badly at the hands of the gin bottle. Cathleen wasn't against drink but seeing what it did to her mother left her with a healthy respect for it. Consequently, she only drank occasionally at birthdays and other special occasions.

Cathleen's relationship with both her grandparents ran deep. They had been surrogate parents to her and as their only grandchild Cathleen was the centre of their world.

Sean and Caitlin McClung hailed from Dararra a small village near Clonakilty in County Cork in the southwest of Ireland. They had married there in 1908 and emigrated to America in 1911. They initially settled in Boston where Sean found work in a foundry and Caitlin as a cleaner to a wealthy Boston lawyer. Both being from farming stock they didn't much enjoy living in the city and before long they had moved to Fairlea in West Virginia to stay with an old uncle and work at the farm he had established on 180 acres just outside the town. On his death a few years later, Sean and Caitlin inherited the farm and renamed it Dararra after the village where they were born. Cathleen's grandparents farmed there happily for over forty years until they passed away several years ago.

In the ground a few yards in front of the tree was a simple wooden cross. No more than ten inches high it was painted white and had the words "Peter Heggerty, Died 21.5.64. 'Forever in our Hearts," inscribed on it. Cathleen paused for a moment and looked forlornly at the cross. She moved back up the hill to where a patch of dark purple larkspur and wild red columbine were growing. She bent down and picked a couple of the larkspur and placed them on the ground next to the cross. They had been her grandmother's favourite flower as they reminded her of her childhood home in Ireland where they grew wild around the farm. Cathleen bowed her head in the stillness of the night and said a short prayer.

Last night's heavy rain had softened the surface of the ground a little, but after weeks without any rain, the soil underneath was still hard, and it was very difficult to dig. Cathleen carefully cut out a sod of turf which measured about three-feet-long by two foot-wide and laid it to one side. She then set about digging down into the hard earth. After about fifteen minutes with sweat dripping off her brow she had dug a hole about two feet deep. It will need to be at least the same again thought Cathleen but the next couple of feet were proving difficult as she kept hitting large stones that were almost impossible to lever out of the ground. After another twenty minutes had passed she had only managed to dig another foot and by now she could feel blisters forming on the palm of her right hand. It will have to do she thought.

Cathleen went back into the farmhouse and after checking that baby Josh was still asleep went into the kitchen to open the trap door to the basement. She felt the chill of the air on her face as she descended the stairs. She made her way to the table at the far side of the room and picked up the apple crate. This time she didn't bother to pull back the grey blanket that was covering her still-born child. Her actions were perfunctory and without emotion. In the cycle of life another more important child had entered her life and now he must be nurtured and cherished. Now was not the time for sentiment. Cathleen had had enough heartbreak in her life. It was time to move on and grasp the opportunity that had so unexpectedly presented itself. Holding the crate in both hands she climbed the nine steps to the kitchen and closed the trap door. As she walked up the hill to the newly dug grave Cathleen's mind drifted back to that day nearly three years ago when she had walked up the same hill with Frank and her grandmother carrying baby Peter in a tiny white coffin. The raw emotions that had been so overwhelming that day were strangely absent this time. This felt very different. She briefly wondered if it was because she was alone this time, but in all honesty, she knew in her heart that it was baby Josh that she now had to love, not the child she was carrying in the apple crate.

Cathleen knelt on the damp grass and lowered the crate into the dark ground. Carefully she started to shovel soil back into the hole. When the hole was about half filled she placed several large stones on top of the soil. She didn't want any wild animal disturbing the grave. Having filled the grave with the remaining soil, she placed the grass sod on the top and trod it firmly down with the heel of her shoes. Cathleen stood alone in the darkness. This grave would not be marked with a cross.

Chapter 3

Baby Josh had only needed fed once during the night and by 7am Cathleen felt refreshed enough to face the day. She reckoned she had managed to get four hours sleep and now her thoughts turned to her own needs. She was hungry and badly in need of a bath. With baby Josh gurgling contentedly in a Moses basket on the kitchen table Cathleen made herself some eggs and a stack of pancakes. The eggs were from her chickens and today they tasted particularly delicious. She would have liked to have soaked longer in the bath but there were many chores that needed to be done amidst juggling the demands of her baby son.

Standing on the porch by the front door was a metal bucket filled with vegetable peelings and other scraps of discarded food. Cathleen picked up the bucket and a tattered old wicker basket sitting next to it. She intended to pick some vegetables from the garden. The peelings were for the five hogs that lived in a byre adjacent to the bigger of the two outbuildings. The hogs were a fairly new addition to the farm, Frank reckoned they made good economic sense as they ate all manner of scraps and leftovers and fetched a good price at market. If all went well the hogs would also provide them with their own supply of bacon and sausages.

Before going to the byre Cathleen wandered up the hill to the vegetable plot. The distinctive garlicky scent of ramps, a variety of wild onion that grew prolifically in the rich West Virginian soil, filled the air and she picked several of the tender shoots. She also picked a couple of artichokes as they were also coming into season. Cathleen would use the ramps to make soup and a chicken stew for Frank's arrival home the following day as the pungent onions were a particular favourite of his. After picking her vegetables Cathleen checked the wire fence which enclosed the vegetable garden and ran all the way from the house to the chestnut tree. No hog was going to be allowed to get through the fence to eat the ramps or her grandmother's precious flowers. In the warm morning sunshine everything appeared in order, so she returned to the byre and fed the hogs leaving the byre door open so that the hogs could wander out and root around the fields and numerous apple trees that grew in small orchards on all sides of the farm. Last autumn, when the hogs had just arrived, disaster nearly struck when they got into the orchard and ate every windfall apple lying on the ground. That wasn't a concern at this time of the year but there was no way they could be allowed anywhere near Peter or the newly dug grave. Before returning to the house Cathleen fed the chickens and collected six eggs.

As well as the soiled shawl, Cathleen decided she would burn the dress she had been wearing last night and Frank's old gabardine coat. She had thought about washing the dress but apart from her precious baby she needed no reminders of the events of that dreadful night. In any case a new baby was a cause for celebration.

She could treat herself to a new dress and Frank could get a new coat.

Cathleen placed the clothes into an old oil drum that stood behind the outbuildings. She poured some petrol from a jerry can over the clothes, lit a match and then dropped it into the drum. Flames immediately leapt up and within seconds the drum was an inferno. No wonder, thought Cathleen, with all the oil and muck that was on Frank's coat this fire could burn for hours. By the time the last of the embers were dying down it was after four and in a few hours, Cathleen would have to head into Lewisburg for her meeting with Officer Wilder. Before then there was time to feed and change Josh and just sit a while together. A mother with her son, just as it should be.

The late afternoon sunshine was hot and shone directly onto the porch. Cathleen moved her chair to the far side of the porch beyond the kitchen window where there was at least some shade. Supporting Josh in her arms she fed him his bottle which he sucked on contentedly. There was next to no breeze now. She watched a pair of buckeye butterflies flutter above a verbena bush that was growing in front of the porch. Each wing bore a large orange and black spot and its blue centre gave it the appearance of a deer's eye. Their wings were delicate like painted silk and fragile in the way rice paper is. Cathleen marvelled at their beauty and thought they looked like flowers in the air as they continued their endless search for nectar. High in the sky above her, chimney swifts soared effortlessly on the thermals catching flying ants to feed to their newly hatched offspring. In the run at the front of the hen coop a couple of chicks scratched and pecked at the grit and grains of seed that covered the ground. Though only days old, the chicks were already independent and spending time away from their mother, not like the helpless babe that she cradled in her lap. All around her new life was flourishing. Cathleen felt happy in a way that she had not felt in quite some time.

Cathleen leant back in her chair and closed her eyes. In her mind she could see her grandmother picking vegetables from the garden for the evening meal. She remembered her Grandpops holding her hand and taking her up to the chestnut tree after he finished his work on the farm to push her on the swings for what seemed like hours. She would excitedly tell her grandfather what she had been doing at school or with her friends that day and he would tell her tall tales of what he'd been up to on the farm. It had been a very happy time in her life and she missed her grandparents terribly. As she gently rocked baby Josh in her chair she longed for the day when she would relive those childhood days. This time it would be Josh who would get to sit on the swing.

It was almost six-thirty when Cathleen turned off the farm track and onto the Lewisburg road. As she drove along it was still possible to see evidence of last night's torrential downpour. Stones of various sizes were strewn across the highway and the Haney Creek, a tributary of the Greenbrier River which ran parallel to the road, looked more like the Greenbrier itself such was the volume of water flowing down it. Cathleen didn't notice the stones on the road or the height of the creek, her mind was on other things. She had dressed Josh in a fresh sleep suit and tucked him snugly into his Moses basket. It hadn't taken long for the movement of the car to send Josh to sleep and she hoped he would stay asleep while she spoke to Officer Wilder. It wasn't her intention to take the baby into the police station, officer Wilder knew nothing about Josh and Cathleen intended to keep it that way.

As she drove Cathleen started to feel her heartbeat quicken and her chest tighten. The events of last night were spinning in her head and she was having difficulty concentrating on the road. It wasn't the image of the crashed vehicle or its deadly contents that were distressing her, it was the words of Susan McDowell that were playing on a seemingly never-ending loop in her head. "I can hear a baby crying. Can you hear the baby crying? It sounds like a crying baby." On and on it went.

Cathleen didn't see the other vehicle coming but as it passed her she heard the long blast of its horn. She had been very lucky, by the time she came to her senses she realised she had crossed the white dividing line of the road and the nearside of her vehicle was at least two feet into the lane of the oncoming traffic.

Cathleen pulled into the first available lay by and came to a stop. She closed her eyes and took several deep breaths. After a minute or so she felt calmer and her heart was no longer racing. She knew she had to focus. She was sure that the police would want to interview Susan. What would she say to them? Would she mention that she thought she had heard a baby cry? She remembered that she told Susan that it was a fox that she'd heard crying and Susan had seemed to accept that. Surely it wasn't important. But what if she did mention it? Much better that I mention it too thought Cathleen. Just mention it. Don't make a big deal of it but don't ignore it. That way if Susan does mention it, then I will have too. If she doesn't then no big deal, it will be a minor detail. The officers will concentrate on more important matters anyway.

Her mind was made up. She had a plan and she intended to stick to it. She once again felt in control. Cathleen put on her indicator and glanced over her shoulder to check for oncoming traffic, to be doubly sure she checked all was clear a second time before heading cautiously onto the carriageway. The rest of the journey passed uneventfully and as she drove into Lewisburg it was ten minutes before the hour.

*

Ewart Wilder was in his office on the third floor of the police office. He had only been at his desk for ten minutes but was already finishing his second cup of coffee. Another long evening lay ahead. It had barely been eight hours since he had gone off duty and he had had little more than four hours sleep. The shots of caffeine would be very welcome as he needed to finish his report, so it could be with the District Court in the morning. The accident paperwork and dealing with the hospital and relatives had taken longer than expected and with the witness statements still to be obtained he was in for a busy night. The phone on his desk rang; it was the desk sergeant from reception informing him that a Cathleen Heggerty was in the office to see him.

"Can you show her to the lift?" said Ewart, "I'll meet her when she gets out." He walked the short distance along the corridor to the lift and was waiting for Cathleen when the doors opened.

"Thanks for coming. Did you manage to get parked alright?" asked Ewart.

"I wasn't sure about the parking, so I'm parked in a side street next to the library just around the corner," replied Cathleen.

"That's fine," said Ewart. "Did you know that Jennifer Saltman worked at the library? Funny to think she was working only yards from my office and yet we'd never met. I never forget a face, so I'd have recognised her if we had met. You'd have thought we'd have bumped into each other at Annie Mack's shop, everyone round here gets their sandwiches from Annie Mack's. Just think it's strange I'd never seen her."

Cathleen was again struck by Wilder's abruptness; he was just so matter of fact. Did he not care? A poor woman had died, and he finds it strange that he'd never met her in a sandwich shop. His lack of empathy was starting to irritate Cathleen, but she knew she mustn't show her frustration. She needed to concentrate, answer any questions, give her statement and then go. She didn't want to spend a minute longer than was necessary in this place. In the back of her mind she was worried that Josh would wake up and start crying. She had left the pick-up windows slightly open for ventilation, but if he started to cry, somebody would hear and questions would be asked. She tried to put those thoughts out of her head. Now, more than ever, she needed to be thinking clearly.

"Would you like a coffee? asked Ewart, "I'm having one."

"No, no thanks," replied Cathleen, "I had one just before I left the house. Can I ask how the baby is?"

"Seems to be doing fine," replied Ewart. "The hospital says they're going to keep him in for a few days, just for checks and stuff. When I spoke to the family last night Jennifer's sister Ruth was going to be taking the boy. She lives up Marlinton way. She's got two sisters you know, the other one lives in Georgia, but she can't take the baby as she and her husband both work away from home a lot, not ideal but there you have it."

"No, not ideal, but good to know the baby's doing well," said Cathleen. "What about Susan McDowell, have you been able to contact her?"

"Yep, got to speak to her last night at the hospital. Shads, sorry, Officer Coutts, is away to Fairlea to get a statement from her. Hope she's doing better now. She was real shook up when I saw her last night."

"I expect she was in shock. Not surprising though, it's not something you'd want to have to deal with." said Cathleen, "I hope she's going to be alright."

"She'll get over it. Nothing else for it, you've just got to move on." said Wilder. "Anyway, you seem okay and you had more to deal with than her. What is it you do?"

"I'm a midwife at Fairlea," said Cathleen, "and I'm fine, as you say, you've just got to deal with it. Now, can we get this statement done I've got to be somewhere in an hour."

As she waited for the lift to take her down to reception Cathleen read the posters that were pinned on a notice board wall next to the lift. One poster in particular caught her eye. It was a picture of a car smashed into a large tree. The caption underneath read 'A tree never hits an automobile except in self-defence'. The poster was warning against the perils of drunk driving. How stupid thought Cathleen, you didn't have to be drunk to have the misfortune of crashing your car into a tree. It could happen to anyone, literally anyone, just ask the Saltman family. Cathleen ripped the poster from the wall and crumpled it into a ball. She tossed it into a bin that was next to the water cooler in the corridor. She decided to take the stairs. She did not want to be in the police office a moment longer.

As she walked to her car Cathleen went over the statement she had just given to Officer Wilder in her head. To give him his due he had just said to her, "You just tell me what happened, and I'll write it down, that's how this works." Cathleen had done just that and bit by bit she described the dreadful events of the previous night. When she was finished, Officer Wilder read the statement back to her. And there it was, the bit about the fox crying, in amongst all the other details that she had provided. Cathleen smiled to herself, mission accomplished she thought, she quickened her step in her eagerness to get back to the car.

Cathleen woke before six the next morning, shafts of bright light shone through the shutter at the side of her bed casting a checker board of brilliant early morning sunlight onto the dark floorboards. Particles of dust danced in the white light and outside she could hear the leaves of the beech hedge rustling in the gentle spring breeze. Cathleen felt invigorated and recharged.

Baby Josh was still sleeping so she headed out to feed the hogs and chickens. The night dew still clung to the grass and droplets of moisture glistened on the ramps and lettuces in the vegetable patch. There was washing to be done and a soup and stew to prepare before Frank arrived home that evening, but on a morning like this all tasks seemed joyful.

Chapter 4

Fifty miles away in Hinton, Frank Heggerty had one last task to help George with before he could pack his bag and head home to see Cathleen. Five lambs had still to be dipped but at this moment in time neither George nor Frank knew where they were. They should have been dipped three days ago but the tin of iodine that they used to sterilize the umbilical cord and stop infections had run out before the last five lambs could be done and now they could be anywhere on the hillside. Eighty-two lambs had been born this year which was only four short of George's best ever total. That was an impressive number as the season had got off to a difficult start when seven lambs were lost in one night on account of very wet and cold weather that had hit early in March when the first of the lambs were born. Only three more had been lost since; two had been killed by raptors and George thought the other had been taken by a rogue coyote. Finding the missing five was a priority as without being dipped the number of loses could easily increase and every one that didn't make it to market meant less money in George's pocket.

After an hour of fruitless searching George drove his battered old Buick truck to the top of the rise overlooking Bluestone Reservoir, a ten-mile expanse of water that impounds the New and Bluestone river systems. In the far distance they could see a number of sail boats on the sparkling water enjoying the spring breezes, in the foreground the blue white limestone of the dam glinted in the sunshine. It was an idyllic location and Frank could see why his brother so enjoyed living here. There was a rhythm and simplicity to George's life that was often lacking in his own and, despite his brother's social awkwardness, Frank coveted the peacefulness and contentment that his brother appeared to have found.

Standing at the bottom of the hill near the fence they could see three ewes and half a dozen lambs. The lambs were still small so were definitely no more than a couple of weeks old.

George peered through a pair of ancient field glasses, "I think we may be in luck, Frank," he said. "I can't see any mark on the belly of the one lying down. Time to do your stuff Bess."

Frank released the tailgate of the truck and Bess jumped down and raced down the hill. On George's whistle the dog stopped and crouched down no more than twenty feet from the sheep.

"We've got them now Frank, with the dog in front of them they'll not move. Can you grab the brush and tin?" shouted George as he headed down the hill.

Four of the six lambs hadn't been dipped so Frank gave each a generous splash of the iodine solution as George held them down.

"Don't know where the last one can be," said George. "I thought they would all be here, of course, a predator might have got it."

George searched his pockets for a biscuit for Bess who was standing in front of him expectantly wagging her tail.

"Do you want to continue looking?" asked Frank with a distinct lack of enthusiasm.

"No, no I'll think we'll call it a day. It might turn up yet with any luck, but I'll sort it if it does. You've done your turn for this week and I'm grateful to you little brother."

By the time they had climbed back up the hill Frank's foot was aching. Since his accident the pain in his foot would come and go but recently even relatively short walks were painful. Especially when the terrain was steep and uneven.

"That foot of yours giving you trouble again?" asked George.

"Pretty sore after walking up the hill if I'm honest," replied Frank.

"Nothing the doctors can do for me apparently. Keep taking the acetaminophen they tell me, but it hardly touches it. Only thing that seems to get rid of the pain is marijuana. Illegal but effective. A friend of mine smokes it and gives me some when the pain gets really bad. Cathleen doesn't know I take it, I don't think she'd approve somehow."

Frank continued, "Stupid thing is they lock you up now for smoking weed, one time not that long ago you could get it from your doctor for, guess what, pain relief!"

"Crazy." said George as he shook his head.

Back at the truck George pulled a large canvas bag from under the driver's seat. It was a strange faded green colour and clearly very old. On the front it had a tarnished brass buckle and the words US Navy were just about legible.

"Still got the bag then," said Frank.

"Sure have," replied George. "Nearly lost it a couple of months ago. I caught it climbing over a barbed wired fence and it ripped the bottom out of it. Repaired it though." George lifted up the bag to show Frank.

"You'll never make a surgeon, not with stitching like that!" laughed Frank.

The bottom of the bag had been crudely stitched with what appeared to be string.

"Doesn't need to be pretty just has to be functional. Anyway, I'll never get rid of it; it's the only thing I still have from dad. Think I was fourteen when he gave it to me, long time ago now."

"It was dark green when I got it, look at it now!" laughed George. "Spent too much time in the sun."

"I don't think I have anything that belonged to dad." said Frank. "To be honest I don't really remember much about him, only what you tell me."

"He looked very like you." said George. "About your height and same stocky build. He was broad across the shoulders and strong. A good sportsman he was. That must be where you got it from. He played middle line-backer in high school."

Frank smiled. It was a big hole in his life not knowing his father. George had told him many times before what their dad had been like but he never tired hearing about it, especially the part about being a good sportsman. Frank had been a gifted footballer and baseball player. In 1944 he had been in the Fairlea team who won the County Pennant and had been runners up in the state football championships. Frank still had his pennant and medals somewhere and one day he hoped he might have a son who, like his grandfather and father before him,

48

might also play football for Fairlea High School. Frank's thoughts drifted to home and his pregnant wife. He really didn't mind if the baby was a boy or a girl as long as it was healthy. He couldn't go through the pain and anguish like last time. But if he was to be given a choice Frank really wanted a boy, not that he'd let Cathleen know that.

In the bag were a couple of sandwiches. The bread was roughly cut, each slice must have been nearly an inch thick and brimmed full of egg and cheese. From a large jam jar George produced some pickled corn, a George Heggerty speciality, which had always been a favourite of Frank's. George hated wasting food so just about every left-over vegetable or fruit found its way into a pickle jar. Some of his experiments worked better than others. The corn, dill cucumbers and onions were great, but the pickled strawberries and melon - not so good.

The meal was washed down with a bottle of home-made lemonade. Having eaten their fill, the brothers lay back on the soft grass and dozed for a while in the warm sunshine.

It was gone four when Frank loaded his bag into the back of his Chevy flatbed to head home. "I'll see you in September then," said George. "I'm hoping for a bumper harvest this year. Those Jonagold trees I planted three years back should start to crop this year and the Grimes Golden were great last autumn. Here's hoping for another good year. As long as we get some rain," he added, "the apples won't grow if we don't get enough rain."

"Tell Cathleen I'm asking for her, you'll need to bring her out with you next time. It would be great to see her," said George.

"She might be a bit busy, what with the new baby and all," replied Frank sarcastically.

"Jeezo, sorry Frank, I just forgot, man I feel bad. When did you say it was due again?" asked George.

"Next month, should be here about the middle of May." said Frank.

"That's great, you'll let me know when it arrives Frank, won't you?" said George.

"Yep you bet, I'll phone you immediately. Oh, no wait I won't, will I! You don't have a phone, I'll need to send a postcard!" exclaimed Frank in an exasperated voice.

"Jeezo Frank, I said I was sorry. I just forgot."

Frank started his engine and as soon as the vehicle began to move Bess did as she always did and started barking and snapping at his tyres. Frank wound down his window and called across to George who was leaning against an apple tree next to the farm gates.

"I'm not mad George, I'm just joshing with you, but seriously you need to think about getting a phone installed. You're not getting any younger and if you're taken unwell, you're completely stuck! And you never know I might actually want to speak to you now and again, stranger things have happened."

George nodded his head and gave a rueful sigh.

"You're probably right, I'll think about it. Good luck with the baby and give Cathleen my best."

With a final wave Frank headed out the gates and down the farm track towards the main road. As long as I don't get stuck behind a John Deere I should be home by six he thought to himself.

It was twenty past five when he pulled up outside Moller's bakery in Fairlea. He wanted to pick up some moonpies for Cathleen, the delicious chocolate covered biscuits with soft marshmallow centres were her favourites and Moller's made the best and biggest moonpies in the town.

"Could you do me a favour and put them in a box with one of your fancy ribbons on it?" asked Frank as he ordered six of the biscuits.

"Sure thing," said Steffen, "all part of the service, is it a special occasion?"

"They're for my wife, she's expecting a baby soon and she loves moonpies. In fact, she seems to love anything chocolatey right now, got a real craving for it ever since she got pregnant."

"Well I'm sure she's going to love these." said Steffen as he tied the box up with a bright red ribbon. "They are the best moonpies in the county!" he said laughing. "Then again I'm biased. Best of luck when the baby comes."

"Thanks a lot, I'm sure she'll love them." said Frank as he carefully picked up the box. At $1.40 for six they were a special treat, but it isn't every day that your wife is expecting your first child, thought Frank. Besides it had been a cheap nine days as there had been nothing to spend his money on at George's. They hadn't even gone into Hinton for a beer after work as George was teetotal and had been all his life. Anyway, after ten hours work with the lambs you only wanted to have your dinner and put your feet up. Most nights they were in bed and asleep by ten.

Frank crossed the road to Pike's Liquor store and went into the shop. He headed straight for the chilled cabinet in the corner of the shop. He knew exactly what he wanted, a six pack of ice cold Stroh's. Frank had got a taste for Stroh's beer when he first worked in the mine. After work most Fridays, Frank and his colleagues would head into town for a couple of beers in Bursley's bar on Logan Street. Bursley's sold Stroh's on draft and just about everybody drank it. It made buying a round simple and ever since those days it had always been Frank's beer of choice. Sometimes two beers became five and Frank would catch the wrath of Cathleen when he wandered in after eight well the worse for wear. Many a Friday evening she would make Frank sit alone at the kitchen table while she presented him with a plate of burnt vegetables and congealed gravy that two hours ago had been a tasty plate of sausage casserole. Cathleen would take some pleasure from watching Frank's feeble efforts at eating the scorched offering. Mercifully for both of them those occasions were now a distant memory as Frank's capacity to drink beer had reduced as the years advanced. He still enjoyed a drink but if he had more than three beers he would need the toilet every ten minutes, so it just wasn't worth it anymore.

Frank paid for the beer and walked back to his truck, as he was pulling away from the kerb he noticed someone coming towards him in a yellow Chevy Camaro. The driver was leaning out the window and waving frantically at him. It was Jed Gosling. When Frank realised who it was he wound down the window just in time to hear Jed shout, "Congratulations Frank, great news about ..."

Frank didn't catch the end of what Jed had shouted and as he turned his head to follow the car the Camaro was already disappearing into the distance. What was all that about thought Frank. He'd known Jed for years, so it wasn't as if Jed had mistaken him for someone else, and anyway he'd called me Frank.

Frank was still trying to make sense of what Jed had said when he turned off the highway and headed up the track that lead to Dararra. He had only been away nine days but somehow it felt much longer. He missed Cathleen and he was desperate to get back to see her, though he was equally keen to get some proper home cooking. George had very limited skills in the kitchen and his own efforts had been no better. In little over a week the farm somehow looked and smelt different. The recent rains had refreshed the parched countryside and everywhere Spring was in full bloom. The track up to the farm was lined with redbud trees and their delicate flowers formed a magenta coloured carpet on either side of the road. In the fields barn swallows chased clouds of tiny insects swerving effortlessly between the apple trees as they feasted on nature's bounty. It was good to be back home thought Frank, as he parked the Chevy next to the hen coop at the side of the house.

Cathleen was sitting on the porch with baby Josh when she saw Frank's truck coming up the track. She felt suddenly nervous and butterflies filled her stomach. She was worrying that Frank might be angry with her for not making more of an effort to contact him and tell him about the baby. But then she thought, Frank hadn't made much effort either. He'd only phoned once during the time he was away and that was just after he arrived to say he was safely there. Anyway, what did it matter, he's here now and he's going to meet his son.

Cathleen had dressed Josh in her favourite dark blue baby suit, it had a golden Teddy Bear holding a red ball on the front. She had bought it at a church sale in Lewisburg when she was expecting Peter, now was the first opportunity she'd had to put it on Josh and show it off. Cathleen had also gone to some effort for her husband's return. Her hair was freshly washed and pinned neatly in its usual bun; in her ears were a pair of silver stud earrings that Frank had given her last year as an anniversary present. Her cream coloured dress was short sleeved and printed with large pink and purple flowers. She was wearing her best Sunday shoes. They were light pink and flat with a square heel, the front fastened with a single Mary Jane strap. They were made of vinyl which although very fashionable had a big down side as they made her feet sweat. Nevertheless, Cathleen was delighted with them. She'd had to make a special trip to Macey's in Charleston to get them.

Frank slung his bag over his shoulder before picking up his beer and the neatly wrapped box of biscuits from the front seat. In the late afternoon dappled sunlight streamed through the leaves of a maple tree that was growing next to the outbuildings leaving intricate shadows and patterns on the ground. Silhouetted on the porch steps he saw Cathleen. She appeared to be holding something in her arms.

His bag dropped from his shoulder and he stood motionless staring at Cathleen, something in his brain wouldn't compute and he couldn't quite comprehend what he was looking at.

Several seconds passed before he cried out, "The baby, you've had the baby!" Frank ran towards his wife and the force of his embrace nearly knocked them all over.

"Wow, our baby, you've had our baby!" I can't believe it Cathleen." Frank held Cathleen's face between his hands and kissed her deeply on the lips.

"When did it happen? Are you both alright? Is it a boy?" Frank's questions came thick and fast and all the while he was shaking his head in disbelief. Cathleen just managed to get out "Yes, Frank, it's a boy," before he was off again.

"I can't believe it you've had our baby, just look at him. He's beautiful."

By now Cathleen's nerves had disappeared. Frank wasn't angry, he was clearly overjoyed. Tears were rolling down his cheeks.

"I couldn't be happier, Cathleen. It's unbelievable, I'm a dad and you've had our baby!"

Cathleen's heart swelled as she saw how much it meant to Frank. She had hoped that he would be thrilled but she was taken aback by how emotional he was. Frank was not a man given to outpourings of emotion.

"You're starting to sound like a broken record now. Yes, I've had the baby and we're both doing just fine. Come and sit down and hold your son. His name's Josh just like we agreed," added Cathleen. Frank smiled and nodded in approval. He sat down, and Cathleen carefully put the baby into his arms.

"Just make sure you support his head," said Cathleen.

"Like this?" asked Frank as he tentatively moved the crook of his arm under the baby's head.

"Just like that," said Cathleen. "See you're a natural, nothing to worry about."

"I'm not sure about that, I'm as nervous as a kitten," whispered Frank so as not to startle Josh.

For several minutes Frank studied his son not saying anything but taking a mental note of every detail. The baby was kicking his legs and waving his arms, he stared back at Frank and tiny bubbles blew from his mouth. Finally, Frank spoke, "He's got my blue eyes and your button nose, but I've no idea where that blond hair has come from."

"His nose will grow you know, hopefully not as large as yours!" laughed Cathleen. "Anyway, lots of babies have blond hair when they're born. I expect it will turn red like yours when he gets a bit older"

"Let's hope it stays blond," replied Frank rather seriously, "I don't want him teased like I was."

"Don't be worrying about that just now Frank, anyway I don't think he's going to have red hair. Expect he's going to be a brownie like me," said Cathleen. "Let's just enjoy our son, isn't he the most gorgeous baby you ever saw?"

"That is for sure," replied Frank as he leant down and kissed Josh gently on his cheek.

"I've held many things in these hands, but I've never held anything as precious as you," he whispered to Josh.

Frank glanced up as Cathleen opened the front door to go into the house,

"Hey, Cathleen, that dress you're wearing, it's just like the one you had on when we first met," said Frank beaming with pride. "I've got a beautiful wife and now I've got a gorgeous son."

"Ah, that's sweet of you to say, Frank, and I've got a lovely husband too," said Cathleen. "Just for your information, it's the same dress that I wore that night. It's just a little tighter now, but hey I did have a baby five days ago so that's not too bad don't you think?" she added laughing.

Frank had met Cathleen at a miner's dance in Maxwelton ten years ago. Cathleen had been dragged along by Cynthia Lehman who wanted to go as she knew a fella called Roger Crider would be there. She'd met him a couple of times at the hospital when he had taken his sister to see Vernon Schilling when she was pregnant. Cynthia was keen on Roger from their first meeting and it wasn't long before she had established that he wasn't married and worked at Middleton mine. It transpired that Roger was good friends with Frank Heggerty and while Roger turned out not to be the slightest bit interested in Cynthia, Frank was rather keen to get to know her friend. To this day Cynthia insists that it was she who had introduced Cathleen to Frank. That always made Cathleen laugh as she remembers Cynthia being in a huff for most of the night after being ignored by Roger. Frank on the other hand had plucked up the courage to ask a pretty girl wearing a cream coloured floral print dress to dance and it was the start of a beautiful courtship.

Frank and Cathleen married in October 1959 in St Catherine's Roman Catholic church in Ronceverte two miles south of Fairlea. Since that day they had always lived at Dararra. Initially they had only intended to stay for only a short time while they saved for a place of their own. But when Cathleen's grandfather died four years ago there was no way that Cathleen was going to move and leave her beloved grandmother alone. As it happened Caitlin McClung passed away only fourteen months after her husband and on her death the farm passed to Cathleen and Frank.

After a couple years of married life their thoughts turned to starting a family. They hadn't been trying for a baby for long when Cathleen fell pregnant with Peter. The pain of his loss had been a big hurdle for them to overcome, so when she fell pregnant for a second time neither Cathleen or Frank would talk about it much, nor did they let themselves get too excited, they didn't want to tempt fate. The birth of the baby would not replace the loss of Peter, but they hoped it would bring them happiness and allow them to make plans for the future.

"Cathleen, Josh is starting to fret, I think he's hungry. Do you want to try feeding him?" asked Frank.

"Good idea," said Cathleen, "bring him into the kitchen and I'll show you how to make up his bottle and then you can feed him."

Frank was confused, "I thought you were going to be feeding the baby yourself," he said.

"It's a long story," replied Cathleen, "get yourself into the kitchen and I'll explain everything. The first ramps of the season are ready, so I've made soup and a chicken stew, bet you've not eaten a decent meal since you've been away."

"That's a fact," replied Frank as he carried his son into the house.

Chapter 5

In her flat above the bakery Susan McDowell was stuffing some clothes and toiletries into a canvas holdall. It had been a traumatic week and Susan was heading home to spend the weekend with some old school friends at her aunt' lodge. The morning following the accident she had somehow managed to make it into school. She hadn't wanted to miss the parents' afternoon but when the Principal found out what had happened she wanted Susan to go home and rest. Susan thought that would only have made things worse. She didn't fancy being stuck in the flat staring at four walls and reliving the horror of last night, so she insisted on going ahead with the afternoon as planned. She couldn't remember much about it and she was struck by how life just seemed to go on. None of her children's parents were affected by the accident, in fact they were probably not even aware that it had happened. They just wanted to know how Julie, John or any of the other twenty-four kids in her class were getting on. That's just how life is thought Susan. If we all stopped what we were doing every time someone died or there was a disaster reported nothing would get done. Still, it all seemed a bit surreal.

Susan hadn't slept well since the accident, she wasn't waking up in the night with nightmares or anything like that, she just couldn't get off to sleep. Her mind seemed to be racing as she endlessly went over the events of that night. Her most vivid memory was of the woman's face just after Cathleen had delivered the baby. She knew she had been unconscious, but it was as if she knew what was happening and her expression changed suddenly to being tranquil and peaceful as soon as the child was born. It was as if Jennifer knew that it was done, and the baby was safe. Susan liked to think so anyway, and she took some comfort from knowing that in the horror of that night there was one bright light of hope.

Susan picked up her bag and guitar and headed down the stairs to her car that was parked outside. She loaded her belongings into the trunk and went into the bakery to let Steffen know she was away for the weekend.

"How're you doing Susan? I heard you'd been at the accident the other night. Just been reading about it in the paper. Must have been terrible for you," said Steffen.

"It's just so sad," replied Susan. "There was nothing I could do for the poor parents, but the baby is safe. The other woman who was there did a great job. She saved that baby's life."

"Well from what I heard you both deserve a medal!" said Steffen. "You take it easy driving all that way tonight. Shock can do funny things to you so take care you hear me? And here, take these for a bite to eat on the journey. Made fresh today but I won't sell them now, so I want you to have them."

Steffen handed Susan a bag containing two ham and cheese baguettes.

"Gee, Steffen, that's kind of you!" said Susan. "I'll be careful, no choice really, my old Chrysler doesn't do fast driving anymore so it's the slow lane all the way for me!" laughed Susan trying to lighten the mood as she headed out the door.

Susan was not relishing the three-hour drive, but it would be compensated by meeting her friends Anna and Colette. Anna Hayburn and Colette Swan had been best friends with Susan since they all started elementary school aged five. They had spent all their schooldays together, but this weekend would be the first time all three had been together since they left Harpers Ferry High School more than four years ago. While Susan had gone to Charleston to do her teacher training, Anna had gone to Philadelphia to study to be doctor and she was about to start her fifth and final year of study. Colette on the other hand had never managed to leave Harpers Ferry and she was still working as a waitress in Riley's Burger Bar.

The three friends couldn't be more different in character. Susan always considered herself to be the most 'normal' one, which compared to the other two was probably reasonable enough. She was an above-average student, not super intelligent but clever enough, and she got on with just about everybody. She was okay at sports but excelled at music and art. She never made school captain, but she was hardly ever in trouble either.

Anna was the highly strung one. A grade 'A' student throughout school she was always top of the class. Her father was a doctor and the family lived in a large detached house on the edge of town. Tall and good looking she was even good at sports. There was not much wrong with Anna's life growing up. She did, however, have an Achilles Heel, she was a control freak. You'd better look out if things weren't done just how Anna wanted. Once in second grade, Colette had taken

Anna's pencil case where her coloured pencils were meticulously organised with pastel colours on the left and dark colours on the right and shuffled them, so they were in a state of disarray. Anna cried for the rest of the day and wouldn't speak to Colette for a week. Worse was to follow in fourth grade, Colette thought it would be a good idea to bring her brother's pet ferret into school in a cardboard box. She didn't tell anyone and placed it on the floor under her desk. By mid-morning the creature had gnawed through the side of the box where Colette had made some ventilation holes with a pencil. The ferret escaped from the box and darted around desks and between feet. The whole class was in uproar. Anna was petrified and stood on her chair refusing to come down until the wretched animal was caught and removed from the classroom. Colette was in a whole heap of trouble after that episode. Minor dramas like that punctuated most of Anna's schooldays and she maintained a love-hate relationship with Colette.

Colette was a total scatterbrain. She couldn't sit still and was always up to mischief. It wasn't as if she was stupid, but the teachers despaired of her antics and as a consequence she never seemed to be given the benefit of the doubt. Consequently, she was labelled as disruptive. Her studies suffered and with it any hope of going to college. Colette was a free spirit and she had a most unconventional dress sense. She liked to dress in bright colours and nothing she wore seemed to match. Unlike the other girls, she didn't worry too much about what anybody else thought. Colette was a one off and her quirky dress sense suited her personality. She was also kind to a fault. If you needed help she would always be there for you. She would give you her last dollar and often it would be the only one she had as she never had much money. There just wasn't a bad bone in Colette's body and Susan and Anna loved her kind nature. Over the years she had proved to be a loyal and dependable friend.

Colette was also a very talented singer. When the girls were teenagers Colette would sing all the latest hits and Susan would accompany her on the guitar. For her small frame Colette had a powerful set of lungs and could belt out a tune with her deep husky voice. In 1961 the pair of them won the school talent show, with their version of the Shirelles hit, 'Will You Love Me Tomorrow'. For a while they dreamed of becoming famous, they had even chosen a band name. They were going to call themselves 'Swan Song' as a play on Colette's surname. Sadly, this idea, like many teenage dreams, petered out when Colette met her first true love in the shape of a boy called Eric Hefferman. The romance lasted through that summer but by early fall she had realised that while Eric was handsome he was also deadly dull, and so he was unceremoniously ditched.

Susan smiled to herself as the memories of those happy times came flooding back. After the week she had had, it would be great to let off some steam with good friends. She switched on the radio and the first song to come on was Ray Charles, 'Hit the Road Jack'. Susan giggled to herself, just perfect for a road trip she thought.

*

"What you up to Frank?" shouted Cathleen who was at the sink rinsing dishes.

"I'm out the back chopping some kindling. Why? What's the problem?" replied Frank.

"No problem," said Cathleen, "but do you think you can change Josh's diaper, he needs cleaned up before supper? He's in his cot; I'm going to bring the washing in."

"Sure, no problem," replied Frank. "Is the stuff in the bottom draw?"

"Yep, it's all in the drawer," replied Cathleen.

Cathleen had begun to feel anxious as soon as she saw the police vehicle coming up the farm track. Her chest felt tight and her heart was racing. Small beads of sweat started to appear on her forehead. What did they want? Had someone said something? Were they coming to take Josh away? Endless negative thoughts filled her head. Grabbing the washing basket from the kitchen table Cathleen headed outside. If she could get to the other side of the outbuildings before the car reached the top of the track she could speak to the officer there. Frank would be changing Josh, so he wouldn't see the police car and, more importantly, the officer wouldn't see Frank or Josh.

The police vehicle drew to a halt as Cathleen rounded the corner of the hen coop. In the car was Officer Wilder. Cathleen gave a breezy wave and managed to force a weak smile. Wilder leant out the driver's window.

"Hello again," said Cathleen, "Is everything okay?"

"All good thanks," said Wilder. "Just stopped by to tell you that the baby is out of hospital and now at Marlinton with Jennifer's sister and her husband. They are going to formally adopt the baby. Have I told you this already?"

"You did mention the baby was going to be staying with her sister, but I didn't know about the adoption. That's great news," added Cathleen.

"I've just been with the family," said Wilder, "they wanted me to let you know that the funeral is going to be next Wednesday in White Sulphur Springs. Emmanuel Methodist Church, 11am. They wondered if you might want to go?"

"Yes, yes of course." replied Cathleen. "Next Wednesday at eleven, fine yes, I think I can make it."

"That's good, they seemed keen for you to be there, I'm sure they would appreciate it." said Wilder. "I'm hoping to go myself, so I'll probably see you there. Oh, I nearly forgot, the family wanted you to know that they've named the baby, Todd."

"Todd, that's a fine name," said Cathleen. "It's just great that he's doing well and going home. 11am next Wednesday at the Methodist church in Sulphur Springs. I know it." added Cathleen. "I'll go and write it in my diary right now."

"That's good, I'm glad I caught you," said Wilder as he turned his vehicle and headed back down the track to the main road.

Frank was carrying Josh through from the back bedroom when Cathleen walked in the front door carrying the empty washing basket.

"Where's the washing? I thought you were going out to get it?" asked Frank.

"Err, well I was. But it needs another hour. It's not quite dry yet, don't know what I was thinking of," mumbled Cathleen. "Anyway, supper's nearly ready so sit yourself down. I've made meatballs with grape jelly. Thought we might go into town tomorrow. We need to register Josh's birth and I must take him to the hospital to let Cynthia and the other girls see him."

"That'll be fine," replied Frank, "and I'll pick up some rope when we're there. I want to put the swing back up on the chestnut tree."

"No hurry for that Frank!" laughed Cathleen. "He's not even a week old yet. I know you think he's marvellous, but it will be a while till he can sit on a swing!"

"I know, I know, but I want to do it. You can hold him on it and I'll push you." said Frank.

"Yep, that'll work," laughed Cathleen as she leant across to kiss her husband on the top of his head.

*

It was after seven when Susan took a left turn off highway 340 and drove down the slip road that led to her home town. She found a parking place next to the Seasons Motel and walked the last couple of hundred yards down to the Point. Wow thought Susan as she leant on the metal fence, it's still majestic. Susan had stood at this very spot dozens of times before, but it never failed to take her breath away. The Point was so called because it was here that the mighty Shenandoah and Potomac rivers met in a boiling swirl of turbulent dark water. Susan was standing on the northern tip of West Virginia, but to her left on the other side of the Potomac was Maryland and to her right across the Shenandoah was Virginia. On either side of the rivers maples, beech and white oak trees formed a canopy of green around outcrops of ancient granite rock that in turn formed the gentle slopes of the Blue Ridge Mountains. Even in the fading light and quiet of a late

April evening it wasn't difficult to see why tourists flocked to Harper's Ferry. The views were simply stunning.

Over to her right Susan noticed a young woman sitting on a bench staring out into the distance. She was wearing jeans and a light blue jacket. Her long blonde hair was tied in a ponytail and she was smoking a cigarette. Susan recognised her instantly, it was Anna Hayburn.

Susan walked quietly across to the bench where Anna was sitting and stood silently behind her.

"Well, I've learned one thing," said Susan in a stern voice, "I never knew Anna Hayburn smoked!"

Anna, jumped to her feet immediately, "Susan! Oh my God you gave me such a fright creeping up on me like that!"

They both started to laugh and hugged each other warmly.

"It's great to see you Anna," said Susan.

"You too," replied Anna. "I can't believe it's been four years since we were last together!"

"Seems crazy doesn't it?" said Susan. "Years just go by, I can't believe I'm twenty-two!"

"You shouldn't worry," scoffed Anna. "I'm already twenty-three! It's scary."

"Seems like it was only five minutes ago that we used to hang out down here eating pizza and drinking beer. At least the view doesn't get old, it's still as beautiful as ever," said Susan. Anna nodded in agreement.

"When did you get here?" asked Susan.

"About an hour ago. I took the train down as I reckoned the weekend would involve quite a lot of alcohol if you and Colette were involved, so the drive back didn't appeal," said Anna.

"Also, I've just finished my exams. Only one more year and I'll be done, so that deserves a celebration!" said Anna mischievously pulling a bottle of Wild Turkey bourbon out of her bag.

"Do you know that'll be eighteen years in school by the time you finish, I've just worked it out," said Susan.

"I know, sometimes I think it'll never end," said Anna with a resigned sigh.

"Good thinking about the train though," said Susan. "Typical Anna, always calculating what the best options were. Wish I could have taken a train, but then again, I should be grateful there was a road from Fairlea to get me here. It's a bit of a backwater!"

"How's the job going anyway?" asked Anna.

"Really good thanks, I'm enjoying teaching and love the kids, but it's hard graft. I'm exhausted at the end of the day!" replied Susan.

"Ah that's great Susan. I mean it's good that you're doing a job you love, nothing worse than being stuck in one you didn't." said Anna.

"Oh, and about the cigarettes, I only smoke the odd one, just to relieve stress you understand," added Anna.

"Stress, what stress? You just said your exams were finished, it's party time now!" said Susan.

"The stress, my friend, is not knowing what awaits when we walk in that restaurant to meet Colette! Anything could happen, she might have that damn ferret with her!" laughed Anna as she stubbed out her cigarette butt on the bench.

"Ah, yes the ferret, I was thinking about that day on the drive up," said Susan giggling, "You've got to admit there was never a dull moment with Colette around."

"That's an understatement if ever I heard one," laughed Anna. "She was crazy! But you've got to love her, heart of gold. Bet she's got purple hair or something now."

"Wouldn't put it past her," said Susan. "We better get over there, she said she was finishing her shift at 7.30 and we're going to eat there. She also says we'll get her staff discount and the food will be extra good as she's been sleeping with the chef!"

"Brilliant. Classic Colette!" said Anna. "Let's go then, I'm starving."

The two friends chatted happily as they made their way along Shenandoah Street to Riley's Burger Bar which sat on the corner of West Washington Street. Susan opened the door and the two girls went in. The restaurant was jammed full of people and there didn't appear to be an empty table or seat in the place.

The girls scanned the room looking for Colette, suddenly they turned to each other and in unison shrieked, "Purple hair, she's got purple hair!"

Colette spied her two friends standing by the door and gave them a wave as she squeezed her way through the throng of people to the door.

"Great to see you both!" said Colette as she gave them both a welcoming bear hug. "What are you laughing at?"

"Sorry, Colette, it's your hair. Anna was joking before we came in that you would have purple hair and here you have!"

"It's just a little bit of purple at the front!" said Colette indignantly. "Well at least I've changed my hair style," she continued, "you've still got the same pony tail you had when you were six!" exclaimed Colette pointing at Anna.

The three friends looked at each other and laughed.

"This is going to be great," said Colette, "just like old times, only with more alcohol involved I expect. I've managed to reserve a booth over there in the corner. We're not really allowed to reserve tables, but staff perks and all that."

"Are you sleeping with the manager as well then?" laughed Anna, "Susan told me about you and the chef!"

"Hey! No, I'm not, but it's not for the want of trying. He's a bit tasty is Paul."

"Now is Paul the chef or the manager?" asked Susan.

"The manager!" replied Colette with just a touch of exasperation, "John's the chef. He's a nice guy, a bit fat but a nice guy. Paul now he's just cute. Anyway, enough about my love life girls, I want to hear about yours and what you've both been up to."

Colette led them to the booth in the far corner of the restaurant. On the table was a paper sign that said, 'reserved Swan + 2.' Next to it was a large pitcher of beer and three glasses.

"Just to get us started," said Colette, "I take it you both still drink beer, don't you?"

"Is the Pope a catholic?" replied Anna. Susan looked at her aghast.

"You may still have the same hairstyle, girl, but you've sure developed a bit of attitude! I think I'm going to like the new Anna just fine," said Susan.

"I agree!" squealed Colette as she poured three glasses from the pitcher. "This weekend's going to be a blast."

*

At 9 o'clock the next morning Mike Rawlingson and three friends were in Knoxville, three miles east of Harpers Ferry, preparing to go white water rafting as part of Dave Ellison's Bachelor Party Weekend.

"Are you sure you don't have a bigger size?" Mike asked the instructor who was handing out helmets and life jackets ahead of the first run of the morning; 3 ½ miles of fast water passing through three sets of rapids to the finish at Harpers Ferry.

"That's the biggest one we have," he said. "The yellow helmets are the biggest size and the white ones are a size smaller. Anyway, it's not supposed to be comfortable it's supposed to keep you safe and it'll do that. I've checked it and it's fine."

"It just doesn't seem to sit right on my head," continued a perplexed Mike.

"For God's sake, man up Mike!" said Dave, who's wedding in three weeks was the reason the friends were gathered for this adventure weekend.

"If I thought you were going to be all girly about it I would have told you to go fishing with my father. I thought policemen were tough all action type of guys!" said Dave who was clearly losing patience with Mike.

"Just want to make sure it's on right that's all," said Mike sheepishly.

Mike and Dave had met six years ago when they found themselves roommates at the university of Chicago. After graduating with a degree in psychology,

Mike had joined the city of Chicago Police Department two years ago and he was now preparing to sit his detective exams. Dave had done a business degree and now he worked for Chase Manhattan Bank in Chicago. He hated banking, so his weekends were a release from the mundane routine of his work and he liked to spend them climbing rocks or canoeing down rivers. It was therefore no surprise that he had chosen an adventure weekend in Harpers Ferry for his Bachelor Party.

Most of the time Mike and Dave got on just fine but occasionally, like at this moment, Mike's rational head would kick in and he would find himself at odds with his thrill-seeking friend. Mike didn't really know Chris and Eric the other guys on the raft trip. They had known Dave since school and as it later transpired neither of them were particularly relishing the rafting, but they had clearly chosen to say nothing, so Mike somewhat against his better judgement found himself acquiescing and getting into the raft.

Mike and Chris being the tallest were instructed to go to the rear of the raft while Dave and Eric sat in the front. The instructor handed them each a paddle and talked them through some basic instructions on how to manoeuvre the raft. Dave wasn't listening to a word and was clearly itching to get started. Mike was trying to concentrate on what the instructor was saying. He was stressing the importance of picking the proper line when they approached the rapids and of making sure that they keep the raft facing in a straight line as they went through the rapid itself. If they hit the rapid side on they were toast. Mike didn't like the sound of that and found himself wondering why the guy wasn't with them in the raft as there was clearly room for him.

"…When you reach Harpers, I'll be waiting with the trailer and we can get loaded up. The second run will be a bit more challenging and more technical with bigger drops through the rapids," he said.

"Brilliant!" said Dave.

Shit thought Mike.

The first part of the journey passed without incident. The raft meandered through the slack water of the upper stretch at a leisurely pace and there was time to take in the magnificent scenery that surrounded them. They had even managed to navigate the first rapids without too much difficulty. The water had been more turbulent certainly but the length of the rapid was no more than seventy-five feet and the drop off was less than ten. They had done what the instructor had said and kept the raft in a straight line, so apart from being slightly damp from water splashing over the sides everything was going to plan.

"How you all doing?" shouted Dave as the raft crashed through the foaming white water and raced through the second set of rapids. Whether anyone heard him or not it was difficult to say but Mike was concentrating hard and was desperately trying to keep the raft going in a straight line. That was proving almost impossible as the force of the water battered his paddle which he was trying to keep steady and use as a rudder. The constant pummelling of the water made his arms and shoulders ache and each time he lost control of the paddle the raft lurched violently to the side. Freezing water showered over them each time they hit a wave and the cold water numbed Mike's hands and fingers. Chris was no help at all he didn't even have his paddle in the water. He was slumped in the bottom of the raft with his arms outstretched holding onto the side ropes for all he was worth. Rocks swept by on either side of the raft and low hanging branches touched the raft where the river narrowed in the fast water.

"Doesn't get much better than this!" yelled Dave. Before Mike had time to disagree he felt a huge wave smash into the side of the raft, the impact ripped the paddle out of his hands. The raft was now out of control and it swung violently to the left. Mike glanced at the river ahead and he could see the last set of rapids fast approaching. Well that's just great thought Mike sardonically, rapids ahead and we're going sideways, couldn't be better.

*

It was just after nine thirty when Susan dragged herself out of bed. She would have stayed there longer, but she was desperate for the toilet and her throat felt dry as a bone. Her head was pounding, and she badly needed some aspirin and a drink of water. It had been some night. The other two were still sleeping but the carnage of last night was everywhere to see. Empty beer cans littered the kitchen work surfaces and the bottle of Wild Turkey that Anna had brought sat on the coffee table in the den. It was three quarters empty.

Susan switched on the kettle before taking a couple of aspirin and drinking two large tumblers of water. She took the largest mug she could find out of the cupboard and made herself a mug of strong black coffee grabbed a croissant and went outside to sit at the picnic table at the front of the lodge. The sun was shining but there was still a freshness to the air, Susan pulled her dressing gown tight around her and wished she had put on a pair of socks as her toes were cold in her open toed slippers.

Holding the mug in both hands Susan sipped at the steaming coffee and breathed in the rich vapours hoping it would help to heal the headache she was nursing. An eastern towhee bobbed up and down as it perched on the far end of the picnic table hoping that some crumbs from the buttery croissant might come its way. Susan stared at the bird and thought how beautiful it looked. It was about eight inches long with a jet-black head and a white coloured body. Delicate feathers of apricot edged its wings but its most striking feature was its piercing red eye that now seemed to have fixed its gaze on Susan's plate.

"I'll give you some on one condition," said Susan tearing a corner off the croissant.

"Promise me you'll never drink beer and bourbon together because I'll guarantee it'll give you a sore head." The towhee bobbed up and down again.

"Good, I'll take that as a yes then." said Susan and for several minutes in the stillness of the spring morning they shared their feast.

Her Aunt Claire had bought the lodge twenty years ago primarily as a base to return to when her work took her to Washington. Susan had known it all her life and, as her aunt didn't manage down as often as she used to, Susan could usually use it when she was home for a weekend. It was a traditional log cabin with a kitchen dining area, a den, two bedrooms and a small bathroom. There was a log burning stove in the den that in winter would heat the entire cabin. Susan liked to curl up on the sofa with a good book, or just relax and play her guitar with the fire blazing in the corner.

Outside there was a grass area where the picnic table and an old swing stood. Apart from the log store and some hard standing, enough for a couple of vehicles, that was about it. Well apart from the view that is. The lodge sat on a piece of land about sixty feet above the Shenandoah River. A hundred yards to the right from where Susan was sitting were the Compton Rapids a fast-flowing section of the river that was popular with rafters and kayakers. When the river was high and in spate, like it was now after the recent heavy rain, it was a treacherous stretch of water and hidden rocks made it particularly hazardous to the inexperienced paddler. Over the years Susan had watched many people capsize at this very spot and today it looked like the raft heading for the rapids was destined for the same fate. She could see that there were four people in the boat which was travelling sideways when it hit the first section of turbulent water. The impact of the wave lifted the raft high out of the water tilting it viciously on the left-hand side. Momentarily it appeared that the vessel might have righted itself, but then, a second even bigger wave crashed into the raft. As the surge of water hit, the front of the raft was driven violently upwards causing the occupants in the rear to be catapulted backwards into the depths of the freezing water.

They couldn't have chosen a worse place to capsize, jagged rocks jutted out from the river bed and crashing waves and swirling currents formed whirlpools of foaming water which sucked and spun anything that got caught in its maelstrom.

Susan stood up and ran to the edge of the bank. She could see two helmets bobbing in the water, further down-stream two men were pulling the raft onto a gravel bank on the other side of the river. The paddler wearing the white helmet was now swimming towards the far bank where two other men held out their hands to help him ashore.

The other paddler was removing his yellow helmet on some rocks directly below the bank where Susan was standing. He was examining his right elbow and his left knee both of which were bleeding. Gingerly, Susan started to climb down the steps that led to the water's edge. After only a few steps she dispensed with her slippers as they had next to no grip and they were making her descent precarious. She winced as the cold damp stone numbed her bare feet. When she reached the water's edge a young man was sitting on a rock bending and straightening his arm.

"Are you alright?" asked Susan.

"Think so," replied Mike, "some cuts and bruises but I don't think anything's broken."

"That's good news." said Susan. "I saw you being thrown out the raft, it looked pretty spectacular."

"Yep, I suppose it must have done. It feels like I've been tossed about in a washing machine," said Mike. "I'll tell you another thing that water is darn freezing!"

"I've got a first aid kit up in the lodge," said Susan, "I'll nip back and get it." She paused before adding, "Better still, why don't you come up and we can sort you out up there? Looks like you could do with some hot coffee?"

"That's the best idea I've heard in a while," said Mike smiling. "I'm Mike by the way, pleased to meet you."

Susan smiled back, "Pleased to meet you too, Mike, I'm Susan."

As they started to climb the steps Mike could see Dave standing on the opposite bank. "Have you still got your paddle? We're missing one!" yelled Dave.

Mike shook his head despairingly. "No, I don't have the damn paddle it could be half way to Washington by now!" he yelled back sarcastically, before adding, "I'm fine, nothing broken thanks for asking!"

"Sorry Mike, glad you're okay," replied Dave pretending to show some concern, "It's just that if we've lost the paddle we'll have to pay for it, so It's worth looking for. "No worries though, you get yourself sorted, I take it you're not coming for the second run?" enquired Dave.

"You are correct Dave; wild horses wouldn't get me back in that damned raft." replied Mike.

"Fine. You take care we'll see you at six in Meckleburg's, you better have the beer in when I get there, it's going to be a great night!" said Dave before returning to the gravel bank where Eric and Chris were loading the raft onto a trailer.

Up at the lodge Mike changed out of his wet clothes and was coming out of the bathroom wearing Susan's dressing gown and a pair of pink pyjama bottoms that he had just about managed to squeeze into when he bumped into Colette who was waiting to use the toilet.

"Oh hello!" said Colette winking at Mike, "who are you with then, Anna or Susan? I'm pretty sure you're not with me, I am drunk but I'm sure I would have remembered pulling you!" she giggled. "So, who is it then?"

"It's neither of them, well it's Susan but it's not what you think!" spluttered Mike. Realising how pathetic that sounded he was about to explain more clearly why he was dressed in Susan's clothes when Susan walked into the hallway.

"I see you've made Colette's acquaintance," said Susan in a stern voice much like the one she used at school to tell off misbehaving children, "please follow me, I need to see to those cuts."

As she turned to go out the door Susan winked at Colette who immediately winked back. The two friends started to laugh, and a confused Mike followed Susan out to the picnic table where she began to clean and dress his wounds.

"I think you've been lucky," said Susan, "it's mainly superficial cuts and grazes from what I can see. The one on your elbow is a bit deeper but I don't think it'll need stitches. You'll be sore and bruised tomorrow though."

"That's good news, I really don't fancy a trip to the hospital," replied Mike.

"A couple of beers tonight and you'll be right as rain," said Colette who had now joined them outside. "Always great for some fun pain relief, well I think so."

"Are you kidding me," said Susan ruefully. "Try telling that to my head, I've already taken two aspirin and my head is still thumping."

"A bit of a heavy session by the sound of it" said Mike. "I better be careful, Dave seems to have something similar planned for us tonight."

Susan, Mike and Colette sat in the morning sunshine chatting. Susan told Mike all about the lodge and why the girls were there, and Mike told them about Dave, the wedding and the Bachelor weekend.

Susan was hanging Mike's wet clothes on the washing line when Anna appeared out of the lodge carrying a tray laden with plates, rolls and a huge pan of eggs and bacon.

"Thought we'd better get our stomachs lined, girls, there's another long day ahead of us!" said Anna in a matronly sort of a way. "And who is this lovely specimen of manhood that fate has brought us?" asked Anna in her best posh voice.

A bemused Mike sat and didn't say anything while Susan and Colette burst out laughing.

"I'll tell you something Anna, getting out of Harpers has done wonders for your sense of humour. I'm seeing a completely different girl from the one I knew at school" said Colette, "we're going to have to get together more often this weekend's been way more fun than I'm used to."

After Susan had properly introduced Mike to Anna the four of them sat chatting and eating the splendid breakfast that Anna had prepared.

After she had finished eating Susan pushed her plate to the side and announced, "Funnily enough I do feel much better after eating that, my head isn't nearly as sore."

"Best hangover cure there is; food and plenty of liquids to rehydrate. Four years at medical school wasn't wasted on me you know," said Anna with a grin.

"Will you excuse me," said Mike politely, "I need to get out of these pyjamas they're killing me."

"I'm not sure your clothes will be dry yet," said Susan. She got up from the table and felt the t-shirt that was hanging on the line.

"Still feels a bit damp, another half hour and they should be fine," added Susan.

"It won't matter that they're not quite dry, I'll be changing anyway when I get back to the hotel. I don't want to take up any more of your day, I expect you've got things planned."

"Nothing really planned till later," said Susan, "Colette and I might play a few tunes, it'll be just like old times."

"Just as long as it's not the Shirelles," said Anna, "that would bring back my headache!"

The three friends started laughing again, Mike wished he was in on the joke but after they had calmed down a little he asked Susan, "What do you play?"

Before Susan had a chance to answer Anna piped up, "She plays the guitar, she's really very good and Colette's a great singer."

"And what about you, do you play or sing?" asked Mike.

Anna looked at Mike and laughed, "Can't play or sing a note I'm afraid!"

"You can't be good at everything, but I need to tell you she is the brains of this outfit," added Susan. Mike smiled, "I can't sing a note either, think I must be tone deaf, I'm told that I do have a brain though, only I'm not sure it's always functioning the way it should if you know what I mean."

Susan smiled at Mike, she found his self-deprecating humour attractive and she found herself wanting to get to know him better. But with Colette and Anna there that was going to be difficult.

"Get changed if you want," said Susan, "I'll give you a lift to your hotel when you're ready. Where are you staying?"

"The Clarion," said Mike. "I'd be grateful of the lift if it's not too much trouble."

"No trouble at all," replied Susan, "I'll run you round when you're ready."

"Great, thanks, I'll just go and get changed," said Mike has he unpegged his clothes from the line and headed into the lodge.

"Beautiful manners," whispered Colette, "I think he might be a keeper!"

"Stop it, Colette, I only met him two hours ago!" said Susan, "But he sure is good looking," she added with a sigh.

The three friends looked at each other and started to giggle, it had been that sort of a weekend.

The drive to the Clarion Hotel took no more than ten minutes and during the journey the two of them chatted about the weather and other inconsequential things. As he was getting out of the vehicle Mike turned to Susan, "I'm coming back down to Frederick in four weeks for Dave's wedding, it's the Memorial weekend so I don't have to head back till the Monday. It would be great to see you over the weekend if you were around. Perhaps I could take you out for dinner? I'd like to say thank you for your help today."

"I'd like that," said Susan smiling, "that would be really nice."

"That's great then Susan, I'll look forward to it," said Mike.

They exchanged telephone numbers and then Mike leant across and kissed Susan gently on the cheek.

"I'll call you in a few days and we can firm up the arrangements," said Mike, "and thanks again for your help today."

With a final wave, he headed up the steps and into the hotel. Susan leaned back in her seat and smiled to herself, this weekend was proving to be even better than she'd hoped for. As she turned to drive away she noticed a large damp patch on her passenger seat. I told him those clothes weren't dry but typical man wouldn't listen; with that thought she turned her car around and headed back to the lodge. Susan was thrilled at the prospect of meeting up with Mike again, lots to tell the girls she thought, but after a moments consideration a voice in her head was saying to her that perhaps some things are best kept to yourself, well for the moment anyway. Besides if she told Colette the whole of Harpers Ferry would know about it, including her mom and dad. Plenty time for that thought Susan, no need to say anything about it just yet.

*

It was just after 8am when Cathleen tapped on Cynthia's office window. Cynthia glanced up from her desk and looked over her horn-rimmed spectacles, a broad grin breaking out across her face. "It's the baby!" she cried in a shrill and excited voice. Cynthia opened the rear door of the office and the two friends hugged each other warmly. "Wow, Cathleen, look at him he's gorgeous. I knew you'd had the baby because I met Jed Gosling the other day and he told me. It is a he, isn't it?" she asked somewhat cautiously.

"Yep, he's a boy alright, his names Josh. You're right he is gorgeous, isn't he?" replied Cathleen.

"He certainly is. Can I get to hold him?" asked Cynthia.

"Sure can," replied Cathleen as she handed over the baby who was wrapped snugly in a cream coloured shawl.

"Oh, look at him! I love his blue eyes, and he's so alert, must be my glasses that's fascinating him. And he's got blond hair! Where did that come from?"

"No idea," replied Cathleen, "I expect he'll grow out of it and it'll end up plain brown like mine."

"When was he born?" asked Cynthia.

"A week yesterday," said Cathleen.

"You are a monkey, Cathleen, why didn't you call me? I knew you must have had the baby at home as I hadn't seen your file. I double checked the other day after Jed told me, just in case I'd missed it," said Cynthia with just a hint of annoyance.

"I did try to call you," said Cathleen, "I rang you three times last Thursday, it was around 6pm so I must have just missed you. Anyway, it's all a bit of a long story," continued Cathleen. "It happened so suddenly, one minute I was making some bread and the next minute I was having my baby on the kitchen floor, it was a bit surreal to be honest, there wasn't time to get to the hospital or call for help so I just had to get on with it! Being truthful the next few days were the worst, I just felt exhausted, so for a while afterwards I took it really easy, just me and Josh."

"Good grief, Cathleen, that must have been horrendous for you! Just as well you're a midwife, at least you knew what to do. Just a pity Vernon's retired he would have loved to have delivered your baby," said Cynthia.

"It certainly helped that's for sure, looking back I suppose I didn't panic and when the baby arrived I just

84

knew what I needed to do. I'd done it hundreds of times before just not for my own baby. Even Vernon wouldn't have been able to help there just wasn't time," explained Cathleen.

"Actually, I've just posted off a letter to Vernon, did I mention that he'd sent me a postcard asking when the baby was due?"

"No, I don't think you said. I got one too which was nice of him. I do miss him, not been the same since he left," added Cynthia.

"I know what you mean, he was such a big part of this place. He was always going to be a difficult man to replace that's for sure," said Cathleen. "Well, I'm glad I'm here now, after Frank I wanted you to be the first to see the baby."

"Oh, that's lovely of you Cathleen, I'm touched" said Cynthia.

"I'm sorry it's a flying visit but I'll have to dash now I've got to get Josh back to Frank and then head over to a funeral in White Sulphur Springs for eleven," said Cathleen.

"Of course, in the excitement of meeting Josh I haven't asked about the accident. I read about it in the paper. That was a truly awful thing, so sad. I'd heard you'd saved the baby's life though which is just wonderful. The family must be so grateful it was you that came across the crash," said Cynthia handing the baby back to Cathleen.

Cathleen nodded, "I'll phone you soon, perhaps we could catch some food one night after work next week?"

"Sounds great." replied Cynthia, "Let's do that."

As Cynthia watched Cathleen drive out of the car park she reflected on their conversation. Cathleen had said she had tried to phone last Thursday around 6pm. That's odd thought Cynthia, last Thursday I was here till after eight catching up on some filing and I swear the phone never rang. Not once.

*

"I don't think I'll be more than a couple of hours," said Cathleen as she handed baby Josh to her husband. "He's just been fed, I've changed him, so he should be okay till I get back."

"We'll be just fine," replied Frank, "if the rain goes off I'll take him for a walk in his pram. First time since I got back from George's that my foot hasn't been sore, so I could do with the exercise. If the rain stays on, then we'll just stay in the house and have fun. You'd better get going it's after ten now and it'll take you at least thirty minutes to get there. Drive carefully please, those roads are treacherous in the wet. Have a care, won't you?"

"Of course I will. Don't overdo it with that foot of yours, I'll see you in a couple of hours," said Cathleen as she ran to the pick-up to avoid getting wet.

When Cathleen arrived at Emmanuel Methodist Church the car park was already full, and a steady stream of mourners were heading up the steps and into the smart red brick church. Cathleen looked at her watch it was just leaving 10.35, this was clearly going to be a busy funeral. She managed to find a parking place a few hundred yards up the street. As she walked back to the church she was careful not to step in any of the puddles that were starting to form on the walkway. She was wearing a smart navy suit and black shoes and she was glad she had taken an umbrella as the rain showed no signs of easing up.

As she made her way up the path to the church she passed a white painted noticeboard, written in large black letters on the board were the words 'Seven days without prayer makes one weak'. The words made Cathleen stop abruptly and she felt a chill go up her spine. She thought about turning back, she suddenly felt that she shouldn't go in. Cathleen was a lapsed catholic and hadn't been to chapel since her grandmother died and she couldn't begin to recall when she last went to confession.

But standing there in the pouring rain she had a very vivid memory of herself sitting on the front pew of St Catherine's Catholic Church being addressed by Father Francis a rather old and stern priest whose job it had been to prepare her and her fellow communicants for their first Holy Communion.

Cathleen must have only been about eight, but the memory was so clear it could have been just yesterday. Each week leading up to the communion Father Francis would meet the children and deliver a talk about what it meant to be a Catholic. He explained about Mass, the Eucharist and prayer and the liturgy of the word. Most of this passed Cathleen by but the lecture he gave one day on the Sacrament of Penitence and Mortal Sin was indelibly imprinted on her mind. God knows everything about you and you can never hide from God Father Francis had bellowed in a gravelly and slightly threatening voice. Cathleen remembers feeling scared as he went on to tell them that as baptized Catholic's all the sins they committed were sins against God and only God himself could forgive their sins.

As she stood outside the church a sense of foreboding came over Cathleen, she understood all too well the sanctity of this holy place and she knew she had committed a mortal sin. She wanted to be sick. If only she could be back home with Frank and Josh. She didn't want to be in a church, she didn't want to be judged or told that she was a sinner - she already knew that. Most of all though she didn't want to be near God.

As the rain continued to fall a voice behind her said, "Glad you could make it the family will be pleased." It was Officer Wilder. He was dressed in his best uniform and before Cathleen had a chance to respond he took her by the arm and shepherded her up the steps. "Come on, we'd better get in," he said, "if we stand out here we're going to get soaked."

An elderly gentleman in a dark suit offered them an order of service as they entered the church and ushered them through the centre door into the sanctuary. Most of the pews towards the front of the church were already full but there were still spaces in the rear pews. Cathleen looked down the centre aisle to the front of the church. The aisle and chancel were carpeted in royal blue and gold carpet runners delineated the three steps that lead to the chancel. On two metal framed trolleys stood identical coffins made of the finest white oak with ornate brass handles. An arrangement of yellow and white roses sat on top of each coffin. The mourners sat in silence and the only noise was the sound of the organ playing Schubert's Ave Maria, it was hauntingly beautiful.

Once more Cathleen found herself feeling profoundly sad, she understood that God was angry with her but in that moment, she was angry with God. She wanted him to explain, what was the purpose of this? Why did they have to endure such suffering?

Officer Wilder scanned the congregation before nodding to a man towards the rear of the church who was dressed in a grey suit and holding his order of service aloft.

"That's Richard Patterson," said Wider. "He was at the accident last week, he's here representing the ambulance service. Do you recognise him?" Cathleen shook her head. Before she had time to ask, Wilder pre-empted Cathleen's question, "Susan McDowell isn't able to be here, she was asked, and the family were keen for her to attend but her school commitments didn't allow it. To be honest I got the impression that she really didn't feel up to being here, so the school thing was a convenient get out."

At that moment Cathleen wished she could have been anywhere else as well. Cathleen let Officer Wilder sit next to Richard Patterson while she sat at the end of the pew. To avoid eye contact she buried her head in the order of service and pretended to read. The words were just a blur, so Cathleen turned the order of service over. On the rear was a picture of David and Jennifer Saltman standing holding hands at the edge of a lake. It was obviously a recent picture as Jennifer was heavily pregnant in the photograph. Cathleen could feel sweat starting to trickle down the side of her face and her head was starting to hurt, sadness had visited Cathleen often during the last week and today that feeling was almost too much to bear. As she looked down she was aware that her hands had started to shake, Cathleen put down the order of service and clasped her hands tightly together, she didn't want Wilder or anyone else to see her like this. A voice from the front asked them to rise and everyone stood up. A door to the side of the pulpit opened and a dozen or so people all dressed in black filed into the church and took their places in the front two pews. Cathleen could see that a young woman with short blonde hair was carrying a baby in her arms. Baby Todd, thought Cathleen and tears started to well up in her eyes.

The Pastor welcomed everyone to the service and reminded them that even in tragedy there was hope and reasons to give thanks to God. Cathleen couldn't think what those reasons might be right now, God didn't seem to have been around when the car hit that tree.

Pastor Philip Whitehead was very short and a bit over weight, he had a thick thatch of brown curly hair framing what Cathleen thought looked like a kind face. He spoke with a soft north-eastern accent very different from the southern drawl that Cathleen and most of the other mourners spoke. He was originally from Rhode Island and like many New Englanders had a habit of dropping his r's at the end of syllables. It was so noticeable that Cathleen became fixated on it and in doing so missed much of what the Pastor said in his lengthy tribute to the young couple. That, she thought, was somewhat of a blessing.

When he had finished his tribute, Jennifer's middle sister Elaine read a passage from 2nd Corinthians.

"Praise be to the God and Father of our Lord Jesus Christ, the Father of compassion and the God of all comfort, who comforts us in all our troubles, so that we can comfort those in any trouble with the comfort we ourselves receive from God. For just as we share abundantly in the sufferings of Christ, so also our comfort abounds through Christ."

Although her voice never wavered, and no tears flowed, her voice seemed distant and remote. Perhaps she was all out of tears. Her pallid face was devoid of expression, yet it reminded Cathleen of the one she often saw staring back at her in the mirror when she grieved the loss of Peter.

As Elaine read the words "God of all comfort, who comforts us in all our troubles," Cathleen found herself wanting to scream. There was no comfort, there will be no redemption from your misery. Your God has forsaken you she thought to herself clenching her fists tightly.

Cathleen was still fighting her emotions as Jennifer's younger sister Ruth read Henry Scott-Holland's well-loved funeral poem 'All is Well'. The words were evocative of love and loss and Ruth read them with great tenderness and sensitivity. But they hardly even registered with Cathleen who by now was completely gripped by anguish.

The final torment was delivered during Pastor Whitehead's closing prayer. "We give thanks to those whose actions on that fateful night now bring succour and strength to David and Jennifer's families. We hold up the actions of Officers Wilder and Coutts, Crewmen Patterson & Dodds, and Susan McDowell and Cathleen Heggerty."

As the words seeped into her consciousness Cathleen felt as if she was asphyxiating. Blood pounded round her head and her heart thudded in her chest, her hands began shaking uncontrollably and she could feel bile rising in her throat. She needed to get away. Before the Pastor had concluded the prayer, Cathleen stumbled from the end of the pew and out the rear door into the vestibule. Through blurred eyes she could see a ladies' toilet. She pushed the door open and almost fell inside, her hand trembled as she tried to lock the cubicle. Eventually the door locked, and she slumped down on the toilet seat. She held her head in her hands and wretched into the toilet bowl. Cathleen spat out the sour and acidic taste that clung to her throat. She took several deep breaths and slowly lifted her head till she was looking at the ceiling, in through the nose and out through the mouth. It was a familiar routine for Cathleen, but she knew that in a few minutes it would help her to feel calmer. She scanned the room for something to concentrate on. Fixating on something completely unrelated was another tactic that Susan used to distract herself from what was making her anxious.

Cathleen looked up at the ceiling, she could see that a moth had got itself trapped in the plastic cover that was protecting the fluorescent light above her. She watched attentively as the insect flittered and danced along the length of the glass tube. Back and forwards it went repeating the journey several times in just a couple of minutes. The moth seemed transfixed by the light. She was starting to relax, and she could now hear the murmur of voices outside the toilet door. The service must be over she thought and with that there was a gentle knock at the door. "Will you be long?" said a voice from outside, "I'm desperate for the bathroom."

"No, won't be a minute," said Cathleen. She took a drink of cold water from the tap to rinse the foul taste in her mouth and then quickly washed her hands and face before drying herself with some paper towels that were lying on the window ledge. Feeling more composed she looked at herself in the mirror, I've seen worse she thought to herself, another couple of minutes and this will be over. Cathleen switched off the light and looked up at the moth. As the neon light flickered and died the moth sat motionless at the bottom of the plastic cover, "looks like your God has forsaken you too," whispered Cathleen.

Officer Wilder was waiting for her in the vestibule.

"Are you okay?" he asked, "I wondered where you had gone."

"I'm fine now, but I was desperate for the toilet, so I thought I'd go before the service ended," said Cathleen.

"Fine service don't you think? Sad of course but I thought the Pastor's eulogy was right on the money," said Wilder.

Cathleen nodded, but she found Wilder's use of the term 'right on the money' inappropriate and mildly offensive.

The last of the mourners were now shaking hands with the family members who along with Pastor Whitehead were lined up on the far wall of the vestibule near to the front door. David's mother Elizabeth was being supported on each arm by Elspeth and her husband Paul. The old lady was clutching a photograph of David and Jennifer in her hand. She was completely bereft and sobbing uncontrollably.

Standing at the end of the family line was Jennifer's sister Ruth holding baby Todd across her left arm. Ruth had greeted each mourner in turn and had remained stoically composed throughout. Officer Wider shook Ruth's hand and passed on his sincere commiserations for her family's loss. After a brief exchange of words Officer Wilder turned to Cathleen and said, "Can I introduce you to Ruth Woodburn, Jennifer's sister."

Ruth and Cathleen looked at each other and smiled warmly.

"I'm so pleased you were able to come," said Ruth shaking hands with Cathleen. "It has been an awful tragedy and we will never get over the loss of Jennifer and David but having the baby is giving us all comfort and some hope for the future."

Cathleen stared at the tiny baby lying in Ruth's arms, the baby had sparkling blue eyes and soft tufts of blond hair, Cathleen briefly closed her eyes and thought of Josh.

"I didn't do anything that anyone else wouldn't have done, I'm just grateful I was able to help." Said Cathleen. "Your baby is a gift from God, you must treasure every moment you have with him."

Cathleen smiled, and the two women hugged each other. As they broke apart Ruth said,

"Our family will never forget what you have done for us, we will be forever in your debt."

Cathleen forced a weak smile before turning and heading out the front door. It was time to get back to the farm. It was time to get back to her son.

Chapter 6

May 1984

On a hillside high up in the Allegheny mountains, not far from the summit of Briery Knob, Henry Jarret and Eustace Brownlie were unloading demijohn jars from the rear of their dilapidated GMC flat-bed truck. Back in January they had started to construct a still to produce moonshine and today was the first time they were going to see a return for their labours. The still itself was housed within a rickety wooden shack made from timber planks that they and helped themselves to when the lorry transporting the wood was left unattended in a car park in Addison. The roofing felt had been removed from an outbuilding at the railway yard in Durbin and the condenser, copper pots and demijohns had been stolen from locations the length and breadth of Greenbrier County. In fact, nothing they had used building the still had been paid for.

From the top of the track where their truck was parked it was still a couple of hundred-yards walk up-hill through thick shrubs and trees to the still. The location had been carefully chosen as it was impossible to see from the track and was therefore hidden from prying eyes. The shack had also been built only feet from the Briery Creek which provided the necessary fresh water needed to make the precious liquid. Over the last four months the two friends had sweated blood heaving all the materials and equipment up the mountain's steep slopes. Today's journey was particularly difficult as the delicate glass jars were large and difficult to hold. They could carry one under each arm, but each step was precarious as the soft soil and old leaves made underfoot conditions very slippery.

"Be careful, will you?" shouted Henry as Eustace again lost his footing on the wet ground. "We've only got the eight jars and we're gonna need them all so don't you go breaking any."

Henry Jarret and Eustace Brownlie had been friends since their early school days. Now in their late thirties Eustace, or Brownie as he was universally known, was a year older than Henry. They had been in the same year at school as Eustace had been held back because of his weak academic skills. Eustace's had been a difficult upbringing. He never knew his parents and in his early years he lived between grandparents, an aged aunt and, occasionally, sympathetic neighbours. It had been rare for him to have spent more than a week in the same bed as he was growing up. The Brownlie's were also dirt poor and Eustace can remember once spending an entire summer without shoes. His grandparents just didn't have the money to buy him any. He had also been bullied at school. It later transpired that he was dyslexic which explained many of the difficulties he encountered reading and writing. He was taunted relentlessly by his peers and received little or no support from his teachers. His only true friend growing up had been Henry and the two boys had remained close ever since those early days.

Henry Jarret made no bones about the fact that he was a thief. He wasn't proud of it but when circumstances dictate, there are things you must do to provide for your family. So, Henry liked to think of himself as a thief with principles. He would never be violent, and he would never knowingly steal from someone he considered to be poor or who found themselves in unfortunate circumstances.

Henry still lived at home with his mother and younger brother Charlie. Henry's elder brother and his younger sister left home years ago desperate to escape the grinding poverty that bedevilled the family. Poverty was an everyday occurrence in West Virginia and Greenbrier county had more than its share of it. But even by these standards the Jarret's were poor. Their hardships just seemed unending.

Henry's father Joe and been killed in a mining accident when Henry was just four. After the death of his father, his mother, Alice, had tried desperately hard to provide for the family but, with no compensation from the mine and work scarce, it was an almost impossible task. To make things more difficult Charlie, the youngest child, had developed Polio when he was two. The Jarret's had no running water in the house when the children were small, and the toilet was no more than a latrine at the rear of the small yard. It is likely that Charlie caught the virus because of this terrible sanitation. Henry often thought it was a miracle that none of the other siblings had caught the horrible disease that left Charlie wearing a calliper on his right leg and using crutches to get around.

Henry's mother had suffered mental illness for most of her adult life. By her mid-fifties it had manifested itself as severe agoraphobia and the thought of leaving the house terrified her. Now sixty-two, it had been more than seven years since Alice had been out with the house or yard. She was a self-made prisoner and the thought of meeting people or going into Fairlea brought on panic attacks and severe anxiety. All possibility of work had gone for Alice and, like Charlie, she was now wholly dependent on Henry to provide for her.

Henry had held down a variety of jobs after leaving school and he was far from stupid. However, the demands of full time work had made it difficult to balance the needs of his mother and brother. He had started with petty theft. Foodstuffs and clothes mainly but of course the inevitable happened, and one day he found himself in court charged with stealing coffee, bacon and whisky from the local store. Having got himself a conviction for theft he lost his job at the timber mill and finding another job after that proved impossible. A life of petty crime became the only means by which he could put food on the table, but it was a vicious circle. The more often he stole; the more times he got caught. His third conviction lead to three months in the state penitentiary. After that, well, Henry had lost count of the times he had been sent to jail. He was trapped, and when he was in jail his mother and Charlie suffered, and did he know it.

Throughout all Henry's transgressions with the law Brownie was inevitably with him. On the odd occasion Brownie wasn't in jail with Henry he would go out of his way to try and look after Mrs Jarret and Charlie. Henry and Eustace were quite literally as thick as thieves.

Henry Jarret was seldom called by his proper name. Like Eustace, Henry had a nickname, and though it

98

irked him greatly there was nothing he could do about it. Apart from his mother, Charlie and Eustace, everybody that knew Henry called him Screech.

Throwing stones after school with other boys when he was aged eight, Henry had been hit in the eye by a well-directed rock. He had been taken to the hospital in Fairlea and for a while the doctors hoped that they would be able to save the sight in his right eye. But it proved to be of no avail and three months later he was blind in that eye. The doctors removed the eye and fitted him with a glass replacement. In 1954 such procedures were crude affairs and the eye that was fitted, while being a reasonable colour match, appeared to be two sizes too big. This unfortunately left Henry with a very prominent right eye which, being truthful did not look unlike the wide-eyed stare of an owl. It wasn't long before every child in the school was calling him, 'Screech' and the nickname just stuck. As he got older the over-sized eye became a little less obvious, but he was never able to lose that boyhood nickname. So, Screech it was, whether he liked it or not.

"Line the jars up over there," said Henry, pointing to a flattish area of ground adjacent to the hut. "And stand well back, I'm going to light the burner." He opened the valve of the gas bottle and lit the burner. Blue flames immediately leapt up and started to heat the base of the large copper pot that contained the corn mash, malt and yeast.

"That will heat in no time," said Henry, "you keep your eye on the worm box and open the tap."

The worm box was a wooden barrel containing a length of coiled copper pipe. Fresh water from the creek fed into the top of the box and back out via a pipe at the bottom. On the side of the barrel was a tap. Underneath it stood a metal bucket into which Henry hoped the clear whisky would soon be pouring.

"Let me know a soon as we get any liquid," said Henry "we're gonna need to test it for purity."

"Sure will," said Eustace nodding enthusiastically.

After a few minutes liquid started to drip from the tap.

"It's coming Henry!" said Eustace who could now hardly contain his excitement, "we'll be drinking moonshine tonight alright!"

"Okay, grab that metal spoon and hold it under the tap till it's full," said Henry gesticulating at the spoon that was lying on a wooden bench by the hut door.

Eustace grabbed the large spoon and held it under the tap. The drips were becoming more frequent and in no time the spoon was full.

"What happens now?" asked Eustace with a quizzical expression on his face.

"Just hold the spoon steady in both hands," instructed Henry, "I'm going to light it. We want it to have a blue flame. A blue flame is good, means it's safe to drink. We don't want a yellow flame, that'll mean it's contaminated and no use." Henry lit the clear liquid and both men held their breath.

"It's blue, Henry!" shouted Eustace, "that flame is definitely blue!" Eustace was shifting his weight from one foot to another, it was all he could do to stop himself dancing with joy.

"So far so good," said Henry in a calm voice, "but we need to do one more test before we can taste it."

"What test?" said Eustace impatiently.

"We need to see how much alcohol is in it," said Henry. "The more it has the better the price will be for us when we come to sell it."

"So how we gonna test that then?" asked Eustace whose frustration at not being able to sample the liquor was in danger of boiling over.

"See that plastic bottle?" said Henry pointing to a small plastic milk bottle that was also on the wooden bench. "Fill it nearly full, put the lid on and give it a good shake. If it makes large bubbles then we've got good moonshine."

Eustace asked the obvious question, "What if we've only got small bubbles?"

"Then it won't be as strong, and we'll not get as good a price for it. But don't fret Eustace, I'm expecting it to be just fine," said Henry confidently.

Eustace trusted Henry, as he had always been the brains of their outfit, so Eustace reckoned he must know what he was talking about.

Eustace took the bottle and held it under the tap. When it was about three quarters full he put on the lid and started to shake the bottle vigorously. Suddenly, the lid of the bottle flew off and liquid started to fly everywhere.

"Watch what you're doing you idiot!" shouted Henry, but it was too late. Most of the liquid hit the copper pot containing the mash but some splashed on the ground and still more landed on Henry's trousers. Realising the danger they were now in, Henry grabbed an old rag and frantically wiped at the sides of the copper pot, but it was to no avail. The liquid dripped off the pot and onto the gas burner igniting instantly. Fierce flames licked up the sides of the pot and the rubber pipe that connected the gas canister to the pot started to melt in the intense heat. Flames leapt from the ground where the liquid had splashed onto the floor.

"I'm sorry Henry, I thought the lid was on proper!" wailed Eustace.

"Get out! Get out the shed before it explodes!" screamed Henry. The fire had now engulfed the gas bottle next to the burner and Henry knew it would blow, he just didn't know when. Henry grabbed Eustace's arm and pushed him towards the door.

"Just get outside this thing's going to explode!" The floor of the hut was now ablaze, and flames licked at Henry's trousers as he headed for the door. The moonshine soaked legs of his dungarees were now alight, and Henry knew he risked being badly burnt if he didn't act soon. As he exited the door he flung himself to the ground and started rolling down the steep slope. Over and over he went until a large mountain holly bush prevented him from rolling any further. When he came to a stop he was soaking wet and covered in leaves, but at least his trousers were no longer on fire. Henry looked to see where Eustace was. To his horror, he could see Eustace walking towards the shed carrying a bucket of water that he had filled in the creek which he was now about to throw onto the roof of the shed.

"Eustace, get the hell out of there!" cried Henry. "The gas canister is going to explode!"

"I know," replied Eustace, "but this is my fault! I caused the fire Henry!"

"Eustace put the bucket down and get your ass down here right now! That's an order!" barked Henry.

Eustace put the bucket down and made his way down the steep slope towards Henry.

Henry grabbed Eustace by the arm and the two friends started to run. Slipping and slithering down the muddy slope through entanglements of arrowwood and wild raison shrubs towards their truck. The explosion ripped across the tree tops just as they reached the vehicle scattering scores of roosting stock pigeons in all directions. Plumes of acrid black smoke drifted over the forest canopy and the bitter smell of sulphur stung their nostrils.

"Well there goes four months of work!" said Henry in an ironic voice.

"Suppose it could be worse," said Eustace, desperately trying to see a bright side. "At least we didn't lose any money this time, so that's a good thing, right?"

Henry gave Eustace a withering look and shook his head, "Some town somewhere is missing an idiot, and I think I've just found him," said Henry.

Eustace looked at Henry clearly confused, "Not sure I follow you," said a bemused Eustace.

"Just get in the truck, will you? Someone's going to be reporting this real soon, so better we're not here," said Henry as he started the truck and made his way slowly down the twisting track.

*

Chief Wilder answered the phone in his office. The call was from the duty officer Sergeant Coutts informing him that a highway patrol had arrested Henry Jarret and Eustace Brownlie at Fat Sam's diner in Ronceverte on suspicion of arson and operating an illicit still.

"Apparently Jarett's dungarees are badly burnt and Brownlie has all but confessed in the rear of the police vehicle," said Sergeant Coutts.

"That's the news I was waiting for Shads, I knew it would be them," said Wilder. "Do we have any update from the fire department about the extent of damage?" asked Wilder,

"Just an estimate at the moment, sir. The fire officer is saying more than four acres of woodland has been completely destroyed. The fire is now under control, but they expect to keep a tender there overnight just as a precaution."

"That's all noted," said Chief Wilder, "now I need you to find me Mike Rawlingson, and have him report to my office."

"I can see him right now through the window, looks like he's heading to his vehicle. Probably heading home, it's after five thirty."

"Well stick your head out the window and tell him to get his ass up here! I need him to interview Screech and Useless."

Sergeant Coutts opened the window and shouted across to Mike Rawlingson who was taking off his jacket and about to get into his car.

"Mike, Mike!" shouted Sergeant Coutts. Mike turned around to see his colleague leaning out of the office window.

"What's up, Phil?" said Mike.

"Sorry about this Mike, I know you were heading home but Bull wants to see you in his office right away. It's about the fire up at Briery Knob, cops have arrested Screech and Brownie and they're en route here. He wants you to interview them, really sorry about that.

You know what's he's like, especially when Screech and Brownie are involved."

"God damn it Phil, I'm supposed to be picking Keegan up after his softball practice and Susan is at the High School with her music group," said Mike, clearly annoyed.

"I knew there had been a fire, I could see the plumes of smoke from my office," added Mike, "but I didn't think it was criminal, just assumed it was a forest fire."

"Not sure it is criminal, well, the fire bit anyway," replied Phil. "It appears Screech and Brownie had an illegal still up there and have somehow set fire to it."

"Can you print me off the incident?" asked Mike who was now putting his jacket back on and walking back across the car park.

"One step ahead of you Mike," said Phil holding out several sheets of paper.

"Thanks, Phil," said Mike as he grabbed the paper from Phil's hand. "Can you do me a favour? Phone the High School and get a message to Susan, tell her that she'll need to pick up Keegan from his practice? I may be stuck here for quite some time by the sound of it, and apologise for me, won't you?" asked Mike.

"No problem, Mike, I'll phone the school and let her know. Better read the incident before you see Bull," added Phil.

"Don't worry about that," said Mike, "I always do my homework before speaking to Bull. I've been caught out like that before and I don't intend for it to happen again."

Ewart Wilder had been promoted to Chief of Lewisburg Police Department six months ago. At forty-two he was the youngest Chief of Police in Lewisburg's history. His move up from Deputy Chief had been fortunate to say the least as the incumbent in the post, Chief Nicol, suffered an aneurism only weeks into the job and had to retire from the service on ill health. Timing is everything as they say, and on this occasion, there was no doubt that Ewart Wilder was in the right place at the right time. It would also be fair to say that his promotion was not universally well received, and his dictatorial style of management had ruffled more than a few feathers.

Wilder's dislike for Henry Jarret and Eustace Brownlie bordered on the obsessive. Throughout his police career he had always been on their case. He had lost count of how many times he had arrested them. It was an obsession that had been handed down from his father. Bill Wilder had been in the same year at school as Henry's dad, Joe and the two had never got on. It was difficult to know why it all started but throughout their time at school the two of them would regularly get into fights. More times than not it was Joe Jarret who would emerge victorious.

When Bill Wilder joined the police department it gave him the perfect opportunity to revisit old grudges and he took every opportunity to persecute Joe and make his life a misery. He would arrest him for any and every misdemeanour and of course arrests led to convictions, fines and occasionally time in jail, the impact on an already impoverished family was devastating.

By the time Henry hit his late teens he found himself the victim of Bill Wilder's vendetta. When Bill retired, Ewart simply picked up the mantle from where his father left off and the persecution of the Jarret family continued.

As Henry's constant companion Eustace frequently found himself caught up in Ewart's hate campaign. Ewart didn't hold quite the same malice towards Eustace but he still regarded him with contempt and as easy prey. Arresting Eustace Brownlie was like shooting fish in a barrel he would say. When he started his police career, arresting soft targets were just as important as any other ones to Ewart. He was young and out to impress and every arrest was a tick on the Captain's tally sheet. Quality wasn't important, it was the number of arrests that counted and Ewart was more than happy to oblige.

Ewart's progression through the ranks didn't stop the persecution of Henry and Eustace. Now sycophantic young officers, keen to impress their new boss, all knew that any arrest of Screech or Brownie would be looked on favourably by the Chief and many seemed more than willing to harass the unfortunate pair.

Mike Rawlingson hated such petty vindictiveness. It was not what he joined the police service for and his disdain for Wilder and his ilk was palpable. Mike knew it didn't do him any favours not dancing to Wilders tune, but he would rather maintain his principles, and be able to look himself in the mirror each morning, than sell out to a megalomaniac like Ewart Wilder.

Mike was the senior detective at Lewisburg but that, of course, was not down to Ewart Wilder who, if he had his way, would have Mike back in uniform kicking tyres on patrol duty. No, Mike's promotions had come when other, more reasonable, chiefs had been in charge. From a professional point of view, Mike would have liked to have moved back to Chicago where he'd started in the police nineteen years ago. The opportunities, particularly for detective officers, would be far better in a big city. But love had intervened, and he was now settled and happily married to Susan. They had their nine-year son, Keegan, to think about now so for now Mike was staying put.

Mike and Susan had married three years after their first meeting when Mike had capsized whilst white water rafting on the Shenandoah. It had not been a particularly lavish wedding, Susan had been keen to avoid it being too formal or posh as that really wasn't her style. The service and reception were held in the Clarion Hotel where Mike had stayed when he first met Susan. They were both only children and neither of them had particularly large families but on the day of the wedding it felt as though half of Harpers Ferry had been there.

Susan had worn a simple wedding dress of white cotton which had long sleeves and a scooped neckline. Everyone agreed that she'd looked beautiful and very elegant which particularly pleased Susan as her pre-wedding diet and fitness regime had seen her manage to lose the half stone that had crept on since she'd started teaching. Her two bridesmaids were of course Anna and Colette. Carrying posies of yellow and white freesias, they looked stunning in their tangerine full-length charmeuse dresses.

There was something of a panic in the lead up to the wedding as Susan's mother had got sight of a recent picture of Colette sporting bright green streaks in her hair. Fearing that Colette might end up looking rather like a carrot, Mrs McDowell contacted Colette and asked if she wouldn't mind changing her hair colour so as not to spoil the photographs. Colette didn't take offence at the request and was happy to oblige. Susan knew nothing of this of course, as she would have been horrified if she'd known what her mother had done. Susan wouldn't have dreamed of asking her friend to change her hair colour. Thankfully, Colette's accommodating nature saved a diplomatic incident and the wedding went off without a hitch.

The music and dancing continued late into the evening and the night was capped off by Susan and Colette giving a slightly tipsy reprise of the Shirelles hit 'Will you Love Me Tomorrow' that Mike had specially requested as he had never heard them sing it before. It brought the house done but Susan swore it would be the last airing of the song as from now on she intended to be more rock chick than disco queen.

Unfortunately, Mike's friend, dangerous sport loving Dave hadn't managed to make the wedding as the week before he had broken his leg while mountain Biking. Looking back Mike and Susan still laughed at the wedding present Dave sent them, a gift voucher for a weekend zip lining and learning how to abseil. Poor Dave never appreciated that neither Mike or Susan shared his love for extreme sports and the voucher ended up as a prize in Susan's school Christmas raffle.

For the first few months after they met, Mike would make the long trip south to stay with Susan whenever he had a long weekend off work. Eventually, after fifteen months of trying he secured a transfer from Chicago to Lewisburg Police Department and the moment that confirmation came through he moved into Susan's flat above the bakery.

The Rawlingson's moved into their present house on the outskirts of Fairlea just before their son Keegan was born. Since then family life followed the familiar routine of kids sports and musical activities with busy weekends spent walking, cycling and catching up with friends. Harpers Ferry remained a firm favourite, but now when the family goes Mike and Keegan fish for trout in the quiet waters below the lodge and stay well clear of any rafts.

Susan Rawlingson took up her current position as deputy principal of Ronceverte Elementary School three years ago. Since then her creative and musical talents helped the school forge an enviable reputation for its drama and musical productions. For the last two years, Susan had also helped to run the music club at Fairlea High where she taught the teenagers acoustic and electric guitar and occasionally piano. The spectacular end of year concert had become one of the highlights of the school year.

*

Mike knocked on the door of Chief Wilder's office.

"Is that you Mike?" said Wilder looking up from his desk, "come in and sit down, I need you to do something for me."

"Okay Sir," said Mike, "and what might that be?"

"Have you heard about the fire up on Briery Knob? Well Screech and Useless have been arrested and I need you to interview them," explained Wilder. "Arson and whatever the charge is for operating an illegal still, court in the morning for both of them."

"I had heard about the fire sir, and I think you'll find his name's Eustace sir," replied Mike tersely.

"Don't be a smart ass with me Rawlingson! I know what his fucking name is," said Wilder pointing his finger at Mike.

"Anyway, as I was telling you, I need you to interview the useless Eustace and his sidekick. Shouldn't take too long, from what I hear Brownlie is singing like a bird already," added Wilder. "Should be a quick interview formal caution and charge and jobs done."

"Might not be quite as simple as that sir," replied Mike. "I don't think operating an illegal Still will be a problem, but the evidence for Arson looks flimsy to say the least."

"What do you mean flimsy?" asked Wilder with a frown. "Setting fire to growing wood has always been Arson, ever since I joined the job, unless of course you know better detective," said Wilder sarcastically.

"Setting Fire to growing wood is Arson, you're quite right sir. But it's not a felony unless it's done knowingly or maliciously. I think we're going to find that Jarret and Brownlie have somehow managed to accidently set fire to the still and its then spread to the surrounding forest. Just surmising you understand, but if that's the case the charge will be Reckless Burning and not Arson," continued Mike. "Also, as I don't think the still was in production, we won't be able to charge them with selling the liquor, just trying to make the stuff. What I'm trying to say sir is, at the end of this we're looking at a fine, not perhaps the term in jail you were looking for." After a short pause he added, "Of course all that will depend on the court finding them guilty, never a given these days."

"I'm familiar with how our judiciary works Lieutenant Rawlingson," said an increasingly exasperated Wilder. "Now get out my office and go interview them, and don't disappear home till you've personally given me an update, understand?"

111

"All understood sir," said Mike in a perfunctory voice. Just as he reached the door Mike turned towards Wilder and with a dead pan tone added, "Trees and legislation, tricky things sir, aren't they, very tricky."

"I'll say something Lieutenant Rawlingson, you're one cheeky son of a bitch. Now get out and get them charged."

Mike smiled to himself as he headed for the stairs. His last remark had been intended to touch a nerve and, judging by Wilder's response, it had hit its mark. Mike couldn't think of too many times when anyone had got one over on Ewart Wilder, but last Christmas was one such occasion, and it was made all the sweeter as it had been done by Henry Jarret and Eustace Brownlie.

In the weeks leading up to Christmas, Screech and Brownie had been working hard. What they were doing was still illegal of course, in fact it was blatant theft. However, unusually for them, this particular money-making scheme had been well thought out. It had involved a lot of hard graft but for once it was destined to make the two friends some serious money. Henry had heard that old man Deans had gone into hospital in Charleston with a serious bout of pneumonia. His wife had gone to stay with her daughter, who lived near to the hospital, as it would make visiting easier. All of which meant the estate and house that the Deans owned over at Huntersville was empty and unattended. The Deans were extremely wealthy, Robbie Deans, who was now in his late seventies, had inherited a fortune from his father's publishing company when he died twenty years ago. Using some of his inheritance, Deans bought the estate at Huntersville. For the last twenty years the

Deans had grown Christmas trees, thousands of them of all shapes and sizes.

Henry knew the mountain tracks around that area like the back of his hand and his plan was to drive up to the plantation in the dead of night. He and Eustace would then cut down the trees which they would store and then sell in the run up to Christmas. Henry reckoned the flat-bed truck he owned could carry at least twenty-five trees. They would need to cut the trees by hand, it would be slow, but they couldn't risk using a chainsaw as someone would be bound to hear it. Henry calculated that if they used a two man saw, they could have the trees cut in a couple of hours. Half an hour to load the trees, factor in the two-hour drive there and back and the night's work would take them less than five hours.

Sam Coombs was a longstanding friend of the Jarret's. Years ago, he had worked with Henry's dad in the mine. But after Joe Jarret's tragic accident Sam lost his appetite for mining and started his own joinery business in Fairlea. He had recently retired and had sold off most of his lathes and cutting machines, but he still owned a large shed near the centre of town. In front of the shed was some hard standing, enough for six cars. The rear of the shed had a set of large double doors, easily big enough to fit Henry's truck. The lane at the rear of the shed was hardly ever used and as there was no street lighting, it was perfect for what Henry had in mind. The biggest bonus though was the fact that the lane provided a back way out of the town and a mile down the Lewisburg road was a junction that took you high up into the Allegheny mountains and past the Dean's estate in Huntersville.

Henry had got Sam's agreement to use his shed, so since the beginning of November, Henry and Eustace had been making nightly trips to Huntersville and by the week before thanksgiving, Sam's shed was crammed full of more than 400 hundred Christmas trees.

By the time they were finished both Henry and Eustace were exhausted. The work was demanding. Cutting trees by torchlight in the middle of the night was not without its difficulties. After the first few days, Henry realised that it was taking them much longer to cut the trees and load the truck. All the trees that were near to the track had already been cut so they had to venture further into the forest to get the right sized trees. Each tree had then to be carried back to the truck. Henry lost count of the number of times they had cut or poked themselves on stray branches. It got so bad that he went and bought a couple of pairs of protective glasses. Having already lost one eye, Henry was keen to hang onto his other one. The glasses worked well enough but when Henry and Eustace started to sweat the glasses steamed up. Every couple of minutes the friends would have to stop and wipe the glasses with a cloth. What had started as a couple of hours work soon became three and sometimes even four. Add on the journey and the loading and unloading time and it was nearly six hours before they got home to their beds. The energy sapping work combined with only snatching a few hours' sleep during the day was fast taking its toll and by the end of November Henry and Eustace were shattered.

Of course, Sam knew that the trees were stolen, Henry had been up front about that. But as he didn't much like Robbie Deans and he liked Ewart Wilder and the Lewisburg Police Department even less he wasn't at all bothered. If he could help Henry and his family out he would. There would be more than a few dollars in it for Sam who had agreed to sell the trees from his shed. Sam also arranged for his grandson Bradley to give him a hand. Bradley was only sixteen, but he was strong as an ox. His job would be to tie the trees up and lift them onto vehicle roof racks or wherever the customer wanted. He had recently left school and was always looking for ways to earn a little cash.

Henry and Eustace's trees sold for ten dollars less than any of their competitors in the area, so it was no surprise that they sold like hotcakes. By the time several of the other shop keepers had complained to the police about the cut-price trees it was too late. That Christmas, half of Fairlea had Henry and Eustace's Christmas trees adorning their front rooms. Indeed, Mike Rawlingson took great delight telling everyone at the senior officers' morning meeting that Ewart and his wife Bridget's tree had been purchased from Sam's shed as Susan had seen Bradley loading it into the rear of Mrs Wilder's station wagon one afternoon after school.

Ewart Wilder, like most other people in that room, believed that Screech and Brownie were behind the venture and he was apoplectic with rage. No evidence was ever found to prove that the trees were stolen or that Henry and Eustace had been involved, but the thought that Henry Jarret had got one over on him nearly made Wilder demented.

Mike was still chuckling to himself when he walked into Sergeant Coutts office, as no matter how bad his day was going the story of Henry Jarret and the Christmas trees always brought a smile to his face.

"I've just finished booking them in Mike," said Sergeant Coutts. "I'll just get you the key for the interview room and you're good to go. By the way, I spoke to the caretaker at the school, he was going to make sure that Susan got the message about picking up Keegan."

"Thanks, Phil, that was good of you, appreciate it," said Mike who was still smiling to himself.

"What you so pleased about?" asked Phil, "I thought this interview was going to be a pain in the butt."

"It will be," said Mike, "but, oh never mind, I'll explain later." With that he headed down the corridor to the interview room.

In the annex behind the main school building at Fairlea High Susan Rawlingson was speaking to the caretaker while searching her handbag for her car keys.

"Thanks for letting me know Kenny, and if you're sure I'll let the kids know that you'll lock up after they've finished," said Susan with a smile and a grateful nod.

"Listen up everyone," continued Susan, "somethings come up and I've got to shoot off early to pick up Keegan. Kenny says he will lock up when you've finished so you can keep practising till 1815 hrs just like we usually do."

"Josh, can you look after Maisie, Joe, in fact all of the senior group? Pauline, if you could take charge of the juniors just now that would be great," added Susan clutching her keys which she had found at the bottom of her bag.

"Homework for next week Seniors, Dire Straits, Sultans of Swing. I know some of you have played it before but it's not an easy piece. Getting the right speed and groove is difficult so you'll need to practice it. It's likely going to feature in the show so it's important we get it right."

"I'm leaving the music with Josh, so if you don't already have a copy you can get one from him?"

"Juniors, I need you to keep practising Knockin on Heavens door. You all know the chords we just need to be syncing a bit better so plenty of practice this week please."

"Okay everyone, have a good weekend and I'll see you next Tuesday," said Susan as she hurried out the door to the car park. It was 1745 hrs, if the traffic wasn't too bad she could still make it to Keegan's softball practice by 1800 hrs. Damn it thought Susan, if Mike's held up at the office I'll need to get the dinner organised as well, funny how he always seems to get held on at work when it's his turn to cook the dinner.

By the time 1815 arrived Josh was glad to finish the practice. Nobody was deliberately being obstructive but trying to keep some semblance of control and get people to listen to him was far more difficult than he thought it would be.

"Definitely don't fancy being a teacher after that," said Josh as he and Maisie strolled out the school gates and headed for home.

"Just shows you how good a teacher Mrs Rawlingson is," added Josh. "I just don't think I would have the patience. If someone was really trying it on I'd just want to thump them, so perhaps teaching isn't for me!"

"No, doesn't sound like it is," said Maisie, who as usual was hanging on every word that Josh said.

Maisie Foster was two months short of her sixteenth birthday and was in the year below Josh. She and her little sister Becca, who was fourteen, came from a musical family. Their father, Dave and been a successful session musician playing keyboards with several bands throughout the late 60s and 70s. The Grateful Dead, who he played Keyboards for on their infamous European tour of 1972, being about the most famous. It was in Amsterdam during that tour that Dave claims he developed his lifelong addiction to marijuana. Something he was now desperate to keep away from his two daughters. Dave was now semi-retired, he still played occasional local gigs with his band the Ragtails but nothing too serious. Strangely, Dave could hardly play a note on the guitar. As neither of the girls showed much interest in the Keyboard he was more than happy for Susan Rawlingson to teach them guitar as she was a gifted player who could really make the instrument sing.

Maisie Foster had a big crush on Josh Heggerty. But so far that affection had not been reciprocated although Maisie remained hopeful. It wasn't as if Josh didn't like Maisie because he did. He also happened to think she was a pretty good guitarist and of course, the fact that her dad had once played keyboards with the Grateful Dead was a huge bonus as far as Josh was concerned. So, taking all that into consideration Maisie knew that all was not yet lost when it came to a potential romance with Josh. And anyhow, Maisie Foster still had her ace card to play. Jerry Garcia, lead guitarist of the Grateful Dead, was one of Josh's guitar heroes. What Josh didn't yet know, was that Maisie's dad had a signed Gibson SG guitar hanging on the wall in their den that Garcia had once played. When she thought the moment was right she intended to tell Josh about the guitar and maybe invite him over to the house to see it, she was pretty sure that he would be impressed. What might happen after that she wasn't quite so sure about, but she was confident it could only be a positive step towards her ambitions for Josh. But for the moment, she would keep plugging away and hope that he would begin to notice her.

Her situation wasn't helped by the fact that she could never find a way to be alone with Josh. They only time when that might be possible was walking home after music club but everywhere Maisie went Becca was sure to follow. That wasn't exactly Becca's fault, Dave and their mother insisted that Becca didn't walk home alone as the route, which was less than a mile, took them past the rear of the Fairlea Hotel, along a quiet footpath past the school sports fields and through a small wooded area none of which was particularly well lit. The Fosters weren't that keen on Maisie walking home but since it only happened on rare occasions they would tolerate it, but at fourteen Becca was still too young, and she required to be chaperoned.

Being truthful Maisie didn't much like walking home herself, so she could understand why her parents didn't want Becca doing it. Of course, the consequence of all of this was that Maisie's opportunities to be alone with Josh were few and far between.

Maisie Lily Foster was a fine looking young lady. She was tall, willowy and very slim. She took her figure from her mother who had been a dancer in her younger days. Maisie had long dark hair that she wore parted down the middle. The sides were feathered into short curled back layers, it was very much the in style of that time. Perhaps Maisie's most distinctive feature was her flawless alabaster skin. It was like porcelain and looking at her, you would have thought that Maisie had never been exposed to the sun. That wasn't entirely true, while Maisie didn't seek out the sun, she didn't avoid it altogether either. But for someone with such dark hair it was unusual to see such pale skin. Maisie's mother thought she must have a pigment deficiency as she was so white and for most of the summer Maisie didn't go anywhere without her floppy cotton white sunhat as she didn't want to risk burning her delicate skin. The hats wide brim covered her face, but it gave her a distinctive look and everyone that knew Maisie also knew that hat.

Little sister, Becca was in many ways quite like her big sister. She wore her dark hair a bit shorter and she wasn't as tall as her sister had been at the same age, but she shared Maisie's pale complexion so physically there was no mistaking the pair as sisters. They liked the same types of clothes and shared a similar taste in music. Most of the time the pair got on just fine, but after music club Maisie found her little sister's constant presence more than a little irritating. This was time that Maisie craved to be alone with Josh, but that never seemed to happen. Becca never said very much, most of the time she just trailed behind daydreaming or singing to herself, but she was always there, like a shadow that couldn't be thrown off and Maisie found it infuriating.

As the three of them ambled along the path, Maisie turned the conversation to Josh's favourite subject; who were the best guitar players and what made them so great. This was slightly unusual as normally it would be Josh who wanted to talk about bands and favourite guitarists, once Josh got started there was usually no stopping him. Predictably Josh trotted out his list of all-time greats. Page, Garcia, Clapton and of course the king of them all Hendrix. Josh's list never really changed and while he could add in many more, his top four were head and shoulders better than the rest, well according to Josh they were.

"Why do you never have any women on your list Josh?" asked Maisie provocatively.

The question caught Josh slightly off guard. He stopped walking and thought for a moment before adding, "I'm not saying they aren't any good, but rock music's more a man's thing, so it follows that there isn't as many women", said Josh authoritatively," that's just the way it is I'm afraid."

Maisie scoffed loudly. "Rock's more a man's thing, you've got to be kidding me," said Maisie sarcastically. Even Becca who hadn't really been following the conversion stood and looked at Josh with a puzzled expression on her face.

Josh could see that Maisie looked annoyed and was clearly not convinced by his reply, so he hurriedly tried to repair the damage. "Of course, there are some really good female guitarists."

"Yeah, well at least that bit's true," said Maisie. "So, who would be in your all-time top three females," asked Maisie with just a hint of mischief in her voice. Josh wasn't sure where this conversation was heading. As far as talking about bands and guitarists he was the font of all knowledge, but at this precise moment his mind was a blank, he was struggling to name any female guitarist let alone a top three. Eventually Josh managed to splutter a reply, "Joni Mitchell for one," said Josh, "and Nancy Wilson for another, she was great in Heart with her sister, can't remember her name though."

"Okay," said Maisie, "That's two, so who would be your third?"

Josh was stumped. How difficult could it be he thought, there must be hundreds of female guitar players but at this precise moment, he couldn't conjure up a third name. Then, suddenly, out it came. "Susan Rawlingson is a great guitar player," said Josh "and she's definitely female, so that's three."

As soon as the words were out of his mouth Josh realised how pathetic that must have sounded.

It was Becca Foster who laughed first. Maisie just stood with an incredulous look on her face. By the time Maisie started to laugh Josh could feel his face turning red. He was embarrassed and didn't enjoy being made to look ridiculous by a couple of girls.

"That's it, I'm done with this conversation," said Josh curtly. "I'm late already, I'll need to go," and without another word Josh broke into a jog and headed off up the path.

Maisie was crestfallen, what had she done? She had only wanted to be mischievous, perhaps even a little flirtatious but somehow, in the space of just a few moments, she had managed to embarrass and annoy Josh. This was not how it was supposed to happen.

Becca looked at her sister and sensed that she was upset.

"I know you fancy him," said Becca, "but I think you've probably gone and annoyed him now. If it'll help, I'll just tell him that you fancy him, what do you think?"

Maisie looked at her sister but didn't say anything. She knew that Becca meant well but at this moment she didn't think that Josh would even want to speak to he let alone regard her as a potential girlfriend. To make matters worse she had forgotten to ask how his mom was. She had intended to, but in their stupid conversation about female guitarists, it had escaped her mind completely. It had been a while since she had asked Josh about his mother and that made her feel bad, he'll think I don't care thought Maisie to herself. As if he hasn't got enough on his plate already thought Maisie, and then I go and make things worse.

As she walked home with her sister by her side Maisie wanted to cry.

Chapter 7

"God damn it," said an increasingly exasperated Josh, as for the umpteenth time his fingers failed to complete the sequence of notes he had been trying to master for the last two hours. E string – middle finger, B string – Thumb then back to E string and index finger he said to himself. Finger picking like Mark Knopfler was proving impossible. He could play all the sequences in the first part of the song but the last guitar solo at the end needed to be played super-fast and Josh just couldn't master it. Susan Rawlingson hadn't been kidding when she said it was difficult to get the right tempo playing 'Sultans of Swing.' Josh looked down at his hands, "It's my fingers," he cursed. "Look at the state of my fingers, they're too fat and not long enough." At that moment in time something or someone was going to get the blame as Josh's frustration at not been able to play the solo was boiling over. Josh threw his guitar onto the chair in the corner of his room and slumped down on his bed. He lay back with his hands behind his head and shut his eyes. It took a lot to get Josh annoyed and he was not used to failure.

Josh Heggerty had just had his seventeenth birthday. He still had to complete one more year of high school before deciding what he might do in the future, but the time was fast approaching when that decision would have to be made. He was academically bright and his SAT scores across all subjects were well above average. Josh wanted to go to college to study music but financially that was always going to prove difficult. College didn't come cheap and the Heggertys were far from wealthy, now with his mother's health problems, going to college looked almost impossible.

His father was dead against it anyway. He wanted Josh to take a job at the local mine, just as he had done at the same age, but Josh was having none of it. He'd seen too many men like his father suffer illness or disability through working in the mine. Josh could name two friends of his fathers who had died in mining accidents and at least another three who had emphysema or some other respiratory disease. His own father was now walking with a permanent limp and was in almost constant pain as a result of the injury he had suffered while working at the Middleton mine.

His father's attitude made Josh angry, if he wasn't going to be able to go to college he would find some other work, but it certainly wasn't going to be down any mine.

Josh looked older than his seventeen years, at 6'2" he towered over his father and he had a powerful and athletic build that in part could be attributed to years of working on the farm. Broad across the shoulders and with long legs and a slim waist Josh looked more like a sportsman than a musician. Apart, that is, for his hair. Josh had thick blond hair which he wore a couple of inches over the top of his collar. If it had been solely down to Josh it would be much longer, as who ever saw a rock guitarist with short hair. But his father wouldn't allow it, not while Josh still lived in his house, or so he said. So, the length Josh wore his hair was on the absolute limit, half an inch longer and his father would go off on one and experience had taught Josh that it wasn't worth the battle.

Frank Heggerty just didn't get the music thing. He didn't have a musical bone in his body and when Josh was growing up much of the time they spent together was either on the football field or softball park. It wasn't as if Josh wasn't any good at sports or didn't like them, if fact he excelled at most of them and for a while that wasn't a problem as Josh played football and softball for the school. He proved to be even better at track where from the ages of eleven through fifteen he was his years 400 metre champion. It was after his fifteenth birthday that things changed.

For his birthday his parents gave him a Sony Walkman and from that moment onwards there was no turning back for Josh. Music was his passion and over the next year or so, much to the annoyance of his father, Josh listened to more and more music and did less and less sport. There just wasn't the time for both and anyway the school music club met after school on Tuesdays and Thursdays which were the days the football team trained. He couldn't continue with both, so Josh chose to follow the musical path and football was put to one side. To this day Frank couldn't understand it and it caused endless arguments and tension between them.

Cathleen Heggerty found herself stuck between a rock and a hard place. She wanted to be loyal to her husband but at the same time be supportive and sympathetic to her son's situation. Cathleen steadfastly tried to remain neutral, but it wasn't easy.

Josh had been listening to Classic Rock on AOR Radio for a couple of years, but the Walkman, which came complete with a set of Sony Headphones, meant that he could now take his music just about anywhere. So long as Josh remembered to carry some spare batteries he was never without his music. Most evenings after dinner Josh would sit on the swing on the chestnut tree listening to his Walkman. The views across the valley to Fairlea and the Allegany mountains beyond were spectacular. At this time of year when the larkspur and columbine were out it was a favourite place to just sit and relax. It also brought Josh close to Peter, the brother he never knew. Cathleen had told Josh about Peter and the small white cross that still stood in the shadows of the chestnut tree when he was only small, now years later, he still liked to think about Peter and what he might have been like whenever he sat on the swing.

Josh could sit there for hours listening to his favourite bands and his father soon began to rue the day he ever bought Josh that Walkman. But that was just the start of things, shortly after his birthday Josh used the money he had saved doing chores around the Farm to buy a Fender Stratocaster and a Dynaco ST-70 amplifier. For Josh Heggerty that was about the best $150 dollars he ever spent. Both the guitar and amplifier were second hand but that didn't matter as they were both in great condition. The body of the Fender was bright red, and it had a cream neck, just like the one he had seen Jerry Garcia play at a concert in the Uptown Theatre in Chicago which Josh had watched on television.

Over the next few months, Josh started to teach himself how to play the guitar. He picked up a copy of

Bert Weedon's 'Play in a Day – Guide to Modern Guitar Playing' at a second- hand bookshop in the town, and while it took him longer than a day, Josh was playing recognisable tunes within a couple of weeks. When he joined the music club at school his playing really started to improve. Susan Rawlingson's predecessor at the club had been a colourful character called Conrad Blewitt, who for a number of years worked as a peripatetic music teacher in Greenbrier County specialising in both the acoustic and electric guitar. Conrad thought Josh showed real potential and it was under his guidance that Josh's playing ability really took off. Conrad was a big rock fan and pointed Josh in the direction of several bands and guitar players that he had previously never heard of. The world of Robert Johnson, Charlie Christian and the legendary B.B King were suddenly accessible, and Josh soaked up their music with relish. Within a year Josh gave a solo performance of the Deep Purple classic, 'Smoke on the Water,' at the end of year school concert and it was then that he made his mind up that he wanted to study music at college.

When Josh turned his amplifier up to full volume in his bedroom at the back of the farmhouse the noise nearly blew the roof off. It was so loud that Josh only ever played his guitar that loud when his parents were away. Once when they had gone to Hinton for the weekend to visit Frank's brother, Josh played a medley of 'Stairway to Heaven', 'Ace of Spades' and 'White Wedding' at full blast for several hours. For the next 3 days none of the hen's produced any eggs which dumbfounded Frank when he returned home. Josh always suspected that his playing had been responsible.

Only goes to show that chickens didn't appreciate good rock music thought Josh.

As he lay on his bed Josh gazed at the poster of Jimi Hendrix that hung on the wall next to the door. Over the years the sun had faded the image which displayed a young Hendrix, dressed in a purple shirt with his wild afro hair tied back in a blue bandana, leaning backwards while holding vertically a black and yellow guitar. His left arm hung by his side and his left hand, that magical left hand, was tantalisingly not shown on the poster. Judging by the grimace on Hendrix's face, Josh had always imagined that his left arm would, at any moment, sweep into view and seconds later the first bars of Purple Haze would blast from the wall and attack your senses in the way only Hendrix could.

On the top of a chest of drawers was a small wooden box with a glass fronted door. Sitting on a green velvet cushion inside the box was Josh's prized possession, an orange coloured plectrum. This was no ordinary plectrum, it had been given to him by Conrad Blewitt after his solo performance at the end of school concert. According to Conrad the plectrum had belonged to Eric Clapton, or Eric the God, as Conrad always referred to Clapton. Apparently, Clapton gave the plectrum to Conrad in April 1979 after he had attended three of his hero's concerts on consecutive nights. With his distinctive red curly hair, moustache and wire rimmed glasses Conrad's was not a face you would easily forget. He had arrived at each venue hours ahead of the scheduled performance, so he could secure a position at the front of the stage. At the end of the encore on the third night, Clapton leant down from the stage and presented

Conrad with the plectrum, a reward, he said for his dedication and support.

Josh hadn't wanted to take the plectrum, but Conrad had insisted. It was time to hand over the baton, so to speak, to someone else and he knew Josh would treasure it. More importantly, Conrad said he hoped the plectrum would inspire Josh to keep practising and maybe one day he would play as well as Eric the God.

Josh leapt from the bed and picked up his guitar. Hendrix and Clapton must have had their set-backs, he thought, it must have taken years of practice to play the way they did. Josh didn't like being second best at anything and he wasn't a quitter.

"Okay," he said, "let's give this son of a bitch another try." "E string – middle, B string – thumb, back to E string – Index and repeat. "That's more like it Josh, that's more like it."

An hour or so later Josh reckoned he had just about nailed the solo, there was still the odd mistake, but by and large he could now play the whole song fingerpicking, just like Knopfler did and the tempo was good even during the fast, last section. Only yesterday that had seemed out of reach, but he was now excited and itching for Tuesday to come around, so he could show Mrs Rawlingson that he'd nailed it.

As he sat on the edge of his bed wondering whether Maisie, or any of the others had mastered the song, the smell of something cooking wafted through the open door. Like most seventeen-year-old boys Josh was usually ravenous and by dinner time after school he was as hungry as a bear. For the last sixteen months eating in the Heggerty household had become a purely functional activity, much like putting fuel in your car. His mother used to make the most delicious meals and no two days were ever the same. Soups, stews, fruit pies the list just went on and on. Most of the produce, certainly all the fruit and vegetables, were grown on the farm, and Josh loved all of it. Suddenly, with his mother's illness that all stopped. Sure, there were still times when the vegetables were fresh from the garden, but Josh's father, who had now taken over the cooking duties, had a habit of steaming them to mush and they tasted horrible. Now every other meal seemed to be a frozen meal, bought in bulk from Kroger's in Lewisburg. On the rare occasion, like tonight, when his father tried to cook a meal using fresh ingredients it invariably ended up burnt and was often barely edible. Frank Heggerty was not a natural cook.

Josh knew complaining about the food was futile, his father would simply say if you think you can do any better then do it yourself. Even Josh appreciated that was not an unreasonable argument, but as he had even less skills in the kitchen than his father it was better to suffer in silence. So, for nearly a year and a half meal times had become no more than a re-fuelling operation and Josh cringed whenever he heard his father shout that dinner was ready.

"Your dinners on the table," shouted Frank Heggerty from the kitchen, before adding, "can you go and give your mother a hand she's out on the porch."

The euphoria and buzz that he had felt only moments ago when he had cracked the solo evaporated immediately he heard his father's voice. What horror awaited was still to be revealed but whatever it was it smelt burnt. As Josh walked through to the kitchen he glanced at the table where three white dinner plates were piled high with some dark coloured gruel. Steam rose from the plates, so it was at least hot, but other than that it was difficult to say what lurked on the plates.

Josh opened the door to the porch; his mother Cathleen was sitting on a pile of cushions in an old wicker chair at the shaded end of the porch. Josh looked at his mom and his heart sunk. The frail and vulnerable women that sat hunched up in the chair was unrecognisable from the mom who had loved and nurtured him. It was his darling mother who had taught him to read, soothed him to sleep singing Irish lullaby's and thrilled him with exciting stories of Irish giants and Pukwudgies, mythical little people who lived in the bogs that surrounded his grandmother's house in Clonakilty. Looking at her now it was hard to believe that she was only fifty-three, she looked at least twenty years older.

As Josh looked at his mother's expressionless face, he remembered the time, not long after she had got out of hospital, when his dad had sat his mother down on the porch in the very same chair and left her there while he went to repair the fence by the bottom orchard. He was only gone a couple of hours but by the time he returned to the house the right side of his mother's face was burnt to a crisp. The early afternoon sun had crept around the porch and the chair that had been in the shade when Frank had left was now exposed to the full intensity of a hot sun. Trapped in a body that wouldn't move Cathleen had slowly fried. The scar from the second degree burns she suffered that day was still clearly visible and Josh shuddered at the thought of the pain and trauma his poor mother went through that afternoon. It was only one of many examples of suffering that Cathleen

Heggerty had endured since that fateful day in October 1982 when her life changed forever.

Josh took his mother under her left arm and helped her to her feet, after months of effort and rehabilitation she could now walk a few steps with the aid of a tripod walking stick. Her right side was completely immobile, and her steps were slow and awkward, as Cathleen shuffled her left foot forward her right one limply dragged behind. The distance from her chair to the kitchen table was no more than twenty feet but it took Cathleen the best part of three minutes to walk there. Josh helped his mother into her chair at the table and tucked a napkin into the top of the blouse she was wearing. Josh noted the large red stain which was the result of pasta sauce dripping off her spoon and onto her blouse. That had happened on Monday, and this was now Friday, so his mother had been wearing the same top for at least five days. Josh looked at her trousers, they told the same story. Old food stains covered the grey sweat pants she was wearing, this was verging on neglect. He understood the strain his father was under put surely, he could take the time to make sure that her clothes were clean. Josh had never dressed his mother, that wasn't what seventeen-year-old sons were supposed to do, but if his father wasn't going to take responsibility for doing it Josh vowed that he would, day by day what little dignity his mother still had was ebbing away and it left Josh feeling angry and sad.

He took the table spoon from the table and put it into her left hand. Slowly and very deliberately Cathleen placed the spoon into the dark congealed slop that sat on her plate and began to eat.

"Before you ask its bean stew, I'm sure it will taste alright it's just slightly overdone that's all," said Frank in a voice that would have struggled to convince himself let alone anyone else. Josh didn't say anything. Mercifully the ordeal was not made worse by an accompaniment of pulverised vegetables, well that was until Josh found what he presumed to be carrots hidden under a thick coating of gelatinous gravy. Josh prodded at the wretched things with his fork, they immediately disintegrated and any notion that Josh might be able to eat this offering passed. He glanced over to his mother, she must have managed three maybe four spoonsful of the evil stuff. It was as well that his mother had the build of a small bird, at least she didn't need much sustenance. Josh took the spoon from her hand and replaced it with a glass of water which he was willing her to drink. At least it will take the taste away mom, he thought which in some small way would be a blessing.

Throughout the meal not a word was spoken. His mother could be excused as since her stroke she had been without speech. In the last couple of months, she had started to make the occasional sound but even these were inconsistent, and it was impossible to make any sense of what she might be trying to say. It was also not possible to communicate through facial expressions as the right side of Cathleen's face remained frozen and immobile, she couldn't even raise a smile. Although she could hold a pen she was unable to write any letters or words. Initially Josh wondered if that was because she had been right handed but the physician treating his mother, assured him that wasn't the case. It was a direct consequence of the damage that had been done to his mother's brain when she suffered the stroke and unfortunately the long-term prospects of regaining her speech or the ability to write were not good.

The doctors were surprised that after nearly a year of complete immobility, Cathleen had regained a little movement and could now manage a few steps with her walking aid. Despite all her physical disabilities, Josh still believed that his mother was aware of all that was going on around her, he could see it in her eyes. This was not a view that was shared by his father. Her inability to communicate and frequent bouts of incontinence had undoubtedly had a negative impact on Frank who nowadays showed little love or affection towards his wife. He rarely made the effort to speak to Cathleen and while Josh had never seen his father be physically abusive to his mother the emotional abuse was glaring.

The silence was eventually broken by his father, "I saw coach Simpson in town today, he told me he asked you to do track this term and you refused."

"That's not what happened," said Josh wearily. "He did ask me, but he knew I was committed to doing the end of year concert and that track training clashed with rehearsals, so I just explained that I wouldn't be able to run this term, I wasn't rude or anything."

Josh was tired of his father's constant efforts to undermine his musical interests. He never complemented Josh on his playing and wouldn't dream of attending the concert. The only comment he ever made about his music was to tell him it was too loud or that it was disturbing his mother.

"Coach tells me that you'd still win the school 400 metres regardless of whether you trained or not and with just a bit of work you could be challenging for the county title," said his father.

It was relentless. No matter how many times he told his father he wasn't interested in running or playing football for the school the penny just never seemed to drop.

"Don't know why you bother with that guitar, it's not like you're that good is it? You should have stuck with your sports at least you were good at sport," said his father seemingly oblivious to how hurtful that last remark had been.

Josh couldn't say exactly when his relationship with his father had started to deteriorate. It must have been around the time he started to play his guitar, but it wasn't only the music that was causing a rift. Frank Heggerty resented the closeness of his relationship with his mother. Josh never knew his grandparents, but he knew how close his mother had been to them and he was always fascinated to hear stories about their time in Ireland and like his mother, he was proud of his Irish heritage. On St Patrick's day, Cathleen would pour herself a glass of Jameson's and he would sit on the couch with his mother to watch the St Patrick's day parade live from New York. Not once could Josh ever recall his father joining them.

His father also seemed to resent the fact that Josh was smart and popular at school. Everything that Frank had achieved in his life had been achieved because of hard graft. He didn't much care for his sons laid back and easy-going approach to life. Life was difficult, it wasn't meant to be easy, it was meant to be a challenge, it all came too easy for Josh as far as his father was concerned. His son was wasting his god given talent on the sports field and now his recent obsession with music, well it nearly drove him to distraction.

"I've got a hell of a better chance of making something of my life through music than I would ever do running around a stupid track," said an exasperated Josh.

His father didn't respond, he just looked at Josh coldly. Josh knew that he had annoyed his father and one more comment could well tip him over the edge as it had done many times before. It was now time to back off, it just wasn't worth the hassle and he certainly didn't want their argument to upset his mother.

"If you'll excuse me I've got homework to finish for tomorrow, I've got some stuff needing cleaned, so I thought I'd put a washing on, is there anything you or mom are needing washed? asked Josh politely.

"No, we're both fine, you just see to your own stuff," replied his father tersely.

It didn't appear that his mother would be getting to change her blouse anytime soon and that left Josh feeling despondent. You take more care looking after the hogs than you do your own wife, he thought. He desperately wanted to help his mother, but he felt helpless, he just didn't know what he could do.

"Come on Mom, I'll take you back to your chair on the porch," said Josh as he went to help his mother up from the table.

"Just leave your mother," said Frank brusquely. "She'll be going to her bed soon, I'll see to her."

Josh looked at his watch, it was just after quarter past seven, he gave a resigned sigh, and kissed his mother affectionately on the cheek and headed back to his bedroom.

*

137

The Marlinton apple fair took place on the first Saturday in October every year. For the last ten or so years Cathleen, Cynthia, and two other work colleagues, Anne Grey and Edna Billings had been in the habit of attending the fair as it was one of Greenbrier County's great social occasions. It was much more than just an apple fair, nowadays most people went for the music, dancing and drink. The apples were still of course the centre-point, but it was the floats and sideshows, live bands and street food that drew the four friends each year. They always stayed at Mrs Wadkins bed and breakfast. Her house was close to the main street where most of the activities were centred and over the years Elma Wadkins had become a good friend. The Marlinton weekend was one of the few occasions when Cathleen could let her hair down and enjoy a few drinks. She and Edna were the temperate members of the group. A couple of glasses of cider and the odd beer was more than enough for Cathleen and Edna. Cynthia and Anne on the other hand were seasoned drinkers and from Friday when they arrived until Sunday afternoon when they had to return home, the two of them were hardly without a glass in their hands. Cider, beer, bourbon you name it they drank it but Strangely, it didn't seem to affect them. They were neither up nor down with it and Cathleen could never say that she had seen either of her friends the worse for drink. A life time of drinking hard liquor with two older brothers is what Cynthia put her capacity for alcohol down to, what gave Anne the ability to drink such vast amounts without getting drunk, nobody knew, least of all Anne.

It was Saturday afternoon around four o'clock and the friends had returned to the bed and breakfast to relax and freshen up before heading out for their evening's entertainment. Cynthia, Anne, and Edna were chatting and having coffee with Elma in the conservatory, but Cathleen had decided to go and lie down for a while as she had a bad headache and was feeling unusually tired when she got back to their accommodation.

As she lay on the bed a strange feeling came over Cathleen. Suddenly she was aware that she couldn't lift her right hand off the bed. She tried several times, but it wouldn't move, and she had no feeling in it. She made a conscious effort to lift her right foot but that wouldn't move either, now afraid that something was seriously wrong Cathleen tried to call for help but no words came out, only incoherent gibberish. Although her thinking was still lucid Cathleen's vision was becoming blurred, she closed her eyes and started to pray, she knew she was having a stroke.

It must have been after four-thirty when Cynthia, who was sharing a room with Cathleen, went up to use the bathroom. On entering the bedroom Cynthia saw her friend lying on her back and assumed that she was sleeping. As she passed the foot of the bed to go into the bathroom she noticed that the right side of Cathleen's face appeared lopsided and droopy.

"Cathleen are you Okay?" asked an already worried Cynthia. When her question met with no response Cynthia grabbed her friends foot and shook it. "Can you hear me Cathleen? Please wake up, please Cathleen." Her friend lay unresponsive and motionless on the bed. Cynthia rushed to the top of the stairs and screamed, "Someone call 911, I think Cathleen's had a stroke."

The ambulance radio couldn't be heard above the noise of the Eagles tribute band that was playing before a sizeable crowd outside the Apple Tree bar just off the main square. An ambulance was usually on stand-by at the Marlinton Apple Fair because of the size of the crowds but they were hardly ever called upon, but they were going to be needed today. The ambulance crew were leaning on the hood of their vehicle drinking sodas and chatting to the crowd while listening to Hotel California being played at full volume on a small make shift stage. Neither of them heard the radio above the noise of the guitars and drums and when they eventually took the call the ambulance controller was irate. She had been trying to contact them for nearly fifteen minutes, it had taken so long to get them to respond that due to the seriousness of the call she had dispatched another ambulance from Lewisburg, but it would take at least another half an hour to get there so she needed them to attend immediately. A woman had suffered a suspected stroke at Wadkins Bed & Breakfast in King Street and was now unconscious.

By the time that the ambulance arrived at Charleston General Hospital it had been an hour and twenty minutes since Cynthia had found Cathleen unresponsive on the bed. No one was sure how long before that she had suffered the stroke but Doctor Petterson, the on-duty consultant, was extremely concerned about the length of time it had taken to get Cathleen to the hospital. The MRI scan was taken a couple of hours after her admission and it confirmed Doctor Petterson's worst fears. Cathleen had suffered a catastrophic Ischaemic Stroke caused by a blood clot in her brain. She didn't regain consciousness for three days and didn't leave ward 11C of Charleston General for the next six months.

These were desperate times for the family. The journey from Fairlea to the hospital was over a hundred miles and as Frank had the farm to look after and Josh had school and important exams coming up, getting over to see Cathleen was extremely difficult. A trip to the hospital took the best part of a day and what started out as weekly visits on a Sunday soon dropped off to every fortnight. For the last two months Cathleen was lucky if she saw her husband and son twice. Josh felt guilty at not being able to visit more often but as he didn't drive he was wholly dependent on his father to take him. Josh wasn't sure why Frank hadn't gone more often as he never said, but he suspected that his father didn't see the point as his mother was so unresponsive. There had been some hope of recovery to begin with, certainly with regards to regaining her speech, but as the weeks turned into months the prospects of any meaningful recovery receded.

Cathleen's most loyal visitor was Cynthia who each Saturday made the journey to see her friend. On a couple of occasions Josh had gone with her when he had other commitments on a Sunday. He was struck by how good Cynthia had been with his mom. She would sit by the bed holding Cathleen's hand and talk none stop for an hour and a half. Josh was always struggling for things to say to his mother when he was at the hospital and his father, well, he was even worse. Cynthia on the other hand seemed to have unending patience and the ability to talk engagingly about just about anything and it didn't seem to matter that she never got any response. She always said she was just glad to be able to do it and Cathleen would have done the same for her if the roles had been reversed. Josh suspected that it was Cynthia's unstinting loyalty and weekly visit that had allowed Frank to stop going every Sunday, he could salve his conscious in the knowledge that Cathleen would still get a visit from Cynthia. Josh resented his father's apparent indifference to his mother's situation and their relationship, that deteriorated after he dropped out of football and took up the guitar, certainly worsened after this latest setback.

*

In the bathroom next to their bedroom, Frank Heggerty washed his wife's hands with cold water and soap. He didn't bother to open out and clean the fingers of her redundant right hand which were curled tight and stiff. After drying her hands with a cursory wipe with a towel he brusquely brushed her teeth before sitting her on the toilet. He saw no need to wash her hands again after she was finished. In the bedroom he undressed her and put on an incontinence pad. He then lifted a threadbare old pink linen nightdress which was draped over a chair and put it on his wife. Throughout this time Frank said nothing to Cathleen, it was a routine that he would repeat each morning and night, it was demeaning and de-humanising for Cathleen. Frank could just as easily have been dressing a department store dummy such was his level of apathy to the task. Having finished his obligations, he put his wife into bed and turned on the radio which was on a table at the side of the bed. He then switched off the light and closed the bedroom door. The clock on the wall by the window said 1935 hrs, it would be another twelve hours before Cathleen would stand on her feet again.

Cathleen lay in the bed looking at the ceiling, the sunlight outside cast strange shaped shadows above her as shafts of light flickered through gaps in the curtains as they rippled and swayed at the play of the evening breeze. Cathleen watched as the shadows stretched and slid into geometric shapes before the next breeze morphed them into ghost like figures and creatures. The bizarre light show continued until darkness filled the space and Cathleen found herself alone once more, entombed in a body that no longer functioned and, in a world, almost completely devoid of love and stimulation.

As usual the radio was tuned to the CBS Sports Channel that Frank liked to listen to in the mornings. He never gave it a moment's thought that Cathleen wasn't in the slightest bit interested in sport, he could have tuned the wretched radio to any number of music stations that she would enjoy, but he didn't. It was just another example of how Cathleen's needs were ignored.

Cathleen's mind was still alive, it hadn't withered or become dormant like the rest of her body. It was still eager and restless but found itself trapped in a state of suspended animation, she had a brain that could no longer connect with the world around her. Cathleen resented the coldness of her husband's touch, theirs had been a happy marriage full of love, hope and joy, but at the stroke of God's hand that had wilted and died. She understood why God had forsaken her, but she couldn't comprehend why her husband had too.

The stroke of God's hand; Cathleen could recall the exact time that Vernon had explained that expression to her. A young mother had suffered a terrible stroke

143

shortly after giving birth to her baby. She was not married, and her God-fearing father had remarked to Cathleen that it was God's will that his daughter had suffered the stroke. A judgement on her for having a child out of wedlock he said. Vernon explained, it had been a belief in the sixteenth century that a stroke only occurred as the result of direct intervention from God, it was a belief that had clearly not died out.

Cathleen had been shocked that a father could say such a cruel thing about his own daughter, but now years later she firmly believed it was the stroke of God's hand that had judged and punished her. Hers had been a mortal sin and for fifteen years she had lived the lie, and all had been well, but, as Father Francis told her as a young child you can't hide your sins from God. There would be no redemption for Cathleen, she understood why she had to suffer, she had incurred God's wrath, and this was her punishment.

Chapter 8

By the time Maisie came down the path into sight, Josh had been sitting on the wall at the entrance to the school for about twenty minutes. He had wanted to arrive ahead of Maisie and his well-rehearsed apology was primed and ready to be delivered. He had felt badly after last Thursday's stupid argument and it had been bothering him most of the weekend. He had thought about phoning Maisie but after careful consideration had decided it would be better to apologise in person.

As Maisie approached Josh could see that she was carrying two guitar cases. Maisie's own case was unmistakeable, it was lime green and covered in bright purple and pink flowers that Maisie had stencilled on. Josh thought that the second case couldn't be Becca's as hers was brown and made of canvas. Anyway, Becca would already be in school for the junior rehearsal, so it didn't belong to her. This was a black, hard case. It looked a bit battered and bruised, but Josh was sure he hadn't seen it before. He was intrigued, why had Maisie brought a second guitar to practice?

Before Josh had a chance to speak Maisie smiled and greeted him with her usual breezy welcome, "Hiya, big guy, how's it going?"

This caught Josh off guard. This wasn't how he had planned it, he was supposed to take the initiative and apologise, set the record straight so they could move on. He had been distracted by the second guitar case and for a few seconds it appeared that he may have lost his opportunity, but, regaining his composure he just about managed to retrieve the situation by blurting out, "Fine thanks, Maisie. Look, I just wanted to apologise for last Thursday, I don't know what came over me and storming off like that, well, that was pretty immature. I shouldn't have said it or ran off, so I wanted you to know that I'm sorry."

Maisie looked Josh in the eyes and a smile broke out across her face.

"Wow, I wasn't expecting that. There was no need for you to apologise," she said, her face turning a deep shade of crimson.

"It was as much my fault as yours. It's funny 'cause I was going to phone you at the weekend because I felt bad about it, I wish I had now."

"That's spooky because I was going to phone you too!" said a clearly relieved Josh.

"Really? That is spooky," said Maisie. "Do you think we could just forget about it then? I really hate falling out with people," asked Maisie hopefully.

"Sounds good to me!" said Josh. "Anyhow, how did you get on with the Dire Straits number? Difficult wasn't it?"

"You can say that again," said Maisie, "I found that last section impossible! My fingers couldn't keep up! How did you get on?"

"Took a long time but I think I've just about got the hang of it. Did you use your thumb for the B-string? I think that's the key. I watched a video of Knopfler playing it and that's how he does it," replied a now animated Josh.

"Come on, let's go in and I'll show you. By the way, why have you brought another guitar?" asked Josh.

"Actually, it's a surprise for you," said Maisie who was now tingling with excitement.

Inside the music room Susan Rawlingson was talking to Mr Crawford, one of the school's music teachers as the junior group packed up their instruments after their rehearsal. As Maisie walked into the classroom her sister grabbed her by the arm, "Have you shown him yet? The guitar? Have you told him?" Becca could hardly contain her excitement.

"No, not yet," said Maisie pulling her arm away, "and don't you go telling him either," said Maisie sternly. "Anyway, mom told me to remind you that that you're going home with Julie's mom tonight. And don't you dare say anything to Josh."

"I'm not going to say anything," said Becca with a frown, "but you must tell me everything when you get back, promise?"

"Okay, okay," said Maisie, "now you'd better go, Julie's mom will be waiting for you."

Josh was already sitting on a table with his feet on a chair tuning his guitar when Maisie placed the black case on the table next to him. He kept a close eye as Maisie carefully unclipped the three metal catches and opened the lid of the case. There it was in all its glory, a 1971 Gibson SG electric guitar. The guitar's body was brilliant white and made of mahogany while the fingerboard was a deep coffee colour and made of solid rosewood. The bridge, volume controls and input jack were all made of chrome. It may have been nearly fifteen years old, but it

147

still looked magnificent. Josh stared at the guitar in disbelief. There in black ink and written in large letters just to the side of the pickguard, was the signature of his hero, Jerry Garcia. Josh didn't say anything, he couldn't! He was so taken aback that he just stared open mouthed at the guitar lying in its case before him.

It was Joe Phelps who broke the silence, "Holy shit, Maisie, is that for real?" Immediately realising that he had just sworn in front of Mrs Rawlingson, Mr Crawford and the rest of the group Joe quickly tried to apologise.

"Ma'am, Sir, really sorry about that, it just came out! Sorry, I'm really sorry."

"Okay Joe, that's the last time we hear any language like that. If I hear that again from you or anyone else for that matter, you'll not be doing the concert do you understand?"

"Yes Ma'am," said Joe looking at his feet to avoid making eye contact with anyone else. He really wanted to make a plea of mitigation, after all it wasn't every day that someone brought a guitar owned by a rock idol into class, but he thought better of it and stood silently leaning on the radiator next to the door.

By the time Mrs Rawlingson had come across to see what was causing all the fuss Masie had lifted the guitar out of the case and handed it to Josh.

"I thought you might like to play it," said Maisie, "my dad's had it hanging on the wall in the den ever since Jerry gave it to him and I can't remember the last time anyone played it. I've checked with dad and he's happy for you to try it out, I'm afraid you can't keep it though, he said he wants it back!" said Maisie with a chuckle.

Josh's smile filled the room as he took the guitar from Maisie and placed the black leather strap over his shoulder.

"This is brilliant, Maisie! Jerry Garcia's guitar! I can't believe you never said, I would have been telling everybody, this is just amazing!" said Josh. "It feels a bit different from mine, more solid, it's much heavier too."

"You've got to remember that it's a much older guitar," said Susan who had now realised what was going on. "That guitar is likely made of mahogany or some other hardwood, the denser the wood the better the sound, or so they say," she went on. "They use different materials now, cheaper to make so it's not surprising it feels different from yours. Is it in tune Maisie?"

"I did try to tune it but I'm not the best at that as you know so it might be a bit out, but I don't think it's too bad."

"Okay Josh, your big moment has arrived, time to see if you've done your homework! Let's cut to the chase, let me hear the last section of Sultans of Swing. I've every confidence in you, Josh, you're playing with Jerry Garcia's guitar after all!" said Susan folding her arms and with a broad smile on her face.

"Happy to give it a go," said Josh plugging the lead into the amplifier, "but I'll get my excuses in early, I have been practising, just not with this guitar you understand!" said Josh laughing. With that Josh picked up his plectrum and started to play.

"Not bad, Josh, not bad at all!" said a clearly impressed Susan. "However, I think we may need to tighten your G-string a little, Maisie." Before she had time to clarify what she meant the room erupted into laughter. Joe, who had just taken a mouthful of soda

149

desperately tried to suppress a laugh, but it was too late. He started to splutter like an old water faucet, fizzy liquid exploded out of his mouth spraying everyone around him as he convulsed into fits of laughter.

This situation was not recoverable, there was nothing Susan could do other than laugh along with everybody else. It had been an innocent remark, she had got caught up in the moment but then most of life's funniest moments are unintentional thought Susan and for several minutes no-one in the room was capable of saying anything such were the shrieks of laughter that brought tears to their eyes and made their sides sore.

"That was a classic, Mrs Rawlingson!" said Josh, "an absolute classic!"

When he had regained some sense of composure Josh looked across to where Maisie was sitting. Having nearly ruined things last week he didn't want to repeat that mistake now. After all the joke had been made at her expense and he wanted to be sure that she was okay. Josh gave a sigh of relief, Maisie's face had turned its usual colour of red, but she was still in fits of laughter. Just when it seemed that she was about to regain her control off she went again. Joe was even worse he had had to remove himself from the classroom and was now rolling about on the grass outside punching the grounds with his fists as a bemused Mr Crawford looked on. Mr Crawford was so alarmed he returned to the class-room to check that everything was alright, and only left when Mrs Rawlingson assured him that it was, and she would explain everything in the morning. That Tuesday rehearsal was destined to live long in the memory of everyone who had been there.

"If I can be serious for a moment," said Susan, "it is worth knowing that of all the strings on a guitar, it is in fact the G-string that is the most difficult to tune. There I've managed to say what I had intended to say ten minutes ago!"

The class listened carefully. "Absolutely correct, Mrs Rawlingson," said Josh pretending to be serious, "especially Maisie's G-string which we can see has a tendency to be loose!" And with that the whole group erupted into laughter once more.

*

At the Domestic Arrivals Terminal of Yeager Airport, three miles east of downtown Charleston, Elaine and Howard Ritchie were waiting for the arrival of flight EB325 from Portland, Oregon. It was Elaine's fiftieth birthday tomorrow and her youngest sister Ruth was due to arrive with her husband, John, and their children Todd (17), and twin daughters Louise and Pamela (14), to help her celebrate the occasion. Elaine had decided to hold the celebration in Tuckahoe as her birthday was close to the anniversary of the death of her sister Jennifer and her husband David. Elaine had felt for some time that she wanted to combine her birthday with a service of remembrance for the sister she had lost all those years ago and it seemed fitting to hold it in Tuckahoe where Jennifer and David had lived and where both families had spent many happy times together.

Ruth had agreed it was a lovely idea. Having moved to Oregon a number of years ago when her husband took up a teaching position at the Lewis & Clark School of Law in Portland, it would be the perfect opportunity to see her family again and come back to the area where they had spent the early years of their married life. Todd had been only seven, and the twins four, when they had moved away so Ruth was looking forward to showing them just how beautiful Greenbrier County was.

Since the death of Jennifer, Elaine had kept in touch with David's sister Elspeth and her husband Paul and she was delighted that they had agreed to travel up from Tallahassee to join them for today's memorial service and her birthday lunch which was being held the following day.

As the terminal doors opened Elaine felt tears well up in her eyes. It had been eighteen months since she had last seen Ruth and it must be nearer three years since she last saw John and the children. Elaine spread her arms wide and walked forward to embrace her sister.

"Gosh, Ruth, it's great to see you!" said Elaine as the two sisters hugged each other warmly, "And look at you, you seem to look younger every time I see you! I'm so glad you all could make it."

"Wouldn't have missed it for the world, it's not every day your sister's fifty!" said Ruth mischievously.

"I know, I know," said Elaine, "next you're going to tell me it's five years till yours."

"Six actually," said Ruth. They both started to laugh and hugged each other once more.

"And look at the kids," said Elaine, "I can hardly believe how much the girls have grown, and as for Todd, well, he's not even a child anymore! Look at him, what a handsome young man. Girls, Todd, come and give your old aunty a hug. Sorry John, you can have one too, I didn't mean to miss you out it's just the kids! I can't get over how grown up they are now."

Pamela and Louise rushed forward and gave their aunt a big hug.

"I can't believe the size of you girls, you must be six inches taller than when I last saw you. And your lovely long hair, it reminds me of your aunt Jennifer's, she wore it like that when she was about your age," said Elaine.

As Elaine turned to give Todd a hug she noticed that he had a cut and a large bruise just under his nose.

"I'm going to have to be careful giving you a hug," said Elaine, "that looks like a sore one!"

"It's just a bit tender now," said Todd, "the batter hit the ball back at me when I was pitching, and it hit the edge of my glove and ricocheted up and struck me under the nose. You should have seen the blood! Still managed to strike him out and win the game, that was the main thing," continued Todd.

"Glad to hear it," said Elaine, "I wouldn't have expected anything less. Your mom tells me you're in the all state squad this year and the Rockies have been scouting you? That sounds fabulous Todd!" said Elaine proudly.

"Yep, it's going well this year. Still got another year at high school but after that, who knows? The Rockies coach who saw me play said if I continue to progress I might get invited to their Spring training camp," said Todd. "That would be awesome as it would mean training with their top stars."

"That's just great, Todd, I know your mom and dad are very proud," said Elaine.

Todd had known since he was about eight that Ruth and John were not his birth parents, they had both been very open about that. He always called Ruth and John, mom and dad, but he knew about the accident and how they had come to adopt him. In their lounge Ruth and John kept a couple of photographs of Jennifer and David on display. The one taken at their wedding usually caused visitors to remark how like his father Todd was. He was tall and powerfully built just like David and his mane of blond hair with its side parting was just the way he used to wear his.

"I can't get over how like David, he is," said Elaine to her sister, "Elspeth is going to be gobsmacked when she sees him. When I spoke to her about the arrangements for today she said it had been more than six years since they met up with you during that holiday at Disney. I know she's looking forward to seeing you all but she's going to be thrilled when she sees Todd. By the way did you know that Elizabeth had died? She passed away over a year ago now and I know Elspeth is bringing some of the ashes with her. She always said she wanted them shared between Jennifer and her husband Bert, so we're going to incorporate it into the service."

"I'm sorry I didn't know that Elizabeth had died, though it must have been a blessing after all those years living with Alzheimer's. It certainly must be a relief for Elspeth and Paul," said Ruth. "Anyway, it'll be great to see them again, what time are we meeting them?"

"I said we'd see them at the cemetery around four," said Elaine, "so we've got a couple of hours before we need to head over. Howard brought the old Pontiac which seats eight so there's plenty room for the five of you and us. You must be hungry after the flight; do you fancy a bite to eat before we head over?" asked Elaine.

"Now that sounds like a plan," said Ruth.

It was just approaching four when Howard parked the Pontiac in the small car park that sat adjacent to Tuckahoe Cemetery. A small wrought iron fence surrounded the rows of granite headstones that stood silently in tribute to departed loved ones. The smell of freshly cut grass filled the spring air and the edge of perfectly manicured lawns touched herbaceous borders blooming with brightly coloured azaleas and delicate pink and cream rhododendrons.

In the far corner of the cemetery Elspeth and Paul Ward stood at a graveside chatting with Pastor Philip Whitehead. The minister's thatch of thick brown curly hair had managed to avoid the ravages of the passing years, but his waistline had clearly not been so fortunate. The buttons of his frock coat strained against his considerable girth.

"Comes with the territory I'm afraid," he said patting his ample stomach, "every hatch, match or despatch always seems to be accompanied by a mighty fine purvey, something as you can see I find difficult to resist!"

"Well, I don't think we're having anything today but be sure and leave room tomorrow, Elaine has planned a splendid lunch at the Lake View for her birthday, our taxi driver said it's about the best eating place round here," said Paul.

"It's splendid, one of my favourites! The roast meats are particularly good," said Pastor Whitehead.

Elspeth smiled as she saw Elaine and the others approaching. In her right-hand she was holding a small bouquet of yellow and white roses and in her other hand was a small blue velvet bag the top of which was tied with a bow of gold coloured cord.

Apart from Pastor Whitehead, all the others present were dressed in light spring clothes as the late afternoon temperature was nudging 80 degrees. Elspeth, Elaine and the other family members greeted each other warmly. Elspeth gasped as she saw Todd.

"I'd be lying if I said I didn't recognise Todd. I knew who he was of course, but doesn't he just look like David?" said Elspeth shaking her head almost in disbelief. "I wasn't sure how I was going to feel about today," added Elspeth, "but you know, any sadness is going to be made so much better by being with all of you. It will also give Paul and me some closure knowing that mum is going to be reunited with David and Jennifer. And having Todd with us, well that's just an added bonus."

Elaine smiled and gave Elspeth another hug.

"I'm glad you feel like that Elspeth," said Elaine, "I wasn't sure whether having this service at the same time as my birthday celebrations was the right thing to do, but now we're all here I feel sure that it is. It just feels right."

As the family gathered around the simple grey gravestone Elaine opened the bag she was carrying and gave Todd, Pamela and Louise a small bunch of miniature yellow and white roses. As they stood there together Elaine noticed the bouquet that Elspeth was carrying, and a smile broke out across her face.

"I see that you remembered too. That's so sweet of you, yellow and white roses were always Jennifer's favourite," said Elaine as Elspeth and the children laid their flowers at the foot of the gravestone and bowed their heads.

Pastor Whitehead's prayer had been carefully crafted. He began by giving thanks for the lives of Jennifer and David and spoke of the deep love that they had for each other. He gave thanks for that love that lived on through their son, Todd, and he paid a fitting tribute to Ruth and John and the rest of their loving families who had gathered today to remember their loved ones, now at peace and embraced in the loving arms of God.

The Bible reading that followed had been chosen by Elaine, it was from chapter 40 of the book of Isaiah. Elaine had always loved the passage and its message of hope and encouragement. Over lunch she had asked Ruth whether she thought Todd might like to read it. Ruth wasn't sure but was happy for Elaine to ask him. Both families had always been regular church attenders, but recently Todd, like many other seventeen-year-old boys, had been a little less inclined to go. However, somewhat to his mother's surprise, he had said he would be honoured to do so when his aunt had asked him.

Todd had visited the cemetery only once before. He had the vaguest recollection of laying a bunch of flowers on the grave when he was aged about nine. While he had known about the tragic circumstances that led to the death of his real parents it had never really upset him, after all he never knew them. His mom and dad since the day he was born had been Ruth and John. Rarely, if ever if he was being honest, had he given much thought to his birth parents. That was until today. Standing at the graveside he felt a profound sense of loss, the constant reminders of how like his father he was; his father's achievements on the sports field; and his mother's graceful beauty and loving nature, left him with an empty, hollow feeling. Sadness was not an emotion that Todd was used to. As he looked down at the Bible his hands started to tremble, he wasn't sure that he was going to be able to do this. He didn't want to let his mom, dad or aunt Elaine down, and he certainly didn't want his sisters to know that he was feeling emotional. He looked down at the ground and took a deep breath, lifting his head he started to read

"Do you not know? Have you not heard? The Lord is the everlasting God, the creator of the ends of the earth. He will not grow tired or weary, and his understanding no one can fathom. He gives strength to the weary and increases the power of the weak. Even youths grow tired and weary, and young men stumble and fall; but those who hope in the Lord will renew their strength."

His voice was brittle, and his throat felt dry. Each line wobbled worse than the last one and there was still one more sentence to go. Todd took a final breath and in a weak and quavering voice read the last line, "They will soar on wings like eagles; they will run and not grow weary, they will walk and not be faint."

For a minute or so the group stood in respectful silence each with their thoughts of times long past. Ruth's instinct had been to go over and hug her son as she could see how difficult an ordeal that had been for him, but she didn't want to break the solemnity of the moment. It was Pastor Whitehead who eventually spoke.

"And may God add a blessing upon the reading of his holy word". Pausing briefly, he thanked Todd for reading the passage so well. Ruth felt proud of her son and gently squeezed Todd's hand as she stepped forward to read 'All is Well' by Henry Scott-Holland that she had first read at her sister's funeral seventeen years ago.

Elaine had forgotten just how beautifully her sister read. The calmness and assuredness of her personality seemed to lend itself effortlessly to the words of the poem. Every syllable, every word, and stanza delivered with great care and precision. Feeling warm and comforted by the words of the poem and surrounded by her family and friends, Elaine felt close to Jennifer in a way that she hadn't felt since she had said her goodbyes at the funeral.

As Ruth read the last few lines of the poem Elaine began to weep quietly.

"It is the same as it ever was; there is absolute unbroken continuity,

Why should I be out of mind because I am out of sight?

I am but waiting for you, for an interval, somewhere very near, just around the corner.

All is well.

Nothing is past; nothing is lost. One brief moment and all will be as it was before only better, infinitely happier and forever we will all be one together with Christ."

"Beautiful, Ruth, that was just beautiful," said Elspeth, "I don't think it could have been any more perfect. Somewhere up there my brother and your sister are smiling right now," added Elspeth looking up into the sky, and I just know that mum is there with them. I'm so glad you arranged this Elaine, it's been good to be able to share this time with you all."

"Sorry to be a nuisance," said Pastor Whitehead, "but I was wondering if it was still the plan to scatter the ashes at the lake? It's just that I've got a circuit meeting in Williamsburg at six-thirty so without wishing to hurry you do you think we could head down now? It'll take me thirty minutes to drive to Williamsburg."

"Of course, no problem, Philip, I remember you saying you had a meeting to go to. We'll head down now. Can you park at the jetty along from Jennifer and David's old house? We thought that would be the best spot."

"That's fine," said Philip, "I'll see you there in five minutes."

The view from the jetty was stunning. The late afternoon sunshine glittered and sparkled on the rippling water making the lake appear as if it were filled with diamonds. A blue heron stalked the shallows looking for an early evening meal and red maples and flowering pear trees, resplendent in their spring foliage, lined the far side of the lake. Dotted along the shoreline to their left were a dozen lakeside houses of different sizes and styles, each affording their occupants sublime views of this beautiful spot.

"It hasn't changed much I suppose," said Elaine to her sister and Elspeth who were standing together looking at the house where Jennifer and David had lived. On the lawn in front of the house was a large trampoline, swing and plastic slide.

"It's nice to see that a family are living there, a house like that needs a family don't you think?" Said Elspeth. "Mom was so looking forward to having grandchildren. She always loved children. Even in her last years when her Alzheimer's got really bad, she would still respond and smile whenever small children were around," explained Elspeth. "Do you know when Jennifer and David moved here she used to take a fold up chair from the garage and after dinner she liked to sit on this jetty with a cup of coffee and watch the sunset. That's why we chose to scatter her ashes here, it just seemed like the perfect place."

"I don't think you could have chosen a better spot," said Elaine,

"I agree," added Ruth, "it's the perfect place."

After a short prayer and reading by Pastor Whitehead, Elspeth untied the bow and opened the velvet bag. Paul stood at her side with his arm wrapped around her waist as Elspeth tipped the contents of the bag into the air. Puffs of grey powder drifted briefly in the gentle breeze before settling quietly on the water's surface. Elspeth and Paul threw magnolia petals, picked from Elizabeth's favourite tree in their garden, onto the shimmering water while Pastor Whitehead said a closing prayer. With that the time for mourning was over.

"Thanks again, Philip, it was a beautiful service and it was so nice that you were able to conduct it for us," said Elaine, "I hope we haven't made you late for your meeting?"

"No, it's fine honestly, I'll be in good time," said Philip, "I was delighted to be able to take the service for you."

"That's great," said Elaine, "we'll see you tomorrow at the Lake View, lunch is booked for one o'clock."

"You certainly will, I'm looking forward to it immensely," said Philip as he got into his car and made his way to the main road.

"If we might borrow the Pontiac we thought we'd take the kids up to Marlinton and show them the town and their old house? We'll grab some food when we're up there," said Ruth. "Hope Patty's is still on the go, they used to do the best burgers. The girls can't see past Burger King, but I've told them Patty's are way better so time to put that to the test!"

"That's fine, Ruth," said Elaine, "you're all checked in, so we'll see you at the hotel when you get back." Howard and I are going to get something to eat with Elspeth and Paul, so no hurry. We'll catch up later for a drink no doubt."

Todd looked despondently at his mother, "Mom, I don't think I can be bothered going to Marlinton, not really feeling like it," he said, "I'd rather just stay and hang out here if that's okay?"

Before Ruth had a chance to say anything Elaine stepped in, "Todd can grab some food with us later if he feels like it. It would be great to hear more about school and his plans for next year."

"Are you sure you don't mind?" said Ruth who could tell that her son really did not want to go. "I think today has affected him more than he was expecting it to. That goes for me too, it's been a bit of an emotional rollercoaster, so if you really don't mind."

"Don't mind at all, it would be our pleasure," said Elaine. "That's as long as Todd doesn't mind eating with us old fogies"

"No, that would be fine," said Todd with a smile, "but I'm going to hang out down here for a while if that's okay."

"Not a problem," said his aunt, "we'll see you in the restaurant at seven."

As the others departed Todd sat on the end of the jetty thinking about the day and the mom and dad he never knew. It was a really strange feeling. For the first time in his life he realised that he was technically an orphan. In fact, there was nothing technical about it, he was an orphan. He wasn't quite sure how that was supposed to make him feel, but at that precise moment, he did feel different. He couldn't help wondering what his life would have been like if he'd lived with his birth parents, right here on the shores of Lake Tuckahoe. Would he have even liked them? Just because everyone said they were great people didn't mean they were. Would his name still have been Todd? Probably not he thought, that name must have been chosen by Ruth and John. None of his friends would have been the same either, it was all just a bit weird.

Ruth and John were great parents. They loved him, and he loved them back. His relationship with his mother could sometimes be tense, they were both strong willed and determined characters. Stubborn might be a better word for it and occasionally this would lead to a clash with neither party willing to back down. Perhaps they were just too similar. His father had a much more placid character and Todd unashamedly used his father's good nature and wish for a peaceful life to get his own way, which at times infuriated his mother. But all things considered he got on pretty well with his parents and he certainly didn't want that to change.

Also, this might be a beautiful place, but he couldn't imagine living here, Greenbrier County was a quiet backwater compared to Portland. He began to wonder if they even played baseball here, he'd never heard of any team coming from West Virginia.

The musky sweet smell that now hung in the air was unmistakeable, it was marijuana. Todd looked down to his right and standing on the shore was a fisherman casting a lure into the shallow waters of the bay. Todd watched mesmerised as time and again he cast his lure towards a batch of cattail reeds that were growing in the water some thirty feet or so away. As the lure hit the water the man paused for a couple of seconds, just enough time to let the lure sink and allow him to take a long draw of the reefer he was holding in his left hand. As he started to slowly retrieve the line he gave the rod a series of sharp jerks to try and entice any fish lurking near the reeds into grabbing the lure in the mistaken belief that it was an injured fish. Todd watched the man for several minutes.

What was fascinating was how he was able to cast his line and land it just a few inches or so from the reed bed, every cast was the same. Even a foot more would have meant that his lure would have got tangled in the reeds, but it never happened. It wasn't that dissimilar to pitching a baseball thought Todd as the key to that skill was precision and being able to repeat an accurate throw through nine innings of a game. Todd watched on in admiration.

Todd jumped down from the jetty and walked towards the fisherman.

"That's pretty neat casting," said Todd, "I can't get over how you can land it on the same spot every time."

The fisherman gave a wry smile. "Trade secret, son," he said. The man appeared to be in his late thirties and had shoulder length brown wavy hair and a full beard. He was wearing a pair of long green shorts and a blue Hawaiian style shirt that had palm trees printed on it.

"Take it you're not a fisherman then?" said the man.

"No, not really, tried it a couple of times but nothing serious," said Todd, "why you asking?"

The fisherman laughed.

"I wish it was my skill that was making me land the cast like that every time," he said. Todd looked puzzled.

"I've got a line clip on," said the man, "it means the line can't go any further than the clip so once the line hits the clip it stops. When you've got it adjusted to the right distance it will land on the same spot every time," said the man. "If I was as good as you thought I was I might have caught a fish by now, looks like nothing doing tonight, sun's too bright and there's not enough breeze." The man reeled in the line and took another long draw on his joint.

"Do you smoke weed?" asked the man.

"Now and again," said Todd, "usually just at weekends, maybe at a party, that kind of thing."

"Cool," said the man. "I'm Steve by the way."

"Good to meet you, I'm Todd."

"Cool," said Steve. "Where's that accent from? It's not from round these parts."

"No, I'm from Portland, just down visiting for a couple of days, although I was born here but we moved when I was seven."

"Great city Portland," said Steve, "I lived in Eugene for a few months in 1975, just after I came out of the army after the war."

"Were you in Vietnam then?" asked Todd.

"Sure was," said Steve, "that's where I got into the weed, been smoking it ever since."

Steve started to laugh.

"What's so funny?" asked Todd.

"Folk from Oregon, they're sometimes known as reifers, did you know that?" said Steve

165

"Never heard that before," said Todd, "are you kidding me?"

"No seriously, man, they're known as reifers, kind of cool that don't you think as we're talking about weed?" said Steve. "Here, Todd, have a spliff."

Steve reached into a canvas bag and pulled out a silver coloured cigarette case. Inside were six joints. Go on take one, no in fact take a couple, this is top quality weed, grow it myself you see," said Steve.

"How do you manage that?" asked Todd, "bit risky, won't the police arrest you if they catch you?"

"They're not going to catch me though," said Steve, "I grow the plants in amongst the tomato plants, they look very similar, been growing them for years in the back yard, never been caught yet."

Todd smiled and took two of the joints from the cigarette case.

"I can pay you for these I've got twenty dollars on me," said Todd.

"Not a problem," said Steve, "I don't want any of your money man, just be careful with them, they're good shit. Strong and it's a real hot smoke, so don't say I didn't warn you."

"Cool," said Todd, "and thanks, I'll bare that in mind."

Todd put the joints into his back pocket and looked at his watch, it was quarter to seven. Time to head up to the hotel and meet Aunt Elaine and Howard and have some food. He was now feeling famished.

Todd turned and gave Steve a wave as he headed up the path, "Hope you catch something soon," shouted Todd.

"So do I, dude. If I don't get anything I'll not be eating dinner tonight!" laughed Steve, and with that he cast his line landing it expertly a foot short of the reed bed.

The Lake View Hotel was only a two-minute walk from the jetty and was located just the other side of the main road to Fairlea. The hotel had only opened in the last ten years, so it hadn't been built when David and Jennifer Saltman had bought their lakeside house. The 3- storey hotel had been built on top of a small hill and its position on the lake's south shore afforded panoramic views across the lake and to the Allegheny mountains in the far distance. A sun terrace with numerous tables and chairs ran the entire length of the front of the hotel and as Todd reached the main road he could see aunt Elaine sitting with Elspeth and Paul having a drink.

As Todd waited to cross the road a white Buick coupe went past heading west on its way to Fairlea. Driving the vehicle was Anne Grey, Cathleen Heggerty's friend and former colleague who was heading to the hospital to start the nightshift at the maternity wing. It had only been the most fleeting of glances, but Anne was sure the boy at the side of the road had been Josh Heggerty.

It must have been more than a year since Anne last saw Josh, but his thick blond hair and athletic build was unmistakeable. As soon as Anne saw Josh, pangs of guilt swept over her. She couldn't remember when she had last visited Cathleen, it was at least six months ago probably even longer. By the time she had driven another couple of miles Anne reckoned it must have been the time when she last saw Josh. She felt ashamed, how could it have been more than a year since she had last gone to see her friend? What day is today thought Anne to herself? It's Wednesday, I'll phone Frank tomorrow and see if would be alright to go over and visit on Friday when it's my day off. That's what I'll do, thought Anne, I'll phone tomorrow and get it organised. I can't believe it's been over a year, where does the time go?

Chapter 9

"Before we eat let us join hands bow our heads and give thanks to God for what we are about to receive, now let us pray," said Pastor Whitehead.

"We thank you Lord, for all you give; the food we eat, the lives we live;

And to our loved ones no longer with us, please comfort them with your blessings,

Lord we pray. And help us all to live our days with thankful hearts and loving ways.

Amen.

"Thank you, Philip, for that lovely Grace," said Elaine who for her birthday lunch had chosen to wear a smart navy-blue dress, the hem and sleeves of which were edged with delicate white lace. A morning spent in the hotel's spa resulted in a facial, manicure and new hairstyle all courtesy of the voucher that Ruth and the family had given her as a birthday present. Elaine's ensemble, which included new diamond tear drop earrings and an unusual lariat silver necklace that Howard had commissioned especially for her birthday, was topped off with a pair of silver sling back shoes and matching clutch bag. Elaine looked very elegant in her fine clothes and beautiful jewellery, but the thing that had given her most pleasure was the large 'fabulous at fifty' pink badge that Louise and Pamela had bought for their aunt in a card shop in Marlinton.

"I would like to say a few words of thanks to you all, but I think that should wait till after we've eaten. There is a selection of appetizers on the table immediately behind where John is sitting, so please help yourselves, after that we will be having a hot buffet with a selection of roast meats-

"Oh, how splendid!" purred Pastor Whitehead to nobody in particular.

"- the wines on the table," said Elaine, "but if you'd like anything else to drink please speak to one of the waiters, I just want everyone to enjoy themselves."

As the others perused the array of appetizers Elaine went to speak to Ruth.

"I was really thinking of Todd when I said people might like something other than wine to drink, I know he's only seventeen, but I wondered if he might like a beer instead?" said Elaine.

"I'm sure he would. I've told him he can have a couple of bottle of beers but no more," said Ruth, "anyway his coach would have a fit if he thought I was allowing his star pitcher to be drinking alcohol at lunchtime, and on a Thursday as well!" laughed Ruth.

The twins giggled as they watched Pastor Whitehead pile his plate high with assorted cuts of roast beef, pork and turkey. The plate was so full of meat there was hardly room for any potatoes or vegetables on the plate.

Pastor Whitehead noticed that the girls were watching him, so he turned to them and said,

"I can see you are wondering how I'm going to fit my vegetables onto my plate. The answer to that young ladies is that I'm going to put them on another plate!"

Louise and Pamela laughed even more as true to his word, the Pastor piled a heap of vegetables onto a second plate before he returned to the table and set about the serious task of eating the mountain of food.

"Don't be surprised if he goes up again once he's demolished that plateful," said Elaine to Elspeth, "I've never known anyone with an appetite like Philip's, he's insatiable! I'm just glad I don't' have to feed him every day, I'd be broke!"

"Just as well his thirst doesn't match his appetite," said Elspeth, "or you really would be bankrupt. He's been nursing that same glass of wine since we had the toast," said Elspeth with a smile.

"I'm more concerned about Todd to be honest," said Elaine, "He's had a couple of beers, but I see he's now drinking red wine, and I've seen him have at least two big glasses. I don't think Ruth or John's noticed. I hope it's not going to give him a headache, they've to fly back to Portland later," said Elaine.

"What time's their flight?" asked Elspeth.

"I think it's an hour or so after ours, must be around nine," said Elaine.

"I'm sure he'll be fine," said Elspeth, "anyway, it's been a great party and a super couple of days. Thank you so much for inviting us, we've really enjoyed it," said Elspeth giving Elaine a hug.

"It's been terrific, hasn't it?" said Elaine, "and yesterday was really special too, I'm so glad we did it."

By four o'clock the party was coming to an end. Pastor Whitehead surprised everyone by not returning for a second main course but by way of compensation he did manage two trips to the sweet trolley. Howard gave a lovely speech in which he paid a wholesome tribute to his lovely wife and thanked everyone for travelling such a distance to join then on this special occasion. Finally, he wished Pastor Whitehead safe travels as he and his wife Jane were heading to the UK for six weeks holiday to visit Jane's sister and various cousins who resided there.

As people were starting to say their goodbyes, Todd felt in need of some fresh air and wandered a bit unsteadily outside into the garden at the rear of the hotel. He wasn't sure how much he had drunk, but the hit of fresh air made him feel dizzy and quite nauseous. For a moment Todd thought that his lunch was about to be expelled onto the manicured lawn of the hotel. He breathed deeply and leant against a wall out of sight of everyone else. A few minutes past and with it the feeling that he was going to be sick. As he walked back through the door into the hotel corridor he became disorientated. Opening a side door, he found himself in a large function suite. The aftermath of a raucous lunch was evident by the large number of empty glasses and half empty bottles that littered each of the rooms tables. At the far end of the room on the wall above what looked like the top table was a large banner which read 'Sigma Phi Delta – 75th Anniversary Lunch'.

A waiter appeared with a tray and started to collect glasses from the tables. The waiter looked at Todd and smiled,

"I think you're in the wrong room," he said, "are you part of the 50th birthday lunch?"

"Yes, I am," said Todd trying desperately not to slur his words. "I must have come in the wrong door."

"That's okay," said the waiter, "you're looking for the next door down on the other side of the corridor.

Gosh man, that nose of yours looks sore, how did you do that," asked the waiter.

"Got smacked in the face with a baseball a few days ago, the bruising is just starting to come out," replied Todd with a rueful sigh.

"It sure looks painful," said the waiter, "I hope you didn't mind me asking."

"No," laughed Todd, "Not a problem."

"I'm Donald by the way, pleased to meet you," said the waiter as he emptied ashtrays into a bucket.

"I'm Todd, good to meet you too. By the way, do you know what that banner is all about?" asked Todd pointing at it.

"I'm told it's a fraternal for engineers, got groups set up all over the country apparently," replied the waiter. "I'll tell you something, they sure can shift some booze, been going at it since twelve o'clock and only just finished. Most are staying in the hotel tonight so after a couple of hours sleep this afternoon they will be back at it this evening."

Having picked up his tray, Donald pushed open the door with his foot and left the room.

As Todd turned to follow him out he noticed a half bottle of Wild Turkey bourbon sitting on the table nearest the door. There was no more than an inch out of the bottle and as no one was around Todd lifted the bottle and put in the side pocket of his jacket.

"There you are," said Ruth as Todd returned to the function room, pulled up a chair and sat down. "I was wondering where you'd got to," Ruth looked at her son suspiciously. Your aunt and uncle have kindly agreed to drop us in Fairlea on their way back to the airport. We're going to call in and see the Johnstons for an hour or so, and we'll get a taxi back to the airport from there," said Ruth.

Todd leaned back in his chair and groaned. "I know you said we were going to visit them, but I don't even remember who they are," said Todd with more than a hint of indifference.

"They were our next-door neighbours in Marlinton and they were always very kind to you and your sisters, especially at birthdays and Christmas time," said his mother. "And anyway, they must be in their late seventies now, so this will probably be the last time we will get to see them."

Todd didn't say anything but made a groaning noise twice as loud as the last one.

Half an hour later the Pontiac pulled up outside a neat chalet style house. It was painted grey and had white window shutters and blush coloured roof tiles. Rows of lavender plants lined the path to the front door.

"Thanks again for a lovely couple of days, I'm glad we were all able to be here for your birthday. And the service for Jennifer and David, that was special too," said Ruth hugging her big sister tightly. "And thank you Howard for chauffeuring us all about, that saved us a lot of hassle not having to hire a car."

"My pleasure," said Howard as he and John lifted the last of the bags out of the trunk of the car.

As Howard and the twins picked up the bags Ruth turned to Todd. "I don't know how much you've had to drink but it's way more than the couple of beers we agreed. You could hardly stay awake in the car and you're stinking of drink. I'm not having you see the Johnstons looking and smelling like that."

174

Todd didn't say anything, but he was smirking from ear to ear.

"Don't think you've got away with this," said Ruth who was clearly angry with her son. "We'll talk more about it when we get home, but you can expect to be grounded, and if that means missing practice so be it!" continued Ruth.

Todd glared at his mother.

"I suggest you go for a walk and sober up, there's a park just over the road. Be back here in an hour. Don't go wondering off anywhere else, and don't you dare be late, you hear me?" said Ruth.

Todd nodded. He wasn't happy being chastised like that, especially in front of his sisters, but he was glad he didn't have to go in and see the Johnstons. By the time they got back to Portland he was confident that his mom would have calmed down a bit. She better have, he thought, there's no way I can afford to miss practice, not at this stage of the season.

Todd crossed the road and wondered through the gates that led into the park. He reached into his jacket pocket and took out the bottle of bourbon, removed the cap, and took two large swigs from the bottle. He winced as he swallowed the dark liquid, it tasted smoky with hints of spice and nutmeg. A burning sensation filled his mouth and throat. It didn't taste pleasant but the warm feeling it left him with was satisfying. Satisfying enough anyway for him to take a third mouthful of the fire-water.

From his rear pocket Todd took out the second joint. He had smoked the first one late last night on the balcony of his hotel bedroom. Steve had been right, he had nearly burned his throat on the hot smoke but that aside it had made him feel good, really relaxed and chilled. Right now, he thought he needed to feel like that again. His mother's angry words and tone had annoyed him, he was surprised she had reacted like that especially given the circumstances of the last two days. She may have lost a sister, but he was grieving the loss of his real mom and dad, she should have cut me some slack for that he thought.

Todd didn't light the spliff as nearby a young woman was pushing a baby in a pushchair and over to his right an elderly couple were exercising a pair of cocker spaniels.

Through the trees at the far end of the park Todd could see what looked like school playing fields. He could make out a set of football posts and what liked like some bleachers and a small stand for spectators. In front of the stand there appeared to be a running track. Nobody seemed to be using the pitches, so it seemed like the ideal place to smoke his joint, well away from prying eyes.

*

Over at Dararra farm, Frank Heggerty was loading a small overnight case into the back of his Ford pick-up. He was about to leave for Charleston General Hospital where his wife was due her annual assessment the following day.

"We'll aim to be home by seven tomorrow, but that will depend if we get finished on time and get away from the hospital before the rush hour traffic builds up," said Frank.

"I know you're supposed to be at practice tonight, but I need you to repair that section of fence, Josh. Two of the posts have rotted through and another three are about to go the same way. All eight will need replacing, I'm not having a repeat of last time. I'm sorry, Josh, but you'll need to stay and fix it," said Frank.

Josh gave a weak smile and nodded without saying anything.

Last year when the hogs had got through the fence they ended up in Hector Balen's front garden on the other side of the valley and ate all of Mrs Balen's prized dahlias. Josh agreed with his father that Hector had probably kept the fifth hog for himself, by way of some sort of compensation, as they only ever got four back. All in all, it had proved to be an expensive episode and was clearly one that they didn't want repeated.

"I've left the posts and concrete mix up by the chestnut tree, the spades and toolbox are in the shed next to the coop. You'll need to make the post holes a couple of feet deep at least, that was part of the problem last time, holes weren't deep enough," said Frank.

Josh looked on as his father lifted the tiny frame of his mother into the front seat of the truck. He leaned through the open window and kissed his mother gently on her cheek.

Josh watched as the pick-up disappeared down the farm track and onto the main road. He hadn't given up entirely on making tonight's practice. He looked at his watch, it was a little before five, he reckoned if he could get half of the holes dug in the next forty-five minutes or so, he could take his bike and still be the practice for six. He would skip his social studies class last thing tomorrow afternoon and finish the job then. It would all be done before his parents were due to return home. Well that was the plan anyway. Josh picked up a shovel and pick axe from the shed and grabbed his father's toolbox before heading up the hill to the fence. As he passed the small white cross marking Peter's grave he thought how good it would be to have had a brother's help now. "We'd have had this fence done in no time bro," said Josh with a smile, "no time at all."

*

"There must be at least twenty poles in that pile alone, Eustace," said Henry Jarret. "There could well be more on the other side that we can't see."

Screech and Eustace were sitting in their van in the far corner of the Fairlea Hotel car park. They had been parked there for more than half an hour and through the maple trees that lined the rear of the car park they were watching the groundsmen build Fairlea High's new football stand that was being constructed ahead of the new season in September.

"I haven't seen anybody for the last ten minutes," said Henry, "it's after five now so I expect they're finished for the day. We'll give it another five minutes and if nobody shows I'll turn the van around and you can start loading them into the rear."

"Fine," said Eustace, "What do you think they're made off Henry?"

"Most likely be aluminium," said Henry, "most scaffolding is made of aluminium these days."

"Are we going to take them to Arnold's?" asked Eustace.

"Yep, that's the plan. If we get a move on we can get over there by six. He usually closes about half past so if we get a hurry on we should be okay," said Henry.

"Hopefully we'll get enough for them to pay off that fine you got me after that fucking shambles up at Briery Knob."

"I got a fine too," said Eustace somewhat sheepishly.

"Sure am glad to hear it, "said Henry sarcastically, "you deserved yours, it was your stupidity that set fire to the thing in the first place."

Eustace didn't reply, years of experience had taught him when it was best to shut up and say nothing and right now was one of those times.

"Right, still no-one about," said Henry, "I'm going to turn the van and reverse it back. Get your gloves on Eustace and get ready, we're not going to be hanging about any longer than is necessary. Okay, let's earn ourselves some cash."

As Henry turned the van around Eustace made his way to the piles of poles and brackets that were lying neatly in rows on the ground under the bleachers. Tucked away by the corner of the stand was a mound covered in thick sheets of black plastic. Eustace lifted the sheets and looked underneath, there must have been upwards of fifty poles of various sizes in that pile alone. Eustace couldn't contain himself and, in his excitement, shouted to Henry.

"Fifty, Henry! There must be at least fifty here!"

"Shut the fuck up, Eustace, you dumb-ass, someone's gonna hear you!" said Henry in an exasperated voice. "Just shut up and start loading them into the van."

*

At five thirty Elliot Manning was setting the alarm and locking the door of his pharmacy on the main street. Manning's pharmacy was an institution in Fairlea and for the last twenty years Elliot had managed the shop that his grandfather first opened in 1944 just before the start of the Second World War. Elliot was a former mayor of Fairlea and a longstanding elder in the first Presbyterian church in the town. Consequently, Elliot seemed to know just about everybody in the town.

As he made his way to his vehicle in the lot across the street he was carrying a large white paper bag containing an assortment of pills and tablets that would have stocked most people's medicine cabinet for years. Incredible to think she was still alive, thought Elliot, as he placed the bag on the passenger seat and started his engine. Every Thursday after work he delivered Mrs Brew's prescription to her son, Eddie, who owned and ran the Fairlea Hotel. Elsie Brew, who was now in her early nineties, had been largely confined to her upstairs bedroom for the last couple of years as she had trouble walking and was suffering from a list of ailments that were too numerous to mention. Elliot shuddered at the thought of how many chemicals must be in her system. She must be taking a dozen tablets three times a day, she would rattle like a nickel in a collection box if you shook her, he thought. Yet despite all that she was still very much alive, and her memory was sharp as a tack. According to Eddie she spent her days listening to her Benny Goodman records and watching endless re-runs of the Carol Burnett Show.

As Elliot indicated to turn right into the hotel car park a white transit van containing two males turned out of the car park and drove off in the direction of Lewisburg. Elliot immediately recognised the driver as Screech Jarret and the passenger as being Eustace

Brownlie. Henry's mother had been another who Elliot occasionally made home visits to, so he'd gotten to know Henry over the years and of course if you knew Henry you got to know Eustace as they were almost always together.

Elliot parked his car at the rear of the hotel and lifted the medicine bag from the passenger seat. As he was locking his door he noticed the figure of a young man leaning against a stanchion of the bleacher stand by the football park. The afternoon sunshine was casting long shadows from the maple trees that stood immediately behind the stand but in the bright sunlight the figure, with his blond hair and muscular build, was unmistakeable. It was Josh Heggerty and he was smoking a cigarette. Elliot watched for a few moments as Josh, dressed in a white T-Shirt and blue jeans, took several long slow puffs of his cigarette. Holding his linen jacket over his shoulder, he leant back his head and blew several small puffs of smoke into the air.

Elliot didn't know Josh well, but he had met him several times in the past, most recently outside his shop when Josh had been pushing his mother in her wheelchair. Over the years, Elliot had been a regular visitor to the maternity ward delivering drugs when the hospital's own pharmacy had run out. That was of course before Cathleen Heggerty had had her stroke, but occasionally during those visits he would meet Josh who was usually waiting for his mother to finish work, so he could get a lift home after school. Of course, he looked much bigger now, but the fresh face and distinctive blond hair hadn't changed.

*

By five-thirty Josh had managed to dig one and a half holes. The soil was rock hard and every few inches he would hit a large stone and have to dig it out with the pick axe. His plan to make that evenings practice was clearly not going to work. He couldn't afford to just leave the fence and go because if it wasn't finished by the time his father got back there would be hell to pay and Josh didn't want to risk being grounded as that would potentially make him miss other more important practices. He wasn't happy about it, but he reckoned after Tuesday he was someway ahead of the others, so perhaps he could afford to miss practice just this once.

Josh decided he would phone Maisie and let her know he wouldn't make practice, she could explain to Mrs Rawlingson what had happened, he didn't want to just not turn up. He hurried back down to the farm house, if he was lucky Maisie wouldn't have left her house yet.

*

"Just take the bike home with you tonight Nelson if it helps and you can bring it back with you tomorrow. By the time you get back from the Rossiters it will be nearer seven and I don't want to keep you late. Anyway, Mrs Latimer doesn't like me being late as the dinner will spoil and the pain that would cause me just isn't worth the hassle," said Mr Latimer with a chuckle.

"Remember that, Nelson, if you're ever stupid enough to get married!" continued Mr Latimer.

"I'll do that," said Nelson laughing.

"Did you remember to put the jar of pickled onions in? If Deke Rossiter doesn't get his onions my life won't be worth living and you'll be getting the sack," laughed Mr Latimer.

"I've checked the list," said Nelson, "everything's in. I'll see you tomorrow after school then and thanks for letting me take the bike home."

"That's okay son, that's what considerate bosses do for their employees," said Mr Latimer smiling as he watched Nelson head off on his bike.

Nelson Parker was fifteen and each day after school for the last year he had run deliveries from Mr Latimer's convenience store. Today he was running late, and the last delivery was to the Rossiters, an elderly couple who ran a smallholding just beyond the Heggertys' farm a few miles out of town.

Nelson dropped a gear and got out of the saddle in an effort to get up the hill without having to get off his bike. The road really wasn't that steep but the basket of groceries that sat over the front wheel did nothing for the aerodynamics of the bike. He grimaced as he tried to keep the bike steady. If he leant too far to the side the weight in the basket would easily cause the bike to topple over. It was an occupational hazard, but it hadn't happened for a while and Nelson was determined it wasn't going to happen now. Funny how the last delivery always seems to be uphill he thought to himself, at least the cycle back will be a breeze. He could see the bridge that ran over the Haney Creek just ahead and the road end that ran up to the Heggertys' place and the Rossiters' just beyond was just across the road from the bridge. His goal was to make it to the bridge and then he would take a well-deserved rest.

By the time he reached the bridge Nelson was hot and he could feel beads of sweat rolling down the side of his face, but he had made it without having to get off and push his bike and that made him feel good. Nelson was not a natural athlete, he was a bit chubby and a little overweight, he was more interested in nature and fishing than sports. But with all the cycling he had been doing with his after-school job he had never been fitter.

Nelson leant the bike against the bridge and peered over the wall into the clear water below. The water was no more than a foot deep and at this time of year was running very slowly. Towards the far bank and under the branches of a willow tree was a deeper pool and it was that which had Nelson's attention. He stood perfectly still being careful not to cast his shadow onto the water, clumps of emerald green coontail weed drifted leisurely in the slack water and shafts of sunlight illuminated the smooth stones and gravel that lined the river bed. Suddenly Nelson spotted what he had been looking for, a good-sized brook trout, maybe three quarters of a pound or more darted out from the shadows breaking the surface of the water as it snatched a caddisfly. In that fleeting moment he could see the orange belly of the fish and the delicate red spots that lined its flanks. Nelson felt a frisson of excitement, he had never fished this far up the Haney, but he made a mental note that it would be well worth a return trip.

Feeling refreshed and elated by this new discovery Nelson turned his bike around and headed across the road to the farm track that would take him to his destination. If he could manage it in one go he should be at the Rossiters' in about five minutes, at this rate he would make it home by just after half six, that's only fifteen minutes later than normal. It's just as well I don't have to return the bike tonight, thought Nelson, otherwise I really would be late.

*

As Todd took the last few draws of his joint he was already starting to feel strange. He couldn't keep his hands still. For the last few minutes they had been twitching and jerking involuntarily and his head was now feeling very hot. So hot it felt as though his brain was on fire. Then quite suddenly his whole body felt cold, freezing cold and he began to shiver uncontrollably. Worse still he was starting to hallucinate. The branches of the trees ahead of him were filled with weird monkey like creatures with talons for fingers and blood red eyes. Todd didn't know what was happening to him and he felt scared. Yesterday it had all been so different. It had felt so good, so relaxed he had been in a good place. This just felt horrible. The alcohol in his system was making him feel dizzy and disorientated. The ground underneath his feet appeared to be moving and he felt sick. The vomit came up in waves, Todd sank to his knees and leaned forward, his body wretched as his stomach disgorged its contents onto the soft soil. He thought it was over but as he was about to stand up bile and the last remnants of his half-digested lunch filled his mouth as his stomach turned over one more time.

*

Maisie was heading out the door when she heard the phone ring. She hesitated for a moment wondering if she should answer it. Becca was already at the school for her practice and her parents were at Walmart doing the weekly shopping. It's not likely to be for me thought

185

Maisie, so with a shrug of her shoulders she picked up her guitar case, locked the front door and headed down the path.

Maisie couldn't have been happier, it was a beautiful day and only yesterday she had finally mastered the fast section of Sultans of Swing. She couldn't wait to show Josh. The school concert was less than three weeks away and it was shaping up to be the best one yet. By ten to six Maisie had reached the path by the school playing fields, she had a spring in her step, life was good, and she was relishing every moment of it.

As Maisie strolled down the path towards the school she saw a familiar figure standing in the shadows underneath the football stand leaning against one of the stanchions. What is Josh doing over there? Wondered Maisie. He was standing facing the other way and hadn't seen Maisie. She thought she would surprise him, so she carefully picked her way across the rough ground being careful not to make a sound. When she was only a few feet away she called out, "Hiya big guy, wondered if you might like to tighten my G-string, seems to have worked loose again," said Maisie with a giggle. "Nice jeans by the way, I like your hair you've had it cut! You told me you wanted to grow it longer and now you've had it cut." Maisie started to laugh.

As Todd turned around to face her Maisie could smell the distinctive sweet herby aroma of cannabis. Her father still smoked it regularly, never in the house and deliberately never in front of Maisie or her sister, but the smell was familiar to her.

"What's going on, Josh?" asked Maisie, who was now feeling confused and a little uncomfortable. "Are you alright? I can smell cannabis and you stink of alcohol, and what have you done to your nose?"

Todd didn't reply, he looked at Maisie through glazed eyes and grabbed her right wrist. Pulling her roughly towards him Todd placed his hand onto Maisie's breast and leant into her in an attempt to kiss her.

Maisie dropped her guitar case, "Stop it, Josh! What are you doing?" said Maisie, her voice anxious and shaking. Instinctively she tried to pull away from Todd's grasp, but his grip tightened, preventing her from breaking away.

"Let me go, Josh, let me go! You're scaring me!" said a distressed Maisie who was now sobbing and desperately trying to wrench herself free from the vice like grip that held her. Todd squeezed Maisie's breast hard and she felt a shooting pain in her chest, as he let go of her breast, Maisie felt his hand move underneath her dress and she twisted and squirmed as his fingers slipped under the elastic of her underwear and touched her skin. Fear now coursed through her body, frantically she pulled and bucked as she fought to break free. Repeatedly she swung her arm and lifted her knee as she tried valiantly to strike his groin and attack his vulnerability, but no blows were landed. Her energy levels exhausted Maisie summoned one final effort and with the palm of her hand struck out hard contacting her foe across the bridge of his nose, a scream of pain pierced the balmy evening and blood started to pour from Todd's nose. Large drops fell staining his white t-shirt, yet more ran down his arm onto Maisie's yellow dress.

Suddenly she realised, "Who are you? You're..."

Before she could finish her sentence, a metal bar came crashing down on the side of her temple. A second blow immediately followed, and Maisie's body crumpled beneath her. She slumped to the ground and lay motionless on the dark earth her unseeing eyes wide open with the fear of her final moments.

*

By the time Josh had finished digging the fifth of the post holes it was ten past six. He was hot, his hands were raw from the digging and his back was starting to ache. That's enough for tonight he thought. He could do the remaining three tomorrow afternoon and attaching the barbed wire fence wouldn't take long. He may have had to miss the practice but at least the fence was on schedule to be finished before his parents got back. As Josh picked up the wire fence to prop it up against the tree a barb caught in the back of his hand and ripped the flesh open.

"Jeezo, that was sore," said Josh screwing up his eyes and winching in pain. As he looked at his hand, blood was pulsing from the open wound. In his efforts to get his hankie out of his pocket he only succeeded in getting blood all over his jeans and white vest.

Shit thought Josh, I could have done without that, it won't be easy digging more holes with a cut hand. He wrapped the hankie round his hand but within no time the white linen cloth was a bright scarlet colour and saturated in blood. Josh held his hand in the air remembering his first aid training from school. It seemed to be working as after a couple of minutes the blood was no longer oozing from the cut. He hoped he could get it to stop as he didn't much fancy a trip to the hospital to get it stitched.

*

Nelson Parker was not defeated by the gradient, it had been the sheer number of potholes that littered the farm track that had necessitated him getting off his bike and walking the last few hundred yards to the Rossiter's farmstead. As Nelson passed the entrance to Dararra farm he noticed Josh Heggerty standing on a hill near to a large chestnut tree, he couldn't have been more than seventy yards away. Josh was two years above Nelson at school and while they didn't know each other well, Nelson would have given Josh a friendly wave had he been looking. But Josh seemed pre-occupied and he was staring at his right hand. Nelson could see the blood-stained cloth wrapped round Josh's hand and what he presumed was blood on the white singlet he was wearing. Looks nasty thought Nelson as he wondered what had caused the injury.

By the time Nelson passed by again after making his delivery to the Rossiters', Josh was nowhere to be seen. Nelson jumped on his bike and started to freewheel down the track taking care to avoid the craters on the way down, at this speed Nelson was sure he could be home in less than fifteen minutes.

*

Ruth was standing on the sidewalk outside the Johnson's house when Todd appeared from across the street.

"Well at least you're not late," said Ruth as she saw her son approaching, "but what on earth have you done to yourself Todd?"

Todd was covering his nose with his hand as he walked towards his mother, but his face, hands and t-shirt were covered in blood.

"Looks worse than it is," said Todd, "I went to swot a fly away and my hand caught the end of my nose. Can't get it to stop bleeding, have you got some tissues mom?"

"I've got wet wipes in my bag, come here and let me have a look at it."

"It's fine, mom, honestly," said Todd, "can you just give me the wet wipes and I'll sort it? It's kinda tender, just easier if I do it," added Todd calmly. "Could you get me my other shirt out my bag, don't think they'll let me on the plane like this."

Ruth took the wipes out of her handbag and handed them to Todd.

"Just wait here and I'll go and get your shirt, I don't want the Johnston's to see you looking like that."

By the time Ruth had returned with his shirt Todd had managed to wipe most of the blood off his face and hands.

"I think it might have stopped bleeding," said Todd as he took off his blood-stained shirt. Ruth handed him his other shirt and put the soiled shirt into a plastic bag she was carrying before handing her son a packet of tissues.

"Tear off a couple of pieces and use them to plug your nostrils," said Ruth. "Can't afford to have it happen again as you've run out of shirts!" she said, trying to lighten the mood with some humour.

"Your fathers called the cab, so it should be here soon. Expect you'll looking forward to getting home, it's been a tough couple of days for you."

Todd, who was now sitting on the Johnson's front wall leaning his head backwards, nodded but didn't say anything.

"You're not forgiven for having all that drink this afternoon, but maybe I was a bit hard on you. I'm not going to make you miss your practice next week. I didn't want you worrying about it on the plane home. Six hours on a plane is a long time to be worrying about something, so I hope that makes you feel a bit better."

Todd nodded and managed a weak smile.

"That looks like good timing, here's the cab and your nose does look as if it's stopped bleeding," said Ruth. "John, girls, the taxi's here! Can you bring down the bags?"

"Can you help dad load the bags, son? I'm just going to quickly say cheerio to the Johnstons."

Chapter 10

"I'll get it," said Mike getting up from the couch to answer the phone. It was nearly nine-thirty and Mike and Susan were drinking coffee and relaxing in the den having just got Keegan to go up to his bed.

"Yes, Susan's here," said Mike, "can I ask who's calling?"

"Susan, it's Dave Foster on the phone, he's wanting to speak to you. Not sure what it's about but he sounds a bit stressed," said Mike as he handed Susan the phone.

"Okay, yes, yes of course, no you're not bothering me in the slightest," said Susan.

"No, she wasn't at practice, I was expecting to see her, but she didn't turn up.

I did wonder where they'd got to as Josh Heggerty wasn't there either and they usually arrive together.

Yes, I expect that's the case, they will probably be back soon though.

Yep, I've got Josh's number somewhere, but I'll need to go look for it, I'll tell you what I'll call Josh when I find it and ring you right back Okay.

Try not to worry, Dave, I'm sure she will be back soon, she's a sensible girl.

Yep, that's a good idea, ask Mary to check Benny's when she's out. I know a lot of the kids like to hang out there after practice. If she's not there someone there will probably have seen her.

Okay, I'll get back to you as soon as I can," said Susan putting down the phone.

"What was all that about?" asked Mike, "is everything alright?"

"I'm sure it's fine," said Susan. "Dave says his daughter Maisie hasn't returned home after practice, only she wasn't at practice." Susan was starting to feel slightly anxious.

"Dave said she left the house with her guitar, but nobody's seen her since. Her mom and sister are away to check the arcade and Benny's so fingers crossed she's there," continued Susan.

"Josh Heggerty wasn't at practice either. Not like either of them to miss it. I expect they're together and forgot what the time was. I know Maisie fancies Josh as her sister told me, not so sure how Josh feels about Maisie. Anyway, I said I would try and phone Josh and then get back to Dave. I've got Josh's number in my folder somewhere," said Susan leafing through a black ring binder. "Ah, here it is," she said with a sense of relief. Susan let the phone ring for a good couple of minutes but there was no reply.

"If she isn't back when you speak to Dave tell him to contact the station and report her as a missing person," Said Mike. "The patrol cars will be given her description and I expect they will quickly trace her. That's what usually happens. Anyway, the more eyes out looking for her the better."

"Do you think I should head out and look for them as well?" asked Susan.

"No, I don't," said Mike, "I meant the more police eyes that were looking the better at this stage. I think the fact that you couldn't contact Josh might not be a bad thing. Kind of suggests that she will be with Josh," added Mike.

"You might want to mention that to Dave when you phone him back, might help to reassure him. I know what a worry it must be but it's just past quarter to ten now. You said the practice finished at eight and by the time they walked home, well she's just a little more than an hour late at the moment, so let's not get ahead of ourselves," said Mike trying to give Susan some sense of perspective.

"Yes, you're right, I know," said Susan. "It's just... no, you're right, it'll be fine. Must happen all the time, youngsters going missing."

"Everyday occurrence, Susan, and invariably it all works out just fine," said Mike. "Now come on, you'd better phone Dave back, he might have some good news you never know. Remember to tell him that not getting Josh in wasn't necessary a bad thing."

Susan couldn't sleep all night and by five she was showered and sitting in the kitchen sipping a mug of strong coffee. Maisie hadn't returned by the time she phoned Dave back, but Mary and Becca hadn't got back from checking Benny's either so perhaps that was a good sign. Dave hadn't actually said he would phone back when Maisie arrived home and she hadn't exactly asked him to either. Susan just assumed that he would have and as the phone hadn't rung she was starting to feel uneasy.

Mike usually left the house a little after seven most mornings to head for the station but today he was up a little earlier too, so it was only quarter to when he kissed Susan at the door and headed for work.

"You'll phone me at school and let me know what's happening, won't you? Leave a message with Diane in the office if I can't take the call," said Susan.

"Of course I will," said Mike. He could tell how uptight his wife was feeling but years of experience had taught him to stay calm and not to jump to conclusions. After all, nearly every missing person turned up safe and well. Why should this turn out to be any different? He started his engine and reversed slowly out the drive onto the main road.

"Phil, have you got a minute?" asked Mike as he walked into the front office of the station.

"Be right with you, Mike," said Sergeant Coutts who was counting the petty cash from the office cash box that was sitting on his desk. "Just got to sign it off in the register and then that's me," said Phil. He returned the cash box to the safe and locked the door.

"What can I do for you, Mike?" asked Phil.

"Can you tell me if Maisie Foster has been reported as a missing person?" asked Mike.

Phil nodded. "Yes, she has been, her father reported her missing about ten thirty last night. Why, do you know her?" asked Phil.

"I don't but Susan does, teaches her guitar at the music group at Fairlea High. Jeez, I was expecting her to be home by now," said Mike.

"Has a Josh Heggerty been reported missing as well?" asked Mike.

"Funny you should say that because when Mr Foster reported his daughter missing he thought she was with Josh Heggerty," said Phil, "but when we sent a station

195

up to where he stays he was in the house. In fact, he was in bed asleep, took some time for the officers to waken him. I spoke with Jamey Davidson at the handover, he had been up at the house last night, apparently the boy was pretty upset, his folks are away for a couple of days and they're not due back till tonight."

"It's Cathleen Heggerty's boy. Remember the lady who helped Susan save that child from the road accident at Greenbrier bridge? Must be more than fifteen years ago now."

"Yep, I know who he is. Susan teaches him as well, bit of a star pupil she says. And it's seventeen years since that accident, quite incredible," said Mike. "Anyway, what's happening with the missing person enquiry? Any suggestion of a fall out with her mom or dad? Must be a reason for it, there always is," added Mike.

"Too early to say, Mike, I had a squint at the initial report but there's no indication of any argument or falling out, bit of a mystery at the moment," said Phil. "The uniforms are getting a briefing just now from Bull and Brad Curran, he's been brought in as search advisor, I'm just running off the maps now. Usual stuff, town split into 3 sectors, once they've finished their enquiries at the house, sector one will be the route from the house to the school and spreading out from there once that's done," said Phil. "I'll keep you posted of any developments, Mike, but nothing for you detectives at the moment. Let's stay positive, how many times have we been here before and things turn out fine?" he added.

"I know," said Mike. "That's exactly what I said to Susan. But she's starting to worry now, so any news would be appreciated Phil. I said I'd let her know as soon as I'd heard anything."

In the briefing room on the first floor Ewart Wilder was stressing the importance of professionalism to the officers' present.

"It will be all over the town already. My wife called me to say our son got a call at breakfast from a friend who already knew she was missing, so it will be all round the school by nine o'clock. Amy, I want you to get down to the school and link in with Mr Peters the Principal and be a conduit between the enquiry team here and the school. I want everyone to be positive and professional. No off the cuff remarks or speculation you hear me. Sergeant Woods will be running things from this end. Any inquiries from the press to be directed to Sergeant Woods and sanctioned by me. Amy, did you get that?"

Amy nodded as she wrote in her pocket book.

"They're likely to turn up at the school looking for information so remember say nothing and refer them to Sergeant Woods. The incident room number is on the board make sure you've all got it in your books," said Chief Wilder.

"Where are those darn maps?" said Wilder impatiently, "John, go and tell Sergeant Coutts I need those maps immediately, I can't deploy the resources without them."

"That appears to be him at the door now, sir," said Officer Jones.

"Don't just stand there, man, come in!" barked Wilder.

Sergeant Coutts stood stern faced at the door and gestured to Chief Wilder to come to him.

"Oh, for God's sake, Coutts, what is it?" said a clearly annoyed Wilder in a voice that everyone could hear. "This had better be good, Coutts, these officers have work to do and we've a missing girl to find." He continued as he opened the door.

"Ok Shads, what is it?" said Wilder, who not for the first time made his frustration with Sergeant Coutts very apparent.

"Sir, I don't think you'll be needing the maps, the control room has just taken a call from George Burroughs, the school's head groundsman. They've found a body of a girl hidden under plastic sheeting under the new football stand they've been building. Apparently, she's suffered an horrendous head injury."

"Fuck," said Chief Wilder, "when did they find the body?"

"Not long ago, maybe twenty minutes at most," said Phil, "they've been told not to touch anything."

"Okay, so now we have ourselves a murder enquiry. Do we have confirmed ID?" asked Wilder.

"Not yet, sir, but they have found a green guitar case next to the body. I'm afraid it is going to be her, sir," said Sergeant Coutts.

"Who have we got down there just now?" asked Wilder.

"Nobody yet, they're all in the briefing with you. Who do you want me to send?" asked Sergeant Coutts.

Chief Wilder scanned the briefing room. "Send Sergeant Claybourne and two patrol cars initially and get Rawlingson and Finch to my office soon as. I'll give the troops a heads up and I'll see you and Sergeant Woods after I've spoken to Rawlingson," Said Wilder.

"Oh, one more thing Shads, see when it's an incident as serious as that, don't fanny about, come and find me and give me the facts straightaway! No delays, got it?" said Wilder.

"Got it, sir, Yep I've got it," said Phil but before he had finished replying Chief Wilder was already through the door and was about to address his officers. It was moments like this that Ewart Wilder lived for.

As Phil walked into Mike's office he was lifting the phone to make a call.

"Mike, can you put the phone down? It's important," said Phil.

"Sure," said Mike putting down the phone, "I was just going to give Susan a call. Is it news about Maisie?"

"Afraid so, Mike, and it's not good news. Ground staff at the school have found a body. It's Maisie Foster for sure, they said a green guitar case was lying nearby. Some fucker's hit her over the head, she's a real mess, Mike," said Phil barely able to control his anger.

"Holy shit, Phil, I was sure she was going to turn up. Oh shit, that poor girl, she was only fifteen. Her parents will be devastated," Mike put his hands over his face.

"It's tragic, Mike, just tragic. We've both got kids, my girls nearly thirteen, I can't begin to imagine," said Phil. "It says on the incident that they found her under some plastic sheets underneath the football stand. Looks like whoever did it tried to cover her up, might get some forensics," said Phil hopefully.

"Might be a long shot, Phil, it rained heavily through the night, but you never know," said Mike.

"Look, Mike, I know you want to speak to Susan, but you'd better be quick, Bull's looking for you and Charlie in his office now. Sorry, Mike, but you know what he's like. Here's the incident." Phil handed Mike some papers. "Not much on it at the moment, but you'd better read it before you see Bull."

"Susan's going to be devastated, Phil, I mean broken, she was close to those kids. I can't phone her now and then have to hang up, I'll call her when I'm finished with Bull," said Mike. "I need another favour, Phil, Charlie's not in yet, he usually drops the kids at school before he comes in, should be here any minute. Can you look out for him and give him the heads up before sending him to see the chief?"

"Will do, Mike, anything else you're needing just give me a shout," said Phil.

"Appreciate it, Phil, thanks."

The meeting with the chief didn't take long. At this stage there really wasn't much that could be said as there was so little information. As Mike and Charlie headed out the door Chief Wilder reminded them that he intended to visit the crime scene.

"I'll be down in an hour or so," said Wilder, "give you a chance to get the scene cordoned off and the doctor and forensics organised. If any press turns up just tell them to wait, I'll speak to them when I get down there," he added. "And remember, de-brief in the incident room at 1800 hrs, don't be late and I want everyone there, you hear me? You only go home when I say, I want this fucker caught."

"Well that was clear enough," said Charlie to Mike as the two of them headed downstairs.

"You know, he can do all the damn media he wants as far as I'm concerned. One less thing for us to worry about, just as long as he lets me get on with my job," said Mike.

"I don't think you need to worry on that score, boss, he hasn't been a detective for more than twelve years and even then, it was for less than a year. You know what's he like, he's a blowhard. If we keep him in the loop he'll stay out of it, but boy he can be one giant pain in the ass, can't he?" said Charlie.

"You're not wrong about that," said Mike with a knowing look. "Do me a favour Charlie and make me a coffee will you, I need to phone Susan right now and tell her what's happened."

Ten minutes later Charlie entered Mike's office carrying two mugs of coffee. "How did Susan take the news?" asked Charlie.

"Completely devastated, she can't believe it, but then I'm struggling to believe it too," said Mike. "She's phoning the headteacher to see if they want her to go across, she knows a lot of Maisie's friends through the music group, so she wanted to offer her support. What else can you do in circumstances like this?"

"I know, I think people just feel helpless. At least we've got the investigation to focus on, I always find that helps," said Charlie.

"Do you know it's more than three years since we had a murder in Fairlea?" said Mike.

"Really, I knew it had been a while but didn't think it was three years," said Charlie. "last one must have been when Cliff Yates shot his brother at the truck yard over the unpaid debt."

"That's the one," said Mike ruefully, "but I've got a feeling this one isn't going to be quite so straight-forward."

*

"Sir, can you park your car on the other side of the street?" said a young officer in uniform who was standing at the entrance to the Fairlea Hotel preventing any vehicles from entering the car park. "Sergeant Claybourne wants this whole area kept sterile because of its proximity to the crime scene," added the officer.

"Sure, no problem," said Mike as he turned the vehicle and parked across the street. "Looks like the uniforms have done a decent job with their cordon." Charlie nodded in agreement. A large area surrounding the football stand was now cordoned off with yellow barrier tape and uniformed officers were stationed at strategic points preventing any unauthorised access.

Mike waved to Sergeant Claybourne and indicated for him to come across.

"Aren't we just going in then?" asked Charlie innocently. "Think I'll need to send you on a scenes of crimes refresher," said Mike, "there will be a single point of entry into here so as not to disturb the scene any more than is necessary. At this moment, Charlie, I don't know where that is, so we better wait and let Sergeant Claybourne tell us, don't you think?"

"Sorry, boss," said an embarrassed Detective Finch. "Don't know what I was thinking of."

"Lesson learned, eh?" said Mike. "But I need you to switch on now, this is going to be a challenging enquiry and all eyes will be on us."

"Sure thing, Mike, it'll not happen again."

"Good timing, Mike," said Sergeant Martin Claybourne. "The medical examiners just arrived, and the district attorney is apparently on his way. Single path of entry is from the other side by the football pitch.

Thought that would be best as its where most of the foot traffic has been coming and going since they started to build the new stand" added the Sergeant.

"The rain last night made the footpath quite muddy, so you might want to put your boots on."

"Good work, Martin. So, what can you tell us?" asked Mike.

"I've been across and had a look, didn't need to check if the poor girl was dead or not, it's a devastating head injury she's suffered," said Sergeant Claybourne.

"What about the groundsman who found her? Have you had a chance to speak to him yet?" asked Mike.

"Yep, managed a quick word. His name's George Burroughs. Found her just over an hour ago when he and his team were coming to start work. One thing of interest he did say was that a large number of scaffolding poles are missing that were definitely here last night when they left," said Martin.

"Any idea how many have gone?" asked Mike.

"He says at least fifty, probably more," replied Martin.

Mike nodded as Charlie noted the information in his pocket book.

"That's interesting, anything else?" asked Mike.

"Couple of things. There is a pole lying on the ground quite near to the girl. It isn't piled neatly the way the others are. It's lying in shadow so it's difficult to see if it's got blood or anything else on it, but it looks like it might be the weapon," said Martin. "The only other thing that's immediately apparent is an empty half-bottle of Wild Turkey that's lying about 10 feet from the edge of the path. It's been exposed to last night's rain but might be of interest," added Martin.

"Oh, I nearly forgot, there's a pile of vomit a few feet from the girl's body, looks pretty fresh. I can't see any signs of vomit on the girl, so it might be the assailant's."

"Thanks, Martin, that seems pretty comprehensive and very helpful," said Mike. "You should have been a detective, you're wasted in uniform," added Mike with a hint of a smile.

"I'll speak to the doctor first and then we'll grab a word with the ground staff," said Mike to Charlie. "But for now, I need you to keep the chief happy while I speak to the doc," said Mike pointing over to where Chief Wilder was remonstrating with the young officer who was stoically trying to explain why he couldn't park his vehicle in the hotel car park.

*

It was just before nine when Josh approached the playing fields on his way to school. He hadn't slept at all since the police had woken him last night and told him that Maisie was missing. He felt agitated and anxious and had a queasy feeling in the pit of his stomach. None of this made any sense. Why would Maisie go missing? Last time they spoke she couldn't have been happier, he was the same. They had the concerts to look forward to and the long summer holidays after that. Josh couldn't think of a single reason why Maisie wouldn't have gone home.

As the path wound its way through the trees towards the football pitch Josh could see a police officer on the path about a hundred yards or so away. The officer was standing immediately in front of some yellow tape which was strung across the path. The tape appeared to continue to some trees that stood on rough ground to the right-hand side of the footpath. It was difficult to see but it then seemed to continue to the fence that encircled the football field. In the far distance Josh could see the football stand where a number of people appeared to be standing next to a small white tent.

"What's happened, officer? Is anything wrong?" asked Josh with a deep sense of unease.

"Sorry, I'm going to have to ask you to cut through the trees here onto Melville street. If you're headed for the school you'll be able to get in from there," said the officer.

Josh could feel his heart thumping and he was starting to sweat. He knew this wasn't right. Why was the path closed off? Why were so many police here? But it was the image of the white tent that sent his mind racing uncontrollably. One thought came crashing in on top of another and he felt overwhelmed and completely helpless, deep down he knew something dreadful had happened and he couldn't bare it. The tape and the white tent could only mean one thing, this was a crime scene. He starting to run through the trees and into the street beyond. Small knots of people stood speaking in hushed tones outside their houses and on street corners. Josh was oblivious to them all, he just wanted to reach the school and shut out the horror that was unfolding, he wanted to see Maisie and be done with this nightmare.

At the school teaching staff were positioned at each entrance and concerned parents stood huddled in small groups many protecting their children with a comforting arm.

It was Susan who saw Josh first. The call of his name stopped him dead in his tracks. He turned around and walked across to where she was standing, he buried his head in her shoulder and burst into tears. Her own voice trembling with emotion, Susan held the back of Josh's head and whispered, "It's okay to cry Josh, it's okay to cry.

*

"Cynthia, it's Anne Grey speaking, have you got a minute?" asked Anne who was phoning Cynthia from the kitchen of her house.

"Of course, Anne, good to hear from you. It's been a long time, what can I do for you?" replied Cynthia.

"Far too long," said Anne, "I'm really sorry about that, time just seems to disappear. Anyway, it's bad enough not having spoken to you, but yesterday I realised it's over a year since I saw Cathleen, I'm feeling ashamed to be honest."

"Don't be so hard on yourself, it's been a difficult time for all of us, it's easy to put it off and before you know it months have passed," said Cynthia sympathetically.

"I tried phoning Frank yesterday to see if it was alright for me to come over and visit, but I couldn't get a reply," said Anne.

"Ah, that's because they were away overnight for Cathleen's check-up in Charleston, she has to go once a year," said Cynthia.

"Oh, I see," said Anne. "Can I ask, do you usually still see her on a Saturday?"

"Try to as much as I can," said Cynthia. "I saw her last Saturday, she's really much the same as when you last saw her. Perhaps her walking's a little better, but still no speech or much movement on her right side.

I can't go tomorrow though, I said I'd take my niece shopping as it's her birthday next week," said Cynthia.

"Well then," said Anne, "perhaps this phone call has come at a good time. I could go tomorrow instead. Do you think Frank would have a problem with that?" asked Anne. "It would certainly salve my conscious if I went."

"Frank will be fine with that. Helps me too and it means Cathleen still gets a visit," said Cynthia. "I usually go around two and stay about an hour. She'll be pleased to see you. Frank says she doesn't recognise people or understand, but she definitely does. I can see it in her eyes and just occasionally she'll squeeze your hand. But please do go, Anne, it'll do you both good," said Cynthia.

"Thanks, Cynthia, I feel better about it already and that's just after this call. Listen we'll need to get together with Edna and have a night out, catch up with all the news. It's been too long," said Anne. "I'll be seeing Edna during the week, so I'll speak to her and get back to you."

"I'll look forward to that," said Cynthia, "hope it goes well tomorrow and thanks for the call."

*

Those assembled for the end of day de-brief in the incident room at Lewisburg Police Office watched the television intently.

"Very good interview, sir, if I might say so," said Sergeant Woods as he switched off the television. Several heads nodded in agreement, but Mike and Charlie stood motionless at the back of the room.

"Hopefully that will start to get the phones ringing, most people won't have seen the earlier broadcast but this one should catch them as they get home from work," added Sergeant Woods.

"Did we get any calls from the earlier showing?" asked Chief Wilder.

"Yep, a couple," said Sergeant Woods. "First on was Robert Chudley claiming he killed the girl. That's the third time he's done that. Last year he wanted to confess to the rape at Brooklands park and then he said he'd stolen all the fridges from the break in on the industrial estate. I've checked and he's still in the psychiatric unit at the hospital, so we can safely rule him out," said Sergeant Woods to ripples of laughter in the room.

"The one significant call was from Eddie Brew at the Fairlea Hotel. He's still checking the tape but says his security camera has picked up a white van leaving the hotel car park at 1755 hours yesterday. He said the tape is very jumpy but reckons that's just his machine playing up and not necessarily the tape," said Sergeant Woods. "I've sent Tony Whetton down to get it, he should be back with it anytime," he added.

Chief Wilder nodded in agreement. "Okay everyone, decent start to the enquiry so let's keep that going. Morning briefing here at 0730 hours tomorrow and then be ready to hit the ground running there will be plenty actions to follow up on. Mike, Charlie, Sergeant Woods see me in my office in five," said Wilder with his usual brusque tone.

As Mike and Charlie walked along the corridor Tony Whetton came bounding up the stairs.

"Is that the tape from the hotel?" asked Mike gesturing at the package Tony was holding in his hand.

"Yep, that's it," said an out of breath Tony.

"Have you looked at it?" asked Mike taking the package from Tony.

"Nope," said Tony, "there wasn't time. Anyhow, I thought you'd want to see it as soon as possible."

"That's great Tony many thanks," said Mike, "I'll see you tomorrow, 0730 sharp."

"Sure will, sir, see you then," said Tony who had decided to take the lift back down as he hadn't yet caught his breath.

Charlie switched on the monitor in Chief Wilder's office and inserted the tape.

"I fucking knew it, just knew it," said Wilder clenching his fist and punching the air.

On the screen as clear as day peering out from the windscreen of the van was Screech Jarret and his cohort Eustace Brownlie.

"Wow, that couldn't be clearer," said Sergeant Woods latching quickly on to the chief's sense of euphoria. "That artificial eye and stare gives him away every time, we might have struck lucky here."

"Re-wind it Charlie and play it again," said Wilder jubilantly. "Halle, fucking, lujah!" he yelped slapping Sergeant Woods on the back. Chief Wilder was almost beside himself with glee.

"They've been there stealing the scaffolding poles and been disturbed by Maisie Foster. They've panicked and one of those fuckwits has picked up a pole and battered her over the head with it," said Wilder. Sergeant Woods nodded his head in agreement.

"We just need to work out which one," added Chief Wilder.

Mike didn't say anything. He watched the tape again carefully while chewing on the end of his pencil. Finally, he spoke. "This is clearly significant, but if I can just add a word of caution."

"Oh, here we fucking go," said Wilder, "Detective Rawlingson's not buying it."

"I didn't say that," said Mike, "It's just that in all the years we've been locking up Screech and Brownie, it's never been for anything violent, not even once. It's always been for theft."

"First time for everything," said sergeant Woods.

"Exactly," said Wilder. "First action tomorrow, find those two sons of bitches and bring them in. We'll interview Brownlie first, he hasn't got the brains and will burst like a ripe peach."

"Nice metaphor, sir," said Sergeant Woods. Mike didn't say anything and behind Wilder's back Charlie just rolled his eyes and quietly shook his head.

Chapter 11

With the last of the post holes dug, Frank and Josh had started to erect the first few fence posts. Josh held each post steady as Frank poured the cement powder into the hole. He then poured water over the cement and prodded the hole with a stick to get rid of any air pockets. Using a spirit level, Josh checked that each post was vertical and in no time, they had the first three posts in place. As they were preparing to fix the next post, a white Buick coupe came up the farm track and parked a few yards away next to the hen coop.

"Hello, Frank," said Anne as she stepped out of the car, "I hope you don't mind me calling like this, but I was hoping to see Cathleen. Cynthia isn't able to come this afternoon, so I hoped I could visit instead. It's been such a long time since I've seen Cathleen and I feel terrible about that."

"That's alright," said Frank, "no need to apologise. It's nice to see you Anne, it has certainly been a while."

"As I say Frank, I'm sorry about that. I did try phoning on Thursday, but Cynthia said you had been at the hospital in Charleston. How's she doing now?"

"Much the same," said Frank, "no better, no worse." Doctors don't think her speech will return now it's been too long. Same with her paralysis, her right side is useless, although she can walk a little bit with help. She won't know you Anne, but you're welcome to visit, she's sitting on the porch. If you could encourage her to drink her glass of water that would be great. Doctor said she was a bit dehydrated and needed to up her fluid intake."

As they were talking Josh walked past carrying more bags of cement. If he had looked across Anne would have said something, but Josh seemed to be avoiding making any eye contact.

"Your son's a fine-looking boy," said Anne, "I know Cathleen is just so proud of him."

Frank nodded his head. "It's been a tough couple of days for him. The girl who was found murdered near the school was a friend of his, she played guitar with him in the music group, so he's pretty cut up about it as you can imagine," said Frank quietly making sure Josh didn't hear him.

"Oh, I'm so sorry Frank, that's just awful," said Anne. "I heard it on the news yesterday but had no idea she was a friend of Josh. The poor lad. Would it be better if I just went?" asked Anne.

"No, no, you weren't to know. Go and see Cathleen now you're here," said Frank. "I think keeping Josh occupied is the best thing at the moment, so if we've finished this fence there are some trees needing pruned in the bottom orchard which we might do after. If we're down there when you go can you just make sure Cathleen's in the shade, that would be great," said Frank.

"Of course, no problem," said Anne.

As she walked towards the porch Josh passed her again carrying more bags of cement. Anne looked at Josh closely, there was something different about him than when she'd seen him at Tuckahoe just two days ago. He was wearing a boiler suit today but that wasn't it. It suddenly struck her, it was his hair. It looked wavier and seemed to be a couple of inches longer. How strange, thought Anne, his hair couldn't have grown that much in two days, but unless he was wearing a wig, it sure looked like it had.

*

"Making coffee Charlie, you want one?" asked Mike as Charlie sat down at his desk by the window.

"Yeah, milk and one please," replied Charlie.

"Well, how did it go?" asked Mike.

"Fine, been a while since I've attended a PM but always find them fascinating. Just a verbal update for now, Doctor Roberts says he'll have the written report by tomorrow," said Charlie.

"Okay, that's good," said Mike, "so what's he saying?"

"Cause of death is two blows to the left side of the head. Doc says the temporal plates were shattered and that's lead to a massive brain haemorrhage. Skull is thin there; poor girl didn't stand a chance," said Charlie. "I took along a scaffolding pole identical to the one we've sent to forensics like you suggested. The doc says he's ninety-nine percent sure that's been the murder weapon. You can see the round shape of the pole where it's hit her head," he added.

"Did he find any other injuries?" asked Mike.

"Only other thing was small fingertip bruising on her left breast, but nothing other than that," said Charlie.

"Other than the bruising any other evidence of a sexual assault?" asked Mike.

"Nope," said Charlie. "No injuries at all on her lower body and she was still wearing her underwear. Doc says she definitely wasn't raped."

"A small mercy I suppose, thanks for the update," said Mike. "We'll go and personally brief Wilder and I'll give a brief summary at the evening de-brief."

"Anything of interest come in since I was away?" asked Charlie.

"Surprisingly yes," said Mike.

"Two potential witnesses. Times are a little sketchy, but they seem to be corroborating each other. Elliot Manning, you know from Manning's pharmacy on the main street, contacted the incident room saying he saw Screech and Brownie leaving the car park of the Fairlea Hotel in a white van. Now, we already knew that, but the other thing of interest is he's saying he saw Josh Heggerty standing near the football stand at around the same time," said Mike. "Says he was smoking a cigarette!"

"Huh," said Charlie, "I take it he must know Josh if he's naming him? Anyway, that's going to need followed up, so who's the other witness?"

"Eddie Brew's mother, Elsie," said Mike. "She lives at the hotel and was sitting at her window around six last night going through the docket box of pills that Elliot had dropped off. From what I've been told her room looks directly onto some trees and the football stand. Eddie says she saw a young guy with blond hair hanging about the stand, and he says she saw a young dark-haired girl come down the path around the same time who then cut across the rough ground towards the stand where the male had been standing. She says the girl was carrying some sort of bag."

"Did she mention if she saw the male and the girl together?" asked Charlie.

"Didn't say so in the message that was passed to me," replied Mike, "but we'll obviously have to check that out."

"Hum," said Charlie, "I suppose the bag could just as easily have been a guitar case. What age is Eddie's mom, must be getting on some, is she a credible witness?" he asked making notes on a pad on his desk.

"Same thought went through my head," said Mike, "I spoke to Phil Coutts who knows Eddie well, says his mom is certainly in her early nineties. But according to Phil there's nothing wrong with her memory as far as he is aware."

"The fact that Manning's naming the male as being Josh Heggerty is hugely significant. He could, of course, have mistaken him for someone else. We just don't know yet," added Mike.

"Grab yourself a quick sandwich and then we'll head over to see Manning, if we have time we'll try and speak to Mrs Brew as well," said Mike.

"God, I hope Josh has nothing to do with this, Susan would be heartbroken. She already is about Maisie, but this would be too much," said Mike. "Same for the parents, it would just add to their misery. However, let's stay positive we're a long way from that at the moment," said Mike.

"Also, with the blood that was on the pole and goodness knows what might be on her dress, the forensic report could take us in another direction altogether, who knows?" said Charlie trying his best not to jump to any conclusions.

"Yep, spot on, Charlie, I've been involved in too many investigations to make premature judgements on what might have happened. We need to check out those witnesses, then things might be clearer."

Charlie was stuffing some statement paper into his folder while eating his sandwich and trying desperately to avoid getting relish on his shirt when the phone rang. Mike smiled and told Charlie that Susan was always saying that men were not genetically programmed to multi task, so he had better not even think about answering it. "You just concentrate on finishing that sandwich, lucky that's a short-sleeved shirt, it's all over your arm!" said Mike shaking his head

Mike lifted the receiver, "Mike Rawlingson speaking. Oh, hi Phil, what's happening?"

The smile on Mike's face was quickly replaced by a frown. Charlie looked on watchfully sensing that something wasn't right.

"You have got to be fucking joking, Phil, are they that stupid? Don't answer that, clearly, they fucking are. What on earth were they thinking of?" said Mike angrily, and with a face the colour of puce.

"Don't you apologise, Phil, it's not your fault, who accepted the arrest?"

"I know he's new in that role, but for fuck's sake Phil, why didn't he ask you or anyone else for that matter?"

"Oh, that's just marvellous, you've answered my next question. So not only does Wilder know, he's high fiving them in his office as we speak."

"No, no just leave it, Phil," said Mike, "I'll brief Charlie and then we'll go and see Wilder. And one more thing, don't let Chris or Angela leave the office, I'm going to need them to go and get a couple of witness statements right away so can you find them and send them up? I'll phone you back in ten when I'm finished with that halfwit upstairs."

"I'm guessing what you're going to tell me isn't good news then," said Charlie knowing that was going to prove to be somewhat of an understatement.

"Those clowns, Mitchell and Price have gone and arrested Screech and Brownie for Murder and the duty officer has accepted the arrest and booked them through!" said Mike incredulously. "Phil says they heard Woods banging on about what Wilder had said yesterday after we'd seen the tape and how Screech and Brownie were responsible. So, they thought they'd make a name for themselves and go and arrest them. Doesn't matter that they didn't have the evidence, oh no, just as long as it would impress the chief! Pair of fucking clowns," said Mike slamming the drawer on the desk.

"They were the ones laughing at Wilder's jokes and smiling inanely whenever he spoke at the de-brief, they are so far up Wilder's ass it isn't true," said Charlie. "So, what are we going to do now. If they've been arrested, we'll have to interview them, won't we?"

"Yep, we will," said Mike. "But before we do we'll go and rain on Wilder's parade because I think we can prove that Screech and Brownie didn't kill Maisie Foster." Mike looked at Charlie knowingly.

"Funny that, Mike, I was thinking just the same thing," said Charlie with a grin.

Mike pursed his lips and gently nodded. "Go on then detective, impress me. Why aren't they the killers?" asked Mike.

"Alright, I'll tell you," said Charlie. "Remember you said to me that Mrs Brew had seen a male at the football stand from her bedroom window? Well, you also said she saw a girl cutting across the path around the same time"

"That's correct, I'm with you so far," said Mike.

"Well we know from the tape and from what Elliot Manning's saying that Screech and Brownie were driving out the car park when he arrived," continued Charlie.

"Okay, go on," said Mike who was listening intently.

"So, here's the rub," said Charlie, "if Mrs Brew was at her table checking her pills when she saw the girl coming down the path, then Screech and Brownlie can't be the killers as they'd already left in the van before Elliot Manning had delivered Mrs Brew's prescription."

"Bingo," said Mike with a rueful smile. "The times don't stack up. If she got her pills after they had already left, they can't have killed her. I'll make a detective of you yet."

"As long as that is the sequence of events we can prove it wasn't them. I'll guarantee they stole the scaffolding poles though," said Mike.

"Right, here's the plan, we'll brief Chris and Angela and they can head off and get proper statements from Elsie Brew and Elliot Manning. We'll go up and ruin the chief's day and then we'll have to think about interviewing Screech and Brownie, but not before we've had confirmation back from Chris and Angela."

Charlie smiled and nodded at his boss. "Don't know how you put up with it, Mike, must be a real pain in the ass having to take orders from a boss who doesn't have half your brains."

Mike chuckled and nodded his head. "Can be sometimes," said Mike, "but sure makes it easier to manage your manager when you're brighter than them, and believe me, that's important too."

"So, what are you telling me Mike?" asked Chief Wilder who had clearly had the wind taken out of his sails by Mike and Charlie's revelation.

"Sir, we will have to interview both of them about the murder," said Mike, "as that's what they've been arrested for and anyway Lawyers have been contacted so it needs dealing with properly. Screech isn't stupid, he'll deny the murder of course, not unreasonably so, since he didn't do it, but he might well confess to the theft. If that proves to be the case, he can be charged with the theft and released, and we might just get away with this fuck up."

"Alright, Mike, that's enough. They were just showing willing, it's good to have keen officers," said Wilder desperately trying to find something positive to say.

"No use being keen if you're also incompetent. Actually, that might overstate the abilities of Wayne Mitchell and Jerry Price," said Mike sardonically.

"That's enough, Rawlingson, you've made your point. I said I would speak to them and I will. You just make sure we get this enquiry back on track. Pity we don't have the forensic report though, when is it due?" asked Wilder.

"Tuesday or Wednesday at the latest," replied Mike. "Now if only we had waited to see what it said before we went and arrested our suspects..." before Mike could finish Wilder exploded with rage. "You think you're so fucking smart Rawlingson don't you?" spluttered Wilder. "Well you better be right about this cause if you're wrong you'll be back in uniform before you know it. Do you hear me?"

"Loud and clear sir, loud and clear," said Mike getting up and heading for the door.

"Jeezo Boss that was pushing it a little," said Charlie as they waited for the lift. "What if we are wrong?"

"I can't help it he's such a monumental pain in the butt," said Mike. "Anyway, we're not wrong, Charlie, you took the call from Angela, she's confirmed the times, and Elsie Brew saw Maisie after they left the car park in their van, so they can't be the killers. Angela says Elsie's going to be a great witness, she might be frail but mentally she's really sharp, so relax."

"I know you're right, but it might make our lives a little easier if you laid off Bull a bit," said Charlie trying to be diplomatic.

"Don't worry about it, it'll be fine. But I'll be a bit more guarded in future, I appreciate you've got a career to think about," said Mike.

"Now you make me sound like a pussy," said Charlie feeling slightly deflated.

"Now that is garbage, listen, you wouldn't be working with me if I didn't think you were any good. So come on, we've got two murder suspects to interview," said Mike with a wink. "First rule of detective work, Officer Finch, always keep an open mind."

Charlie smiled to himself, there was no one better to work with than Mike Rawlingson, even if he did like to antagonise senior officers. At least life was never dull he thought as he pushed the button for the ground floor and the custody suite.

"Just had a thought Charlie," said Mike as they headed along the corridor to the interview room. "Slight change of plan. I think we'll interview Screech first, something in my water tells me he might want to tell us about the whereabouts of some scaffolding poles."

"Yep," said Charlie nodding in agreement, "I think you may just be right."

"I'm hoping the pair of them may have seen whoever murdered Maisie hanging about. We know they were at the locus shortly before she died so you never know," said Mike.

"Do you think they would tell us even if they had? They're not exactly on great terms with the police, not after the way they've been persecuted by Bull over the years," added Charlie.

"That's true," said Mike, "but you know, deep down I think they've both got a conscious and are decent enough people. I always think the pair of them are now just stuck being criminals, they've got no other way of getting a job or earning money. I'm pretty sure they will be appalled at what's happened, so if they do know something I think they would tell us, I sure hope so anyway."

*

Screech was sitting on a wall across the street smoking a cigarette when Eustace emerged from the front door of the police station. Spotting his friend sitting on the wall, Brownie waved, and his face broke into a broad grin.

"What you so pleased about?" said Screech suspiciously, he always found it disconcerting when Eustace appeared pleased with himself. Experience had taught Henry that confidence in his friend was almost always misplaced.

"Didn't say a word, Henry," said Eustace with a grin a Cheshire cat would have been proud of.

"Nada, zilch, nothing," said Eustace proudly. "I didn't say anything, not one word."

Henry looked at his friend quizzically. "Didn't say anything, huh?" said Henry in a deadpan voice. "First time for everything Eustace, bet McKie was amazed?"

"He sure was. Said in all the time he's been my lawyer he's never known me to say nothing," said Eustace who was now wondering what was going on. Henry didn't seem to be too pleased.

"I don't understand, Henry, I said nothing. You're always telling me to keep my mouth shut and say nothing, so I did what you said, I didn't say didly," said Eustace. "And now you don't seem too pleased 'bout that."

Henry took the last draw of his cigarette before stubbing it out on the top of the wall. He fixed Eustace with a cold gaze, narrowing his good eye to a slit. Henry leant forward and whispered menacingly to his friend, "Just as well one of us has a brain," said Henry.

Eustace didn't have the slightest idea what Henry was on about, but it wasn't going to be long before he found out.

"I've got to tell you, Eustace, I sang like a bird," said Henry quietly, "coughed it all up, got it off my chest."

"You mean you told them we stole them poles?" said Eustace who still didn't understand what Henry was on about.

"Yep, even told them that we took them to Arnold's and sold them for $300."

Eustace stood shaking his head. "We'll go to jail for this one Henry, and it's gonna be your fault, I didn't say nothing!" said Eustace with a pained expression on his face.

"You're probably right for once, Eustace, expect we'll go to jail for it, I'm guessing three months maybe six, who knows," replied Henry.

"But I'll tell you this, Eustace Brownlie, that's a hell of a sight better than the thirty years they were trying to pin on us for the murder of that girl!" snapped Henry.

"But we never killed that girl, Henry," said Eustace who was still struggling to work out why his friend had confessed to stealing the scaffolding poles.

"I can see you've still not quite got this, Eustace," said Henry, "so I'll explain again."

"Wilder and those cops thought we'd murdered that girl and arrested us. It wasn't looking too clever as we were there close to the time she must have been killed. I told them that we'd stolen the poles to prove we didn't kill the girl, are you with me?"

"I think so," said Eustace scratching his head.

"They were asking questions about the time we were at the football stand, they knew we were there 'cause they've got a tape from the hotel security camera with us in the van, comprende?" asked Henry.

Eustace nodded.

"Well, I knew if I told them we sold the poles to Arnold they would get cops to check that out. Now if you were paying any attention when we were there you would remember Arnold telling us that he has to record the exact time and date of any sale in his register, also the type of metal it was and how much he paid for it. Well my friend, that helped save our bacon, cause the time Arnold recorded in his book meant we couldn't have been in Fairlea at the time the girl was murdered," said Henry.

"Ah, I see what you mean," said Eustace, "by admitting we stole the poles you proved that we didn't kill the girl."

"Exactly," said Henry who was just relieved that the penny had finally dropped.

"That was real clever, Henry, real clever," said Eustace patting his friend on the shoulder.

"I'll remember that next time we find ourselves in bother," said Eustace trying to sound intelligent.

Henry just shook his head.

"Come on, Eustace, let's go to Bursley's and have ourselves a beer," said Henry.

"Good idea," said Eustace who never declined an invitation for a beer.

"What, another good idea?" said Henry sarcastically, "that's the second one I've had today then."

Eustace looked puzzled, "The second one, what was the first then?" asked Eustace innocently.

"Oh, give me strength," said Henry looking skywards, "give me strength."

*

224

"Angela, Chris, listen in for a moment, will you?" said Mike who was pouring himself a coffee in the detective's office. "The interviews went pretty much as we expected. Well apart from Brownlie keeping completely schtum. That threw old McKie, he didn't know what the hell was going on. Anyway, luckily Screech isn't stupid, he could see that admitting to the theft was going to help them prove they didn't murder Maisie. I'm also sure if he'd seen anyone at the locus he would have told us, but that drew a blank," explained Mike.

"They've been charged with the theft and have now been released," added Charlie.

"Okay, before we go and update Wilder, just wanted to go over some things from the forensic report that's just arrived," said Mike opening a buff coloured folder on the desk.

"First up: the murder weapon was the scaffolding pole as we suspected. They found some of Maisie's blood and hair on the end near to the hinge. Also, there are saying that there are two types of blood on the pole. One is Masie's and the other we can presume is our murderer."

"That must mean the killer was cut somehow," said Angela, "poor girl must have put up some fight trying to defend herself."

"It certainly looks that way," said Mike. "They found blood under her fingernails on her left hand and the blood's not hers. It's not Screech or Brownlie's either, neither of them had a mark on them."

"Maybe she managed to scratch her attacker, that would explain the blood under her fingernails. Hopefully she got him on the face, might make him easier to find," said Chris.

"Lots of assumptions there, including that it's a male who's attacked her. We don't know yet so let's not start assuming anything," added Mike. "While we're talking about blood, the other thing of interest is there are two blood types on Maisie's dress as well. Not specks either, fairly large spots of blood, as if the blood has dripped onto her dress."

"Anything in the toxicology report to suggest that she'd been drinking or had been sick?" asked Charlie.

"No, nothing," said Mike. "And other than the head injury and fingertip bruising on her breast no other injuries. Oh, I nearly forgot, they didn't find any fingerprints on the plastic sheeting that was covering her body, or on the whisky bottle. Alright, that's about it, anything to update us on regarding your door to door before I go and see Wilder?"

"Turned up one that looks interesting boss," said Chris. "Delivery boy by the name of Nelson Parker, works for old man Latimer at the convenience store. He was on his bike making a delivery to a Mr Rossiter who lives on the farm next to the Heggertys'. Anyway, he was pushing his bike along the track when he says he saw Josh Heggerty standing on a hill near to a large chestnut tree. The boy says Josh looked as though he had a nasty cut on his hand as the cloth wrapped round it was soaked in blood. Knew it was significant after you mentioned that Elliot Manning was claiming he'd seen Josh Heggerty at the football stand around the time we know that the girl was killed," Chris continued.

Mike sat with his elbows on the table, his chin rested on his clasped hands as he listened carefully to what Chris was saying.

"Good work, folks," said Mike stroking his chin. "Does the boy know Josh Heggerty? Also, what time is this supposed to have happened?"

"He's not a friend but he does know him. Says Josh is two years above him at school," replied Chris, "as for times the boy is pretty adamant it was between twenty-five and half past six. Says he was home by twenty to seven and it's three miles all downhill from the Heggertys' place to his house."

"Okay fine," said Mike, "I want you to get a full statement from the boy before end of play today, understand?"

Chris and Angela nodded. "On it now, boss," said Chris.

"I want that statement and the ones from Manning and Elsie Brew on my desk by five. I want to read the three of them together. The whole enquiry looks like it might depend on their testimony," said Mike.

"I take it we're going to bring Josh in for interview soon?" said Charlie. Mike gave a resigned nod. "The evidence is starting to mount up, there might be a reasonable explanation for all this but at the moment I don't see it," said Mike.

"We'll not be bringing him in till tomorrow at the earliest. We'll have the blood results back for Screech and Brownie tomorrow, so that should completely exonerate them. Only then will we think about bringing Josh in," added Mike.

"I know it doesn't look great, Mike, but with any luck a blood test will show it wasn't him," said Charlie trying to be supportive.

Mike looked at Charlie ruefully. "Another lesson about policing, Charlie. I know you're saying it for my benefit and I'm not lying when I say Susan will be in pieces if it turns out to be Josh, but it's not my job or yours to make any value judgement on that," said Mike. "If the evidence is there to prove Josh did it then so be it. Justice is what we're about, Charlie, seeking justice for parents who've lost their daughter in the most tragic of circumstances. So, try and remember that. Sentiment, or how I or my wife feels about this enquiry, is not relevant. Finding the guilty party is all this is about, nothing more, nothing less," added Mike as he gathered together a pile of papers from his desk.

"Understood, Mike," said Charlie quietly once again finding himself in awe of his boss. That was just another reason to respect Mike Rawlingson. He was principled, fair and unwaveringly honest. Worlds apart from the megalomaniac chief of police who resided upstairs. I know which of those two I'm having as a role model, thought Charlie as he followed Mike out of the office. And it's not Bull Wilder.

"By the way, Charlie," said Mike as the two detectives climbed the stairs that led to the chief's corridor. "Are you still doing your running?" Charlie stopped on the stairs and looked at Mike with a puzzled expression.

"That's a bit left field, Mike, what's that got to do with anything?" replied Charlie.

Mike smiled. "Yep, bit of a strange question but I need to know if you're still doing your running, you used to be really good," he said.

"Sure, still doing a bit, but not as much as I used to, two or three times a week maximum when time allows," replied Charlie who was still none the wiser as to why Mike needed to know.

"What was your last 10k time?" asked Mike.

Charlie thought for a moment. "Must have been the White Sulphur Springs race last month, finished in about thirty-nine minutes, that's nearly a minute and a half down on my best though."

"I'm impressed," said Mike a chuckle, "it's about twenty minutes faster than I could manage."

"Look, boss, gonna tell me what this has to do with the enquiry? 'Cause at the moment I don't have a clue what you're on about," said Charlie.

"Alright detective, I need you to bring your running gear to work with you tomorrow," said Mike. "We're going to carry out a little experiment."

"Okay," said Charlie, "but I'm still not sure I'm following you."

"Remember Chris said that the delivery boy, sorry can't recall his name,"

"Nelson Parker," replied Charlie.

"Yep, Nelson Parker. Well Chris said he was sure he saw Josh at the farm between six twenty-five and six thirty. From Elsie Brew and Elliot Manning's statements we know it was around six when they saw the boy who we think might be Josh at the football stand."

"Ah, I see what you're getting at," said Charlie interrupting Mike, "You want to see if it was possible to get back to the farm by the time Nelson Parker says he saw him."

"Exactly that," said Mike.

"It's a good three miles, maybe a bit more and nearly all of it is up hill. While it could be done, you'd need to be a pretty reasonable runner," said Charlie. "And also, he was wearing jeans, so that wouldn't make it any easier. Perhaps he took his bike!"

"Yeah, I did wonder that myself, but according to Susan Josh always walked to practice and usually left with Maisie and her little sister Becca in tow. Difficult to cycle with a guitar case and apparently Josh always took his home as he wanted to practice. Also, I know Josh was a very good athlete. Susan told me that he'd given it up to concentrate on his guitar, don't think his father was best pleased. But forget about the bike at the moment, I need you to run it. It will give us a good indication if it could be done in the timeframe we'll looking at. So, no beers after work tonight, you hear me," said Mike with a wry smile.

"Fat chance of that," said Charlie, "the Mrs would have a fit if I was drinking after work midweek, grounds for divorce that is!"

Charlie had never seen Chief Wilder like this before. If he didn't know better, he could have easily been seduced into thinking that the man sat before him listening intently to what Mike Rawlingson was telling him was a reasonable, fair minded individual and a good listener to boot. Listening to the conversation it was apparent to Charlie that Chief Wilder had been chastened by the cock up that had led to the premature arrest of Screech and Brownie. Furthermore, it was obvious from his comments that Wilder was desperately trying to avoid any more mishaps with this enquiry. Crikey, thought Charlie, if I didn't know better you might think that Wilder was being pleasant to Mike. This sudden onset of bon ami was leaving Charlie feeling decidedly uneasy, a leopard like Wilder never changed his spots, so now was not the time to be caught with your guard down. Charlie listened carefully to every word that was said, he wouldn't trust Wilder as far as he could throw him, he was as slippery as a snake and definitely one to be watched.

"Yes, I remember Cathleen Heggerty well, it was Shads and me who attended the accident when Susan and Cathleen Heggerty rescued the baby. Long time ago now. I'd heard from Mrs Wilder that Cathleen had a stroke, now this eh? Funny how tragedy seems to follow some people," said Wilder leaning back in his leather swivel chair clasping his hands behind his head.

"It's far from certain that it is Josh, sir, he's never been in any trouble before, so completely out of character," said Mike. "But we now have two eye witnesses who would appear to place him at the locus around the time of the murder, and Nelson Parker's statement is clearly important too. The cut on Josh's hand would help to explain the blood on the pole and on Maisie's dress," added Mike.

"Yes, yes of course, Mike, I wasn't suggesting he was guilty, but clearly, you'll want to bring him in for interview," said Wilder.

"Absolutely," said Mike, "we'll bring him in, hear his side of the story and get a blood sample from him. That will be crucial to this enquiry. That and an ID parade. If Elsie Brew and Elliot Manning pick him out at the parade, then the evidence might become overwhelming."

"Agreed," said Chief Wilder, "and from what you tell me that's likely to happen. Elliot Manning named him for goodness sake and if what Shads told me about Mrs Brew is true, there is every chance she will pick him out as well."

"There is one thing that doesn't add up or support the theory that Josh did it," said Mike. Charlie leant

231

forward a little to ensure he heard this properly. He hadn't discussed anything with Mike that threw any doubt onto the possibility that Josh had killed Maisie.

"Oh, and what's that?" said Wilder who was curious as to what Mike was going to say.

"It may not be significant, but we have two witness statements from people who said they were walking on the path at about six, or shortly after. One said they were very near to the playing fields and the other was about a quarter of a mile down from the bridge at the Haney Creek, the thing is neither of them saw anyone remotely similar to Josh on the path at that time," said Mike.

"Maybe he took another route home, or perhaps he didn't go home?" said Wilder.

Charlie smiled to himself, Wilder clearly hadn't been listening closely enough.

"Well, if we're going to believe Nelson Parker, and I've no reason to doubt him by the way, Josh was back at the farm by six twenty-five or thereabouts, and to do that he either ran or perhaps cycled home, yet nobody saw him. I just find it a little strange that's all. When we bring him in for interview we'll obviously ask him about it, but of course he may well deny being anywhere near there at all," said Mike.

"Suppose there could be several reasons why they didn't notice him if he had been there, who knows?" said Wilder, "but any court case won't stand or fall on that." Mike shrugged his shoulders and nodded, "Just thought it was interesting that's all".

"Okay, Mike, Charlie, thanks for the update. Keep me in the loop regarding any developments, especially regards bringing in young Heggerty for interview."

"That was just weird," said Charlie as he and Mike walked back down the stairs to their office. "Never seen the chief so mild mannered before. Not sure I like it, I keep waiting for him to revert to type and start growling."

Mike laughed. "Remember what I told you, you need to learn how to manage your manager. You'll need to get yourself a good psychology book, you've got twenty years ahead of you in this job, you've got to understand when someone's playing mind games with you. Anyway, more importantly that's enough for today, time to go home. Don't forget your running gear, we'll do it after the morning briefing if nothing urgent has come in," said Mike patting Charlie on the back.

Charlie gave a little groan, "I'm not looking forward to it, I'm feeling under pressure already. At this moment a pile of paperwork seems more appealing than running three miles uphill against the clock."

"Relax, will you? Nothing to it, it'll be a breeze," said Mike showing his younger colleague no sympathy at all.

"That's easy for you to say," said Charlie, "I take it you'll be driving the car to the finish?"

"How perceptive of you, Charlie, I'll make a detective of you yet," said Mike grabbing his car keys and putting on his jacket. "I'll see you tomorrow and don't be late."

By the time Mike arrived home it was after seven. "Your dinner's in the oven," shouted Susan who was sitting in the den checking Keegan's arithmetic homework. "I'm never sure when you'll get home these days, so Keegan and I have already eaten, hope you don't mind."

"Not a problem," said Mike, "how was your day?"

"Fine I suppose given the circumstances. I had a talk with Stuart Crawford after school and we've decided to cancel the concert now. It wouldn't be appropriate to carry on and I don't think the kids' hearts would be in it anyway, so better to make that decision now," said Susan.

"I think that's the right decision, Susan. Maisie's sister being part of the group, it would be too raw, too emotional, it's definitely the right call in my opinion," said Mike as he lifted his plate out of the oven with a dish towel. "Yikes that's hot," he said putting the plate down on a mat on the table. "Listen, before I eat this I need to tell you something. Can you come and sit down for a moment?"

A concerned frown came over Susan's face, "What is it, is everything alright?"

Mike looked lovingly at his wife, he knew what he was about to say would upset her, but it needed to be said and it needed to be now.

"Look, Susan, from a professional point of view I shouldn't be telling you this, but these are strange circumstances and you're going to need to know," said Mike in a serious voice. Susan looked worried as she pulled up a chair.

"I don't like the sound of this Mike, what is it?" There was a pleading in Susan's voice that was reflected in her eyes. Tiny tears were already rolling down her cheeks as her husband started to speak.

"There's no easy way to tell you this, Susan, but I'm going to have to bring in Josh for interview. I'm not saying he's responsible at this moment, but I have evidence that means I must bring him in and interview

234

him as a suspect." Before he had finished speaking Susan had started to sob uncontrollably.

Mike put his arm around his wife and gently kissed the back of her neck. This was a unique set of circumstances as far as Mike was concerned. Never before had he been leading an enquiry where a member of his own family had been involved with both the victim and now possibly the accused. This would never happen in Chicago. If it did the enquiry would be taken off you and given to someone else. But in Lewisburg, Greenbrier County that wasn't an option. There was no one else to lead the enquiry.

"It might all prove to be fine," said Mike trying to reassure his wife, "Josh might have a cast iron alibi and it's quite possible everything can be reasonably explained. But for now, I'm duty bound to interview him. Now I know you wouldn't anyway, but I've got to ask you not to speak to anyone about this. And I mean no-one. You can't speak to Josh or Becca or anyone else. If you did, I would lose my job and the investigation would be compromised. I'm sorry I had to tell you this, but I couldn't see any other way around it," said Mike who could see how much this was hurting Susan.

"Of course, I won't," spluttered Susan as she dried her eyes with a handkerchief. But I can't believe for one second that Josh would do anything to harm Maisie, they were such good friends. This nightmare just seems to get worse, Mike, I don't know if I can stand much more."

"I know how difficult this is for you," said Mike rubbing the back of Susan's shoulders. "I won't be interviewing Josh before Friday. I wondered if it might be a good idea for you and Keegan to go up to the lodge for the weekend. Maybe see if Colette's around. I'm going to have to work some long hours and it might be easier for all of us if you could get away for a couple of days."

Susan turned around, looked at Mike and nodded. She knew he was right. For all her despair she understood that Mike had his job to do and there was no one she would trust more to do that job properly. Her husband's integrity was impeccable and even in her sorrow Susan knew that Mike would treat Josh fairly and with the upmost respect. That at least was some consolation at this horrendous time. Her love for her husband had never wavered since the day that they married. Now, during such crushing sadness, that love was deep and unyielding and that gave her some comfort.

"Who are the flowers from?" asked Mike who had just seen the bouquet of daffodils and pink tulips that were sitting in a vase by the sink.

"They're not for me," said Susan, "I bought them for Maisie's mom and dad. If I felt up to it, I was going to hand them in with a card. They'll keep another day though, I'll hand them in on Friday when I leave for the lodge."

"That would be nice," said Mike, "that would be really nice."

At 0830 hrs the following morning, Mike and Charlie were parked in the car park adjacent to the school's playing fields.

"I'm going to do a lap of the track and some stretches first," said Charlie who had his foot on the tailgate of the car tying the shoelaces of his running shoes. "Don't want to pull a muscle so I'd better warm up properly."

"Fine, take your time," said Mike sipping his coffee and taking a bite of his doughnut. Mike raised his cup in the direction of Charlie, "perks of the job for those of us who are no longer athletes."

Charlie gave a sigh and shook his head. "Don't know why I let you talk me into this," he said as he started to jog round the track.

"Because I'm your boss and you're supposed to do what your boss says, didn't they teach you that at detective school?" shouted Mike.

"Funny, I must have missed that class," said Charlie as he completed his lap. Standing with his legs straight he bent down and put his head on his knees, "Always stretch the hamstrings Mike, those and the calf muscles are the ones you're most likely to pull."

"I'll take your word for that," replied Mike. "Now are you about ready to go?" Charlie gave a perfunctory nod. "Let's do this," he said.

"Right, before you start remember to stay on the path and stop at the road end leading up to Dararra Farm, I don't want Josh, his father or anyone else for that matter seeing us, got that?" Said Mike.

"Got it," said Charlie. And with that he was off and running. Mike looked at his watch, it was eight forty-five, might as well take a few minutes to enjoy this coffee he thought. It will take Charlie at least twenty minutes to reach the bridge and the road end, so no need to hurry.

Mike was sitting on the bridge at the Haney Creek when Charlie came into sight. The last few hundred yards to the bridge were probably the steepest, a fact confirmed by the pained expression on Charlie's face that was now the colour of a ripe tomato. By the time

Charlie reached the bridge he was exhausted. Bent over with his hands leaning on the bridge, he tried to speak but no words came out. His chest heaved repeatedly as he tried to catch his breath, the yellow cotton singlet he was wearing clung to the contours of his torso and was soaked through with the sweat of his labours.

"Just over twenty-three minutes," said Mike approvingly, "a mere bagatelle! Told you it wouldn't be that difficult."

Charlie tilted his head towards his boss, the expletive he wanted to respond with just wouldn't come out he was so tired. He was just grateful he hadn't been sick, it had been a while since Charlie had put so much effort into a run and felt so, badly.

"We could probably add another four minutes or so to get you to the top of the farm track, can you see the top of that tree sticking up in the distance, that's the tree Nelson Parker says Josh was standing under when he saw him. So, all in I reckon that would have taken you roughly twenty-seven minutes. It's definitely possible for Josh to get from the locus to the farm in the timeframe we're looking at," Said Mike.

*

"Who was that on the phone?" asked Josh, as he removed his boots at the front door having just finished feeding the hogs.

"You're not going to believe this," said his father starting to laugh. "That was your Uncle George over in Hinton phoning. He just got his landline connected today and that was his first ever call. I've been on at him for years to get a phone installed and now he's finally gone and done it!"

"Well I'll be darned," said Josh, "Uncle George finally taking steps to join the twentieth century, he'll be getting a colour T.V next."

"Shouldn't think so," laughed Frank. "Took him seventeen years to succumb to getting the phone, he won't think about a television for a good while yet. I'm just glad we can now get in contact with him, I always worried something would happen to him and he wouldn't be able to contact anyone to get help. It's a weight off my mind that's for sure."

It was strange but in the days after Maisie's tragic death, Josh's relationship with his father had improved immeasurably. They were getting on much better than they had in months and Josh was glad that he'd been able to keep busy by helping his father around the farm.

He hadn't felt able to return to school yet but as tomorrow was Friday, he would see how he felt over the weekend, before hopefully making a return on Monday. Well that was the plan anyway.

*

At eight o'clock on Friday morning Susan was getting ready to leave for work.

"I'll phone you tonight when I get to the lodge," said Susan. "I'm going to pick Keegan up straight from school and then head up, we'll stop for some food in Petersburg. We'll take our time there's no hurry getting up there."

"When are you seeing Colette?" asked Mike.

"She's coming for lunch at the lodge tomorrow," said Susan. "She's bringing her new beau," added Susan with a smile. "His name's Derek Meeler, I remember him from school, he was the year above us. Nice guy.

239

Apparently, he's working at the timber mill in Martinsburg. Anyway, he's into fishing so he's going to take Keegan out for a couple of hours while Colette and I drink wine and have a catch up."

"Sounds good," replied Mike who was now rummaging through the cupboard under the stairs.

"What are you looking for now?" asked Susan, who was waiting at the front door and keen to head off to work.

"My fishing rod for Keegan, it's in here somewhere," said Mike who now had the hall floor covered in suit cases, a toolbox and the vacuum cleaner.

"Don't worry about that," said Susan, "Colette says Derek is going to supply all the gear, one less thing for me to remember."

"Talking of remembering, have you got the flowers?" asked Mike who was randomly stuffing the toolbox and cases back into the cupboard.

"Gosh, just as well you said, I would have been away without them," said Susan as she dashed back to the kitchen to pick them up. "Too many things going on in my head just now, don't seem to be concentrating very well."

Mike hugged his wife. "Please take care driving up that road, I need you and Keegan back in one piece. And please pass on my condolences when you see the Fosters."

"I'll do that," said Susan getting into her car, "and remind Keegan he's to be ready to go straight after school."

"Right, Keegan, we need to get going as well, come on grab your bag and get in the car. I was supposed to

240

be at the office ten minutes ago, so we need to get a shift on," said Mike ushering his son out the door.

*

At the station Charlie, Angela and Chris were drinking coffee and going through the list of actions for the day ahead.

"There hasn't been anything of real significance for the last few days," said Charlie shifting through the paper, "certainly nothing new from the witness side of things since we spoke with Nelson Parker and that was last week." Charlie looked up as a flustered Mike came in the door.

"Everything alright, boss, not like you to be late?" said Charlie.

"Yeah, sorry about that, had to drop Keegan off at school and then got stuck in traffic," said Mike pouring himself a coffee. "Anything come in overnight that I need to know about?"

"Not a thing," said Angela, "Charlie was just saying that there's been next to no new information for the last few days. I'm afraid at the moment it looks like Josh Heggerty is our only potential suspect."

Mike gave a rueful nod of the head. "It's certainly starting to look that way," said Mike who was now scribbling something on a notepad on his desk. He put down his pen. "Has everyone read Charlie's briefing note about the plan for tomorrow?" asked Mike looking at the others sitting at their desks. Everyone nodded. Mike looked across to where Angela was sitting. "I don't expect to have to keep you at the farm for long Angela, but I'll need someone to stay with Cathleen

Heggerty till alternative arrangements can be made. Josh's dad will have to come to the station with us since Josh is still a juvenile, but if it's going to drag on for any length of time I'll get a uniform up to relieve you. I'm hoping his father will suggest someone who could look after Cathleen."

"Just to confirm then, boss," said Charlie, "0700 hr report and we'll look to be at the farm for 0730 hrs."

"That's it," said Mike, "Phil Coutts is custody sergeant in the morning, so I've gone over the plan with him and Wilder also knows we're bringing Josh in. Charlie and I will do the interview as discussed and Chris will take care of lawyers arriving and anything else that might crop up. Any questions?" asked Mike. The others shook their heads. "Right then, I'll go and see the chief and Chris could you check in with Sergeant Woods at the incident room and find out if all the door to door is now complete? The note I've got is ambiguous to say the least so get it clarified, will you?" said Mike.

"No problem," said Chris, "I'll get it checked."

"Charlie, I need you to be on top of the statements from Elliot Manning, Elsie Brew and Nelson Parker. Every time, fact and figure need to be at your fingertips for tomorrow. I'm going to be doing the same so let's find ourselves a quiet space and get reading."

"Will do, Mike," said Charlie, "thought I'd use the doctor's room, always quiet in there, so if anyone's looking for me that's where I'll be."

"Okay, fine," said Mike, "I know it's Friday and we usually have a beer after work, but I think we'll skip it this week, early start tomorrow and I need everyone to be on it from the off, hope that's fine with everyone?"

Charlie, Angela and Chris all nodded, there would be plenty other days when they could go for a beer. Right now, each of them wanted to bring this enquiry to a successful conclusion and just as importantly none of them wanted to let Mike down.

*

Mike was sitting on the settee in the den sipping a glass of Jack Daniel's watching the Friday night baseball game when Susan rang.

"That's us safely here," said Susan, "roads were quiet on the way up, and Keegan wants you to know that he had the three-piece original meal and it was just as good as the last time he was there with you."

Mike laughed. "That's my boy, he always has the three-piece meal and a coke when we go to the KFC, never changes," said Mike.

"Oh, he's now asking if you're watching the game because the Cubs are three nothing down going in to the fourth innings. He says the Cubs suck and if they don't start winning some games he's going to start supporting the White Sox," said Susan chuckling.

"Well you can tell him if he does that he's going to be moving out 'cause I ain't having no White Sox fan living here," said Mike only half joking.

"More importantly, Susan, did you manage to see the Fosters?"

"Yeah, I handed in the flowers and card and they wanted me to come in for a bit but having Keegan in the car gave me enough of an excuse not to stay. They were touched to receive the flowers though. I spoke very briefly to Becca, she says she's going back to school next week," added Susan. "You might have already heard

243

I suppose, but Dave did say that the District Attorney has been in touch to say Maisie's body will be released next week and they can start to make funeral arrangements."

"No, I didn't know that, they do usually let us know, perhaps I was out of the office and someone has just forgot to pass it on," said Mike. "Did they give any indication when the funeral might be?"

"Not really," said Susan, "he just said sometime the week after next, he was hoping that Tom Farringham, the minister at the First Presbyterian might take it for them. They're not church attenders but Becca is friendly with the Farringham's daughter, so they've met socially a few times. Anyway, I thought you'd want to know."

"Yeah, thanks for that. Just to let you know, we're intending to interview Josh tomorrow, so one way or another it's going to be an important day," said Mike.

"Sounds like it will be. I'll be thinking of you, and Josh of course, I'll speak to you tomorrow then. Love you, Mike," said Susan.

"Love you too, Susan, and give Keegan a hug from me, won't you?" said Mike as he put down the phone. I've got to get this resolved now he thought. If this had nothing to do with Josh, then he should be at his friend's funeral. On the other hand, if he is responsible we need to know that before the service. I don't want to make matters worse for that poor family.

*

Charlie had been at the office since the back of six. He hadn't slept well so as he was already up and about he reckoned he would get to the office early and get things ready for when Mike and the others arrived. Charlie was pleased that he'd been chosen to do the interview with Mike, there were other detectives that Mike could have asked, but Mike had said he'd wanted Charlie to do it, so he felt good about that. While Mike would conduct the interview, his was an important role. He needed to listen very carefully to the answers Josh gave to Mike's questions. He would need to pick up on any inconsistencies or contradictions that might occur during the questioning and make sure Mike was aware of them. Charlie cast his mind back to his detective training course. Harry Fosser, the gnarly old detective who had taught him interview technique had a saying that always stuck with Charlie. The truth son is the truth and it will always remain the same. A lie on the other hand will change more times than most people change their socks.

Charlie smiled to himself as he pictured old Fosser in his pin-striped trousers and red braces saying, "And remember, never interrupt them when they start to lie. One lie will lead to another and before long they won't have a clue what they've told you. The guilty, son, have a habit of convicting themselves."

Charlie knew exactly what old Fosser meant, he had worked with so many officers who talked a good game but in reality, most were just blowhards, too fond of the sound of their own voice, and hopeless at interviewing suspects. No, to be a good detective you had to be a good listener, you were born with two ears and one mouth for a reason, so better to listen twice as much as you spoke was Charlie's mantra. He had spent most of yesterday going over the witness statements and now he knew them intimately. On the face of it they seemed straightforward and corroborated each other well, but there were subtle and important differences that needed to be explored. Charlie would be listening extremely carefully to what Josh had to say, if he's being truthful thought Charlie, it will all make sense; if he's not, well then, we might learn how often he changes his socks!

*

It was not yet seven-thirty and Frank Heggerty had already been up for a couple of hours. He had fed the hogs and chickens and hung out a washing. Saturday was no different from any other day as far as Frank was concerned, the animals still needed feeding and there were always chores to be done around the farm. Anyway, by five-thirty he was usually wide awake as the pain from his foot was often most acute first thing in the morning and the nagging ache frequently woke him up. Getting up and walking about usually helped ease the pain but over the years the early rise had become a habit so even on the odd occasion when his foot wasn't sore Frank just got up anyway and found something useful to do.

He would get Cathleen up shortly but before he did there were leeks and his favourite ramps to pick from the garden as he intended to make a pot of soup later. As Frank scoured the vegetable patch for the most succulent plants he noticed two dark blue vehicles turning off the main road and driving up the track towards the farm.

Except for Cynthia Lehman and the postman next to nobody visited the farm and to see two identical Chevrolet's drive up at seven-thirty on a Saturday morning was unheard of. Frank wondered who they could be, and more particularly, why were they coming to the farm.

Frank watched as the cars parked on an area of hard standing next to the hen coop and four occupants got out, two from each car. The men in the first vehicle were dressed in suits while the male and female from the second car were more casually dressed in shirts and jeans. They all had one thing in common though, from the breast pocket of their shirts they were wearing yellow metal badges. Frank realised who they were immediately, but why on earth were they here? Especially at this time on a Saturday morning.

"Hello, sir," said Mike, as the four detectives walked towards Frank. "I'm Lieutenant Rawlingson, would you be Mr Frank Heggerty by any chance?" he asked.

"Sure, that's me," said Frank, "can I ask why you want to know?"

"We're making enquiries into the death of Maisie Foster. I believe Maisie was a friend of your son Josh. Is Josh in the house? We'd like to speak to him and of course yourself, sir," said Mike in a quiet and assured voice.

"He's in the house sleeping. Look what's this got to do with Josh? Or me for that matter? He's hardly left the house since it happened, he's really cut up about it," said Frank, who was now starting to feel quite anxious. Four detectives don't turn up at seven-thirty on a Saturday morning just to have a word. Frank didn't like the sound of this one bit. "I'm not sure what this is all about, but I'll go and wake him up, you can have your word with him in the house," said Frank who was still trying to make sense of what was happening.

"I'm sorry, Mr Heggerty, but we will be taking Josh and yourself to Lewisburg Police Office where we will formally interview your son. We need you to be present as Josh is still a juvenile," said Mike.

Frank could feel his pulse racing and his chest starting to tighten, he knew this could only mean one thing. For whatever reason they suspected that Josh was involved in Maisie's death." The horror that was dawning was etched on Frank's face. "It's got nothing to do with Josh. I can't come to the station, my wife's had a stroke and I can't leave her here," said Frank.

Before he could explain further a voice spoke from behind him.

"What's going on, dad? Who are these people?" asked Josh who had appeared out of the house. He was barefoot and was wearing a pair of white shorts and a black t-shirt with a picture of Jimi Hendrix on the front.

"Josh, I'm Lieutenant Rawlingson and these officers are Detectives Finch, Brown and Carrol. We need to speak to you regarding the death of Maisie Foster and we're going to do that at Lewisburg Police Office" said Mike.

For several moments Josh didn't say anything. He was stunned and completely taken aback by what Lieutenant Rawlingson had just said. Eventually Josh spoke. "I know who you are, you're Susan's husband, is this some kind of sick joke? You can't be serious, you think I killed Maisie," said Josh who was now struggling to stop himself from crying.

"That's not what I said Josh, but we do need to speak to you about it as a matter of urgency," said Mike. "'I'd like you to go and put some shoes on. Detective Finch will go with you and change into jeans or something else if you want to," he added.

"Do I need to pack a toothbrush as well?" asked Josh aggressively. Mike didn't say anything, any response simply risked making an already difficult situation worse.

"I can't believe you think I killed Maisie, she was my friend for God's sake," said Josh as he turned and started to walk back to the house, closely followed by Detective Finch.

For a few moments nobody said anything. The quiet stillness of the spring morning was only interrupted by the soft murmur of a mourning dove that was sitting on an aerial high on the farmhouse roof.

Mike broke the silence to ask Frank, "Is there someone you could contact who could come and be with your wife while we're at the station? Detective Brown will stay with her until someone else can take over." said Mike pointing at Angela.

Frank pondered the question for a moment. "The only person would be Cynthia Lehman, she's a close friend of Cathleen's, she would come," said Frank who was now resigned to the fact that he and Josh would need to accompany the officers to the station.

"I know how difficult this must be for you, Mr Heggerty, but we need to speak to Josh. He'll get every opportunity to tell us his side of things I promise you that. We need to get this sorted as quickly as possible," said Mike.

Frank cut a forlorn character, his world had been turned upside down twice before. First when baby Peter had died and then when Cathleen had suffered her stroke. Now it looked like fate had struck for a third time. Frank desperately wanted someone to comfort him, to reassure him that everything was going to be alright but standing there in front of the farmhouse Frank knew there wasn't anyone who could do that for him. At this moment he needed to be strong for Cathleen, but more importantly for his son whom he loved dearly.

"Cynthia says she can be here in forty-five minutes," said Frank putting down the phone. "Is it all right if I get Cathleen dressed and give her some breakfast before we go? She just has some toast and a coffee, it'll only take ten minutes."

"That's not a problem," replied Mike, "take your time."

It was eight forty-five when Mike and Charlie arrived at the custody suite of Lewisburg Police Office.

"Can I have a quick word, Phil?" said Mike to Sergeant Coutts who was setting up the interview room in preparation for their arrival.

"Sure, Mike, what is it?" said Phil.

"I'm going to need you to organise a responsible adult to sit in on Josh Heggerty's interview," said Mike. "It became apparent on the journey over that Josh's father can't be in the interview. He will also need to be interviewed and sitting in on Josh's interview could compromise the enquiry. I've explained that to him and he says he understands," continued Mike.

"That's not a problem, Mike, I'll get someone organised. It did cross my mind that we might need to do that," said Phil.

"Oversight on my part, Phil, but I'd be grateful if you could sort it," added Mike. "Also, can you contact the doctor? I'm going to need him to take a blood sample."

"I'll get on it right away. What about a lawyer, are they looking for anyone in particular?" asked Phil.

"Not at this stage, so the duty lawyer will be fine thanks."

"Okay Josh, please take a seat by the table," said Mike ushering Josh into the interview room. Before we start I just want to introduce the other people in the room. You've already met Detective Finch and the gentleman on my right is Mr Nellis, who is sitting in on this interview because by law you are still regarded as a juvenile. And you've already met Mr Jackson, the duty lawyer. As Mike finished speaking Charlie reached into his jacket pocket and pulled out a packet of cigarettes.

"Would you like a cigarette, Josh, before we start?" asked Charlie.

Josh looked at Charlie and frowned.

"No thanks, I don't smoke," he replied. "Never have and don't intend to start now."

Charlie glanced across to Mike who pursed his lips and gave a gentle nod.

"Alright, Josh," said Mike, "I need you to listen to what I have to say very carefully. You have the right to remain silent. Anything you say can, and will, be used against you in a court of law. You have a right to an attorney, that's a lawyer..."

"I know what an attorney is," said Josh interrupting, "do you think I'm stupid?"

"If you cannot afford an attorney, one will be appointed for you," continued Mike calmly.

By the time both interviews were concluded it was after twelve and Chris had just returned to the office with a pile of sandwiches from Annie Mack's.

"The prawn mayo's Angela's and the roast beef's mine. Which one of you ordered the rueben's with extra pickle?" asked Chris. Charlie stuck up his hand.

"So, the ham and swiss must be yours, boss," said Chris handing Mike his sandwich and a can of Diet Coke.

"So, how did it go?" asked Angela between mouthfuls of her sandwich.

Charlie looked across to Mike to see if he was going to answer. Mike raised his eyebrows as he was eating which Charlie took as a signal to answer Angela's question.

"Both interviews went fine. Well, in so much as they answered all of our questions. I can't speak for the boss but if Josh killed that girl he must be a terrific actor. He was emotional at the start but after he calmed down he just came across as so genuine," said Charlie.

"Even when Mike went back over some of the detail, like times and the order of events there were no discrepancies or contradictions. Also, he was more than happy to provide fingerprints and a blood sample. He wants to help find Maisie's killer and is adamant he didn't do it. It's difficult not to believe him to be honest."

Mike nodded his head in agreement.

"I've done hundreds of interviews over the years," said Mike, "but never one like that. Everything he said made sense, at no time did I get the impression that he was lying to us. His father was much the same. Turns out he had taken Cathleen to the hospital in Charleston overnight for a check-up, so Josh was alone at the farm. Unfortunately, little of what Josh told us can be corroborated, and that's going to be the problem."

"We can check if he made that phone call to Maisie on the night she was killed," said Charlie.

"True," said Mike, "but he then told us no one answered. So, if all of that is true all we're left with is an unconnected call and the time it was made. Also, we know from your run that it would be possible to get there and back between the relevant times. As I said, the big problem for Josh is we can't corroborate any of what he says."

"What did he say about the cut on his hand?" asked Angela.

"Said he cut it on the barbed wire fence which he was repairing, he showed us the scab on the back of his hand. Perfectly reasonable explanation but again, no one else was there to back him up."

"So, is his story that he was at the farm repairing the fence and he never left there?" asked Chris.

"That's it in a nutshell," replied Mike.

"There were other little things that didn't add up either," said Charlie. "Remember in Elliot Manning's statement he said he saw Josh smoking, well at the start I offered him a cigarette. You should have seen the look he threw me. Said he didn't smoke and never had."

"That could easily be a lie," said Chris.

"You're right it could, but I just didn't get that impression," said Charlie.

"No, me neither," said Mike.

"Did anything come out of the interview with his father?" asked Angela.

Mike sat at his desk looking thoughtful.

"He said something that I've been thinking about because it struck me as slightly strange" said Mike.

"Oh, what was that?" asked Chris.

"Frank said that when he got back to the farm around seven the following evening he found Josh sitting outside the farmhouse completely distraught as you might expect. He also said that five of the eight holes for the fence posts had been dug," said Mike.

"So what? Why is that relevant?" asked Chris.

"Might not be relevant at all. But let's say what Josh told us is true. He dug those holes on Thursday evening, the night of the murder, when he should have been at the music practice. He said he didn't go to the practice because it was taking him so long to dig the holes. That's why he tried to telephone Maisie, to tell her he wouldn't make the practice," explained Mike.

"Alright but couldn't he just as easily have dug the holes the following day?" asked Chris who was struggling to see where Mike was going with this.

"It's possible of course," said Mike, "but we know Josh turned up at the school the following day and was distraught when he found out about Maisie, I know that for sure because Susan was with him at the school. Frank's adamant that five of the holes were dug when he returned. So, if Josh had dug them on Friday, he did it during the afternoon, eighteen hours after he is supposed to have killed his friend. I just find it unlikely, given how upset he'd been in the morning. Don't think he'd be fit for anything to be honest."

"Also, don't forget it was around six-thirty on the Thursday when Nelson Parker saw Josh with the cut hand near to the tree where the fence was being built," added Charlie who had been listening to the conversation. "And Josh told us in the interview that he'd cut the back of his hand on the barbed wire fence on the Thursday evening, so, if he dug them on the Friday he must have done so with a badly cut hand. I'm with Mike, hard to believe he would have been in any fit state to dig them on the Friday afternoon."

"The problem is though, as you've already told us, none of what Josh has told you can be corroborated," added Angela.

"Exactly," said Mike. "But equally, that doesn't mean he's guilty. We're going to have to run an identification parade and see if the witnesses pick him out. That, and the results of his blood test, will decide where this enquiry is going."

The phone on Charlie's desk rang. "Yes sir, the interviews are over," said Charlie after answering the phone. "Yes, he's here, do you want to speak to him? No, Okay, I'll ask him to pop up and see you."

"Wilder?" asked Mike. Charlie nodded. "Grab your notebook and let's get up there," said Mike, "plenty to update our leader about."

"Right guys let me get this straight," said Chief Wilder who was sitting at his desk taking notes as Mike and Charlie apprised him of how the mornings interviews had gone. "If the blood test comes back negative, then we have insufficient evidence to charge Josh Heggerty regardless of whether the witnesses pick him out at an ID parade," stated Wilder who, unusually for him, appeared to have grasped the essence of what Mike and Charlie had told him without any apparent sign of frustration.

"That's correct Sir" said Mike, who was still half expecting his boss to come back at him with a stinging retort. As none was forthcoming Mike continued, "Even if they both picked Josh out, that only proves he was at the locus around the time we know Maisie was murdered. Even the pathologist report only narrows the time of death to between six and eight pm. None of that proves he killed Maisie."

"Sir, I'm assured the results of the blood sample will be here by Tuesday. That's only three days away. So, if it's alright with you, I don't propose to run a parade until after we have the blood results, and only then if the results say the blood belongs to Josh," said Mike.

"And if the blood result is negative? What then?" asked Wilder.

"Well then it's back to the drawing board and we start again. But without a positive blood result I don't intend to charge Josh with the murder," said Mike.

"Alright, I agree," said Wilder. Charlie hadn't said anything up till then, but he had just watched a masterclass in diplomacy from his boss. This was clearly what Mike meant when he said you had to learn to manage your manager, thought Charlie.

"By the way are you aware that the funeral is scheduled to be held a week on Monday at the First Presbyterian? Tom Farringham is going to take the service, I just heard that this morning from the family liaison officer," added Chief Wilder.

"No, sir, I didn't know that," replied Mike, "but it's helpful in terms of planning our timings for this enquiry. One way or another we will have someone charged with the girl's murder or else we'll be back out there looking for the culprit. I really don't want to make an arrest after our suspect had attended the poor girl's funeral. At least with it being a week on Monday we can avoid that happening."

"Right folks, that's all thanks," said Wilder. "I know you've all been working long hours, so I don't expect to see any of you in tomorrow, spend a little time with your families and we'll start again on Monday."

"Thanks, sir, that's appreciated," said Mike. And with that he and Charlie went downstairs to pass on the news of an unexpected day off.

*

"Something smells good," Said Susan as she put down her bags in the hallway.

"Just a chicken stir fry I'm afraid," said Mike whose skills in the kitchen were rudimentary to say the least.

"Well, it's the effort that counts, and if it tastes as good as it smells it will be terrific," said Susan giving her husband a kiss and a hug.

"Good to have you home, Susan, where's Keegan?" asked Mike.

"I'm here," came a voice from the stairs, "mum said I had to shower as soon as I got home."

"He's covered in mud, slipped down a muddy bank racing back to the car after we stopped for lunch," said Susan.

Mike smiled. He would have loved to have spent the weekend at the lodge with his wife and son, but police work meant you got used to missing social and family events. Mike was just glad he had such an understanding wife.

"Did you catch any fish?" shouted Mike to his son, who was pulling off his clothes at the top of the stairs.

"Yeah, got a beauty of a trout and Derek got two!" said Keegan. "That was the best bit of the weekend 'cause the Cubs lost again. You said they would be better this season, but they suck! They're already bottom of the league and the seasons just started. Don't know why I support them."

A broad grin broke out over Mike's face. "Son, you'll just have to get used to it I'm afraid, your team's your team, through good times and bad. You don't go changing your team when things are tough, you've got to stick with them," shouted Mike. That's not a bad lesson in life, thought Mike. I should know, I've supported the Cubs for thirty odd years and they've won next to nothing in that time.

After dinner Mike sat with Susan in the den drinking coffee. It had been a strange ten days for them both and they knew the next few days would prove to be even more difficult.

"So, Tuesday is going to be the critical day then?" said Susan. Mike nodded. "One way or another we'll know what's happening by Tuesday," he said.

"Regardless of what happens I'm intending to go to the funeral," said Susan, "I'll speak to Grace tomorrow and get cover organised, it won't be a problem I'm sure."

"I'll be going too, said Mike, but I'll need to sit with Wilder I'm afraid. It's the usual protocol for the police on these occasions."

"Of course," said Susan, "I completely understand, I wasn't really expecting to be able to sit with you. Now where did you put the Glenlivet? I think we could both do with a large one before work tomorrow."

Chapter 12

It was not unusual for Mike to be the first one in the office in the morning, but this Tuesday morning Mike had not only remembered to bring in milk, he had filled and boiled the kettle and had the coffee in the cups before Angela and then Chris arrived. They finished their first cup with hardly a word and were about to have their second cup of the morning when Charlie, who as usual was last in after dropping the kids at school, arrived. There was a tangible sense of tension in the air, everyone was trying to behave as normally as possible and were busying themselves catching up with routine admin jobs, but everyone knew this wasn't like any other day. It was Charlie who eventually broke the tension. "Did the lab say when they might have the results ready, Mike."

Angela and Chris immediately stopped what they were doing and looked across to Mike who was reading a briefing note left by the nightshift. Mike looked up from his desk.

"When I spoke to Dave Richardson at the lab yesterday, he said he was hopeful that we would have it by mid-morning, certainly before lunchtime. And before anyone asks, I'm not going to speculate on the result, let's just wait and see, shall we?" said Mike.

"And please, nobody bring it up at the morning briefing. If the chief or anyone else mentions it I'll deal with it, let's not let our professionalism slip at this stage of the enquiry."

"No worries, boss," said Chris, "we'll not be speculating about anything, not after that cock up by Mitchell and Price after they arrested Screech and Brownie. Anyway, I saw Sergeant Coutts on my way in this morning, he says most of this morning's meeting is going to be taken up by the arrangements for the funeral next Monday".

"That's well minded, Chris," said Mike, "I've been thinking about that, If It's alright with you and Charlie, I'd like both of you in plain clothes in an unmarked car outside the church that morning. No special duties I just want you there watching for anything out of the ordinary."

"Sure, no problem," said Charlie, "I hate funerals at the best of times, but this one's right off the scale in terms of sadness, I'd rather not be at the service if I'm being honest." Chris nodded in agreement.

"If we're still looking for our killer by then, I don't want to miss an opportunity. It's not unheard of for murderers to return to the scene, so to speak, and watch the proceedings. Seem to take some perverse pleasure in seeing other people's suffering. It's a complete long shot but better to cover every eventuality," added Mike.

"Mike, it's nearly eight-thirty, we better get down there, don't want to give Wilder any opportunity to have a dig at his detectives," said Angela.

"Wilder, having a dig?" said Charlie, "now that never happens does it?"

Mike and the others laughed as they picked up their notepads and headed along the corridor to the briefing room.

It was just after ten when the phone on Mike's desk burst into life cutting the silence that had once again enveloped the detectives' office.

"This might be it," said Mike lifting the receiver. Charlie, Chris and Angela put down their pens and looked across to Mike's desk.

"Hi Dave, yes it's Mike Rawlingson speaking."

*

Five miles away in Ronceverte Elementary School, Susan Rawlingson was laying out instruments for a third-grade music lesson. Since the appalling murder of Maisie Foster Susan had not been sleeping well and focusing on her school work was proving almost impossible. Today it was worse than ever, her concentration was continually interrupted by thoughts of the husband she loved and images of a seventeen-year-old boy whose world might be about to be turned upside down. But it was the picture of a beautiful young girl with alabaster skin and long dark hair that left Susan feeling helpless and quietly sobbing in her classroom.

*

In his top floor office at Lewisburg Police Department, Ewart Wilder was preparing the initial draft of his six-month self-appraisal describing his performance as Chief of Police. He would present the report at a meeting of the Police Authority early next month when they would decide if his position should be made permanent. An early arrest for the murder of Maisie Foster, and a subsequent conviction of course, would be the icing on the cake as far as his appraisal was concerned. As he penned the opening paragraph outlining the case he was careful to erase all mention of the wrongful arrest of Henry Jarret and Eustace Brownlie. However, he wasn't so reticent when he found himself inserting the name of the accused. He took his pencil and mid-way through the second paragraph he wrote the name Josh Heggerty. With any luck, he thought, that name can be inked in by this afternoon and this report will almost be complete.

*

Typing up case notes in her office at Fairlea County Hospital, Cynthia Lehman squinted at the spidery handwriting and tried to decipher what the latest incumbent to occupy Vernon Schilling's old office had written. It was hard to believe anyone's handwriting could be worse than Vernon's, but Doctor Wagstaff's was equally appalling, thought Cynthia. For a few moments her thoughts drifted away, and she found herself thinking about her friend Cathleen. After the police had taken Josh away for interview last Saturday, Cathleen had seemed even more withdrawn than usual. Cynthia could see the sense of fear and bewilderment in her friend's eyes. Like any mother, Cathleen would be desperately worried about her son and Cynthia hated not being able to help her ease the burden of worry that she feared might soon overwhelm her. Cynthia felt wretched, she wasn't used to not being in control and she didn't care for the feeling one bit.

*

In the warm sunshine of a beautiful spring morning, Dave and Mary Foster were planting bedding plants in their front yard. It was the first time in more than a week that their tears had subsided and either of them had felt able to leave the house. Mary had bought purple Michaelmas daisies and pink petunias as they were Maisie's favourite colours and the flowers were just like the ones Maisie had stencilled onto her guitar case. The Fosters had suffered the cruellest of blows, the tragic death of their beloved daughter and while they had been crushed by the horror of it all, they resolved to stay strong, if only for the sake of Maisie's sister Becca.

*

Cathleen sat looking at the moonpie and glass of milk that Frank had left on a small table next to her chair on the porch. She watched as her husband busied himself with seemingly endless chores around the farm and she wondered if this offering that sat before her was indicative of a return to the loving and kind man she once had known. Since the police had taken her son away Cathleen's heart ached with sadness, she longed for him to be able to feel the warmth of his mother's embrace and hear her words of love and comfort but stuck in her frozen body she was tormented by the thought that this again was a punishment from god. Not satisfied with punishing me for my sins she thought, you've turned your wrath against my boy. You're a mendacious and capricious god, and I want no part of you.

*

Y = 1/2 X +2. Becca sat staring at the text book on her desk. The numbers and letters were just a blur, figures and words merged into each other like some abstract puzzle. What had been such a simple equation only ten days ago no longer appeared solvable, nothing seemed to make sense anymore. A week past Thursday Becca's world had fallen apart at the tragic death of her sister. Now Becca longed for her life to return to normal. It had been at her insistence that she had returned to school but sitting at her desk surrounded by her friends Becca just felt bewildered. Nothing she did took the pain of Maisie's death away. She gazed out the classroom window to the school playing fields in the distance and thought of her beloved sister, her childhood playmate, her confidant. The tears of yesterday returned once more and like a river bursting its banks, streams of emotion ran down her cheeks, Becca felt distraught and alone.

*

In the upstairs back bedroom Josh lay on his bed with his headphones on listening to his music. Since returning from the police station Josh had only left his bedroom to eat. His planned return to school now seemed to be further away than ever and he was consumed with grief. The thought that he might now be suspected of killing Maisie was burning him up inside, he didn't know who to turn to or how he could prove his innocence.

Josh pressed the play button once more, Maisie had loved this song, and since waking this morning he had played it on an endless loop. In his pain and anguish at the loss of his friend, the lyrics spoke to him in a way he couldn't articulate. It was all that was keeping him from cracking up.

*All around me are familiar faces, worn out places,
worn out faces.
Bright and early for their daily races, going nowhere,
going nowhere.
Their tears are filling up their glasses, No expression,
no expression.
Hide my head, I want to drown my sorrow, No
tomorrow, no tomorrow.
And I find it kinda funny, I find it kinda sad,
The dreams in which I'm dying are the best I've ever
had.
I find it hard to tell you, I find it hard to take
When people run in circles it's a very, very
Mad world, mad world.*

*

"Okay, Dave, that's all understood, can I just confirm then that you're telling me that Josh Heggerty's blood sample matches the blood found on the murder weapon, under Maisie's fingernails and on her dress?" said Mike who was writing on his notepad as he spoke on the phone. "If you could I'd be grateful, Dave," added Mike, "I'll need to go and update the chief but having the written report by end of play today would be really useful if you could manage it. And listen, I appreciate that you've pulled out all the stops to turn this one around so quickly, that's one I owe you." Mike put the phone down and turned to the others.

"I take it you all got the jist of that?" he asked. Charlie, Angela and Chris all nodded. There was a sombre air in the office. Usually a detection in a major inquiry would be a cause for celebration but at that moment, no-one in that office felt in a mood to celebrate. Somehow this still didn't seem right.

"Wow, I wasn't expecting that, Mike", said Charlie rubbing his chin several times. "After the interview I was sure the blood test was going to be negative. Just shows you that you can never tell, no matter how convincing someone comes across."

Charlie wasn't sure that Mike had heard him, he was gazing out the window and seemed distracted as if he was thinking of something else.

"So, what's the plan now, boss?" asked Chris.

"Eh, sorry, what did you say? I was thinking of something else," said Mike who was now sitting on the edge of his desk.

Charlie was pretty sure that Mike had been thinking about Susan. He knew how badly she had been affected by Maisie's murder and this was now going to compound an already traumatic situation. He felt really sorry for Mike, this must be incredible difficult to manage. Leading a murder enquiry was stressful enough without the added complication of having your wife being friendly with both the deceased and the accused.

"I was just asking what the plan is now, boss?" said Chris, repeating his initial question.

"First up I'll need to go and see the chief and tell him what's happened," said Mike, "I don't suppose that will take too long, so stick the kettle on, and we'll discuss it when I get back. But we won't be arresting Josh today, I think he had intended to be back at school by now, but I don't propose to go anywhere near the school right now, that wouldn't be appropriate. This needs to be done properly so we'll develop an arrest plan when I get back."

*

Mike was sitting on the sofa with Keegan watching Masters of the Universe on TV when Susan arrived home from work. As he heard his wife opening the front door Mike got up and went into the kitchen, he didn't want Keegan to see his mom upset or hear what Mike had to tell her.

"Let me know what happens to Skeletor, I'm just going to get mom's dinner out of the oven," said Mike.

"No worries, dad," said Keegan, "I've seen this episode before, he's about to get zapped by He-Man. Skeletor never wins, only good guys like He-Man win, you should know that dad!" laughed Keegan.

Mike gave a rueful smile, if only that were true, son, he thought, the world would be a much better place.

As soon as Susan walked into the kitchen she could tell by the look on her husband's face that it was bad news.

"I'm sorry, Susan, but the blood tests have all come back positive for Josh, we're going to have to arrest him tomorrow," said Mike.

Susan didn't say anything, nor did she start to cry. She simply pulled up a stool and sat at the breakfast bar in the centre of the kitchen.

"I don't know if you'll feel like eating this," said Mike taking a bowl of spaghetti bolognaise out of the oven.

"Not really to be honest, but I better had, I'll need to eat something," said Susan. "Do you know Mike, I was half expecting this. I don't really know why. Maybe you just try and put a shield around yourself in these circumstances, it's difficult to say. But I just feel numb. Now I feel bad for not crying. It's not like I don't care, I don't know, I can't explain it very well."

"You don't have to explain anything," said Mike putting his arm around his wife's shoulders.

"Sometimes things are just unfathomable. When I told Wilder that the blood test was positive he asked me what I thought had been the motive. I told him I had no idea. There just doesn't seem to be a reason to explain why this happened. I've been a detective for nearly seventeen years and I've never had a case like this where the evidence appears to be so overwhelming but the accused's behaviour, certainly when I've spoken to him, does not suggest he's guilty," said Mike.

"So, what happens now?" asked Susan who was pawing at her plate with a fork. "Will you still need to run an identity parade, even though he's been arrested?"

"We'll hold a parade in due course, to test if the witnesses can identify Josh, but he's going to be arrested regardless," said Mike. "Charlie phoned the school this afternoon, appears Josh wasn't in school today or yesterday. Anyway, it will be an early start tomorrow, he might decide to go back to school so we'll want to up at the farm before he leaves, I want to keep this as low key as possible."

"I can't begin to imagine how the Fosters are going to feel when they hear this news. Becca will be devastated, she always seemed to get on really well with Josh," Susan sighed before qualifying her last statement, "then again everyone seemed to get on well with Josh, that is just the type of guy he is."

*

It was a little after seven-thirty and Frank Heggerty was making breakfast for himself and Cathleen in the kitchen when Mike, Charlie, Chris and Angela arrived at the farm. Like before, they had arrived in two unmarked police vehicles, but unlike last time today they would be leaving with an accused, formally cautioned in strict adherence to Force procedures.

It was Cathleen who saw the officers first. From her chair at the kitchen table she watched as the four officers approached the house. Cathleen's mind was in turmoil, she wanted to scream, to warn her son, to protect him but her useless body failed her once again. Her only response was to stretch out her skeletal fingers on her one functioning hand, a pathetic attempt to reach out and avert danger.

When Frank answered the knock on the door there were only two officers standing there. Chris and Angela had positioned themselves round the back to ensure no escape could be made via the upstairs window or the back door. This was serious, the time for friendliness and sympathy had long since passed. Now was the time for professionalism, they were here to arrest a murder suspect.

Mike took a few moments to explain to Frank why they were there and what was going to happen. Frank had wanted to scream in utter frustration, he knew his son was not a murderer, but the events of the last week had left him exhausted, empty, drained. At that moment his fight had deserted him. He meekly pointed at the stairs and in a hushed voice told the officers he thought Josh was asleep in his room. Mike and Charlie made their way up the stairs to Josh's bedroom. Josh was awake when they entered the room. He didn't say anything when Mike told him he was being arrested. The two detectives stood in silence as a stunned Josh got dressed. There was no screaming or histrionics, at first it didn't appear that Josh had fully comprehended that he was under arrest for the murder of Maisie Foster, later on at the police office it transpired that his quietness and silence was merely a coping mechanism, without which he wouldn't have been able to function at all.

Cynthia was at work when Frank phoned to explain what had happened. She had important meetings that morning and wouldn't be able to get away until much later in the day. Within ten minutes she had called back to say she had got hold of Anne Grey who was going to come over straightaway and would be happy to sit with Cathleen for however long it took.

As Josh came down the stairs he looked at his mother sitting at the kitchen table. He turned to Charlie and asked, "Can I say goodbye to my mom?"

"Of course, take your time," said Charlie.

Josh walked across to the table and stared at this mother. She looked frail and weak. He wondered what on earth she must be thinking. Even in his hour of need Josh was thinking of his mother's feelings. He leant towards her and kissed her tenderly on both cheeks.

"I love you, mom," he whispered as he stepped away and headed for the door.

"I love you more than you'll ever know," replied Cathleen silently. Tears welled up in her eyes and for the first time since her stroke Frank recognised that Cathleen understood, he felt completely crushed.

As he stepped out into the early morning sunshine Josh wondered if he would ever see his mother again, this was a living nightmare and he was now gripped by a sense of fear and helplessness. He was innocent, but minds that should know better were closing down, no one was listening.

*

By the time Frank left the police office it was nearly eleven. He knew that Anne was looking after Cathleen, so he didn't need to hurry home. Right now, the needs of his son had become paramount and Frank was determined to do his very best for Josh. When he left Josh at the police office he was still in the interview room, but Frank knew all too well that he would now be in a cell, alone and frightened, with no understanding of what might lie ahead.

Frank couldn't remember if the office was on Adams Street or Lincoln Avenue, but as he hurried along the sidewalk he saw what her was looking for. Herb Morris, Attorney at Law hung from a sign above an office at the far end of Adams Street. At the entrance to the office Frank peered through the glass door where he saw the man he wanted to speak to sitting at a desk talking on the phone.

Herb Morris was a smallish man in his mid-fifties. Somewhat overweight and balding, he wore dark rimmed glasses that gave him a rather bookish appearance.

He certainly didn't have the good looks or sharp suits of the glamorous lawyers that appeared on T.V.

Herb looked up from his desk and gestured for Frank to come in and sit down.

"I'll be with you in a minute," said Herb covering the mouthpiece of the phone with his hand.

While he was waiting Frank studied the wall behind Herb's desk where three framed certificates adorned the wall. On the left was Herb's Professional Education in Law, while to the right was his Master of Laws. But in pride of place in the centre hung his Juris Doctor Degree from the Marshall University in Huntington. Looks like I've come to the right man, thought Frank.

"Sorry about that," said Herb putting down the phone. "Now, what can I do for you?"

"I'm not sure you'll remember me but my name's Frank Heggerty, you acted on my behalf when my foot got ran over by a coal cart at the Middleton Mine, long time ago now, nearly twenty-one years ago to be exact."

"Yes of course I remember you Frank, as I recall the case didn't work out too well for you, in fact didn't we lose the case? Something to do with health and safety procedures not being followed?" said Herb.

"Yep, that's the one," said Frank, "but don't be too harsh on yourself, you were great, that's why I'm here. It was your boss Mr Pendleman that lost us that case, he was hopeless," said Frank.

Herb shook his head, "Raymond Pendleman, thought he was Petrocelli or some high-flying lawyer like that. All show and no substance I'm afraid. It wasn't long after your case that I set up on my own, couldn't stand losing cases because of his carelessness.

He moved out west, don't even know if he's still practising. Anyway, that's by the by, what can I do for you Mr Heggerty?"

For the next twenty minutes Herb Morris listened intently as Frank went over the circumstances that had led to Josh's arrest. Throughout that time Herb hardly said anything, but at various times he scribbled down some notes on a pad on his desk.

"First of all, Frank, can I say how sorry I am to hear that. It must be a terrible ordeal for all of you, and of course Josh being only seventeen must make it even more distressing. I believe I know who your wife is. My wife, Veronica, is friendly with Cynthia Lehman and I'm sure I've seen Cynthia pass by the office pushing Cathleen in her wheelchair. Anyway, I digress. If I've understood you correctly Frank, you'd like me to represent Josh."

"That's about the strength of it," said Frank, "I don't know any other lawyers, and as I said, I trust you and know you'll do a good job."

Herb stood up and looked Frank directly in the eye.

"I'll level with you, Frank," said Herb, "a case like this is way beyond any court work I usually take on. In fact, I've never represented any client charged with murder before. So, I want you to know that. I could recommend some people if you'd like. Good people who would do a professional job for you," he added.

Frank shook his head. "I don't want anyone else, Herb, I told Josh about you this morning and he said he'd like you to be his lawyer," said Frank. "I wouldn't feel comfortable with people I didn't know, and I know you'll do your best for my son."

For a few moments Herb sat at his desk with his hands behind his head not saying anything. This was not a case that Herb would normally take on. But there was something about Frank's vulnerability and the dire circumstances that his son found himself in that made the request difficult to turn down. Anyway, thought Herb, perhaps I owe Frank Heggerty one, the failure of the case all those years ago didn't sit well with Herb and perhaps this case gave him the opportunity to try and right that wrong.

"Okay, Frank, I'll do it, but on the face of it from what you've told me it seems like it'll be a very difficult case to defend. I don't want that to sound like an excuse, I just want to be honest with you."

"Is that because you don't believe Josh is innocent?" asked Frank who was taken aback by Herb's last remarks.

"No," said Herb, "what I think, and at the moment I've got a completely open mind, is irrelevant. Courts deal with facts, Frank, not supposition, and from what you've told me there seems to be a strong case against your son. That's just me weighing up the facts as you've told them to me. The police have found blood on the deceased girl's dress and on a murder weapon. They've also told you that witnesses have identified Josh as being near to the murder scene around the time the crime took place. And lastly, while what Josh has told you is entirely plausible, very little of it appears able to be corroborated. If you were looking for a model of a prosecution case to teach law students, this might well be it. Alright, that's the negative bit over."

"Is there anything positive in any of this?" asked Frank forlornly.

"Well, the case for the defence hasn't got started yet has it," said Herb with a more upbeat tone in his voice. "There may be witnesses who haven't yet been traced who may be able to confirm what Josh says. Also, we've not tested the credibility of the prosecution witnesses, there may well be parts of their evidence that we can question. What I'm saying, Frank, is until we start that process we won't really know where we stand." said Herb.

"Look I don't want to seem crass, but do you have resources to fund this? If you don't a defence lawyer will still be appointed to act on Josh's behalf," said Herb.

"I've got some money, not that much, but I'm going to speak to my brother to see if he'll help me out. I'm sure he will," said Frank.

"That's fine, Frank," said Herb, "don't worry about it just now, we'll come to some arrangement. My daughter Julia acts as my assistant, that helps to keep down costs. She's not a lawyer but she is an excellent researcher and not afraid of hard work. She's out at a client's just now but next time you're in you'll hopefully get to meet her. Now who did you say was the lead detective in the case? I'll need to contact him and arrange a time for me to see Josh. That might be this afternoon with any luck but failing that tomorrow morning."

Frank looked at Herb and smiled. For the first time in quite a few days he was hopeful that something positive was going to happen, he certainly hoped so for the sake of his son.

As Frank parked his pick up outside the outbuilding at the side of the house Cathleen and Anne were sitting on the porch drinking lemonade.

"Sorry to have been so long," said Frank as he climbed up the porch steps. "After I left the police station I called in to see a lawyer, and it took a little longer than I expected, hope I haven't held you back."

"It's really not a problem, Frank, I'm just so sorry for all of you, especially Josh of course," said Anne. "Cynthia told me what had happened and I'm not looking for any details or anything like that, I just want you to know that if you need me to sit with Cathleen and I'm not working, I'll be here anytime you need me." she added.

"That's real kind of you, Anne, appreciate it. I'm likely to take you up on that offer. Everything's a bit up in the air at the minute, but when I know what's happening with lawyers and the police I'll be in touch," said Frank as Anne put on her jacket and searched her bag for her car keys.

"Not a problem, Frank, just glad to help in some small way, and remember, just call me if there is anything you're needing," said Anne as she kissed Cathleen gently on the cheek and headed for her car.

Frank looked at Cathleen sitting motionless in her chair. Seeing his wife's reaction when Josh was taken away by the police in the morning had left him feeling terrible. He realised now that for months he had been ignoring Cathleen's emotional needs and while she couldn't physically communicate her thoughts she clearly understood what was going on around her. From now on Frank vowed that he would be more considerate of his wife, she was, despite everything that had happened, the woman he loved and the mother of their son. Today had been a dreadful day, Frank was fighting for all he was worth to ensure he didn't lose his son, but in some small way, despite the perilous circumstances, today would also be the day when he reconnected with his wife and for that Frank was grateful.

Frank sat on the chair next to Cathleen and poured himself a lemonade. He reached out and held Cathleen's left hand.

"Cathleen," he said tenderly, "I'm going to explain what happened at the police station and tell you about Herb Morris. He's a lawyer in the town and he's agreed to represent Josh. He's a good man, Cathleen, and he's going to do all he can to help our son."

As Frank finished speaking he felt the smallest of squeezes on his right hand. He looked at Cathleen and tears rolled down his cheeks, at least he wasn't going to face the pain of this alone.

*

"Hello, Hinton 543 – 9845", said the voice at the end of the phone.

"George, it's Frank speaking. I don't really know how to begin to tell you this, but Josh has been arrested by the police and is in big trouble."

"Gee, that's terrible, Frank, what sort of trouble?" asked George in a concerned voice.

For the next few minutes Frank tried to explain the circumstances that had led to Josh's arrest.

"Look, George, this is really difficult to explain over the phone, but I want you to know that I believe Josh is innocent, and I've told him we're going to fight this every step of the way. It's just so hard to tell you all this on the phone, I was hoping you might be able to come up. I could do with the moral support to be honest," said Frank.

"Of course, I'll come up, no problem, Frank. And look I believe you. Josh is a great kid and I don't believe for one minute he is guilty. Just let me feed the lambs and then I'll head right there. Should be at yours by five at the latest," said George.

"That would be great, George, I'd appreciate it," said Frank. "Just one more thing before you hang up, I'm going to have to ask if you could lend me some money. I've hired a lawyer for Josh but I'm not sure I've got enough funds to cover it," said Frank.

"Listen to me little brother," said George, "I've got some savings stashed away and you're welcome to it. You know me, I live pretty cheaply so over the years I've put a fair amount away. It would be coming to you and Josh after I'm away anyway, so you're welcome to it, all of it," said George who was desperate to help in any way he could.

"You're a good man, George," said Frank, "I'll see you about five then."

Chapter 13

"What did Wilder say when you told him that Josh had been remanded in custody?" asked Phil Coutts who was sitting drinking coffee in the detectives' office.

"He was delighted," said Mike. "I suppose if I were in Wilder's shoes I might feel the same to be honest. Did you know we'd got some intel yesterday saying a couple of the local rednecks were threatening some sort of retribution against whoever killed Maisie Foster?"

"No, I hadn't heard that," said Phil. "Probably just a couple of idiots sounding off but might be safer all-round if Josh is in custody."

"It's ironic though, the only reason the judge refused bail was because Josh made a flippant remark about absconding if he got out of court. I'm sure he meant it sarcastically, but old Pearson took him at his word so refused bail and sent him to jail," said Mike.

Phil shook his head, "I know it must be hell for the boy, but he's not making it any easier for himself saying things like that.

Changing the subject, Mike, are you still wanting us to attend at the church in an unmarked vehicle?" asked Charlie. "I know we've made an arrest, but I suppose you never know who or what might turn up. We've nothing urgent to stop us going, but that's only if you still want us to."

"Yeah, let's stick to the original plan," said Mike who was reading through the operational order for the funeral at his desk.

"There will be plenty of uniforms in attendance, but it will do no harm to have both of you there on standby. Angela and myself will be going with the chief. His driver's going to drop us off at ten-thirty and the service is scheduled to start at eleven."

*

By just after ten, Charlie and Chris were in position in their car in the street directly across from the First Presbyterian Church.

"I took you at your word, Charlie, and didn't get you a bagel," said Chris handing a large carton of coffee to Charlie through the driver's window of their vehicle.

"No that's fine, I'm trying to give them up. I need to lose a few pounds, that run the other week was a real eye opener. I really struggled up that hill. Combination of lack of training and too many pies, so I'm trying to cut back for a while," replied Charlie.

"I'll tell you what, it's a great view of the church from here," said Chris between mouthfuls of his bagel. I'm glad Mike said we should still do this, I really didn't want to go to the funeral. I hate them at the best of times and this one's going to be particularly difficult, I don't envy them."

"I know what you mean, I'm glad to be missing it too. I spoke with Phil this morning, he told me the whole of the senior school are going to be attending, I'm not sure the church is going to be big enough for everyone who's wanting to attend," said Charlie. "It's not even half ten yet and quite a few have gone in already."

280

"Look, here comes the chief right on time, bet Mike and Angela are loving this," said Chris somewhat sarcastically.

"Dave Phelps, the man who's never late, and I mean never. You can see why the chief chose him for his driver, always guaranteed to be on time," laughed Charlie.

"Look at him, head back chest out. Wilder's loving this, only thing he's not doing is giving a cheesy grin and waving to the crowd. His ego's bigger than Joseph McCarthy's and that's saying something," said Chris, his voice laced with contempt.

"Mike was telling me that Wilder's got his interview in a couple of weeks to see if he's going to be given the job permanently. The fact that he's got an early arrest in this case is only going to help him more's the pity," said Charlie.

"Look over there, Charlie," said Chris pointing across the street. "Is that not Screech and Brownie? Surely they're not going to the service."

Charlie and Chris watched closely as the two friends crossed the street and headed towards the church.

"Looks like they might be," said Charlie, but as he said it Screech and Brownie didn't turn into the entrance of the church but instead continued walking past and headed into J.C. Penny's on the other side of the street.

"Probably away to do some shoplifting if I know that pair," said Chris.

Charlie was going to suggest to Chris that stereotyping people like that was not always a great idea, but before he got the chance he noticed Susan Rawlingson walking towards the church accompanied by Mr Peters, the school principal, and at least twenty members of staff from the school. Behind them followed a steady stream of students, all dressed in various shades of purple and pink which they had done in response to a request from the Fosters, who wanted Maisie's friends to wear bright colours in celebration of her life. By the time they had assembled at the front of the church Charlie had counted more than one hundred and fifty of them.

"See the lady in the dark blue jacket and white skirt?" said Charlie pointing his finger in the general direction of the crowd across the street. "That's Susan, Mike's wife, did you know that?"

"Nope," said Chris, "pretty sure I've never met her before. How does she know Maisie Foster then, she doesn't teach at the high school, does she?" asked Chris.

"No, she's the deputy principal over at Ronceverte Elementary, but she taught guitar to the music group at the high school. Apparently she's a cracking guitarist. Anyway, that's her connection with Maisie, taught her the guitar. That's how she knew Josh Heggerty as well, he was part of that group," explained Charlie.

Chris puffed out his cheeks, "that's just a bit weird don't you think, especially with Mike being the investigating officer, that's the kind of thing you see on TV. No wonder Mike's been a bit stressed about it," added Chris.

At ten minutes to the hour two black limousines drew up outside the church. In the first car was a white coloured coffin with shiny gold handles. On top of the coffin were two beautiful arrangements made up of purple and pink flowers.

Charlie and Chris watched as Maisie's dad got out of the second car. He was wearing a dark single-breasted suit with a bright pink waistcoat. He carefully helped his wife and Maisie's sister Becca out of the vehicle before returning to assist a frail old lady onto the sidewalk. The old lady was Dave Foster's mother and Maisie's only surviving grandparent. Now in her mid-eighties she had a shock of white hair held stiff in a tight perm and was wearing a black dress with a delicate pink scarf tied around her neck. The old lady, Becca and Mr and Mrs Foster stood in silence as the funeral directors removed Maisie's coffin from the car. They watched respectfully as the four pall-bearers carried their precious girl with great care and dignity towards the front door of the church where the Reverend Farringham was awaiting their arrival.

Mrs Foster wrapped her arm around the shoulders of her younger daughter and whispered words of encouragement into her ear. The poor girl was distraught. Holding her mother's arm, she took a few faltering steps before her legs appeared to buckle underneath her. For a moment it seemed that she might not be able to continue. Reverend Farringham, alert to the situation, indicated for the pall-bearers to stop.

Now supported by her father on her other arm, the four mourners paused for a few moments whilst Becca regained her composure. Then linking their arms together the family climbed the church steps and followed Maisie's coffin into the sanctuary.

Chris shook his head. "I'm nearly crying just watching from here, I don't think I could stand being at the service," he said. "It just isn't right. A parent, or grandparent for that matter, shouldn't be attending the funeral of their child. That's not how it's meant to be," continued Chris. "I don't have kids, but I don't think I'd be able to it, walk behind your child's coffin, it would tear me apart."

Charlie nodded, "I've got two kids and watching this is just heart-breaking, nobody should have to go through that. I'm not a church goer, Chris, but at times like this I struggle to understand why people believe in God. Where was he when that poor girl was murdered?" said Charlie wiping his eye with a tissue.

*

Around lunchtime on Wednesday, Frank Heggerty was chopping wood at the back of the house when the phone rang. Putting down his axe he dashed into the house as he didn't want to miss the call. He was hoping it would be Herb Morris calling with an update about Josh's identification parade which was being held that morning. Frank took a deep breath and answered the phone.

"Yes hello, Herb, I was hoping it would be you," said Frank.

"I'm afraid it's not great news but I'll come straight to the point Frank. Both witnesses picked Josh out at the parade. It's a setback, not ideal for sure, but all is not lost," said Herb trying desperately not to sound too despondent. "Look, I was hoping you might be able to come down to the office this afternoon. I'll give you more details and update you about a couple of things that Julia has turned up that show a bit of promise." said Herb.

"God damn it, Herb, that's not what I wanted to hear," said Frank as he slumped into a chair at the kitchen table.

"But it's not unexpected Frank. We know what their witness statements said, so it would have been a surprise if they hadn't picked Josh out. Look we need to stay positive, what about this afternoon?" asked Herb.

"Yes, this afternoon should be fine, as long as I can get someone to sit with Cathleen. Can we say after three, that'll give me time to get something organised?" Said Frank.

"That's great. I'll see you then," said Herb.

When Frank arrived at Herb's office a young girl was sitting at the desk speaking into a Dictaphone. The girl, who looked as if she was in her early twenties, smiled at Frank and gestured for him to sit down.

"Sorry about that," said the girl putting down the Dictaphone. "You must be Mr Heggerty, dad said you were coming down, he's just nipped across to the store as we've run out of milk. I'm his daughter Julia by the way, pleased to meet you," said Julia holding out her hand.

"Pleased to meet you too, Julia, and please, call me Frank, will you? I get nervous when people call me Mr Heggerty, a bit too formal for my liking," said Frank.

Julia smiled, "No problem, Frank it is then. And good timing, here's my dad coming with the milk. I'm putting the kettle on, would you like a coffee?"

"That would be nice thanks, black and no sugar please."

"Ah, I see you two have met," said Herb hanging his jacket over his chair, "so no need for any introductions. Glad you could make it down, Frank, I take it you got Cathleen organised then?"

"Yes thanks, Cynthia's come over. Honestly don't know what I'd do without her. She's been a great friend to Cathleen, especially the last couple of years since she had her stroke. She's only working part time now so has more time, but still it's a big commitment on her part."

"Yep, Cynthia's a great lady, did you know that she had wanted to be a lawyer? She would have been a good one too, really sharp brain, often thought she was wasted being a medical secretary. There I go again. If you haven't noticed already I have a tendency to digress," said Herb. Julia smiled and nodded behind her father's back. "But as I was saying before, glad you could come today, we've a few things to update you about."

"Firstly, let's get the identification parade out the way. As I said on the phone Elliot Manning and Elsie Brew both picked Josh out. Not really surprised at Manning as he said he'd met Josh before, albeit some time ago, and Elsie Brew, well that was more of a surprise. She's in her nineties and wears glasses but didn't hesitate picking out your son," said Herb.

Frank's heart sank. So far there seemed to be nothing but bad news.

"One interesting thing did come out of the parade," said Herb.

"Oh, what was that?" asked Frank, who was just desperate to hear something positive.

"It was something that Elliot Manning said when he picked Josh out from the line-up. He remarked that Josh's hair seemed considerably longer and wavier than when he saw him on the evening of the murder."

"Why is that important?" asked Frank who wasn't sure he was following Herb's train of thought.

"Well, it might not prove to be that important, but it's only been ten days since Manning said he saw Josh at the football stand, and I don't think his hair would have grown that much in ten days. But it was something that Julia has turned up that might make it significant," said Herb.

"Okay, I think I follow you," said Frank.

"Julia, do you want to pick it up from here?" said Herb sitting down at his desk. Julia nodded.

"Frank, I went to see Anne Grey yesterday, I know she's a friend of Cathleen's from the list of contacts you'd given us. Well, I noticed she didn't appear to have been spoken to by the prosecution as part of their enquiry, so I thought I'd pay her a visit," said Julia. "It turns out that she was driving past Lake Tuckahoe on her way to work around 1845 hrs the day before the murder. She says she saw Josh trying to cross the road near to the hotel at that time. What she said next makes that very interesting. She told me she had visited Cathleen at the farm a couple of days later and you were there with Josh fixing the fence."

"So what?" said Frank shrugging his shoulders, "not sure where you're going with this. The bit about visiting Cathleen and seeing Josh and me repairing the fence is true, but I don't get the bit about Josh being at Lake Tuckahoe. The day before the murder was a Wednesday and he was out with friends after school, well I think he was," added Frank still looking somewhat puzzled.

"That's correct, Frank, he was at Benny's diner at that time I've checked. His social studies teacher Mr Adams bumped into him there. Josh even wanted to continue the discussion they'd been having about President Reagan last period at school that day. Well, when we were going over some things with Josh yesterday, he told us that after school that Wednesday he'd stopped off at Moller's bakery to buy moonpies for

Cathleen with money you'd given him at breakfast." Explained Julia.

"Yes, yes that bits true as well," said Frank who was now becoming more interested in what Julia was saying.

"And he brought the moonpies home and gave them to his mom. Then the three of us ate the biscuits with some coffee on the porch. Yes, I can confirm all that," added Frank.

"Well, all of this means I think we can prove Josh wasn't in Lake Tuckahoe that evening. But the really interesting thing that Anne Grey said was that when she saw Josh at the farm a few days later day his hair appeared much longer and was styled differently from when she had seen him at the side of the road at Lake Tuckahoe."

"So, what are you saying then," asked Frank, who once again seemed to have lost the thread.

"Alright, if we assume that Anne is telling us the truth and I'm absolutely convinced that she is," said Julia, "then the person she saw at the roadside that day can't have been Josh. Also, what she said about Josh's hair backs up what Elliot Manning said at the identification parade," explained Julia. "It might just be that someone who looks very like Josh was at Lake Tuckahoe when Anne was driving to work. If that was the case, could the same person have been in Fairlea the following day when the murder occurred?"

Frank sat back in his chair and clasped his hands. "Well that is interesting, isn't it?" said Frank as he mulled over what Julia had just said.

"Thanks, Julia," said Herb getting up from his desk. "It is certainly something for us to go on, Frank, but I need to add a word of caution, while all this is interesting and needs further investigation, it's no more than a theory. It doesn't explain why Josh's blood is on the murder weapon, on Maisie Foster's dress and under her fingernails. We've still got a lot of work to do to explain that, but at least we have something to get our teeth into."

"I'm going to Lake Tuckahoe tomorrow to make some more enquiries, so here's hoping we can turn something up," said Julia. "Oh, and one last thing. I know you told us that you'd never seen Josh smoke, and Josh himself is adamant that he never has, well I've been asking everyone I speak to if they'd ever seen Josh with a cigarette and so far, no-one has. Still a lot of people to speak to but it's a bit like the hair, what the witnesses have told the police doesn't seem to hold true with what we're finding. Again, it's not a major breakthrough, but it's another inconsistency which we can potentially exploit."

Frank gave a wry smile, "I'm grateful to you both, I know you're doing all that you can for my son and I appreciate it. I feel more positive than I have done for quite some time."

*

By the time Mike got back from work Susan was cooking dinner in the kitchen.

"How was your day?" asked Susan as she poured some stock from a measuring jug into the risotto she was making.

"Fine, thanks," replied Mike picking up a spoon and helping himself to a mouthful of the creamy rice. "Wow, that tastes great. Oh sorry, how was your day, darling?"

"It was okay thanks, but I had a visitor waiting for me when I got out of school. This is ready, so wash your hands, come and sit in and I'll tell you about it," said Susan.

"Sounds intriguing," said Mike drying his hands, "so what happened?"

"Well, when I got to my car Becca Foster was sitting on the wall waiting for me. She'd missed the last period at school and caught the bus across town," explained Susan.

"Really?" said Mike, "how did you think she was? What did she want?"

"Compared to how she'd been at the funeral on Monday she was remarkably composed," said Susan, "she wasn't tearful at all."

"But what did she want to speak to you about?" asked Mike again.

"She wanted to tell me that she didn't believe Josh murdered her sister, she said it must all be some terrible mistake and Josh wouldn't have done anything to hurt Maisie. That was about it really. I didn't think I should question her about it, I just thought it better if I just listened, so that's what I did," said Susan. "I gave her a lift home, but she asked to be dropped off at the corner as she didn't want her parents to know she'd come to see me. Oh, one other thing, she says everyone in the school knows that the police have arrested Josh, but I suppose that bit doesn't come as any surprise."

"Not really, almost impossible to keep something like that quiet in a town like Fairlea," said Mike.

"Do you know what I find strange about this, Susan? Not one person who has had any dealings with Josh finds him anything but completely believable, even the doc taking the blood sample remarked how genuine he appeared when he was talking to him. But weighed against that is the sheer volume of evidence. Looking at it I don't see how a jury isn't going to find him guilty. It's just really weird," said Mike. "Oh, I nearly forgot, I knew there was something to tell you," said Mike pulling up a stool at the breakfast bar. "We just heard today that the trial is scheduled to start on the 13th July. From a purely selfish point of view that works well for us. It should be finished by the second week of August when we're due to go to the lodge, so hopefully we'll not need to change any of our plans."

"I suppose that is good news," said Susan, "do you know who the judge will be?"

"It's not one hundred percent certain, but it looks like it will be Edwin Rowe," said Mike.

Susan raised her eyebrows and blew out her cheeks. "Edwin Rowe, isn't he the judge who had the juror arrested for doing a crossword during a trial?" asked Susan.

"That's him. To be fair she had been warned before, but he's renowned as a stickler for procedure, you don't mess about with Judge Rowe," said Mike.

*

About nine-thirty the following morning Julia Morris parked her car in the car park of the Lake View Hotel. She intended to make some enquiries there, but before she did she wanted to walk down to the roadside where Anne Grey said she had seen Josh Heggerty the day before the murder.

Julia looked up and down the main road. There were no trees or shrubs at the side of the road so there was really nothing that would restrict the view if you were passing in a car thought Julia. A couple of hundred yards away Julia could see a small wooden jetty and set back from the shoreline she counted about a dozen houses. Apart from the odd fisherman, most other people visiting here would either by staying at the hotel or be staying in one of the houses she thought. She intended to do door to door enquiries at each house but her first stop was going to be the hotel, it just seemed the obvious place to start.

In the reception of the hotel Julia saw a lady in a smart suit talking to two chambermaids who were standing next to a trolley piled high with freshly laundered towels and bed sheets. On her lapel the lady wore a badge that said duty manager.

"Can I help you?" said the lady noticing that Julia was waiting to speak to her.

"I hope so," said Julia pulling a photograph from out of the notebook she was carrying. "I was wondering if you or any of your staff might remember seeing this boy at your hotel?" Julia showed the lady a photo of Josh, sitting on the edge of his bed playing the guitar. "He's my brother and he's been missing from home for nearly two weeks. My mother is worried sick and I'm desperate to find him, we need to know that he's okay". This was a well-rehearsed story that Julia had used many times before. If she told people why she was really there they wouldn't entertain her so readily and customer confidentiality would usually be trotted out as a reason why they couldn't help.

"I don't recognise the photo, but why do you think he might have been here?" asked the lady.

"Bit of a long shot really. He had been living in Richmond, but he has friends in Lewisburg and knows this area quite well. I'm just trying to cover all the bases. If he was here it would likely have been a fortnight ago today. We know he was in this area that Wednesday."

"Give me a minute," said the lady, "I'll check our bookings for that day, but I don't know what that would tell us. We get people in here all the time who aren't residents, they just stop by for a drink or some food. If you give me the photo I'll show it to some of the staff and they might remember, especially the girls, he's a fine-looking boy."

The lady left Julia in reception and disappeared down the corridor and into an office. She returned about ten minutes later.

"I'm sorry," she said, "but the photo's drawn a blank, but not all the staff were on that day. I've looked at the bookings as well. We had twenty-nine residents and two functions. An engineer's fraternal and a fiftieth birthday party. I can't give you any of their details as that's private information."

"Of course, I understand," said Julia, "I'm grateful to you, you've been very helpful."

The lady smiled. "I'll give you one name you could try, Donald Hastie, he lives down at the lake with his parents. The house with the green tiled roof you can't miss it. Donald's worked on and off at the hotel for the last four years and he knows just about everybody. Finished with us last week and I know he's off to college in September, but give Donald a try, from the roster he was definitely working that day, he was mostly in the bar, so he probably saw most people who were in the hotel."

"Thanks again," said Julia scribbling in her notebook, "I'll certainly try and speak to Donald."

"And good luck finding your brother, I sure hope he turns up," said the lady.

Julia smiled and nodded and headed out the main entrance of the hotel. She looked across the road towards the lake and immediately spotted what she presumed must be Donald's house as it was the only one with green tiles on the roof. No time like the present thought Julia as she made her way across the road to the house. The knock at the door was answered by a lady who Julia presumed might be Donald's mother.

"Hello, Mrs Hastie?" said Julia politely and with a welcoming smile.

"Yes, that's me," said the lady, "and who might you be?"

Julia introduced herself and repeated the explanation she'd given at the hotel only this time she added that she believed Donald might know her brother through mutual friends.

"I'm very sorry to hear about your brother," said Mrs Hastie, "but I'm afraid Donald won't be able to help you. He left a couple of days ago to go backpacking in Colorado. I believe he's heading to Boulder to meet up with friends, but at the moment I've no means of contacting him."

"That's a pity right enough, but it can't be helped. If he does by any chance get in contact do you think you could ask him to phone me on this number?" said Julia handing Mrs Hastie, her business card.

"Sure, I'll certainly do that. Best of luck finding your brother, I'm sorry I couldn't be more helpful," said Mrs Hastie.

The rest of the morning proved equally fruitless which while disappointing was not altogether unexpected as far as Julia was concerned. For every positive lead she turned up there were dozens more that led nowhere, it went with the territory as far as being a lawyer's assistant was concerned.

Chapter 14

"Have you seen the weather forecast for next week?" asked Charlie to nobody in particular as he buried his head into the pages of the Greenbrier Valley Ranger which he read assiduously every morning over a coffee. It says here hot winds from the south will see temperatures in the mid-nineties by next Wednesday. Well ain't that just marvellous," he continued, "and the very week we're going to be stuck in court with the Heggerty case."

"Talking of the Heggerty case," said Mike looking up from his desk, "can you do a double check that all the statements and productions have been received at the District Attorney's office? I know they went a couple of weeks ago, but let's check just to be on the safe side."

"I'll do it now," said Angela lifting the phone.

Over at the Juvenile Detention Centre in Charleston, Herb and Julia Morris were sitting in an interview room waiting for Josh to be brought in. After about five minutes the door opened, and a warder ushered Josh into the room. After shaking hands with Herb and Julia, Josh sat down at the table.

"Just some final details to go over, Josh, before next week. I'm afraid there isn't much to update you on since we met last week. However, there's no point beating about the bush, Josh, I need to ask you how you're going to plea?" asked Herb.

Josh looked completely calm as he leant across the table. "Nothing's changed since last week Herb. I'm not going to plead guilty to something I didn't do."

"No, of course not, said Herb, "but I just had to formally confirm that before we go to trial. Look Josh this is very difficult, but I just want you to understand that if you're found guilty the sentence will be heavier than if you'd pled guilty, I know that seems unfair but that's how the system works."

"Well, I'm pleading not guilty because I'm not guilty. Hope that's not unclear in any way," said Josh sardonically.

"No, Josh, that's crystal clear," said Herb. "Couple of things then, you're going to be tried as an adult at the circuit court in Lewisburg."

Josh scoffed. "That's ironic given I'm being held in a detention centre for juveniles."

"Well, yes I suppose it is," said Herb, "and I can confirm that reporting restrictions are going to apply so the media can't print your name or photograph."

Josh shrugged his shoulders. "I'm not bothered one way or the other to be honest. I didn't kill Maisie so what does it matter?"

Herb nodded in acknowledgement, "The only other thing to tell you then is that Julia finished her enquiries regarding whether anybody had ever seen you smoking. Well, the good news is no one she's spoken to, and that includes every shop, bar, and diner that sells cigarettes in Fairlea, can say they've ever seen you smoking. It's only a small detail, but at least it's something we can use to question the witnesses' reliability."

Josh sat expressionless not saying anything.

"If I could just add one thing, dad," said Julia, "Josh, you remember that last week we were questioning how well Elsie Brew would have been able to see the football stand given she was sitting at her bedroom window?" Josh nodded.

"Well, I managed to get into the room right next to hers at the hotel and I'm afraid the view from the rear window is pretty clear. It is nearly eighty feet to the rear of the stand and there are a few trees, but they don't really restrict the view. Again, it will come down to whether the jury believe the evidence of a very old lady," said Julia.

*

Monday the 13th July was a glorious day and although it was only just after eight in the morning the temperature was already in the low seventies.

"I suppose it's lovely to be able to sit on the deck and have your breakfast outside," said Susan refilling her husband's coffee cup, "but it feels strange, such a lovely morning but it's the start of a week I've been dreading. I'm going to take Keegan swimming and I think we'll have our lunch at the club. It will be good to keep busy today, but I'll be thinking of you. What time to you have to be at the court?" asked Susan as she helped Mike on with his jacket.

"I need to be at the court for nine, but I said I'd pick Charlie up at the office first, so I'd better get going," said Mike, "I'm beginning to think this dark suit was a mistake, I'm boiling already."

"You're not going to believe this," said Angela, who was standing at the front door of the court when Mike and Charlie came up the steps of the rather austere red brick building.

"Oh, why's that?" asked Charlie.

"Well the air conditioning has apparently broken and they're saying it's going to hit 92 degrees today! And get this, Judge Rowe has already said he won't allow noisy fans in his court, so that room is going to be one hell of a sweatbox," added Angela.

"Splendid," groaned Mike. "Dark suit and a blue shirt, I'll look like I've been in a water fight if I take my jacket off."

*

"It's really no problem at all, Frank," said Cynthia as she helped Cathleen into the passenger seat of her car. "She would want to be there for her son, I've got leave to take and being part time now it really isn't a bother. You might have to speak with the lawyers after the court's finished, so I can take Cathleen home and get her settled. Besides, I want to support Josh as well."

"That's very kind, Cynthia, but don't feel you have to do it every day," said Frank getting into his pick-up. "It's going to be really hot today, so I've packed a few bottles of water. It's important that Cathleen stays hydrated so I'll give you a couple when we get down there. I'll see you there shortly then," said Frank as he gave a wave and headed down the track to the main road.

At precisely nine-thirty the court bailiff stood up. "Silence, all present will rise for the judge of the Lewisburg Court of Greenbrier County. Oyez, oyez, oyez! Silence is now commanded under pain of fine and imprisonment, while the honourable Judge Edwin

Rowe, of the Lewisburg court of Greenbrier County, is sitting.

All persons having motions to make, pleadings to enter or actions to prosecute come forward and they shall be heard. God save the state of West Virginia and this honourable court."

Here goes, thought Herb, as he pushed his chair back and made his way around the table where Josh and Julia were sitting to approach the bench. The imposing figure of Judge Rowe stared down at him. Standing to Herb's right was the state prosecutor, Daniel Ettinger.

Only in his mid-thirties, Ettinger cut an imposing figure with his slicked back black hair and neatly trimmed moustache. He was tall and slim and was wearing light grey pinstripe trousers and highly polished black shoes. His red silk tie looked striking against his crisp white shirt and his attire was completed by a pair of oval shaped silver cufflinks. Ettinger hailed from New York and made no secret of the fact that he was only in West Virginia for a couple of years. He had aspirations to set up his own law firm in New York and chase the big bucks of corporate America. This was just a means to an end, he needed prosecution experience for his CV, so here he was; clever and determined to make his mark.

Edwin Rowe had been a circuit judge for the last ten years. Now in his early sixties he had a fearsome reputation. Herb had never defended anyone when Rowe had been on the bench, but he had done his homework. Rowe had a reputation of being hard but fair, play by his rules and things would be fine, step out of line though and you were destined for serious trouble.

Herb looked at the bench and smiled to himself. There it was, sitting next to a neatly folded handkerchief was an old silver dollar. Herb could see the that the face, that should have borne the head of President Dwight Eisenhower, was almost worn away. At every case he presided over Edwin Rowe would roll the dollar between the thumb and forefinger of his left hand. He did it continuously, hour after hour as he listened intently to the witnesses' testimony. Like water eroding rocks, the constant rotations had nearly rubbed the coin smooth. Now if anyone in the court had dared to produce a coin, fiddle with their watch or do anything other than concentrate fully on what was going on in court, Judge Rowe would be on them like a ton of bricks.

After addressing the twelve members of the jury and listening to counsel's opening statements Judge Rowe interrupted proceedings and asked for the windows on the far side of the court to be closed as noise from the traffic outside was disturbing his concentration and he believed it would not be helping the jurors either.

There were audible gasps from the public benches. The court was already like a furnace and this was going to make matters a whole lot worse. Sensing the disquiet in his court, Judge Rowe showed some benevolence by decreeing that there would be a recess for five minutes every hour in order that those present could take on water and freshen up.

Julia was mesmerised by it all. She made a concerted effort not to be distracted by Judge Rowe rolling his dollar and she paid close attention to all that was said. Her role was to take note of anything that might possibly help their defence, the odds seemed stacked against them and every potential opportunity had to be exploited if they were to stand any chance of returning a not guilty verdict.

As the first day drew to a close, Elliot Manning was already in the witness box being led through his evidence by Daniel Ettinger. If we keep going at this rate this trial will be over in a week thought Julia and I'm not sure a quick trial plays well for us.

*

"How did Cathleen manage in all that heat?" asked Frank as he joined Cynthia and his wife on the porch of their farmhouse for a cooling glass of lemonade after returning from the courthouse.

"Not too badly all things considered I think," said Cynthia. "We were sitting on the side farthest away from Judge Rowe and I don't think he could really see us from the bench, so I was giving Cathleen regular drinks. I'd like to see the Judge try and throw us out if he caught us, outrageous not having the windows open or being able to take a drink in temperatures like that," continued Cynthia. "If it did happen, I'd complain and go straight to the press."

Frank nodded. "You're completely right, I can't be doing with all that formality. Who says oyez, oyez anyway? Not sure what Josh must have made of it all. Herb says we will have a better idea of how things are going after tomorrow. Both Manning and Elsie Brew will have given their evidence and Herb and Julia are going to assess how best to cross examine them when our turn comes. At the moment I'm just trying to stay positive," said Frank.

Mercifully, by the start of proceedings the following morning the air conditioning had been fixed and the temperature in the court was at least twenty degrees cooler than the furnace they had endured yesterday. By lunchtime, Elsie Brew had given her evidence and all present were impressed by the assured way she gave her testimony. Clear and concise, she never deviated from what had been in her initial statement.

"At least I got Elliot Manning to concede that Josh's hair looked quite different when he picked him out at the identification parade," said Herb who was discussing with Julia how they should proceed from here. "There just isn't any mileage in trying to discredit what Elsie Brew said in her evidence," added Herb. "When I asked her why she didn't see anything after Maisie left the path to go and speak with the boy at the rear of the stand, she simply said she'd left her room to go downstairs to have dinner with her son. You've got to hand it to her, she didn't depart from her statement once. If I'd come on strong and challenged her recollection any more vigorously, I risked turning the jury against us and that would be a disaster."

Julia listened carefully to what her father had to say but up till now she hadn't said anything. Then a thought came to her.

"What if we approach Judge Rowe and ask for the reporting restrictions to be lifted?" said Julia. Her father looked slightly bemused by the proposal.

"Our entire case is dependent on us being able to convince the jury that Josh was somewhere else when the murder took place," continued Julia.

Herb nodded quietly. "Yep, that's true. So, what are you suggesting?" asked Herb.

"Well, we've already remarked how strange it is that no other witnesses, other than Manning and Elsie Brew, were traced who could put Josh near the murder scene at the material time," said Julia.

"We do have the evidence of Nelson Parker still to come," cut in Herb.

"I know, I wasn't forgetting about him," said Julia. "But think about it for a moment, we've exhausted our enquiries in Fairlea and the area around here and we've turned nothing up. And neither have the prosecution. I think we need to be casting our net much further afield. With the reporting restrictions the press and TV can't show a photograph of Josh let alone name him, so if you're from out with the local area you won't know anything about this case. And if you were a potential witness you probably don't know a murder even occurred in Fairlea that day. It just won't have been picked up by out of state media," she added.

"You're a pretty sharp cookie," said Herb with a wry smile. "It is a long shot, but I think the broadcasters would pick it up, especially if it turns out to be a slow news day elsewhere. I definitely think it's worth a try. I don't think Josh has anything to lose if we can get the restrictions lifted, but that will be a decision for the judge. Very unusual to have defence counsel ask to have them removed, but do you know Julia, I think we should try, we've got precious little else to go on."

During the lunchbreak Herb explained to Josh and Frank that they'd like to apply to have the reporting restrictions on the case lifted. After hearing the reasons why, both Josh and Frank agreed it was a reasonable idea and gave their consent for Herb to approach the bench to make the request immediately after the break.

Daniel Ettinger listened carefully as Herb made his request to Judge Rowe. The was very unorthodox and Ettinger was caught completely off guard by such an unusual request from defence counsel. As he struggled to make sense of why Herb Morris might want the restrictions lifted, Judge Rowe leant forward and asked Ettinger what the prosecutions view on the matter was.

Ettinger couldn't quite put his finger on it, but he thought he smelled a rat. While he couldn't see what advantage there could be to the defence, he was smart enough to realise that there must be one otherwise they wouldn't be asking for the restrictions to be lifted. Ettinger didn't say anything for a few moments to quite deliberately give the impression that he was giving the request careful thought. He was pleased with how the trial was going up till know. His witnesses had given their evidence with conviction and authority. Nelson Parker was still to take the stand and their strongest evidence, the blood found on the murder weapon and Maisie's clothes was still to be presented to the jury. This case is going to plan, and a guilty verdict is important for my reputation, thought Ettinger. I'm not about to risk that by conceding to a request, the motivation of which I don't fully understand.

"Your Honour," said Ettinger in a reverential voice, "prosecution counsel is only too aware that the accused in this case is only seventeen. Reporting restrictions are put in place for a reason and in the interests of fairness to the accused we would be very concerned if the restrictions were to be lifted in this case. We want to be scrupulously fair and I don't believe lifting reporting restrictions is ever in the interests of a juvenile accused and I would be most concerned if any precedent was set in this case."

Judge Rowe pursed his lips and gave a gentle nod.

"I find myself in agreement with prosecution counsel on this matter and can see no good reason why reporting restrictions should be lifted. Your request, Mr Morris, is therefore denied," said Judge Rowe with a look that was designed to repel any challenge. Somewhat deflated, Herb thanked the judge for his deliberation and returned to his seat.

"What did he say?" whispered Julia to her father.

"He declined the request, the prosecution objected too, so it's not going to happen," replied Herb.

"Did you argue our case?" asked Julia clearly not impressed with what her father was telling her.

"I'm sorry Julia, but that's not how this works. Arguing with Rowe would only have antagonised him, you've got to learn which battles are worth fighting, and this wasn't one of them," said Herb.

"Jeezo dad, just seems that everything is stacked against us," said Julia, "we just don't seem to be able to catch a break."

"We're not out of this yet, blood evidence is not one hundred percent reliable, not even close, we've just got to keep casting doubt on their case anyway we can. But it's made up my mind we're going to have to put Josh in the box. He's genuine and speaks with an honesty that will impress the jury. You saw their faces when Elsie Brew gave her evidence, it will be the same when they hear Josh speak," said Herb. "And another thing, I'm going to call Anne Grey as a defence witness. Her testimony will back up what we got Manning to concede about Josh's hair looking different, we need to sow that seed of doubt in the jurors' minds, I think it can help us."

Julia looked doubtful. "Are you sure about calling Anne as a witness? I think she's flaky and I'm not convinced she'll make an impressive witness, I think you're taking an unnecessary risk with her," said Julia. "But hey, you're the lawyer, it's your decision."

Herb rested his chin on his hands, "I'm not sure I've got much option. I'm not saying it's not a bit of a gamble, but it's getting to the time when perhaps we need to roll the dice," said Herb who was clearly in a quandary as to what was best to do.

It was late afternoon on the Thursday when Anne Grey made her way to the witness stand. As the court officer handed her the Bible to take the oath, Anne noticed Cathleen sitting in her wheelchair with Cynthia beside her at the rear of the court. Anne looked at her friends and just about managed a weak smile. When Herb had first talked to Anne about being a defence witness she was keen. She would do anything she could do to help Josh and her friend of course, but that was then. Now the whole prospect of giving evidence in front of a judge and a packed court no longer seemed to have the same appeal. Anne could feel her legs shaking and her mouth was dry as she read the words of the oath on the laminated card handed to her by the court officer.

So far so good, thought Julia as she listened to her father skilfully lead Anne through her evidence. Like most good lawyers, Herb Morris would have made a fine actor. His sense of timing, his use of silence, the intonation and timbre of his voice used perfectly for emphasis and dramatic effect, this was going much better than Julia had dared to hope. When her father questioned Anne on whether she could have been mistaken about the length of Josh's hair she was resolute. "I am not mistaken," she said, "Josh's hair was much longer when I saw him two days later and styled differently as well."

It was mid-way through Anne's testimony that Cynthia first noticed Cathleen's agitation. She started to make little undecipherable sounds and the fingers of her left hand were spread wide and trembling. Something was clearly not right. Cynthia clasped Cathleen's hand, but her fingers were rigid and shaking uncontrollably. The court officer glanced across as the high-pitched squeals that Cathleen was making grew ever louder.

He didn't do it! It wasn't Josh, he wasn't there! Listen to Anne, she knows. The boy she saw in Tuckahoe wasn't Josh, but that boy killed Maisie Foster. For the love of god somebody please listen. The boy who killed Maisie is called Todd and he's Josh's twin brother. Somebody, please, please, somebody listen, please I beg you, help my son!

"I'm sorry ma'am, but I'm going to have to ask you to take this lady out of the court. Judge Rowe has stopped proceedings and has asked for you to be removed from his court. If the lady calms down, she can come back in tomorrow," said the court officer curtly.

"For your information this lady is the mother of the accused," said Cynthia sternly, "and something of which I'm not aware has upset her. But you may rest assured that we will be back in court in the morning," continued Cynthia as she turned Cathleen's wheelchair around and pushed her out the door into the foyer.

The penny had dropped for Cathleen when Anne said she'd seen Josh standing by the side of the road at Lake Tuckahoe the day before the murder. Cathleen knew Josh had been with friends after school that day and had returned home with moonpies that he'd bought for her. He had been in a happy mood and along with Frank the three of them had drunk coffee and eaten the moonpies.

Surely there was no way Anne could have been mistaken, thought Cathleen. She knows Josh, she's known him since he was a baby. It was only after Anne said Josh's hair looked much longer and wavier when she saw him at the farm two days after the murder that Cathleen knew for sure. The only reason to explain why Anne believed she'd seen Josh that Wednesday would be if that person looked so like Josh, it was impossible to tell them apart. Cathleen hadn't seen Todd since his parent's funeral, but she knew he was Josh's twin. If he was an identical twin then of course he would look just like Josh. Cathleen had no idea why Todd would have been at Lake Tuckahoe that day, but she was convinced that he was. And if he had been there, he could just as easily have been in Fairlea the following day and murdered Maisie Foster. Suddenly it all started to make sense. Horrifyingly though, she had absolutely no means to communicate any of this.

Cathleen desperately wanted to tell the truth, she had lived her lie for seventeen years and now was the moment for her to confess her sin, that mortal sin that Father Francis had warned her about when she was eight and the sin that God had struck her down for two years ago. If only she could explain all this she could save her son.

If you're hearing me God, I will willingly go to hell for this, strike me down, take my life but let my son go free.

"I've no idea what brought that on Frank," said Cynthia as she tucked a blanket around Cathleen in her chair on the porch. "One minute she was listening to Anne and the next, well you know what happened."

"I think we should keep Cathleen at home tomorrow," said Frank, "I don't want her to get anymore distressed and it's likely to upset Josh if it happens again."

"Well Okay, if you think it's for the best, I'll come up and sit with her here tomorrow. A day's break might do us both good," said Cynthia.

No, no, please, I need to be there, I need to tell the judge the truth, I'm the guilty one who needs punished, not my son. I can explain all of this, please, please somebody listen to me, screamed Cathleen. The words rang out like sirens in her head, but as she opened her mouth to tell her story, the words fell silent once more. Only the tears in her eyes and her trembling hand gave any indication of the pain she was suffering.

*

David Ettinger had listened intently to Anne Grey's evidence the previous day. It wasn't as if she had been unsure in her evidence, but there was something about her that seemed vulnerable and he sensed this was his opportunity.

For ten minutes he summarised her testimony for the benefit of the jury without once looking at or questioning Anne. He repeatedly cast doubt on her validity as a witness as he told the jurors' nothing she had said was of real relevance. They were in court to examine the events of Thursday the 5th May, not whether the now accused was at a Lake the previous day. There was a tangible sense of tension as Ettinger turned from the jury to face

310

his witness. Anne's knees nearly buckled underneath her, and she felt dizzy. She reached for the glass of water on the shelf of the witness box and took a large mouthful.

"Mrs Grey," said Ettinger, "I'd like to take you back to the moment you said you saw Josh Heggerty standing by the side of the road," a thin smile spread over Ettinger's lips and Anne felt strangely reassured. "I think you told the court that you only got a fleeting glance, a second or two, but you were sure it was Josh, is that correct?" asked Ettinger who was taking a piece of paper out of his trouser pocket.

Anne smiled and nodded her head, "That is correct, sir."

"Can I ask you then, to take a look at this photograph?" said Ettinger unfolding the A4 piece of paper and holding it up in front of Anne. Almost immediately he folded the paper up again and placed it on the table in front of him.

"I held that photograph up for more than three seconds, longer than the time you would have had to see Josh Heggerty at the side of the road," said Ettinger in a deadpan voice. "So, can I ask you if you recognised the person in the photograph?"

Anne smile and nodded again.

"I did," she said authoritatively, "It was a picture of Elvis Presley."

Ettinger nodded and clasped his hands behind his back as he turned to the jury.

"And what colour was his hair?" asked Ettinger with a menacing tone.

Anne wasn't expecting that question. She had been disarmed by Ettinger's pleasant manner and relaxed too soon. She closed her eyes and tried to remember the photograph and the colour of Elvis's hair, but she couldn't. He wants me to say I don't know thought Anne, but I'm damned if I'm going to, I'm here to help Josh. I know what colour Elvis's hair is.

"Black," said Anne in a loud clear voice.

Ettinger paused for a moment before lifting the piece of paper and unfolding it. Turning to The Jury he showed them the photograph.

"Elvis's hair is blond," said Ettinger, "most definitely blond."

Anne's heart sank.

"Fuck," said Julia through pursed lips.

"Yep, fuck," said Herb looking at the ground.

In an instant the whole atmosphere of the trial changed. In a stroke of brilliance, Ettinger had discredited Anne's testimony and with it any doubts the jury might have had about Elliot Manning's observation about Josh's hair.

*

"It's amazing how often a seemingly insignificant thing can profoundly change the course of a trial," said Mike to Charlie as they sat drinking coffee in their office at the police station.

"Unless something else unusual crops up with the forensic evidence next week this trial is only going to end one way," said Mike.

Charlie nodded and added, "I know one man who's going to be delighted."

By Wednesday of the following week all that was left was the summing up by both prosecution and defence counsel. Herb had performed heroics trying to regain some of the ground he had lost by Anne's testimony last week. He had managed to get Dave Richardson, who had carried out the blood test on the scaffolding pole and Maisie's dress, to admit that the reliability of the blood test was at best only ninety percent. If Anne's evidence had stood up to scrutiny they would have been in with a fighting chance.

As the jury retired to consider their verdict, Frank, Herb and Julia gathered in a side room to gather their thoughts.

"Herb, I just wanted you to know that I'm proud of the way you handled the case. I know Josh feels the same," said Frank. "You couldn't have done any more. I'll tell you this, nobody watching that trial would ever have guessed that you'd never defended such a serious case before. Regardless of the verdict, I don't regret employing you as our lawyer," he added.

"That's very kind of you, Frank," said Herb. "I don't think I've ever been involved in a court case where I've believed the innocence of my client more. Josh was superb in the box. Ettinger got no joy at all from his cross examination, we can only hope the jury were equally impressed."

"You've got to hand it to him though, Ettinger was pretty sharp," said Frank. "I expect we won't have heard the last of him."

"Good lawyers need to be able to think on their feet, and Ettinger had that in bucket-loads. His line when we said to the jury that no-one in the town had ever seen Josh with a cigarette was clever," said Herb.

"I can still hear him now," said Julia. "Everyone who has ever smoked, smoked their first cigarette at some time, who's to say that Josh didn't smoke his that fateful afternoon."

"I'm afraid, Frank, it's lines like those that tend to stick in Jurors' minds. Those words were very carefully chosen," said Herb.

"Even when he was summing up, he didn't try and cast aspersions on Josh's character. No point there was nothing to cast aspersions about. Did you also notice that at no time did he try and suggest a motive, again there was no point as there wasn't one? He did the smart thing and just stuck to facts. If only we had been able to trace one witness who could corroborate what Josh had said, we could have challenged those facts better. I can only hope Frank, that we've done enough for the Jury to find Josh not guilty," added Herb quietly.

Frank forced a weak smile and nodded his head.

"Can I also say Frank, that you were a credit to your son, and to Cathleen too. All through the investigation and the trial you've remained positive and I know that was important for Josh," said Herb.

"He's a smashing boy Frank, I've got everything crossed for him," added Julia.

Having failed to reach a verdict by the end of the day the jurors were instructed to retire to a local hotel by Judge Rowe to continue their deliberations. They were instructed not to speak to anyone other than their fellow jurors about the case and were warned of the consequences if they did.

*

At nine-thirty the following morning, Mike was pouring syrup onto his pancakes in the court canteen when Charlie rushed in looking for him.

"Boss, I've just spoken to the court officer, he says they've reached a verdict and Rowe will take the bench in five minutes, we better get in," said Charlie.

Mike wiped his face and straightened his tie before he, Charlie and Angela took their places at the rear of the court.

Cynthia reached across and took hold of Cathleen's left hand, she looked at her friend. She knew she hadn't eaten in days and it showed on her face, she looked pale and drained. Cynthia said a silent prayer.

Sitting on the front public bench immediately behind his son, Frank leant forward and put his hand on Josh's shoulder. Herb whispered a word of reassurance into Josh's ear while Julia eyed Judge Rowe rolling his silver dollar while he scanned the faces of those before him.

As Judge Rowe turned to face the jury, a hush came over those present, and the court fell silent, the only sound that could be heard was the gentle tick of the clock hanging on the wall above the public entrance door.

"Will the foreman of the jury please stand," said Judge Rowe. A gentleman in a beige suit and open necked shirt stood up. "Has the jury reached a unanimous verdict?" asked Judge Rowe.

"We have, your Honour," said the foreman.

The court officer walked across to the foreman and took the piece of paper he was holding from him. He then approached the bench and handed the paper to Judge Rowe.

Cathleen shut her eyes and prayed. *Please God, my son's future rests in your hands, please don't punish him for my sins, I beg you, please I'm at your mercy.*

Judge Rowe looked at the piece of paper which he then folded in half and returned it to the court officer.

The court officer glanced at the paper, cleared his throat and looked out to the public benches.

"The jury finds the defendant guilty."

Chapter 15

1988

Becca grimaced as she looked up at the bus timetable. Gosh, I didn't think it was going to take five hours to get to Moundsville. It must stop at every town between here and there to take that long, thought Becca. And I must catch the 1515 bus back or I really will be stuck.

As the bus pulled out of Lewisburg bus station Becca put on her headphones and switched on her Walkman. At least I'll get the chance to catch up with some of those albums I've been trying to listen to for ages she thought. I've sandwiches and soda and there's even a toilet on the bus so what's not to like.

September is a beautiful time of year in West Virginia, but for the last week it had rained solidly and today was the first time that the sun had shone, and the air was warm. As the bus meandered its way north across the Allegheny Mountains, the sycamores and mountain ash trees which clung to the gentle slopes were just starting to take on the orange and red hues of the fall.

In the fields of Braxton County farm workers were negotiating flooded fields trying to harvest this year's apple crop. Tractors pulling trailers piled high with ripe fruit destined for distant markets left muddy tracks as they picked a route through the orchards and lakes of water. The September sun would need to burn brightly if this year's hay crop, which lay flattened by the recent downpours was to be saved.

Becca woke with a start as the bus came to a halt outside an imposing four storey castellated stone building. The bus driver leant out of his cab and shouted to Becca who was sitting near the back of the bus.

"This is your stop, dear," said the driver, "you said you wanted the state penitentiary, didn't you? Well this is it."

Surely this can't be it, thought Becca as she looked out the window. With its turrets and battlements, it looked absolutely nothing like she had imagined.

"Don't worry," said the driver, "you're not the first and you won't be the last person to not believe it's the prison. Quite a building isn't it? Becca nodded as she got up.

"Is this where I get the bus back?" asked Becca as she stepped off the bus.

"Sure is, and if it's the 1515 you're getting back you'll have the pleasure of my company on the way home," laughed the driver.

"Funnily enough it is, so I'll see you then," said Becca as she gave the driver a cheerful wave before she started to walk up the long gravel path.

Josh was sitting on a bench in the music room with a set of headphones on playing the guitar when the warden approached.

"You've got a visitor, Josh. Young girl with dark hair, real pretty she is too. Said her name was Becca Foster, do you want to see her?" said the warden.

Josh didn't reply immediately. A visit from Becca Foster was not what he was expecting. Four years had passed since Josh had been given a twenty-year sentence for the murder of Maisie Foster. Since his move from a juvenile facility to the state penitentiary shortly after his eighteenth birthday visitors had been few and far between. It was two hundred and twenty miles to his parent's farm in Fairlea and although his folks tried to manage a monthly visit whether it happened or not very much depended on how his mother Cathleen was keeping.

Josh couldn't understand why Becca would want to visit him. He hadn't seen her since before the trial and the death of her sister, but he could imagine how traumatic the years since had been for her. She must by eighteen now thought Josh. Of course, I should see her, it would be rude not to, she must have travelled a long way to be here.

The first thing that struck Josh as Becca entered the visitors room was how like her sister she was. Her black hair was cut in a bob, it was not nearly as long as Maisie used to wear hers, but it was sleek and shiny like her sister's and set against her beautiful pale skin it looked striking. Strangely, Josh didn't feel nervous, but he found himself wondering what he should say. He smiled at Becca as she sat down at the table and Becca smiled back.

"It nice to see you Becca," said Josh, "but I'm not sure why you would want to come and see me."

"That, Josh, is quite simple," said Becca looking Josh directly in the eye. "I just have one question for you. I want to know; did you kill my sister?"

Josh sat back in his seat. He wasn't expecting Becca to be so blunt. No pleasantries, no lead in, nothing. However, it was a perfectly reasonable question for her to ask.

Josh met Becca's eyes and leant forward across the table.

"No, Becca, I did not kill Maisie," said Josh calmly. For a few seconds nobody said anything.

"Okay," said Becca still looking Josh squarely in the eye. "I believe you, I just needed to hear you say it."

"Thank you," said Josh, "that means a lot to hear you say that. If I had done it Becca, I would have told you. I couldn't be in here living a lie like that."

For the next half hour or so Becca and Josh chatted about their families and what Becca had been up to since she left school last summer. Understandably, Josh didn't want to dwell on his life in prison. He had already wasted four years of his life and many more years of incarceration lay ahead.

Becca looked at her watch, her hour was nearly up, and they still had things to discuss.

"I promise I'll go and see Herb Morris," said Becca. "As I said to you, I've been reading loads of journals about new crime investigation methods, and folk are getting pretty excited about this new DNA test that can be done on blood, bones and even saliva. It sounds from what you're telling me that your conviction hinged on the blood evidence. This new test might be able to prove the blood wasn't yours, Josh. Maisie would have hated to think you were locked up for something you didn't do, and just as importantly it means that whoever killed Maisie is still out there. I'm going to do something about that," said Becca.

"And next time I visit I'll have my own car, so it will be much easier to get here. I'll come again in six weeks or so, but it will be a Saturday, only came today because I was due a day off from work. Hope your mum's doing better when you see her tomorrow. And try and stay positive Josh, we're going to find who really killed Maisie," said Becca.

Josh looked at Becca and smiled. "No point being angry in prison, it gets you nothing but trouble. No matter how long it takes for me to get out of here, I won't stop trying to clear my name, but any help you can give sure will be appreciated."

*

In the front room of her house in Fairlea, Susan Rawlingson was talking to Anna Hayburn on the phone.

"Seven will be perfect, Anna, supper will be ready and I've a nice bottle of Paul Masson chilling in the fridge. And remember to bring boots and your waterproofs, it didn't rain today but hasn't stopped for the last week and tomorrow's forecast isn't that great, but it'll not keep us in," said Susan. "Keegan's dying to meet Alfie, he loves dogs, so we've planned a long walk for tomorrow. Just sorry Luke and Eva couldn't come with you, but I know what's it's like, she wouldn't want to miss the swimming competition. Hopefully next time, eh. Yeah, that's right, Mike's still away, but he should be home by tomorrow lunchtime," said Susan. "He didn't want to miss the last lecture so that meant staying till tomorrow and getting an early flight back. Yep, seems to have been a really interesting conference. It's about new processes for testing blood and other bodily fluids, it's called DNA or something like that. Don't know what it stands for, but Mike seems excited by it. Of course, the fact that the conference was in Chicago might have something to do with why he seems so keen to be there! Take care driving won't you, and I'll see you at seven, can't wait," said Susan excitedly.

*

It was after eleven on Saturday morning when Susan, Anna, Keegan and Alfie reached the bridge at the Haney Creek.

"Well at least the rain's gone off," said Anna as she put her foot on the bridge to do up her bootlace. "Not that it seems to be bothering Keegan or Alfie. So where do we go from here, Susan?"

"Do you see that large chestnut tree at the top of the track?" said Susan pointing to it. "Well, when we reach there we take a sharp right turn and head back along the valley to the town. We're just over half way, but the chestnut tree is the high point, it's downhill all the way from there."

The two friends chatted as they headed up the path, but as they approached the top they could hear Keegan shouting.

"Alfie's chased a squirrel and he's gone under the fence! He's now digging at the ground, I don't know if he's caught the squirrel, but I think he might have," said Keegan in a concerned voice.

"Alfie, Alfie! Stop that, come here now!" shouted Anna as she reached the top of the track. Alfie paid no attention but continued to paw frantically at the ground.

"Alfie, Alfie I'm warning you, come here!" Alfie ignored Anna's commands and continued digging. "Sorry about this," said Anna. "It's typical of lurchers, always wanting to chase rabbits and squirrels. Looks like I'm going to have to climb over the fence and get him, he's not for coming back," said Anna as she carefully straddled the barbed wire fence.

"No problem, but be careful please," said Susan.

The ground squelched under Anna's feet as she approached Alfie who had now stuck his head down a large hole in the ground a few yards from the base of the chestnut tree. Anna grabbed Alfie by the collar and pulled him out of the hole. Anna braced herself, as either a petrified squirrel was going to come shooting out of the hole or its lifeless body was going to be lying there staring up at her.

Anna peered into the hole. It must have been more than two feet deep. Soft mud and several large stones appeared to have collapsed into the hole. Anna gave a sigh of relief as there didn't appear to be any sign of the squirrel. She peered into the darkness and saw what appeared to be a large flat stone that had been partially dislodged.

"Keegan, can you come and hold Alfie please?" said Anna. "I've got a flashlight in my jacket pocket, I just want to be sure that the squirrel isn't lying injured at the bottom of this hole."

Kneeling on the wet grass, Anna shone the flashlight into the dark ground and reached down and took hold of the flat stone with her right hand. As she turned the stone onto its side the light illuminated the bottom of the hole. Anna knew immediately what she was looking at. These were human remains.

"Keegan, can you take Alfie up to your mom please and put him on the lead?" said Anna. "Maybe put the lead round one of the fence posts, but I need you to keep him away from here."

"Why, what's wrong?" asked Keegan, "is the squirrel dead?"

"No, the squirrel's fine, Keegan. Susan, can you come down please?" asked Anna. "We've got ourselves a bit of a situation."

By the time Susan joined Anna at the hole, Anna was reaching down and removing small pieces of wood.

"Looks like bits of an old wooden crate," said Anna. "Here, can you hold the flashlight?"

"Better not touch it," said Susan staring into the hole. "I'll go and phone the police, but I know they won't want you touching the bones or anything else for that matter."

"No, of course not," said Anna, "I was just checking that the wood wasn't a coffin, well you know what I mean, not a proper coffin. Looks like a baby has been but in some sort of crate, it looks like the type you'd store apples in."

"That would make sense," said Susan, "plenty of apples grown around here. Can you tell how big the child was?" asked Susan.

"Tiny," replied Anna. "The skull and skeleton look intact but the bones are really small, this was just a tiny baby, but the bones are definitely human."

"Anna, I know a bit about this place," said Susan. "This is the Heggertys' farm. Do you remember I told you about the girl in my music class who was murdered?" Anna looked up from the hole and nodded.

"Well this farm belongs to Josh Heggerty's parents, he was the boy who was convicted of the murder. I taught him as well, really tragic case," said Susan.

"Yeah, I remember you telling me about it, must have been a few years ago now," said Anna.

"More than four," said Susan, "probably nearer five. There's no signs of life at the farmhouse and there are no vehicles about, looks like they might be away. You stay here, I'm going to the next farm, the Rossiters' live there, and I know them as well, used to teach their granddaughter. I'll contact the police from there."

"I'll tell you what's also strange," said Anna pointing at the small white cross standing in the ground a few feet away. "That appears to be marking another grave, but I don't see any sign of a cross here, do you?" she asked. Susan shook her head.

By the time Charlie Finch parked his vehicle next to the outbuildings, uniformed officers had already cordoned off the area with barrier tape and Susan, Anna and Keegan were standing on the path at the other side of the barbed wire fence.

Susan listened while Anna explained what had happened to Charlie who jotted down notes in his pocket book.

"I'll not keep you all any longer just now, Susan," said Charlie. "We're going to need to get statements from you but that can be done later. I've plenty to be getting on with, but I'd appreciate it if you'd get Mike to phone me when he gets back," said Charlie.

"I'll do that, Charlie," said Susan, "but you know my husband, I expect he'll want to come straight up." Charlie smiled and nodded his head.

"Yep, I'll expect he'll do just that," said Charlie.

By four in the afternoon the photographer was packing up his equipment and the scene of crime officer was taking off his protective white suit, gloves and shoe covers and sealing them in a plastic bag for disposal.

"Joe's agreed we can leave the bones in situ overnight and have them removed tomorrow as long as we protect the site properly. He's put a tent up and uniforms will be here overnight," said Mike, who as Susan had predicted had come straight up as soon as he'd heard the news. "But I don't want the remains removed before we get a chance to question Frank Heggerty about them. Good call by Angela, turns out they are up at the prison visiting Josh, but they will be back late tonight, so we'll speak to him in the morning," added Mike.

"Oh, and last thing, I've arranged for Susan and Anna to call in at the station around lunchtime tomorrow to make their statements. That'll allow Anna to get going after that, she's to be up at her folks in Harpers for six, so those timings should work for her," said Mike.

*

At nine-thirty the following morning Mike and Charlie were speaking to Frank Heggerty in the kitchen of his farmhouse. Cathleen was sitting nearby in a chair at the kitchen table.

"So, just to be clear Frank, you're telling us you have no idea how those remains came to be buried in your front yard."

Frank raised his hands and shook his head, "I'm telling you I don't know anything about them. I told you about Peter, but I've honestly no clue as to how that baby ended up buried there. If I knew anything I'd tell you officers, please believe me," said Frank who was clearly shell shocked by this latest turn of events.

"We know about Peter's grave Frank, I've checked with the District Attorney's office and they've confirmed that his death was properly registered and approval for a home burial was given. However, that doesn't help explain why a second child's body is buried on your property and the DA's office have no record of it," said Charlie.

"Look," said Frank who was becoming a little agitated, "the only thing I can think of is the baby's been there since before we lived here. That's about twenty-five years. Cathleen's grandparents, and an old uncle before that owned the place. Cathleen would know better but, well, she can't help, can she?"

"Couple of things then, Frank," said Mike getting up from his chair. "Firstly, I'm not accusing you of doing anything wrong, but we need to get to the bottom of this. Secondly, the forensic report will give us a good indication how long the remains have been there and, as you say, it could pre-date your time living here. One last thing and this is just routine, while I'm here do you have any objections if I have a look around?" asked Mike.

"Not a problem, you carry on," said Frank.

"Okay, thanks," said Mike, "can you remind me which bedroom is Cathleen's and which was Josh's? I think his was upstairs if I remember."

"That's right," said Frank nodding. "Josh's is upstairs, mine's the one next to the bathroom and Cathleen's the one opposite."

Mike nodded. "While I'm doing that, Detective Finch is going to take a statement from you, and the blood samples for you and Cathleen that we discussed, I'll arrange for the doctor to come here tomorrow to get them, make it a bit easier for you both."

"Fine," said Frank, "that's appreciated."

Mike really wasn't sure what he was looking for as he climbed the stairs. But his detective's experience was telling him that it was always worthwhile to have a good look around, you never knew what you might turn up.

It appeared to Mike that Josh's room hadn't changed much in the years since he was last in it. A few boxes stuffed with clothes, shoes and what looked like old school books lay underneath the bedroom window. Josh's guitar and amplifier stood against the wall at the far side of the room and the poster of Jimi Hendrix still hung on the wall next to his bed. Finding nothing of any significance Mike went downstairs into Cathleen's bedroom. He was immediately struck by how spartan and colourless it appeared compared to Josh's. There were no pictures on the wall or even any family photographs to be seen. Apart from the bed, a chair and a chest of drawers the only other piece of furniture was a mirrored dressing table that stood against the wall next to the window. Numerous postcards had been randomly stuck under the various metal clips that held the oval mirror in place.

Mike walked across and opened the pair of threadbare blue curtains that hung limply from a cast iron curtain rail, but it did little to lift the murkiness of the room. Mike switched on the bedroom light and started to peruse the dozen or so postcards that adorned the dresser. The pictures of faraway places provided what little colour there was in the dark and soulless room. His eye was caught by one of the cards that had fallen off and was lying on the floor by the leg of the dresser. Mike bent down and picked it up. Years of being exposed to direct sunlight had dulled the picture on the front but he could still make out the image of some boats moored to a jetty with a pelican sitting on a bollard. The message on the card read 'Greetings from Longboat Key'.

Mike turned the card over. The ink was quite faded, but the words were still just about legible. From the postmark he could see that it had been sent on 15th April 1967. As Mike read the card, it became apparent that it must have been written shortly before Cathleen had her baby.

'Expect it won't be long now till you stop work and the big day must only be a month or so away. You must let me know when baby arrives, I'm betting it's going to be a boy. Wishing you & Frank all the best for the future.

Regards Vernon.

Mike wondered who Vernon might be. He wasn't sure if the card was significant, it could, of course, mean nothing at all, but the fact it made mention of Cathleen's baby was enough reason for him to put it in his jacket pocket.

Back in the kitchen Charlie was finishing off Frank's statement.

"That's just a quick overview of events," said Charlie. "We may need to get a more comprehensive statement later, but that will do for now, thanks."

"No problem," said Frank removing some side plates from the kitchen table and placing them in the sink.

"Frank, can I ask who Vernon is? I saw a card lying on the floor in Cathleen's room and it was from someone called Vernon. Quite an unusual name, never come across it before," said Mike.

"That'll be Vernon Schilling," said Frank. "He was the obstetrician at the hospital and worked alongside Cathleen for years. She was fond of Vernon. Retired a long time ago now, moved away to Florida if I remember rightly, wanted to be near his daughter and grandchildren who lived there."

As Mike and Frank were talking, Cathleen started to make several undecipherable high-pitched noises and the fingers of her left hand started to twitch.

"I think Cathleen must have heard me," said Frank looking across to his wife at the kitchen table. "I told you she was very fond of Vernon."

"What are you thinking now?" asked Charlie, as he and Mike got back into their car.

"I'm thinking I want you to go and see Cynthia Lehman. You remember, the lady who came to sit with Cathleen when we took Josh in for interview?" said Mike.

"Not really," said Charlie shaking his head.

"She's a former work colleague of Cathleen's from the hospital," said Mike, "so she's bound to know Vernon Schilling. With a bit of luck, she might have some contact details for him. Oh, and while you're about it, try and get a hold of Cathleen's maternity file. I know it's twenty-one years ago, but it might be gathering dust in some store somewhere, see what you can turn up."

"Right you are," said Charlie, "but can it wait till tomorrow? Doubt she'll be working on a Sunday."

Mike laughed, "Yep, no problem, we've waited twenty-one years, another day won't matter. Swing by KFC on the way back to the office, will you? I'm famished."

"See what you were telling me about this new DNA test," said Charlie as the two detectives sat eating their lunch. "Will we be able to use it to test the baby's bones?"

"Bit of a grey area I'm afraid," said Mike. "The technology is just too new, and it's only been used in a few high-profile cases up to now, so little old Fairlea will be some way down the list of priorities at the moment. But I have spoken to Dave Richardson at the lab about it. Like me he's been to a seminar about DNA, and he knows how to carry out the test. The thing is, he's not yet certified to use it officially. But, as a favour for us he's going to run the test on the baby's bones. Of course, anything he finds will not be admissible as evidence, but it will be good to know one way or another. We're not doing anything illegal, but I'd be grateful if you kept that to yourself. Not even Wilder knows about it, you understand?" added Mike.

"Of course, no problem Mike, my lips are sealed," said Charlie.

Shortly after eleven the following morning Mike was sitting in his office going through the weekend's crime figures when Charlie walked in the door.

"How did you get on at the hospital then?" asked Mike looking up from his desk.

"Yeah, fine thanks," said Charlie, "Cynthia Lehman's a bit of a character alright. As soon as I saw her I remembered her from the trial, apparently, she's been taking Cathleen Heggerty out every Saturday since she had her stroke, that's more than six years. That's what you call a proper friend."

"Certainly is," said Mike nodding his head in agreement. "Any joy regarding contact details for Vernon Schilling?"

"Yep," said Charlie, "I've got an address and a telephone number. Cynthia says she still keeps in touch with Christmas cards and the odd postcard. He's not keeping great health by all accounts, but he's in his mid-eighties now. Anyway, the really interesting bit about our conversation was that according to Cynthia, Cathleen didn't have her baby at the hospital. Apparently, she went into premature labour nearly a month before her due date and delivered the baby herself on the floor of her kitchen."

"Huh," said Mike chewing on his pencil.

"The other strange thing was it was a few days later before anyone knew anything about it," said Charlie.

"What, are you telling me that Frank didn't know about it? "asked Mike.

"Well, not according to Cynthia. She said Frank had been away at his brother's farm in Hinton when the baby was born, and Cathleen only told Cynthia when she turned up at the hospital with the baby, as I said, about five days after it was born," added Charlie.

"Remarkable women that Cynthia Lehman," said Charlie putting down a file on Mike's desk. "She knew exactly where the file would be and right enough she opened the store and went straight to it. All the files were bundled alphabetically for each year. Even I would have been able to find it," said Charlie with a chuckle.

*

Yes, I'll certainly do that Mr Schilling, I expect I'll see Cathleen and Frank in the next couple of days, so I'll be sure to pass on your kind regards," said Mike before putting the phone down.

"Well Charlie, Vernon Schilling seems like a really nice fellow. He says his memory is not what it once was which is understandable. Anyway, interestingly he says he has no recollection of Cathleen ever telling him that she'd had the baby early or that she'd delivered the baby herself," said Mike.

"He did say that he remembers getting a letter from her telling him about the baby and she sent a photograph as well. But he's adamant she didn't mention it had been very premature. I'll tell you something though Charlie, his memory can't be that bad as he was able to tell me all about her trauma when she lost baby Peter three years earlier. There's definitely something not right about all of this but I can't quite put my finger on it." Mike frowned.

Charlie shrugged his shoulders. "Not sure we're going to get to the bottom of it either, the person who could probably help us can't speak, and it's strange, I got the same feeling speaking to Frank the other day as I did when we arrested Josh, I didn't get the impression that he was being anything other than truthful," said Charlie.

"I totally agree," said Mike putting on his jacket to head home.

As he was putting his bag into the trunk of his car Mike heard someone shouting his name.

"Mike, Mike!" shouted Angela from out of a ground floor window.

Mike turned around to see Angela leaning out of the window.

"Mike, Dave Richardson from the lab has been on the phone, he's asking if you can phone him back right away, says it's urgent," added Angela.

"Okay, thanks Angela, I'll come right in. Oh, and if Charlie's still about can you tell him to meet me in my office?" replied Mike who was feeling slightly confused. Dave had told him the tests on the baby's remains would take at least a week and as he wasn't waiting on anything else from the Lab, he wondered what Dave wanted to speak to him about.

"Hi Dave, Mike Rawlingson speaking, you asked for me to contact you urgently?"

"Yep, thanks for getting back to me so quickly but I thought you'd want to know," said Dave.

"Know what?" asked Mike, who was gesticulating for Charlie, who had just come in the door, to sit down.

"Well you know the blood samples you sent me for Frank and Cathleen Heggerty? Well I know you didn't ask me too but as I still had Josh's blood sample in the fridge I ran a test and compared it with theirs," said Dave.

"Okay," said Mike slowly.

"And, well, the thing is, the test came back negative. Frank and Cathleen Heggerty are not the blood parents of Josh, Mike."

"Woah, are you sure about that?" asked Mike incredulously.

"Absolutely positive, Mike. I ran the test again just to be sure and they definitely aren't his real parents, I thought you'd want to know straight away," said Dave.

"Yep, thanks for that. But what about the baby's remains, any news on that?" asked Mike.

"Need to do some different tests because it's bones," said Dave, "and that will take a few days yet, but hopefully I'll have something by the end of the week."

"Listen, I appreciate that Dave, that news has just opened up a whole new line of enquiry, good work."

"What's Dave saying that's so important then?" asked Charlie as Mike put down the phone.

"He says he tested Frank and Cathleen's blood samples against one he still had for Josh and it's negative, which means they can't be Josh's blood parents," said Mike leaning back in his chair.

Charlie sat wide eyed stroking his chin pondering what Mike had just said.

"Alright then," said Charlie eventually, "it begs two questions then, doesn't it? One, who are Josh's real parents? And two, who are the parents of that baby that's just been found?"

"No, you're absolutely right Charlie, we need to be able to answer both those questions. And do you know what else?" said Mike jotting down some notes on his pad.

"No, what's that?" said Charlie.

"I've just got a feeling that this has a connection to Josh and the murder of Maisie Foster," said Mike whose mind was now in overdrive trying to remember all the details from that case nearly five years ago. "That conviction never sat well with me Charlie, or any of us, remember? It just felt wrong at the time and it still does."

Charlie nodded in agreement. "Yep, you're spot on Mike," said Charlie. "I remember it like it was yesterday, there was all the evidence in the world, yet I felt sure he hadn't done it. But where do we go from here? The blood evidence swung that conviction, I'm sure of it, and we can't explain that away, can we?" he asked.

"You know, Charlie, we might just be able to," said Mike. "It's just a hunch at the moment, I can't prove it yet, so I'm not willing to say right now. We need to do the ground work, but I think our gut instinct about Josh might have been right," added Mike.

By now Mike had his head down and was writing copious notes on his pad. Charlie looked at his boss and a frisson of electricity went up his spine. He didn't yet know what Mike had come up with, but it felt exciting. This was why Charlie wanted to be a detective. He liked locking up criminals, but solving a difficult and challenging case, well, there was nothing more rewarding than that. If they could prove that Josh Heggerty didn't murder Maisie Foster, that really would be something. From the look on his boss's face, it appeared they might be on the brink of something hugely significant.

"Right, listen up, Charlie, here's what I need you to do," said Mike looking at his list of notes.

Charlie sat with his notebook in his hand and his pen poised.

"Firstly, I want you to go and see Herb Morris. I want you to find out if they had any leads, witnesses, enquiries that they weren't able to bottom out at the time of the trial. I'm particularly interested in Anne Grey's testimony so any notes and of course her statement would be really useful. I'm sure Herb will want to help, just tell him that we think we might be able to prove that Josh was innocent," said Mike.

"Okay, I've got all that, anything else?" asked Charlie.

"One other thing, on your way out can you have a word with Phil Coutts and see if he can dig out the road traffic report for the fatal accident that Cathleen Heggerty was the primary witness at? He'll remember no problem. It was Phil who took Susan's statement back then. I'm sure I've told you about it in the past," said Mike.

Charlie nodded. "Yes, you have. I know the incident you're talking about".

"I hope it's in the archive somewhere. I'm sure it will be, Phil never throws anything like that away," added Mike. "I'll need to go and update Wilder about the blood tests, he's going to want to know. Phone me if you turn anything up, I'll be here for a few hours yet."

*

"I'm sorry but my father's not here right now," said Julia who was typing up some case notes when Charlie arrived at the office on Adams Street. "He's away seeing a client. Can I help you?"

Over a cup of coffee Charlie started to explain why he was there and what he was looking for. Julia listened carefully as Charlie outlined, as best as he could, why Mike and himself were taking a fresh look at Josh's case.

"Of course, we'll do everything we can to help," said Julia, "I've never seen my father so upset after a case as he was with that one. Funny, but it came up in conversation not that long ago, we had a visit from Maisie's sister Becca, she wanted our help to get hold of some legal magazine's containing stated case reviews. Apparently, she's been visiting Josh in prison and is researching about DNA as she seems to think that will be able to prove his innocence. She clearly doesn't believe he's guilty."

"Huh, well I never knew that. I wonder if her parents know she's visiting Josh. Anyway, it seems like the only folk who thought Josh was guilty were the jury. Unfortunately, it was their decision that really mattered wasn't it?" said Charlie.

Julia sighed and gave a rueful nod of her head. "Well, that's true for sure," said Julia, who was now browsing through the top drawer of a filing cabinet.

"Ah, here it is," she said pulling out a beige coloured folder. "Yep, Anne's statement is here but this is what I was looking for," said Julia removing a notebook from the file.

"This is where I kept all my notes. Names, addresses, that kind of thing. Use a different one for every case and then file it. Not the first time it's come in useful I'll tell you," said Julia as she carefully leafed through the pages.

"No, I expect it isn't," said Charlie, "that's a really good idea."

"Found it," said Julia animatedly. "There was a potential witness that I was keen to speak to, but he'd disappeared backpacking with friends for the summer, so I never got the chance. His name was Donald Hastie. He'd worked at the Lake View hotel for years and knew just about everybody. He was working in the bar the day Anne Grey said she saw Josh at the side of the road near to the hotel. She paused scanning her notes again. "The hotel manager gave me his name. Also, I've written here that there were two functions on in the hotel that day, an engineer's fraternal and someone's fiftieth birthday party. The hotel wouldn't give me any details because of confidentiality issues. Anyway, dad and I were working on a theory that someone who looked very similar to Josh was at the hotel that day and well, it was a bit of a stretch, but we reckoned that same person might have been in Fairlea the next day and killed Maisie. Unfortunately, it didn't come to anything and after Anne's testimony, well, you know the rest."

"That does sound interesting, Julia," said Charlie, "do you happen to have Donald's address?" he asked as he took down some notes.

"Funny, I don't seem to have written it down, but you won't miss it. I've written here, house with green tile roof by the lake, brackets, the only one," said Julia smiling. "And look I've even got the photograph of Josh I was showing people, he really is a good-looking boy."

Charlie laughed. "I'm supposed to be a detective, so I should be able to find it from that description. Look, thanks a lot, you've been very helpful. By the way do you think I could borrow the photograph? It would be good to have a picture from around that time."

"No problem," said Julia, "you're welcome to take it if you think it might help."

"Many thanks, I'll let you know how I get on," said Charlie as he left the office and returned to his car. No time like the present, he thought to himself, better get over to Lake Tuckahoe and see if I can find this house.

By the time Charlie parked his car in the hotel car park it was after four. Looking across the road to the shore of the lake he could see about a dozen houses dotted along the shoreline. Lovely looking houses, thought Charlie, bet you need a dollar or two to afford one of these. As he crossed the road he saw the house he was looking for. Julia was spot on, there was only one property with a green roof. Charlie rang the bell. The door was opened by a middle-aged lady wearing a blue housecoat.

"Excuse me," said Charlie showing the lady his police badge, "are you Mrs Hastie by any chance?"

"That I am," said the lady, "and who might you be?"

"I'm Detective Finch," said Charlie, "I was wondering if your son Donald might be in? He's not in any trouble, but I'd like to speak to him regarding an historic crime I'm investigating."

"Well officer, it's your lucky day," said Mrs Hastie, "he's upstairs studying. Usually he'd be away at university, but his finals are coming up, so he's been home for a week studying. I'll give him a shout for you."

"Thanks, I'd appreciate that," said Charlie.

"Donald, Donald! can you come down for a minute, there's someone to see you," said Mrs Hastie ushering Charlie into the front room. A few moments later a young man in his early twenties entered the room.

"Hi there, I'm Donald Hastie. What can I do for you?"

Charlie introduced himself and explained that he was making enquiries about a murder that had occurred in Fairlea nearly five years ago.

"Yes, I remember that case, it happened the week before I left to go backpacking in the Rockies for the summer. It was on the local news. Terrible for something like that to happen to such a young girl," said Donald. "Not sure though how you think I might be able to help."

"I think I'm right in saying Donald, that you'd been working at the hotel before you left to go backpacking," said Charlie.

Donald nodded. "That would be right, I stopped a few days before I left. I'd had part time jobs at the hotel since I was sixteen."

"The particular day I'm interested in was a Wednesday, I've got information that who were working

339

in the bar that day. I know it's a long time ago but if it's any help, there were two functions on that day. An engineer's fraternal and a fiftieth birthday party," said Charlie.

Donald looked quizzical and shook his head. "Not sure that helps being honest, we had functions on every other day at the hotel, and I would have seen hundreds, maybe thousands of people. You'll need to give me some more information if I'm going to be on any help to you," said Donald.

"I do have a photograph," said Charlie pulling out the picture of Josh from his folder. "This is the boy I'm interested in tracing, he'd be about a year maybe eighteen months younger than you."

Donald took the photo and stared at in carefully. After a few seconds he started to gently nod his head.

"Do you know," said Donald, "I do recognise the boy. He's quite distinctive with that blond hair, but that's not why I remember him," said Donald taping the photograph against his hand. "He had a really nasty cut under his nose. It looked fresh and real sore. So much so that I remarked on it, and that's not something I would normally do, frowned upon by the hotel you see."

"I see," said Charlie as he scribbled in his notebook. "That's going to be very helpful, is there anything else you can remember?"

"You know I seem to recall he was attending a relative's birthday party, he'd had quite a bit to drink and slurred his words a bit. He came into the room where I was clearing glasses thinking it was where the party was, and I had to direct him to the other function room. That's weird, I do remember it quite well," said Donald.

"Listen Donald, you've been really helpful, don't suppose you can remember whose party it was," asked Charlie.

Donald shook his head. "The hotel should be able to tell you that," he said.

"Yes, of course," said Charlie, "I'm heading over there next."

"There is something else," said Donald looking at the photograph again, "I remember the fat minister being there. He used to dine regularly at the hotel. Huge appetite and always took the carvery. I don't remember his name, but I'm sure he was from White Sulphur Springs, smallish man with brown wavy hair, but like I said, quite fat. Yep, I'm sure he was at that party."

"Well Donald, you've been a great help. There's plenty for me to be getting on with. I'm going up to the hotel now, and I'll definitely be making enquiries about the minister," said Charlie.

"I'm probably going to have to come back at some time and take a proper statement from you, do you think you could give me your contact details?" said Charlie.

"Sure, no problem, glad I could be of some help," said Donald.

"Hi Mike, it's Charlie, thought I'd give you a quick call for an update."

"You just caught me Charlie, I was thinking of heading home. How did you get on?" asked Mike.

"Pretty good thanks. Didn't get to see Herb but I was able to speak to Julia. That was very fruitful. She gave me the name of a boy called Donald Hastie who she'd tried to trace as part of her enquiry. Turns out that he'd left the area to go backpacking not long after the murder and she never got to speak to him," added Charlie.

"Luckily, I managed to get hold of him. He was working in the hotel the day before the murder and remembers speaking to someone who looks just like Josh at a family birthday party. Julia gave me a photo of Josh she'd been using at the time and when I showed it to him he remembered the boy. Said he had a really nasty cut under his nose that looked like it had been done recently. Now we know Josh wasn't in Tuckahoe that afternoon, but it strongly suggests that someone who looks very like Josh was," said Charlie.

"That really is interesting, did he say anything else?" asked Mike.

"The other thing he told me that might be helpful to us was that he remembers a minister being at the party. He couldn't remember his name, but he gave a good description and thinks he lives in White Sulphur Springs," added Charlie.

"And what about the hotel, did you get any joy there?" asked Mike.

"Afraid not, they were hopeless. It appears that while they've now got all their bookings on computer, but back then it was just paper records and they seem to have lost them during a refurbishment a couple of years ago, so I drew a blank with that one."

"How did you get on; did you get hold of the road accident file?" asked Charlie.

"Took him a while, but good old Phil found it eventually. I'm just reading through it now. I'll take it home tonight, so I can get my head around it," said Mike. "And good work this afternoon, Charlie, I think we're making progress. I want to follow up that enquiry with the minister ASAP, so we'll head up there tomorrow morning."

*

Over in Fairlea Mike and Susan had just finished dinner and Mike was filling the sink to wash the dishes.

"That was a delicious meal Susan, always love your lasagne," said Mike looking under the sink for the detergent bottle.

"Just leave the dishes Mike, Keegan will do them," said Susan sternly. "He's going to be doing them for the rest of the week. Took a call from his school today, apparently our son and three of his friends skipped the last two periods of school yesterday and unluckily for them, they were seen at the mall by Mr Peters. So, he's now grounded and on dishes for a week. And before you ask he's upstairs doing his homework, which I said you'll be checking later".

Mike sighed. Keegan was a good boy, and this was right out of character, but Susan was right, he needed to learn a lesson and Mike wasn't about to overrule his wife.

Mike poured himself a coffee and went and sat in the den. "Sorry, to be antisocial but I've brought some work home, just reading, but might take me a couple of hours to get through it."

"Must be important, darling," said Susan, "It's been a while since I can remember you bringing work home. I'll not disturb you, I've got a great book on the go, Patriot Games by Tom Clancy. Great story you'd love it."

Mike glanced up from his chair and smiled. "Maybe I'll wait till our vacation, I like a good story when I'm on holiday," said Mike.

343

For the next hour Mike read through the report. The summary of the actual accident was relatively short, but there were endless statements, doctors' reports and photographs to plough through. Mike smiled as he started to read the statement that Phil Coutts had taken from Susan. He'd read better statements, but Phil was still relatively inexperienced when he took this one, and regardless of which all the necessary details appeared to be there. Mike stroked his chin and thought for a moment before turning back the page. He had read Cathleen Heggerty's statement just a few minutes ago and now something struck him as strange.

"Susan, I need to ask you something?" said Mike. Susan looked at her husband and put down her book.

"Fine, what is it you want to know?" said Susan.

"This file I'm reading, it's about the fatal road accident at Greenbrier bridge that you were at twenty-one years ago. You remember? Cathleen Heggerty and you helped to save that child," said Mike.

"Of course I can remember it, never likely to forget that night, but it was a long time ago," said Susan. "Why are you reading it now?"

"I'll explain why later," said Mike.

"Look, I understand it was a long time ago, but I've got your statement here if we need to jog your memory. But right now, I want you to try and remember what happened when you arrived at the accident and first spoke to Cathleen."

Susan sat back in her chair and closed her eyes to concentrate.

"Okay, when I first arrived I remember Cathleen asking me if I had a flashlight and then going to get one out of my car. After that, well I saw the dreadful scene

344

in the car and all the blood, I had to hold the flashlight to let Cathleen see properly, do you want me to tell you about all of that?" asked Susan.

"No, you can skip that. Just tell me what you did and what was said, you know, between you and Cathleen," said Mike.

"Well, after the baby arrived I remember her asking me to get a blanket or something out the back of the crashed car to wrap the baby with. Then, I think we just hugged each other and cried for a bit because it had been so traumatic. After that she told me to take the baby to the hospital which I did, and well, then a police officer arrived at the hospital, I can't recall if it was Phil or somebody else and that was about it really," said Susan.

"Yeah, that's good Susan, thanks. But did you miss a bit?" asked Mike. Susan looked confused.

"Miss a bit, what do you mean?" asked Susan.

"You missed the bit about hearing a baby crying, and Cathleen telling you that it was a fox that was crying, not a baby," said Mike looking directly at his wife.

"Do you remember saying that, Susan?" asked Mike in a voice that was barely louder than a whisper.

"Now you say it, yes I do remember that. I did hear what I thought was a baby crying," said Susan quietly.

"Why didn't you mention it when I asked you to go over what happened?" asked Mike.

"I must have just forgotten," said Susan who didn't much care for being rebuked by her husband. "Anyway, I didn't think it was that important."

Mike put down the file and looked at Susan.

"It's not," said Mike in a serious voice. "It's not important, so why is it in Cathleen Heggerty's statement, but not yours?" asked Mike.

"I'm not looking for you to answer that Susan," said Mike, "I'm just thinking out loud. But do you know something, Susan? The conversation that we've just had, might just be the key to getting an innocent man freed from prison. I think I can prove Josh Heggerty didn't kill Maisie Foster."

Chapter 16

"I thought we were going to White Sulphur Springs," said Charlie as Mike took a right at the junction and headed in the opposite direction.

"We are," said Mike, "but first we need to stop in at the hospital and see Cynthia Lehman."

Cynthia looked up from her desk when she heard Charlie's knock at the door.

"Good morning, Detective Finch," said Cynthia looking over her horn-rimmed glasses, "I wasn't expecting to see you so soon."

"No, I suppose you weren't," said Charlie, "but my boss has asked if you could lay your hands on Jennifer Saltman's file. I said you'd be able to find it no bother. She had her baby around the same time as Cathleen Heggerty, so it should be in the same pile."

"Indeed, officer, I know exactly where it is, that's the benefit of a proper filing system you see. I'm intrigued as to why you might want it, but I suspect you're not going to tell me," said Cynthia getting up from her desk.

"Sorry, but I don't even I know why he wants it," said Charlie with a mischievous smile.

"Tragic accident that was, both parents losing their lives that night. If it hadn't been for Cathleen passing by they would probably have lost the baby as well," added

Cynthia shaking her head as she opened the door to the store room.

"I'm grateful to you," said Charlie as Cynthia handed him the file. "I'm not sure how long the boss wants it for, but I'll get it back to you as soon as I can," said Charlie as he headed out the door into the car park.

"There can't be that many churches in White Sulphur Springs," said Mike as he parked the car next to a row of shops in the centre of town. Mike pointed across the road to a large modern red brick building that had a modest bell tower and a grey leaded roof. "We might as well try over there first, it's definitely a church, you never know it might be the right one."

The sign by the side of the main door said St Joseph's Roman Catholic Church. Finding that the door was locked, Charlie rang the bell of the house that adjoined it. The door was answered by a rather stern looking lady holding what appeared to be a duster and a can of polish in her hand.

"Excuse me, ma'am," said Charlie politely, "this might seem a little strange but we're looking for a minister. Unfortunately, we don't know his name, but he's quite short and a bit overweight and has brown wavy hair."

"Well that certainly isn't Father McKirgan," said the lady. "He's over six foot and bald. From the description it sounds like you're describing Pastor Whitehead. He was the minister at Emmanuel Methodist church on the other side of town, but I'm afraid he died last year. It certainly doesn't sound like their new pastor either, he's thin and tall like Father McKirgan."

That's a pity thought Mike, just when things were starting to go our way we come up against another setback.

"You might want to speak to Mrs Whitehead," said the lady, "she still lives in the town and might be able to help you."

Charlie nodded. "Yes, that would be very useful, do you happen to know her address?"

"It's the third cottage from the end next to the library, it's about a five-minute walk from here. Mrs Whitehead goes to the same art class as me. It's the only cottage with a hedge at the front, you can't miss it," said the lady.

Mike and Charlie thanked the lady for her help and made their way down the hill to the library which sat directly across the street from the town hall.

"That was a pity," said Mike, "I'm not sure how much help Mrs Whitehead will be, but here's hoping eh."

"This must be it then said Charlie, it's the only one with a hedge, fingers crossed she's in."

"Hello, can I help you?" said the old lady who opened the door.

"I hope you can," said Mike introducing himself and Charlie and explaining why they were there. "And may we also pass on our condolences for the sad loss of your husband."

"Well, that's most kind of you. Please, will you come in."

Mrs Whitehead was small and quite stooped. Her mobility wasn't good, and she walked with the aid of a tripod. However, it appeared to Mike and Charlie that there was nothing wrong with her mental faculties.

"May 1984, you say?" said Mrs Whitehead, "a function at the Lake View Hotel." Mrs Whitehead started to chuckle. "Philip never needed an excuse to eat at the Lake View, it was one of his favourites, we used to go quite often for the carvery, it really is very good you know."

Mike smiled. "Did you ever attend any functions with your husband, you know, when he was there in his official capacity as a minister? Sorry, I mean pastor?" asked Mike.

"Not really," said Mrs Whitehead, "we always tried to keep ecumenical matters separate, so no, I never used to go to those things. I'll tell you what I can do for you, gentlemen, I can check Philip's diary. He always kept all his appointments in his diary and I've not thrown any of them away. They should still be in his wardrobe. I'll check if you'd like."

"If you could that would be great," said Charlie.

"You did say May 1984, didn't you?" asked Mrs Whitehead.

"Yes, that's correct," replied Charlie, "it would have been around the middle of the month.".

A couple of minutes later Mrs Whitehead returned carrying a red coloured diary.

"Well I've found the diary for 1984 so that's a start," said Mrs Whitehead as she put on her glasses and started to leaf through the book.

"Ah," she said, "I might have found something. There's an entry here for Wednesday the 16th May that says memorial service for Jennifer & David Saltman, Tuckahoe cemetery, 4pm. Underneath that he's written, plus Elaine, Ruth and families," said Mrs Whitehead.

"There's also an entry for the following day that just says 1pm, Elaine's 50th birthday lunch, Lake View. Is this what you're interested in?" asked Mrs Whitehead handing the diary to Mike.

Mike looked at the pages and smiled. "It certainly is, do you mind if I hang onto the diary? I'll take good care of it and get it back to you, but it would be helpful if I could take it just now," said Mike.

"Sure, no hurry at all. I'm glad an old lady like me could be of some help," said Mrs Whitehead. "Would you gentlemen, like to stay for a cup of coffee? I've a homemade Victoria sponge if you'd like some?"

"It sounds delicious," said Mike, "but we're a bit pressed for time so need to get on, I'm sorry about that."

"No need to apologise, you must be very busy, I hope you get what you're looking for," said Mrs Whitehead as she showed the detectives out the door.

"Okay Mike," said Charlie as they made their way back to the car, "I'm still not sure where this is all going, can you tell me what's going on?"

"I'm going to I promise, I just want to be absolutely sure that I've got this worked out properly. But we're really close now Charlie, a couple more enquiries and then you'll know," said Mike.

"Sure hope so," said Charlie, "this is starting to do my head in. I'm starting to feel that I'm stupid not been able to work this out for myself."

Mike laughed quietly. "I can tell you you're not stupid, Charlie, but I've got some information that you don't. You're trying to work this out without all the cards and that's never easy," said Mike.

"Tell me about it," said Charlie sarcastically.

"Pass me the Saltman maternity file, will you?" asked Mike, "and while you're at it, give me the Heggerty one as well please."

Charlie reached across to the rear seat and took the two files out of his folder and handed them to Mike.

"Are you going to be a while reading them?" asked Charlie.

"Not that long," said Mike, "Just want to check a couple of things."

"In that case, I'm going to get us a couple of coffee's, 'cause that's what number twos are supposed to do, isn't it," said Charlie who was still not amused about being kept in the dark.

"Great idea," said Mike, "and I'll have a doughnut with mine while you're at it," said Mike grinning.

"Don't push your luck," said Charlie, "folk can go off people you know."

"Did you find what you were looking for?" asked Charlie as he returned to the car carrying two cartons of coffee and a bag of doughnuts."

"You know Charlie, I think I might just have," said Mike. "Here, take a look at the Saltman file and check the page numbers," said Mike handing Charlie the file. "Notice anything?"

Charlie looked at the file for a minute. "Page three is missing, but I don't see anything else unusual," said Charlie.

"No, that's it, you found it. There is no page three in the file," said Mike.

"Now have a look at the Heggerty file," said Mike handing over the second file.

"It all appears to be here Mike, I don't see any pages that are missing," said Charlie.

"No, you're right, I didn't find any pages missing either," said Mike. "But take a look at page three in the Heggerty file, what do you see?"

Charlie turned to the relevant page and read through it. "Appears to be a note written by Vernon Schilling describing a sixteen-week examination, but it's difficult to tell. The handwriting's appalling, but it's definitely been signed off by Vernon Schilling," said Charlie.

"What's so significant about a missing page? Can't be that unusual," said Charlie, "not with a file that's more than twenty-one years old."

"Sure, you may be right," said Mike taking back the file. "But I think we need to give Doctor Schilling another call, I've got a feeling that page isn't missing by accident. Look, the police office is just around the corner, we'll head over there, I need to phone the office anyway, I've left the road accident report that I was reading yesterday on my desk and I need an address from it. But we'll give Mr Schilling a call while we're there, he may be able to clear something up for us."

"Hi Brad," said Mike, as he and Charlie approached the front desk of the police office.

"Well, Lieutenant Rawlingson, long time no see. What can I do for you Mike?" asked Brad with a broad smile.

"Just need to use a phone to call the office, Brad, got a couple of enquiries to follow up on but need to call in to get a couple of addresses. Anyway, good to see you, how're Kate and the kids?" asked Mike.

"Use the phone in my office, Mike. Kate's great thanks and the kids are nine and seven now. Keegan must be about eleven now is he?" asked Brad.

"Thirteen already," said Mike, "can't believe where the time goes."

"Jeezo," said Brad shaking his head, "thirteen already, I remember when he was born, doesn't half

353

make you feel old eh? If you need anything else Mike, just give me a shout" said Brad, "it's great to see you."

"You too," said Mike as he opened the door to Brad's office.

"Hello, is that you Angela?" asked Mike who was sitting on the edge of Brad's desk. "Great, I need you to go into my office and get the file that's lying on the desk. It's a fatal road accident from 1967, it's got the names David & Jennifer Saltman on the front. Can you look at the back of the report? I think it's about the second last page, there's a list of addresses, can you give me the one for Ruth Woodburn, I think it's Birch drive, or something like that, can you go and get it please?"

"23, Birch Ave, Marlinton. That's the one, Angela, many thanks," said Mike.

"Take it that's where we're going next?" asked Charlie.

Mike nodded. "But first let's see if Vernon Schilling's at home."

"Hello, is that Dr Schilling speaking?" said Mike. "It's Lieutenant Rawlingson from Lewisburg Police Department speaking, sorry to trouble you again, but I was hoping you might be able to answer a couple of questions for me."

"Lieutenant Rawlingson, nice to speak to you again," said Vernon, "how can I help you this time?"

"I won't keep you long Dr Schilling," said Mike, "but does the name Jennifer Saltman mean anything to you? She was expecting a baby around the same time as Cathleen Heggerty and until you retired you had been her obstetrician. We're talking around November 1966, I know it's a long time ago now."

"It certainly is," said Vernon, "I'm sorry, but it's not ringing any bells I'm afraid, my memory's not what it was, lieutenant."

"Sadly, she was killed in a road accident along with her husband while travelling to the hospital to have her baby. Thankfully the baby survived the accident," said Mike.

"I have the vaguest memory of hearing about the accident, but I'm sorry, I really don't remember the lady," said Vernon.

"That's okay, no problem, as I said it was a very long time ago," said Mike.

"Perhaps my second question will be a little easier. I was hoping you could tell me if you were in the habit of conducting sixteen-week assessments with your patients and what that assessment might involve?" asked Mike.

Vernon gave a little chuckle. "That is a much easier question right enough," said Vernon. "Yes, I was always in the habit of doing a sixteen-week assessment. You see, you're well into the second trimester by then, so it's useful for flagging up a number of potential issues. Of course, this was in the days before we could properly scan our patients, so apart from the standard blood pressure and urine tests, the sixteen-week assessment allowed me to check if baby's heart was beating properly," said Vernon. "If you did that much earlier it would be difficult to distinguish the heartbeat as the baby wouldn't be developed enough. But if you used a doppler to listen for the beat, you could usually hear the heart quite clearly at sixteen-weeks."

"I see, that's most interesting, doctor," said Mike. "So what type of unusual things might you find during the doppler examination?" he asked.

"Well, an irregular heartbeat for one thing and sadly on rare occasions no heartbeat at all. Also, it was possible to distinguish if your patient was expecting twins as you could hear two heart beats. Forty years of experience taught you if it was likely to be twins. You can tell by the rhythm and frequency of the beats you see."

"Dr Schilling, that really is fascinating, I'm certainly learning something new today," said Mike scribbling down notes on a pad.

"Oh, forgive me, doctor, one final question. Would you always enter a handwritten note in the patient's file after you completed your sixteen-week examination?"

"Absolutely. In fact, I would add a short note after every examination I carried out on a patient," added Vernon. "Mostly routine stuff like blood pressure would be recorded, but anything slightly unusual would also be noted. It was how I was taught as a young doctor, and it stayed with me throughout my career, I just thought it was the professional thing to do."

"I'm really grateful to you Doctor, that's filled in some gaps in my knowledge for sure and it's been very useful, thanks again for your time," said Mike.

"Not at all," said Vernon, "I'm not sure how I've been of help, but if I have that's great. Nice speaking to you again, Lieutenant Rawlingson."

Charlie looked at Mike. "You seem pleased, even if he didn't remember Jennifer Saltman," said Charlie.

"I am. I wasn't really expecting him to remember Jennifer," said Mike, "but I think what he did do was confirm why the third page of Jennifer Saltman's report is missing."

Charlie scratched his head. Just when he thought he was making some sense of where this was all going, something else cropped up to make him doubt himself.

"Okay," said Charlie as he and Mike walked back to their car. "This is what I think. You clearly believe that someone that looks a lot like Josh Heggerty killed Maisie Foster, and from what Donald Hastie told me that person was at a party at the Lake View the day before. That's now been corroborated by what Mrs Whitehead was able to tell us. But, and it's a big but, I have not a clue who that person is or how it begins to explain away the blood evidence, or why, for that matter, page three is missing from Jennifer Salman's file. Oh, I nearly forgot, and we now know that Frank and Cathleen are not Josh's blood parents, but I don't know what that's got to do with it either. There, that's my cards on the table," said Charlie with a shrug of his shoulders.

Mike nodded and gave a gentle smile. "You're getting there, Detective Finch," said Mike, "perhaps the next call will begin to make things clearer. Take me to Marlinton, Charlie, we'll just about be able to squeeze it in, then we'll call it a day and start again tomorrow. It'll take us an hour or so to get up there, that should give you a bit more time to work it out Charlie".

Give me strength, thought Charlie, as he started the engine and turned onto the main road, this is more complicated than an episode of Quincy.

"This looks like it Charlie, number 23, just park it up over there," said Mike pointing across the street.

Number 23, Birch Avenue, was a smart two storey townhouse. Clad with grey painted cedar shingles, the window shutters and front door were a striking dark green colour. The freshly mown front lawn was edged with an array of brightly coloured bedding plants which made the house look like your quintessential American family home. As the two detectives climbed the steep driveway, Mike noticed that the name of the mailbox said Booth.

"Good afternoon, madam," said Mike holding up his police badge as a woman in her early forties answered the door. "I'm trying to trace the Woodburn family, I believe they may have used to live here."

The woman smiled and nodded her head.

"They did a long time ago," said the woman. "We moved here in the summer of 1974, so, what's that, fourteen years ago. We bought the house from the Woodburns. Is there a problem officer? asked the woman.

"No problem, madam," said Mike. "We're just following up some enquiries, but I seem to have only got this very old address for Ruth Woodburn. You don't happen to have a forwarding address for her, do you?" asked Mike.

"I'm sorry I don't," said the woman. "I do know that they moved because John got a new job at a university somewhere in the North West. Idaho or Oregon, somewhere like that. That's terrible I can't even remember the girls' names. She had twin girls and an older son. His name was Todd, lovely looking boy with blond hair, he must have been about eight when they moved."

"I'll tell you who might be able to help you," said the woman starting to nod her head again. "Mrs Johnston will know. The Johnstons used to live next door but they moved to Fairlea about six years ago. Mr Johnston died a couple of years back, but Mrs Johnston's still on the go. Do you know Fairlea?"

"Yes, I do," said Mike "quite well in fact."

"Well, it's the house opposite the park, you know the one near to the high school's playing fields. I can't remember the street name," said the woman tapping her head, "But it's the first house, small chalet, it's got pinkish roof tiles and the garden's lovely, I'm sure its number two. The Johnstons had lived in the house next door to this for more than forty years, I know she was quite friendly with Ruth."

"You've been a great help," said Mike, thanking the lady. "I'm sure we'll be able to find Mrs Johnston from what you've told us, I'm much obliged."

Well Mike, to use your terminology, I think I might have picked up another card," said Charlie as they returned to the car.

"Go on," said Mike, "I'm listening."

"Well, by the sounds of it Mrs Johnston's house can only be a few minutes' walk from where Maisie Foster was murdered, and you clearly think that Todd Woodburn did it. But I'm still none the wiser as to why you know he did it," said Charlie hoping his boss was now going to reveal all.

"I have to admit, Charlie," said Mike with a broad grin, "You're getting mighty close now, but you'll need to sleep on it. Time for home now. We'll start again in the morning and we'll go and see Mrs Johnston, I think she holds the final piece of this puzzle. Right, come on, let's get going, Mrs Rawlingson is making Lasagne for dinner and I'm starving."

Charlie gave a resigned sigh, he couldn't understand why he couldn't work it out. What was it that Mike knew that he didn't? It was starting to drive him mad.

359

Chapter 17

Charlie hadn't slept a wink. He had spent most of last night just lying in bed trying to piece together all the new evidence they had uncovered that would explain why Mike appeared to be so confident that Todd Woodburn had killed Maisie. Try as he might, he just couldn't make sense of it. Every theory he came up with fell apart when he tried to explain how Josh's blood was on the murder weapon and on Maisie's dress and fingernails. Todd Woodburn may have looked like Josh, but that didn't prove he had anything to do with Maisie's murder thought Charlie.

By the time the others arrived at the office, Charlie had gone over the nightshifts report and completed most of the administration tasks that needed attended to.

"How many coffees have you had?" asked Mike as Charlie filled the mugs.

"This will be my third this morning," said Charlie passing Mike his mug.

"Well if you couldn't sleep last night, drinking that amount of coffee isn't going to help, and your eyes are all bloodshot," said Mike.

"You'll not be able to sleep for days, if you carry on like that, and I'm only half joking," added Mike. "Come through to my office, will you? I'll explain what the plan is for this morning."

Charlie followed Mike across the corridor and into his office. Before he had a chance to explain that he was more than capable of looking after his own welfare, the phone on Mike's desk rang.

"Yes Dave, hello, Mike Rawlingson speaking."

"Mike, I've got a result back for the test I ran on the baby's remains. Now remember I've not done this test before so this is far from guaranteed and it can't be used officially. In fact, I'm not going to give you anything in writing so there will be no physical record of this test. I just wanted to make that crystal-clear from the off," said Dave nervously.

"Fully understand Dave, that is what we agreed after all," replied Mike.

"Okay, fine then," said Dave. "The sample from the baby's bones has come back positive when compared against both Frank and Cathleen's blood samples. The test is showing that they are the natural parents of the baby," said Dave.

A thin smile broke out across Mike's face.

"Dave, I'm most grateful to you. You've just confirmed what I already knew," said Mike. "And just for your peace of mind, this will be the last conversation we'll have about it. I give you my word."

"So, I take it the test has established that the Heggerty's are the parents of the baby?" asked Charlie who had been paying close attention to Mike's telephone conversation.

Mike nodded. "Yep, it has, but I was expecting that. It's really just the icing on the cake," replied Mike. "Grab your jacket and folder, Charlie, let's go and see Mrs Johnston. She's going to help us catch our killer."

"Pinkish roof tiles and an immaculate garden, this is definitely it," said Charlie as he parked their unmarked police vehicle outside number two Park View Drive.

"It's even closer to the playing fields than I thought, you can see the top of the football stand beyond the trees. Just give me a minute, will you?" said Charlie lifting up a folder from the rear seat. "I just want to check the door to door file to see if anything of any note was recorded for number two," he said flipping through the file. "I meant to do it first thing this morning but got distracted by the night shift report." Charlie carefully studied the file. "Huh," said Charlie stroking his chin.

"Huh what?" asked Mike.

Charlie taped the file of papers with his knuckle, "Number two is marked off complete and nothing of note. The interesting thing is it's dated 26th May, that's nine days after the murder. The rest of the street look to have been marked off on the 20th, three days after Maisie died."

Mike raised an eyebrow and gave a gentle nod. "Interesting," said Mike, "it must have been marked up the day before we arrested Josh then," said Mike.

"And here's another thing," said Charlie showing Mike a page from the file. "Look who's signed it off!" Mike stared at the page. "Wayne Mitchell. I might have guessed it would be that son of a bitch," said Mike with a rueful shake of his head.

"Well the good news is, Mrs Johnston appears to be in," said Mike. "I take it the old lady peering around the corner of the curtains is her."

The front door opened as the detectives walked up the path and a rather prim old lady with short grey hair and gold rimmed glasses stepped onto the veranda that ran the length of the well-maintained chalet.

"Now, if I were guessing, gentlemen, I would say you were detectives, either that or a couple of Jehovah's Witnesses. No one else seems to wear suits these days more's the pity," said Mrs Johnston.

"Well, we're the former," said Mike pulling his police badge out of his trouser pocket and showing it to Mrs Johnston. "And may I say how preceptive of you to know we were detectives Mrs Johnston. You are Mrs Johnston, aren't you?" asked Mike with a mischievous smile.

"Yes, I am," said Mrs Johnston, "and I'd like to say how perceptive of you to know that, but of course, you've come to see me, so I expect you had a good idea who I was, didn't you, officer?"

Wow, there's no flies on this old girl, thought Charlie. If she does know something she'll be a fantastic witness.

"Please, do come in," said Mrs Johnston, "would you care for some coffee, or perhaps some lemonade?"

"Lemonade," said Charlie quick as a flash, "that would be lovely, we're both trying to cut down on the amount of coffee we drink. Sorry we didn't introduce ourselves, I'm Sergeant Finch and this is Lieutenant Rawlingson."

"Delighted to meet you both. So, Lemonade it is. Excuse me while I go and get some glasses," said Mrs Johnston as she disappeared into the kitchen.

"Charlie, while Mrs Johnston's out of the room can you find me the photo of Josh in that folder of yours?" asked Mike.

"Sure, here it is," said Charlie pulling the photograph out of his folder and handing it to Mike.

"Now, how can I help you officers?" said Mrs Johnston as she poured the freshly squeezed lemonade into three tumblers.

"We were wondering if you might know the whereabouts of Ruth Woodburn and her family?" said Mike. "We believe you used to be neighbours in Marlinton."

"That's correct," said Mrs Johnston. "Lovely family. They lived next door for about ten years till John took a new job and they moved to Portland," added Mrs Johnston.

"Are you still in touch?" asked Mike. "I was wondering if you might have an address for them?"

"Sure, I still send a Christmas card and I get one from Ruth as well. I used to send birthday cards to the children, but I stopped that a few years ago. Todd must be twenty-one or even twenty-two now and the twins, well they had their eighteenths not that long ago, my doesn't time just fly by," said Mrs Johnston.

"It certainly does," replied Mike. "Can I ask when you last saw the Woodburn's?"

"Well I know exactly when that was," said Mrs Johnston. "They came down for Ruth's sister Elaine's fiftieth birthday, that was four years ago now, 1984. I remember because I was eighty that year and of course, Bill, my husband was still alive then. They had a party at the Lake View at Tuckahoe and all the family were there. They also had a memorial service for Ruth and Elaine's other sister Jennifer. She died in a road accident about twenty years ago. Her husband David was killed as well, baby Todd survived though and that's how

Ruth came to have Todd you see. She and John adopted Todd after the accident."

"Yes, I know about the accident, a terrible tragedy that was," said Mike. Mrs Johnston nodded gently and gave a resigned sigh. "So, did you get to see Ruth and the family when they were down?" asked Mike.

"I got to see Ruth, John and the girls," said Mrs Johnston. "They popped in for an hour after the party on their way back to the airport. We just chatted, they didn't even take a cup of coffee they were that full up after the party."

"Excuse me Mrs Johnston, you said you saw Ruth, John and the girls, but you didn't mention Todd. Didn't you get to see him?" asked Mike.

"He didn't come in with the others," said Mrs Johnston. "Ruth said he wasn't feeling well after the party, had a bit of a headache, so he went for a walk in the park across the road while the others were in here."

Charlie, who was taking notes in his folder looked up and glanced across to Mike.

"So, you didn't see Todd at all then?" said Mike.

"Well, that's not entirely true. I didn't get to speak to him, but when they were getting ready to leave I saw him out the front window," said Mrs Johnston starting to chuckle.

"Just like I saw you today officers, I was peering out the window, I'm a bit of a nosey parker."

"Oh, I wouldn't say that," said Mike. "But you saw him walking back through the park I suppose?"

"Yes, that's correct," said Mrs Johnston. "I remember it well because he'd had some sort of nose bleed, he was covered in blood, all down his shirt it was. Ruth had to get tissues for him and a clean shirt to change into before they could get into the taxi for the airport. And, well, that was the last time I saw any of the family. Don't suppose I'll see them again. Not at my age, and anyway they don't really have a reason to come back now, it's a long way from Portland."

"Mrs Johnston, I take it you're aware that a fifteen-year-old girl was murdered down at the playing fields around that time?" said Mike.

"Yes, I did know that," said Mrs Johnston. "But I didn't at the time. Bill and I had gone to visit my sister in Roanoke the next day and it wasn't until we got back the following week that I got to hear about it." said Mrs Johnston. "Things like that don't happen in Fairlea. Well, of course, that just goes to show that they do. Quite dreadful, so sad."

"Can I ask if you spoke to the police about any of this?" said Mike. "I mean, did you tell anyone about seeing Todd covered in the blood that afternoon?" asked Charlie.

"Funnily enough I did. An officer called at the door a few days after we got back from Roanoke and spoke to me. I told him about the Woodburn's visit and seeing Todd that afternoon," said Mrs Johnston. "I remember he didn't seem that interested, he didn't write any of it down. He took my name and address, that was about it."

"So, he didn't take a statement from you?" asked Charlie incredulously.

"No, he definitely didn't," agreed Mrs Johnston. However, I do remember the officer saying that they already had a suspect and were hoping to make an arrest very soon."

"I don't suppose you can remember the officer's name who spoke to you? asked Charlie.

"No, sorry, I don't recall," said Mrs Johnston, "but he was wearing a uniform. He had dark brown hair and was quite fresh faced.

Charlie looked at Mike who gave a wry shake of his head.

"That's all been very useful, Mrs Johnston. If you don't mind I have a photo that I'd like to show you," said Mike handing Mrs Johnston the photograph.

"Yep, that's Todd Woodburn," said Mrs Johnston looking at the photograph, "he's a very handsome young man, bet he sets a few hearts fluttering."

Mike smiled and nodded.

"Just one more thing to ask, Mrs Johnston, if you could go and find us Ruth's address I would be very grateful," said Mike, "and thanks for the lemonade it was really refreshing on a warm day like this."

As Mrs Johnston left the room to go and look for the address Charlie turned to Mike.

"Okay," said Charlie, "despite another almighty fuck up by Wayne Mitchell this is now becoming much clearer, but you'll still going to have to explain to me how Todd Woodburn's blood came back as a positive match for Josh Heggerty's."

Before Mike had a chance to answer, Mrs Woodburn came back into the lounge carrying a piece of paper.

"Here it is, gentlemen," she said, "153, Burnside Street, Laurel Hurst, Portland."

"What a remarkable woman," said Charlie as they walked back to the car. "She's going to make an impressive witness. I hope I'm as mentally alert when I get to be her age."

Mike nodded in agreement.

"Right boss, what are we going to do about Mitchell?" asked Charlie as they got into the car.

"Don't let yourself get distracted by that idiot at this stage," replied Mike. "I'll deal with Wayne Mitchell later. He's not getting away with this one. What he did was a clear neglect of duty and as a consequence an innocent man has spent nearly five years in prison. I'm going to nail his ass for this one, Charlie, you can count on that, but that's for later.

Charlie nodded as he put on his seatbelt.

"Now what are you thinking?" asked Mike, who could tell that Charlie was mulling something over.

"Okay, this is my final go at this," said Charlie. "I'm close but I've not solved it. I wouldn't have the evidence to prove that Todd killed Maisie. But this is what I know. We can now prove that Todd Woodburn was at the Lake View on the day of the murder. From what the witnesses have told us, we also know he had a remarkable resemblance to Josh, so much so that Mrs Johnston thought the photo of Josh was Todd. Mrs Johnston's testimony will place Todd near the locus at the material time and we now know he was bleeding heavily from his nose when she saw him that afternoon. That could help explain how the blood got on the scaffolding pole and on Maisie's dress and fingernails. I reckon she must have put up a real fight trying to fend him off.

But, this is what I still don't get. How come the lab found Josh's blood on all these things. Surely, if it was Todd's the results would have come back negative and we'd still be looking for our murderer. So, I'm sorry Mike. I believe he did it, but I can't prove that Todd murdered Maisie Foster, so it's over to you, the last part of the puzzle just doesn't fit," said Charlie closing his eyes and putting his head back against the headrest.

Mike looked at his colleague. He'd known Charlie Finch for many years and he was a hardworking detective and loyal and trusted friend.

"I think it's time I put you out of your misery," said Mike. "It's not that I didn't want to tell you how I knew, I just thought having you keep an open mind would be helpful. Just in case I might have missed something. I've seen that happen many times before Charlie. It's called confirmation bias; people interpret new evidence as confirmation of their existing belief, I desperately wanted to avoid that. But now you need to know, so let's head over to Ming's, I'm going to buy you lunch."

"Ming's, are you feeling okay, I love Ming's but a sandwich from Annie Mack's would do fine," said Charlie.

Mike laughed. "No, I insist, it's the least I could do for your patience, I could tell I was driving you to distraction. Anyway, eating your own weight at the lunchtime buffet is right up your street, Charlie," said Mike.

"Aye, you know me too well boss," replied Charlie with a wink.

As Charlie began to tuck into a mountainous plate of ribs and spring rolls, Mike produced two sets of photocopied notes from his folder entitled DNA and Forensic Science, Implications for Policing.

"These are a copy of the course notes for the DNA conference I attended at Chicago a couple of weeks back," said Mike pushing a set across the table towards Charlie. "I've marked the relevant section with a purple marker pen, it's towards the back, page seventeen or thereabouts."

Charlie put down his fork and thumbed through the handout. "Page eighteen, is this it?" asked Charlie looking up at Mike, "Anomalies in DNA testing." Mike nodded, "That's it," he said.

Charlie didn't say anything for the next five minutes. He read the page carefully and then read it again. He wanted to be one hundred percent sure he hadn't missed anything. Eventually, he put down the paper and looked at Mike.

"Of course," said Charlie with a knowing look, "I get it. I totally get it now. Todd Woodburn and Josh Heggerty are identical twins. I still feel kind of stupid though. Not about not knowing that identical twins share the same blood type and have exactly the same DNA, this is new technology after all. I can see how that explains why the blood tests were all positive for Josh. That definitely all makes sense, after all, identical twins are formed from a single egg splitting, yep I get all that. The bit I'm annoyed at is the fact that I hadn't worked out that Josh and Todd were twins. Looking back now there were any number of clues, I just didn't put them together. So, tell me Mike, when did you know? Was it when Dave told you that Frank and Cathleen weren't Josh's real parents?"

"No, funnily enough it wasn't then," said Mike. "But that was the confirmation I needed to be absolutely sure that I'd worked it out properly. Of course, the catalyst for all this was finding the baby's remains buried on the farm, that got me thinking about Josh's trial again.

But believe it or not, it suddenly became clear when I was at home reading the road accident report about the fatal crash that killed Jennifer and David Saltman. If you remember, Cathleen Heggerty had come across the accident just a few minutes before Susan arrived at the scene. I was reading Cathleen's statement and I noticed that it made mention of Susan saying that she thought she'd heard a baby crying when she was getting a flashlight from her car. In her statement it said that she told Susan that it was a fox crying and not a baby," said Mike.

Charlie looked a little confused. "That doesn't seem very significant."

"Exactly," said Mike, "It wasn't significant. So much so it didn't merit a mention in Susan's statement. Then when I asked Susan to tell me what happened that night she never mentioned hearing a baby cry. It was only when I prompted her that she remembered saying it. So, that got me wondering why Cathleen had it in her statement. It was as if she was trying to second guess what Susan might have told the police. She needed to be able to explain it away. Quite clever if you think about it."

"Okay," said Charlie, "I follow that, but surely there was more to it than that, you didn't solve it from that alone did you?"

"No, of course not," said Mike. "Do you remember that Cathleen worked as a midwife?"

Charlie nodded.

"Well then, she would have known what to do when she arrived at the accident and she would have been able to deliver the babies. I think she must have delivered the first baby before Susan arrived and put the child in her car. That was the baby that Susan heard crying. As I said, the bit about the fox was just to cover it up.

"So, what was her motivation for stealing the baby then?" asked Charlie.

"Give me a minute and I'll try and explain that," replied Mike. "Anyway, remember later how we discovered that a page had gone missing from Jennifer Saltman's maternity file. Well you were there when I phoned Vernon Schilling and he said he always entered a handwritten note after every examination. Well, Charlie, that is the bit I think you missed.

He told me that it was possible to identify twins during the sixteen-week assessment by detecting two heartbeats. The missing page would have contained Doctor Schillings notes on Jennifer's sixteen-week assessment. Having taken the baby Cathleen would have known that there would be a note in Jennifer's file recording the fact that she was expecting twins. She needed to remove any mention of twins from the file because if she didn't she was likely to be found out very quickly. The police would have started to investigate where the missing child was. And, of course, getting access to the file wasn't a problem for Cathleen. She worked at the hospital and was best friends with Cynthia Lehman, Cathleen would have known exactly where to find the file. Simple really."

"Wow," said Charlie stroking his chin. "Something else has just occurred to me. Thinking back now, I think we missed a trick back at Josh's trial, didn't we?"

"We sure did," said Mike, "and I'm damned annoyed with myself about that. We were too busy with our prosecution case. Anne Grey's evidence was the key. Think about it. She was adamant that when she saw

Josh at the farm two days after the murder his hair was much longer than when she saw him at Lake Tuckahoe the day before Maisie was killed. Yes, I know that boy turns out to have been his twin, but the bit about the length of hair was hugely significant. We all got side-tracked by Ettinger's clever gimmick with the Elvis Presley picture. We should have given more credibility to what Anne Grey had said. She'd known Josh since he was a baby she knew his hair was different that day, she hadn't made a mistake. And remember that fact was picked up by Elliot Manning who said the same thing after the identification parade."

"Funny how it all now seems to make sense," said Charlie. "Wasn't it during Anne Grey's testimony that old Rowe stopped the trial and had Cathleen removed from the court?"

"That's correct," said Mike. "I reckon it was at that point that Cathleen realised the truth. It became apparent to her that Todd and not Josh must have murdered Maisie. She was the only one at that time that knew the truth about Josh being a twin. That's why she became so agitated. The truth suddenly dawned on her, but she just couldn't communicate that to anyone. I'll tell you another thing Charlie, I truly believe that Frank knew nothing about any of that. For all those years he believed that Josh was his son."

"My God, that's just crazy," said Charlie. "And to think that she worked out what had really happened. That would just be torture. She must have gone through hell knowing all that and not being able to tell anyone," said Charlie shaking his head. "And the baby's remains that were never registered, what about them?" asked Charlie.

"This is where I think we get to the motive Charlie," said Mike.

"We know Cathleen had a stillborn son three years earlier, well, I'm sorry to say that I think tragedy struck for a second time and she had another stillbirth at home. She didn't tell a soul. Not her husband, or Cynthia, no one. I think Cathleen buried the child shortly after giving birth at home. So, coming across the accident like she did was just fate. It presented her with the most unexpected opportunity. She had just lost her own child and suddenly it the midst of that horror she found herself holding another new life in her arms. Mentally, I expect she was all over the place and, well, for reasons only she knows, she decided to take the child for herself. And then later, when we discovered there was no record of her having had her baby at the hospital, Dave Robertson phoned and confirmed that Frank and Cathleen were the blood parents of the baby that had been found, it all started to fall into place."

"Quite incredible," said Charlie puffing out his cheeks. "So, our gut instinct was right all along about Josh, he wasn't guilty. I now feel dreadful about that. That boy has spent nearly five years in prison for a crime he didn't commit."

"For what it's worth Charlie," said Mike, "I feel terrible about that too. Put we can now put right that wrong. I think it's time we went and saw Wilder and explained all this to him. Hope you haven't planned anything for your day off tomorrow, because we've got a plane to Portland to catch."

Charlie smiled. "Never been to Portland," said Charlie, "but I hear it's lovely this time of year."

374

Epilogue

"Just be careful on this rough section, there used to be a really deep pothole on the right-hand side near to where that redbud tree is," said Josh as Becca carefully negotiated the twisting farm track that led up to Dararra farm. "I don't want you damaging your new car, not after you've just got it anyway."

Becca smiled and laughed.

"I know you're being cheeky," said Becca, "I may have only had it three months, but this car is over ten years old as you well know. Yikes, you weren't kidding about the pothole though, it's huge."

"The pothole isn't the only thing that hasn't changed," said Josh, peering out the passenger window, the place looks much the same as when I last saw it. Grass has got pretty long though, that'll be one of my first jobs, get that cut back. Best park on that bit of hard standing next to the hen coop," said Josh.

"By the way what happened to the chickens and the hogs, Josh?" asked Becca.

"Frank decided to sell them when he knew he was moving in with George over at Hinton. Impossible to have livestock when you're not living here. But don't worry we'll get some more. Definitely chickens and a few hogs. But I thought I might try a few sheep as well. Plenty of room, they can just graze around the apple trees."

"How does it feel to be back?" asked Becca wrapping her arm around Josh's waist.

"Do you know, Becca, not as weird as I thought it was going to be," replied Josh kissing Becca gently on her cheek. "It was my home for all those years, and now it's going to be my home again. Well, for a while anyway. I'd still like to go to college and study music, but that might have to wait for a bit while we get the farm going again. I never thought I'd end up running the farm but at least I've got you with me to help," said Josh with a smile.

"It's all been a bit mad, hasn't it?" said Becca, "but now you're free, are you still intending to go and visit your mom? "Gosh this is awkward," added Becca, "but I don't know what to call her."

"Mom's fine," said Josh, "I now know she isn't my birth mother, but she's always been mom to me. I don't understand why she did what she did and I'm not going to make excuses for her. But she's suffered as much as anyone in all of this and I'm not going to disown her. Dr Williams has told me that she's hardly eating at all now, and if that doesn't change she'll not last long as she's so weak. But at least she's getting the proper care that she needs in the care home. Frank was right, it's the best place for her now. He's taken the news better than I expected. I did wonder if he'd just walk away from my mom, his wife, Cathleen I see what you mean, it is kinda weird.

According to Lieutenant Rawlingson, Frank never knew about the stillborn baby, or that Cathleen had taken me away from my natural parents. He's been through a difficult time as well. I thought we might go and see him tomorrow, stop in at the care home and then head across to Hinton and see Frank and George. It's only another twenty miles down the road from the home."

Becca nodded.

"What did Rawlingson have to say about arresting Todd, your brother, twin. Wow, I don't know what to call him either, this is just so bizarre," said Becca feeling slightly embarrassed.

"Just don't call him my brother," said Josh. "He means nothing to me, I don't want to think of him as my twin. He killed your sister Becca and he's going to be punished for that. Lieutenant Rawlingson told me he's sure he's going to plead guilty. Apparently, he broke down and cried when the police arrived at the house. Confessed what he'd done in front of his mother. Rawlingson said it was as if he was desperate to get it off his chest." Becca shook her head.

"His parents, I mean his adoptive parents were devastated. Rawlingson's sure they didn't know a thing about the murder," added Josh.

"Is that why they let you out of prison?" asked Becca. "I mean before he has been to court. Is it because he confessed that they've let you out?

Josh nodded. "That's what Rawlingson said. Judge was satisfied that with this new evidence my conviction was unsafe and, well, here I am," said Josh with a broad smile.

Becca's face broke into a huge smile as she leant her head against Josh's shoulder.

"You're really so kind Josh," said Becca, "that's what I love about you. Even after everything you've been through you're not bitter. You're still thinking about your mom and other people's feelings, that takes a special kind of person. Somewhere up there, Maisie's smiling down at us, Josh, I know she is. She'll be made up that you've been freed and that the police have caught the guilty man. I know you just want to move on now, and that's what we're going to do. But I'm glad the boy who killed my sister is going to stand trial for murder, she deserves justice for what he did to her, and I want to see him go to prison. I want that for my mom and dad's sake and for you too, Josh. But most of all I want it for Maisie."

Josh pulled Becca towards him and hugged her as they walked towards the farmhouse. "I know you do Becca and I want that too. I want it for you and I want it for Maisie."

"Look, you've got a rope swing Josh," said Becca pointing up at the old chestnut tree, "come and push me on it, will you?" said Becca sprinting up the hill.

"Wow, what a magnificent tree, and look at the view from here. I can almost make out my old house in the distance," said Becca sitting down on the swing.

As Josh began to gently push the swing, Becca noticed a patch of blue and purple flowers growing in the shadows of the chestnut tree. "What are those Josh?" said Becca pointing to the elegant flowers that stood tall against the uncut grass.

"Those are Larkspur," said Josh, "my great-grandmother planted them because it reminded her of her home in Ireland."

"Larkspur," said Becca, "I've never heard of them and I don't think I've seen any before. But they're beautiful flowers. Maisie would have loved them, Josh, purple was her favourite colour."